THE LIGHT WITHIN

TJ ROSE

CONTENTS

Introduction

Welcome! The Light Within is part two in the Shadow and Light duology, an urban fantasy MM romance. If you haven't read The Shadows Beyond, please start there!

Before you proceed, please take heed of the following content warnings:

- explicit adult content

- alcohol & substance abuse (side characters)

- historic child abuse

- smoking

- grieving for deceased family members

- mention of trauma

- character exhibits self-harming behaviour while angry

This book is written in British English.

All that you touch and all that you see
All that you taste, all you feel
And everything under the sun is in tune
But the sun is eclipsed by the moon

- Pink Floyd, Eclipse

One

JULIEN

The shadows danced between the gnarled trees, twisting and writhing like living smoke. Julien's heart pounded as he crouched low, his eyes fixed on the elusive creature that darted just out of reach. The shadow cat, a being of pure darkness, moved with unnatural grace, leaving wisps of inky blackness in its wake.

The others were just behind Julien; he could hear the soft crunch of twigs under Cinn's boots, the whisper of fabric as Elliot adjusted his rucksack, and the hitch in Darcy's breathing as she struggled to keep up.

Slinking ahead, the cat snaked amongst the foliage, weaving this way and that, its ethereal form slipping in and out of sight.

They were so close.

So close, yet, so far.

Yes, the cat they were hunting was a nightmare.

A literal monster, yes—eyeless, constructed of shadows, and capable of ghastly hissing sounds that would scare any child straight under the covers.

A monster that was supposedly his sister.

As creepy as it was, the true source of their current terror was letting the slippery creature out of their sight for the tenth—scrap that, *hundredth*—time.

The four of them had been at it for almost sixteen hours now, after Darcy sounded the alarm at the crack of dawn, spotting the fiend napping on the bench in her garden. By the time Julien and Cinn arrived, she was crawling through her flowerbeds, head half in a bush, alternating between soothing, encouraging sounds, and curse words.

An empty cat carrier rested near her. Its metal door creaked in the wind, mocking her efforts. Though, did Darcy really believe it could contain a cat made of shadows?

When Elliot arrived a full thirty minutes later—which was admittedly, by Elliot's standards, fairly on time—he found all three of them covered in dirt and bramble scratches. Elliot plucked a leaf from Darcy's hair, her auburn locks the very definition of a bird's nest. He set his face into a determined line. "We're not letting it get away from us this time."

So began their day of cat hunting, as the shadow demon led them on a wild goose chase through the rural outskirts of Talwacht. This involved a long wade through mud up to their knees, a quick dip into a stream, and a desperate trip to an out-of-town supermarket for various demon-cat-catching supplies. Mainly snacks.

They crested the hill that enclosed the valley the Aurelia Arcanum Institute of Esoteric Sciences sat in, and Julien's feet ached in protest of the many miles they'd walked. Yet the sight of the campus ignited a spark of excitement—if the cat was drawn towards Auri, surely that was a good sign that it was indeed some sort of reincarnation of his dead sister?

Half walking, half sliding down the muddy valley that offered no footpath, they eventually made it to the bottom, to follow the creature through the car park, several courtyards, and then to the glittering glasshouse that was the Solstice Atrium's exterior.

"Act natural," hissed Darcy as a large throng of people passed them.

"What, and pray nobody else wonders what the fuck a cat made of literal shadow is doing, taking a casual stroll through Auri?" Julien hissed back.

"Shut up, both of you!" Cinn pointed to where the cat was rounding a corner. Cinn's face was set in such a line of determination that Julien's mouth twitched into a smile, and he resisted an urge to press a kiss into the deep crevice across his forehead.

Thankfully, their prey seemed to prefer the paths less travelled, weaving between thickets of trees and the back ends of buildings, away from prying eyes. As one, with footsteps as feather-light as the branches littering the ground would allow, they followed their mark's path, trailing after shadowy swishes of tail as they slowly increased their pace to close the gap. The cat was lightning fast—every time they caught a flash of darkness, they'd fall deathly silent and creep towards it, cat carrier at the ready. And every time, the creature disappeared, seemingly melting into the actual shadows of shrubbery.

As the sun set, so did their patience.

Especially Darcy's.

"For the last time, Elliot, it's not an actual cat. It doesn't matter which brand of cat food you try to throw at it!"

Yes.

Animal hunting was decidedly a career that none of them should ever consider.

"This would have all been over hours ago if you'd just let me channel," muttered Elliot, scraping a patch of dried mud from the olive skin of his cheek. "I could have blasted her into that carrier within seconds."

"No!" Cinn all but shouted. "What if it hurts her, or like, sends her back into the shadow realm or something?"

"Dude, can we please not call *it* her? We've got no proof it's actually Béatrice!"

Julien's jaw clenched. All Elliot had done that day was air his complaints and doubts. Though Julien wasn't yet entirely convinced his dead sister had returned to them as a thing made of shadows, he was at least giving it the benefit of the doubt.

"If Cinn says—" He was silenced by Cinn's hand clamping around his forearm, accompanied by a quick shake of his head. Julien turned to him, allowing himself to be calmed by the depths of his wide golden-hazel eyes, just visible in the moonlight.

Stepping closer to Julien, Cinn murmured into his ear, "What about if you tried with your... special mote things?"

Julien glared Cinn's suggestion back down his throat before Darcy and Elliot got wind of it.

Since he'd recounted the tale of defeating the umbraphage using motes in the shadowrealm after a decade of not channelling, his two best friends had been relentless in their encouragement for him to do it again.

What they, and Cinn, didn't understand was how dangerous his nameless motes were.

Even if Julien started with lumenmotes or any other mote, how long would it be until he gave in to the temptation to tap into the awesome power the *other* motes offered?

No, he couldn't go there. It wasn't worth the risk.

Because the last time he'd channelled them, he'd crumbled a church half to rubble, and killed his mother.

"No!" hissed Darcy, snapping Julien's thoughts back to their current crisis. "It's going into the library!"

Indeed, there was a flash of a black, sinuous tail under the portico of the Aurelia Library, before it slunk through the open heavy oak doors. Clearly the rebellious minx wasn't bothered about their no pets policy.

The four of them entered the building to be greeted by a pleasant librarian who snapped, "We're closing in five!"

Bypassing the Greek Mythology section, the cat padded merrily through numerous bookshelves to head straight for...

"Surely not," Elliot muttered in disbelief, as it slipped through the ajar door of their favourite study room. The one they'd spent countless hours in with Béatrice over the years.

A light push on the door, and then all four of them stared into the room, where the creature had already curled up on the ancient Morris chair that Béatrice had favoured.

Julien swallowed, his heart thundering at the sight. There was no denying it now. This was her, his sister that he'd grieved for so deeply every day since her death half a year ago. She had returned to him. As a shadow cat, *oui*, but he'd take what he could get.

"Béatrice." Julien took one tentative step towards her, hand out-stretched. In an instant, she hissed, leapt up on all fours, and turned her head towards the open window just a cat-jump away.

Rude.

Julien's heart plummeted as he bit back a low groan—all these hours, and they were about to lose the goddamned cat, potentially for good this time.

Her eyeless head tilted upwards, and Béatrice poised herself on her hind legs, preparing to leap.

"Oh no. Don't you *dare*, you little bi—"

"Elliot!"

Darcy reached out to slap Elliot's arm, but it was too late—Elliot channelled the large amount of windmotes from the blustery weather outside to send a burst of cool air shooting in through the open window, a powerful blast that yanked the creature away from the ledge, knocking her onto the floor.

The cat made an indignant screech, shadowy fur writhing as she arched her back, claws attempting to find purchase on the polished wood as she tried to scrabble away from them. It was no use—Elliot's powerful air current overcame her valiant efforts, and soon she relented, curling into a dark ball that flew towards them, floating several feet into the air.

Before Julien could react, Cinn lurched forward, wrapping his arms around the cat to bring it to his chest, pressing her firmly against his hoodie. "Shh," he said, as the cat squirmed and thrashed, swiping for

Cinn's face with her left claw. Cinn brought the hemline of his jumper up and over the furious bundle, blocking her escape. He sank to the ground on his knees. "We're just trying to help you, alright?"

It was the most ludicrous sight—Cinn on the floor, whispering sweet nothings into his hoodie-cat-trap, to a wiggling, screeching creature that did *not* seem to appreciate his efforts. If Julien wasn't so exhausted, he'd surely be shaking with laughter.

Eventually, the miracle occurred—the squirming calmed, then ceased, then—

"Is it... *purring*?" Julien couldn't believe his ears.

With a smug grin, Cinn beamed up at him, his eyes wide with childlike glee. The sight of Béatrice curled up in Cinn's hoodie warmed Julien's cold heart, his annoyance at the cat quickly melting. If she preferred Cinn, so be it. Julien preferred Cinn too.

Cinn released the grip on his hoodie slightly to reach in and stroke the thing made of shadows. "There we go. Hello, little friend. Sorry that the mean bloke tried to scare you."

A strangled sound came from Elliot, followed by, "Well, that's one way, I guess. At least it likes one of us. Can we go home now?"

Darcy coughed. "Guys? You realise we're going to have to take it home on the bus, right?"

By the time they'd settled back in Darcy's living room, the cat was practically eating out of the palm of Cinn's hand. Well, licking it. She hadn't wanted any of the cat food they'd offered her, even the gourmet salmon, which looked rather appetising.

Cinn, who hadn't so much as glanced up since he'd sat down on the armchair with the cat on his lap, ran his fingers between her ears. She nuzzled against his palm.

"You can put her down for a second, you know," Julien said.

"Oh, sorry, did you want me to scratch your head instead?" Cinn stared at Julien, batting his eyelashes innocently, sending Elliot into a snickering fit he failed to disguise as a cough.

Ignoring them, Julien shuffled across the rug, reaching towards the creature slowly, compelled to finally feel the texture of its—*Béatrice's?*—shadowy form. His fingers connected with inky fibres that magnetised towards him, attracted to his hand. A cool sensation danced across his fingertips. How could something simultaneously feel so solid and so... *not*... at once?

The cat purred.

Darcy cleared her throat, then eyed the cat with pursed lips. "Look Julien, I think we really need to consider how to send it back."

"*What*? Why? She's clearly here for a reason!"

They'd finally found her, and now Darcy wanted her gone?

Cinn shifted the creature around on his lap before pulling her closer against his chest. "Not a chance. Béatrice didn't like the shadowrealm, Darcy. She was lonely there."

"This... *thing* doesn't belong here. Cinn, did you and Noir ever discuss this? Movement between the two realms?" asked Darcy.

The eccentric academic was supposed to be mentoring Cinn, though Cinn was quiet about the content of their sessions.

"Nope. All Noir told me is that there was only ever one other shadowslipper that brought things back. I've got no idea about the shadowrealm's return policy."

"Darcy, we're not going to 'return' her. She's here to help," Julien bit out, unable to dampen his rising temper. Her negativity was the last thing they needed at the end of the long day.

"*How?* It's not like she's able to talk to us!"

"We haven't asked her anything yet!"

Elliot laughed hollowly, leaning forward from the sofa to address the cat. "Béatrice, take us to the leader of the Arcane Purifiers and we'll buy you some catnip."

Julien didn't miss the glance Cinn threw his way, likely wondering if he was going to continue to deny Béatrice's involvement in the 'controversial at best, terrorist at worst' activist group. AP had been lobbying the consortium for years now. Their theory about mote usage causing the umbraphage emergence was largely disputed.

Julien opened his mouth—

"It's late," Darcy said, abruptly standing in that pointed way she did when she wanted them all out of her cottage.

The cat stretched her front two legs out as if in agreement, before hopping down and padding out of the room, a frowning Cinn hot on her tail. They trailed after the pair of them. Julien almost suggested Darcy make sure all her windows were shut—but a creature made of shadows was unlikely to be contained by mere solid material.

The cat darted straight towards Béatrice's bedroom. Julien's breath caught in his throat. Sniffing at the closed door, the cat scratched at the wood with a frantic urgency, then paused, as if considering her next move. Slowly, she pressed itself lower, her fur rippling and shifting, like water disturbed by a strong wind. Then, with a liquid fluidity, her body began to flatten as it melted into a dark, formless puddle.

Julien blinked rapidly, in case his eyes were deceiving him. His sister, a shadow puddle? It shimmered with an unnatural sheen as it stretched across the threshold, then sucked itself under the narrow gap beneath the door, vanishing.

Point proven.

Slack-jawed, Cinn pushed open Béatrice's door, and for a moment the four of them wordlessly stared at the eyeless cat lying on her bed, flicking its tail.

"Still don't believe it's her, Elliot?" Julien asked, a little smugly. Being right had never felt so good. Yet underneath his facade, his heart drummed, his mind racing to process the strange turn of events.

"Okay..." said Darcy, slowly. "I guess it's welcome to Béatrice's room, but I'm not getting it a litter tray."

"Deal."

"And we probably should tell *someone* about this—"

"No. We don't know who we can trust."

"But—" Darcy cut herself off with a shake of her head, then sighed. There was resignation on her face as she ushered the three of them out of her cottage into the dark winter night.

Elliot hopped on his motorcycle and was halfway down Darcy's road before Julien and Cinn reached Maz.

Soon, the gentle click of the car doors closing removed them from the rest of the world, the exhalation of Cinn's gentle sigh sealing their bubble.

Julien inserted his key into the ignition, then paused.

He would only drive a couple of roads until he had to turn left for Cinn's house, or right for his.

Please, please say you're coming back to mine.

Cinn turned to him, cocking his head.

"Do you want..." Julien started, until his tongue turned to lead.

Words, Julien, words! What on earth was wrong with him? Where had his ability to throw up his usual calm, collected facade gone? That armour that protected him from situations exactly like this? Out the window with his vocabulary, apparently.

Cinn stared, arching a questioning eyebrow that almost disappeared into his olive-green beanie. "You're gonna have to be a bit more specific, mate."

He practised the simple sentence in his mind over and over again as a hot flush prickled the back of his neck. Each time, the Cinn his brain conjured laughed hollowly in response, eyes narrowing.

Facing the windscreen while gripping the wheel so tightly his nails bit into the leather, Julien eventually managed the words: "Do you want to... comebacktomine?"

Cinn's roaring laugh practically shook Maz.

Oh, why did Cinn have to have this infuriating effect on him? It was making his life even more complicated.

"Course I'm coming back to yours. No need to beg—unless you want to."

The white flash of Cinn's satisfied smirk had Julien inwardly groaning as he turned the key, grateful for the sound of his car's engine filling the silence.

"It's just that I'm aware that we still need to talk." Julien kept his eyes firmly planted on the quiet road ahead.

"Yeah," said Cinn quietly. "I know."

Damn.

After Cinn had turned up on his doorstep in the middle of last night demanding Julien's... attention... he'd half convinced himself he'd got away scot free without any awkward conversations.

Julien turned on Maz's radio, tuning it into Cinn's favourite channel, the one that played older British hits, then drove them home.

They didn't say anything in the car.

They didn't say anything in the underground garage.

They didn't say anything in the elevator.

By the time they'd sat down on Julien's sofa, nausea had made its home in his gut, and tendrils of panic seized his heart, squeezing painfully. This was it. The moment Cinn shattered his heart by telling him there was no possible future for them.

"Look, Julien—"

"I want to—"

Julien snapped his mouth shut, waiting for Cinn to continue. But Cinn only sighed. Julien pulled a cushion onto his lap, squashing his tension into it. He softly asked, "Did you get that letter I sent? Did you read it?"

The light in the room was dim, the only source coming from the floor lamp behind Cinn. Yet his face visibly softened, gaze drifting to his rucksack on the floor. "Yeah, I got it. I was planning to talk to you, you know, that day at the lantern parade. I was just trying to work up the courage. I know I was being a stubborn git, ignoring you for so long."

"Well"—Julien picked at a thread on the cushion—"it's not like you didn't have a good reason. I did almost get your ex-boyfriend killed." Precious, oh-so-*precious* Tyler, who Cinn would give the world for.

So when Tyler had gone out with the ten thousand pounds Julien had thrown at him before they left—along with some words he'd rather not remember—resulting in a hospital stay for broken ribs, it had been a *little* awkward.

Regrets.

Julien had them.

Cinn freed a brown curl from his beanie to twist it around his finger. Seeing the hat Julien gave him back on Cinn's head brought Julien immeasurable joy. Cinn said, "The thing is, he's usually pretty good at messing things up all by himself, even on a good day." Then, leaning forward, he grabbed Julien's hand, forcing him to meet his eyes. "I still don't get why you let Tyler shake you up so much. I tried to make it clear on the tube that you had nothing to worry about. Then I was all over you at Bradley's place."

The worried, reflective tone in Cinn's voice—like *he'd* been the one at fault—only compounded Julien's guilt until it was a solid brick in his stomach.

"*Non.*" Julien squeezed Cinn's hand, then stroked his thumb against his pulse. "This is entirely on me. And my self-destructive brain." He shuddered out a breath. "You've been all I can think about. Did you know that? Starting weeks before we went to London. Pretty much from the moment I met you. I guess I didn't know what to do with all these... *feelings.*"

Julien made a face, causing Cinn to laugh, and some of the tension to dissipate. But it was true. The way he felt about Cinn was so intense, so big, so *new,* Julien felt unequipped to handle it. His feelings felt like fire in his chest, burning so hot he didn't know whether to run from it or embrace it.

"I couldn't bear the thought of losing you before I even had the chance to have you. It fucked with my mind. God, Cinn, I still feel like I'm losing my mind right now. I want you so badly but I'm so fucking terrified of screwing it up." The honesty poured out of him before he could stop it, and Julien squeezed his eyes shut, unable to face the look of surprise and mild concern written on Cinn's face at his outburst.

"I know you deserve someone with a normal range of human emotions, who'll treat you like a prince. Someone who won't keep fucking up. Someone who won't ever hurt you."

The warm, comforting weight of Cinn's body settled on his lap, his legs wrapping around Julien's back. Then he pressed a finger to Julien's lips, soft but commanding. Cinn dropped his tone to say, "There's only room for one prince here, and that's you."

Julien pulled his lips into a scowl, though his heart fluttered and his stomach uncoiled somewhat.

"Besides, if I wanted *normal,* I wouldn't be here. I know exactly what I'm signing up for."

The tiniest spark of hopeful joy ignited itself within Julien, and he allowed it to weave warmth through him.

"I can be patient while we sort it all out," Cinn added.

Julien brought his hands up to cup Cinn's cheeks, swiping his thumbs over them before kissing his forehead. "You don't need to be patient. I don't need to figure out how I feel about you."

Cinn pressed his lips against Julien's, running the back of one hand along the column of his throat. With the slowest of gentle pressures, Cinn caressed his bottom lip with his tongue, pressing it against him until Julien's mouth parted. As their tongues tangled, brushing up against each other with soft, languid strokes, a calm settled in the ocean of Julien's mind. The anxious waves, so turbulent in the weeks since Cinn had stormed out of this very apartment, finally stilling.

An almost drugged feeling coursed through Julien, and he gently pulled them both down to lie side by side, tugging Cinn's precious beanie very gently off to breathe in the scent of his hair. Damp from the drizzle earlier, the smoke from Darcy's fireplace didn't quite mask the citrus shampoo Cinn favoured. Julien smiled into his short brown curls, running a hand through them.

Cinn settled on his chest, nuzzling in so close, Julien could match every rise and fall of his rib cage. A thick lump formed in Julien's throat. He swallowed it, sliding his arms as far as they could stretch around Cinn.

They remained like that for an eternity and a half, with Julien staring at the ceiling, content to never move again.

In this dreamlike space, right now, he could do anything. Anything, like...

His gaze turned to the lamp emitting a soft orange light.

The lumenmotes called to him. Whispered his name.

He itched to feel them respond to him, to be bent to his will.

Staring at the lamp, raising his hand towards it, his heart rate kicked into overdrive.

Cinn raised his head from his chest, his gaze boring into him. "Are you going to...?" he said, his breathy excitement contagious.

Julien edged his slightly shaking hand closer to the light. The physical proximity of his fingers to the motes was entirely unnecessary, but it felt right.

"I'm here." Cinn reached for Julien's other hand to squeeze their intertwined fingers. "You've got this."

Cinn's unwavering belief in him was the last layer of motivation he needed. Julien exhaled a last, unsteady breath through his nose.

He reached for the lumenmotes.

The motes became visible only when he focussed on connecting with them. Clusters of tiny specks of light, fairy dust almost, they drifted this way and that, awaiting direction.

A tingling sensation began in his fingertips and spread throughout his every limb—a gentle warmth akin to sunlight finally breaking through dark clouds.

He drifted above himself. He became the light, the air, and the space in between.

He'd thought this part of himself was forever lost.

Now, a revival. A resurgence. A reawakening inside him.

His fog had lifted, leaving laser-like clarity in its place as each of his five senses sharpened. Energy softly buzzed in every place that connected him to Cinn's body.

He drew upon the lumenmotes awaiting his call, drawing them away from the lamp, and manipulated them, binding hundreds of them together to form a tiny bright floating ball of light.

Encouraged by Cinn's gasp, Julien pulled out even more—relishing the euphoric feeling of finally, *finally* allowing himself to do the thing he'd craved every day for years—to create another sphere, then another.

Cinn reached up to flick off the lamp, which had dimmed somewhat. Soon they were immersed in a shower of drifting luminescence, flickering like stars. Their own private universe.

"So beautiful," Cinn murmured, reaching out to trace the path of one with his fingers.

"Almost as beautiful as you."

Cinn made a sound somewhere between a scoff and a retch, but the smile Julien felt against his chest filled him with starlight.

Julien drifted off to sleep with Cinn still entwined in his arms. One final thought fluttered through him: he'd do anything in his power to make this tentative happiness his new reality.

Two

CINN

Julien was snoring when Cinn awoke, the exhalation of his breath tickling his ear. During the night, his head had shuffled off Julien's chest onto a cushion they'd shared. His aching muscles protested that two men sharing a sofa when a king-sized bed was a mere handful of steps away wasn't the best idea, but Cinn had no regrets.

He pulled his head back slightly to study Julien's face: the sharpness of his cheekbones that was softened by the morning light; a tiny, tiny scar on his forehead, unnoticed until now; the shiny blond waves that had annoyed him the night they met. He'd yanked on them, hard. But Julien had seemed to enjoy that, hadn't he?

Cinn couldn't help but smile to himself, resisting the temptation to run his fingers through Julien's hair, feel the silky locks that were as soft as they looked. In such a short time, the arrogant, cocky princeling he'd immediately disliked had become... *his* princeling.

It had been difficult to watch Julien last night, falling apart—falling apart *again*—because of him. Almost as difficult as the two weeks of staying away from him had been.

Undeniably, Cinn had been angry at first. Pissed off. Fuming. Tyler was in the hospital with broken ribs, and the man semi-responsible for setting off the chain of events was the same one Cinn had just started imagining giving his heart to. Fury at Julien warred with fury at Tyler and fury at himself for letting it all unfold that way.

Then he'd read the letter. The letter, the one in the yellow envelope that was waiting on his floor the day after he'd broken his own heart by leaving Julien crying on the floor of his apartment. The letter that had contained so, so many words. So many words, Cinn didn't know what to do with them. The letter, the one that he'd gotten out and read again and again, to the point it became dog-eared, Julien's outlandishly over-the-top inked signature smudged where he'd run his fingers over it so many times.

After its arrival, Cinn waited for Julien to show up on his doorstep, or to surprise him by appearing alongside Darcy for lunch one day. After all, it wasn't like Julien to respect personal boundaries. When he didn't make an appearance, and the space between them began to stretch longer and longer, Cinn began to question everything, including whether Julien had gotten bored with him and moved on.

Now, here he was, waking up next to him.

Cinn untangled himself from their web of limbs as gently as possible, to pad around Julien's apartment barefoot with mouse-like steps.

He needn't have worried—even the noise of the kettle boiling and Cinn preparing the coffee beans using Julien's ridiculously high-effort hand-grinder didn't wake him.

While the cafétière steeped the coffee, Cinn found himself wandering around Julien's living room, picking up several curious-looking objects—motetech?—for further examination. A wooden ladder shelf housed plants that felt real and alive to the touch but were rooted in tiny tree stumps rather than soil. On the top shelf, a photo of four people standing in a row, arms around each other, on a sunny beach, waited for his prying fingers to grab it down. Julien and Béatrice wedged in the middle of Elliot and Darcy, the four of them looking windswept and slightly sunburnt. As Cinn tilted the photo, the sea in the background appeared to move just a fraction, as did the hair of the four smiling friends. He set it back down.

Cinn meandered over to sit at Julien's red-velvet piano stool. Smooth curves and sharp angles melded seamlessly to create an impressive grand piano, its black shine winking at Cinn, begging to be played. For all his love of listening to music, he'd never actually played an instrument outside of the few music lessons he'd bothered to attend in secondary school. In his defence, sheet music was even harder to read than words.

Cinn lifted the piano's fallboard to reveal a mesmerising expanse of glossy ebony keys. He ran a single finger over their smooth surface without pressing down.

"Do you have a secret talent you haven't yet revealed?"

Jumping out of his skin, Cinn lurched backwards on the stool. The seat tipped, sending him flying into Julien's laughing arms.

Cinn scowled at Julien's upside down smirking face, his dimples on full display. "You could have said good morning."

"Now where would the fun be in that?" Julien said, before pressing a soft kiss to Cinn's lips. "When I could watch you nose around every inch of my apartment instead?"

Julien released Cinn, who spun around on the seat to continue glaring at him.

"Move out of the way. I want to play you something I've been practising."

Cinn slipped off the stool to sit on the floor while Julien grabbed a thin glossy book down from a nearby bookshelf, opened it without a glimpse at the page number, and placed it on the music stand. Julien played a few notes, pressing his foot against each of the three pedals.

"Sounds great. A plus," Cinn said, slow clapping. "Definitely give up the day job."

Julien paused. Turned his head to stare at him.

Without breaking eye contact, Julien danced his fingers lightning-quick across the keys, conjuring a cascade of melodies, a musical magician. The room soon resonated with a symphony of layered harmonies, all without Julien even glancing at the keys.

Cinn stopped clapping in shock.

"Fair warning, I've only practised this a few times," Julien said, nodding to the sheet music.

"Okay..." Cinn said slowly, waves of apprehension surging.

After a deep breath and a roll of his shoulders, Julien studied the music for a moment before starting to play.

Cinn knew the song at once.

He felt his eyes widen in disbelief and his jaw drop slightly slack as the very familiar chords of "Go Your Own Way" vibrated through the room.

Each note sent a fresh shockwave of raw emotion through him, threatening to choke him and drag him under. Memories of moments flooded Cinn's mind, intertwining with the music as Julien's rendition breathed new life into the song so beloved to him for as long as he could remember.

He traced the rib where the lyrics to the Fleetwood Mac song had been inked many years ago.

It was his mother's favourite song.

Cinn had an entire catalogue of hazy memories of her playing the song during his childhood. Each of them featured her smiling face as she shouted it as loud as she could, often pulling him down from sitting on a bar stool to spin around their tiny kitchen with her. They'd spin and spin, getting dizzier and dizzier until the final notes faded into their laughter.

"Hey. Come here. Sorry, I didn't mean to upset you."

Cinn rapidly blinked. Julien had stopped playing.

He hadn't realised he'd been crying until Julien swiped across his cheek with his thumb as he pulled him onto the stool with him.

"You didn't upset me. That was... really beautiful, Julien. Thanks." Cinn's voice was thick with grief and barely above a whisper. Once he rested his chin on Julien's shoulder, hiding his face, he continued, "That was my mum's favourite song. She must have played it a thousand times."

"Oh?" Julien's hand came up to stroke small circles onto his back. "I had no idea. I just thought you must like it."

"The tattoo artist and my mates thought I got it to make some kind of statement against her or whatever, but I actually got it to keep her close, even after I left."

"You act like you had a say in the matter."

"She said the song reminded her of when she left home to carve out her own path. She'd sing it to herself whenever she doubted her decision to go. My nan passed away when she was just four, so she was raised by her dad and her older brother. I was only thirteen when I went into care, so I don't remember much, but I know they were shitheads."

How long had it been since Cinn talked about all this? The words felt foreign on his tongue.

Julien hummed before nudging his head against Cinn's. "Do you know where she is now?" he asked. "Is she still..."

Alive? A mess? "Nope. No idea. Lost contact years ago." Cinn fought to keep his voice steady. This was exactly why he avoided thinking about her. "It's alright. It's all in the past now. It's probably for the best. I like to picture her out there, living a good life, dancing around to this song. She was always at her happiest when there was music playing."

Julien touched Cinn's shoulders, pushing him off his shoulder to face him. "It's nice you had that in common with her."

"Yeah." Cinn shot Julien a sad smile. "Anyway. Cold coffee?" He dragged himself away from Julien to pour it out. It was cold indeed, but Julien's golden-threaded motetech mug had the lukewarm liquid piping hot in the ten seconds it took to walk Julien's mug over to him.

The calendar dangling on the wall caught Cinn's attention. He tapped on today's date, disbelief seeping through him. "Fuck."

"What?"

"It's Christmas Day in four days. How did we not notice?" Cinn whirled around to catch Julien pulling a face.

"Urg, *Christmas*. I hoped everyone would forget."

"Don't tell me you're a Christmas Scrooge. I can't stand those types."

"Don't tell me you're one of those people who go crazy for it. Actually, scrap that, you're British. Of course you do."

Bright, tinsel-coloured fragments of memories, almost certainly rose-tinted, crowded Cinn's mind. "It used to be a happier time of year when I was a kid. Then it got pretty shitty in foster care. But the last few years have been great. What's not to love about presents and too much food?"

Sighing, Julien interlocked his fingers behind his head, leaning backwards as if pained. "I suppose I can pretend to love it, just for you. Fair warning, Darcy will go home to her loving parents in Scotland. Can you believe it?" He pulled a face of mock disgust. "But Elliot will probably be around."

Cinn turned back to the calendar. It wasn't too late for him to fly back to England, to spend it with whoever was around. Tempting, but no. As much as Julien presented as all-too-happy to ignore Christmas, Cinn couldn't leave him. Didn't *want* to leave him.

The pages of the calendar shook slightly in a non-existent breeze. Cinn's eyes flicked to the ladder shelf, where a minute hum buzzed. He squinted. The objects were vibrating ever so slightly, the leaves of the plants quivering.

That's when the first tremor became obvious. Subtle, yes, but enough for Cinn to feel the pulse of energy thread through him. "What was that?"

"Construction downstairs?" Julien said slowly, tone lacking conviction. Another minor tremor passed under them, and Julien failed to disguise his alarm, jumping to his feet to head to the glass wall that faced Talwacht's centre.

Cinn followed, grabbing on to Julien's arm. "Should we evacuate?"

"Let's not panic." A small furrow formed between Julien's eyebrows as a rumble tore through the apartment—distant thunder? It didn't sound like it.

Nothing of note was visible outside the window, but as seconds passed, the tremors intensified, growing stronger with each passing moment.

"At what point *do* we panic?" That ship had long since sailed for Cinn. His heart thundered in his chest as he shamelessly clung onto Julien's arm.

The room began to sway almost imperceptibly as the rattle of objects bouncing against shelves increased to a deafening crescendo. Several alarms in other apartments pinged, creating a chorus of warning.

Finally, a gasp from Julien. He pointed across the town to where another high-rise building was visibly shaking.

What were you meant to do in an earthquake, again? Cinn had no real clue, fluctuating between suggesting they hide under the dining table or flee outside. Outside, onto the main road, where things could fall on them. Flatten them like pancakes, crush their bones into dust.

"We need to..." Cinn couldn't finish his thought. Every intake of breath offered him an insubstantial amount of oxygen as his legs turned to watery jelly. The gold band around his wrist warmed with his rising adrenaline-fuelled heart rate. It would prevent him from shadowslipping, but it wouldn't save them from being buried alive.

Then came the unmistakable sensation of the floor beneath them shifting violently, as the earthquake's intensity surged. The glass wall rippled ominously, warping inwards as the largest tremor so far blasted through the room.

"Julien!"

With a horrific crack, the glass succumbed to the relentless force, fracturing into a spiderweb of fissures that spread with alarming speed.

Cinn dove backwards, tripping over something in the process, sending both him and Julien tumbling to the floor.

"Fuck!"

The glass exploded inward in a shower of deadly shards. Cinn's arm flew up to cover his face, and he braced, readying himself to feel the stinging bite of razor-sharp fragments.

They didn't come. Cinn unpeeled his firmly clamped eyelids to find the thousands of shiny shards flying away from them, and Julien kneeling, attention focussed solely on the glassless windowpane. A torrent of strong wind, originating from behind them, pushed every shard of glass outwards to tumble down onto the road.

"You certainly picked a good time to start channelling again," Cinn said meekly, rising quickly to his unsteady feet. "Now let's get out of here."

Julien didn't need persuading. Swiping up their rucksacks en route, they dashed straight to the front door. By instinct, Cinn half moved towards the elevator before Julien yanked on his arm, pointing to a door that led to a staircase. Julien may then have said something, but Cinn's ears rang from the deafening cacophony of alarms and the roar of the continuing series of quake-induced shudders. With gritted teeth, they pounded down the emergency staircase, hands interlocked and squeezing each other to the point of pain. Each concrete step was a precarious dance as the building trembled around them. The treacherous descent was made even more ominous by lights flickering through the choking haze of dust that filled the air, making Cinn's eyes water.

At last, their endless journey downwards came to its conclusion, and they burst through a fire door onto the main road.

Cinn gasped for breath. "Another reason"—he coughed violently, spitting bile and ash onto the ground—"not to have a fancy-ass penthouse suite."

"Is this really the time for that comment?"

Cinn's face split into a grin, the euphoria of their escape sending him doolally. He dusted grey powder from Julien's white shirt before meeting his wide, red-rimmed eyes. He was still panting as he brought their foreheads together. "I can't believe we're alive."

The rush of joy from escaping the building faded as Cinn absorbed the chaotic scene around them. The street was littered with debris, the air thick with the acrid scent of smoke and the distant wail of sirens.

The tremors had finally ceased, however, their sensations petering out into nothing. Around them, strangers stumbled, shell-shocked, many of them clutching crying children to their chests.

"This is madness," Julien said, shaking his head. He was as spooked as Cinn had ever seen him. Blinking rapidly, he stumbled several steps backwards to lean against a lamppost.

"Hey." Cinn grabbed his wrist, sliding his fingers up the sleeve of his shirt to feel the corded muscles of his forearm. "We're okay. It's over."

Julien took a second, tipping his head back to the grey sky. He inhaled deeply, once, then appeared to gather himself. He launched himself from the lamppost, marching straight up to a random local, rapidly reeling off questions in what was presumably Swiss-German before returning back to Cinn.

"He said don't bother driving anywhere." As if to demonstrate this fact, several angry car horns sounded in the near distance. "We'll have to walk."

Cinn's shell-shocked mind struggled to process the information. "Huh? Walk? Where?"

Julien looked past Cinn, down the road, a distant look on his face. Cinn came close to repeating his question, then Julien finally said, "Darcy's. Let's hope her side of town was less affected."

Three

JULIEN

They had to see it to believe it.

Standing on the crest of the valley that overlooked Auri, Julien couldn't tear his disbelieving eyes away from the crack through the heart of it. The colossal fissure split their Institute in two, separating St. Caelum's and the Aurelia Library from the Solstice Atrium and the Nexus Towers.

"It's not *that* bad," Elliot said, then scoffed. "I could easily jump that blindfolded."

They'd spent the previous day, once they'd finally reached Darcy's cottage on foot—Julien mourning the loss of Maz every step of the way—primarily in Darcy's living room. Darcy and Julien warred for hours over who had access to her telephone. Eventually, Julien resorted to using her fireplace to send a note to Eleanor, hoping for any titbit of information.

Very little came.

What they did eventually hear was that their own Auri was the epicentre of the earthquake, which had reached a magnitude over seven. Oh, and there was now a massive crack down the middle of it.

"Ah, yes, Elliot, it's no bother at all. We'll all just jump over it and completely ignore it, shall we?" Darcy's mood had soured throughout the day. She'd been fine when Julien had left her cottage that morning on the back of Elliot's bike to collect Maz—seizing the first opportunity, once the town council had declared the main roads drivable again. Now, she was quick to snap.

Cinn cleared his throat. "At least the buildings look okay?"

Indeed, Auri's structures were entirely intact—they had motetech to thank for that—though many of the lumenmote stone columns had fallen, now lying like scattered branches.

The same certainly couldn't be said for many of Talwacht's buildings. Would the public question why the buildings closest to the quake's epicentre had remained standing, almost completely unharmed? Auri was often the butt of the locals' jokes. That crazy place in the valley where all the foreigners worked, doing their *science things*. Would Auri come under more scrutiny now?

At least they had the other earthquakes that had happened simultaneously around the world to distract them. Every other large moteblessed hub had been affected by similar events, from their Asian base near Bangkok all the way to Vermont.

Darcy, staring towards the glowing barrier that encircled the entirety of the Institute, said, "The media has started questioning if we're on the verge of the second wave of calamities. The world has already seen a rise in natural disasters over the last decade, but this is all pointing towards new levels. Calamities of Nineteen Sixty-Five levels."

The Calamities of Nineteen Sixty-Five. Where everything mote-related had started. Or so they said. Soon after the series of volcano eruptions, earthquakes, tsunamis and droughts had rocked the world, a miniscule handful of people had discovered they could see, and sometimes even channel, the ethereal flecks of energy now known as motes.

"Shit!" All eyes snapped to Elliot. He pointed to the far left of the valley. "Who are those people? Over there, close to the barrier."

About a dozen figures, dressed in dark colours, huddled together near the glowing red line of the barrier. One approached one of the power poles, thin silver sticks containing motecells. Julien's own department,

Mote-Enhanced Engineering and Technologies, had designed the device years ago. Erectable in seconds, it blocked any physical movement of flesh from moving through it, repelling a person or animal several metres back upon an attempt.

"I doubt they're up to any good," Darcy said. She glanced at Elliot. "The gendarmerie must be about, though, surely?"

"Most of us are being sent into Talwacht to help with the clean-up today. I start my shift at three."

A sharp intake of breath from Cinn. "Look!"

The intruders had done *something* to a small portion of the barrier—its red shimmer flickered before fading. *How have they done that?* Filing through quickly, the group moved forward with clear purpose, heading straight for the crack.

"Who are they?" Julien muttered, although he had a hunch. He squinted, unsuccessful in his attempt to zero in. But even if they were closer, it would have been impossible to see their faces, each head shrouded by a hood.

Elliot groaned, rubbing his hand over his face. "I can't ignore seeing this. I've got to run into HQ and see who's on shift to help." A second later, Elliot was partway down the hill, leaving them no room to protest.

Losing sight of the cloaked group was unavoidable, as they had to walk around the large crest of the valley to access the portion of the barrier that had been tampered with. Once they'd slipped through, Elliot insisted that Julien, Darcy, and Cinn remain there while he fetched assistance.

As soon as he'd turned the corner, Julien said, "So, you two are going to stay here while I go find our mysterious guests."

Two simultaneous glares pierced him. Darcy simply sighed, green eyes rolling to the back of her head, while Cinn protested, "As if. Why do you even want to talk to them?"

"He thinks they could be the Arcane Purifiers." Darcy's mind-reading skills were en pointe. "Although why he thinks they'll be receptive to interruption is beyond my understanding."

"Okay... We can try to approach them, I guess."

Cinn took a step forward, but Julien's arm flew out, blocking his path. "You're staying here," he said, more sharply than he intended. He winced. "In fact, go wait up the hill where we just were. They could be dangerous. In fact, we *know* they're dangerous."

A slight flush coloured Cinn's cheeks, and his nostrils flared. "In that case, it's too dangerous for you."

"*I* can protect myself," he stated firmly, before pressing his tongue against the roof of his mouth.

"Fuck that!" said Cinn, stepping towards Julien, unmistakable challenge in his narrowed gaze.

Darcy tugged at Cinn's sleeve. "Don't bother. There's really no point trying to reason with him when he's in this mood. Just let him go."

"They literally blew up a building on my first day here! If it's too dangerous for us all to go, then it's too dangerous for him."

"I'll be back in five." Julien spun on his heels and bolted away from them before Cinn succeeded in making him change his mind. He'd been impressively close.

The temptation to look back was remarkably strong, but Julien urged himself onwards. He'd made the right call. Cinn wouldn't be able to follow him, because that would leave Darcy alone. Darcy, who apparently thought his entire plan ridiculous. But how could he pass up a fleeting chance to speak to the organisation that had potentially got his sister killed?

The cold afternoon sun was bright, forcing him into the shadows it created. Creeping around the edges of buildings, he passed through the numerous interlocking courtyards of the Veiled Gardens, inching closer to the fissure in the earth that had split the Institute in two. On either side of the path, trees stood stark and bare, their branches glistening with frost.

Julien froze.

A lone hooded figure stood underneath a large beech tree, facing away from him. Keeping guard? Julien pivoted, treading quietly as he took the longer route all the way around Caelum Hall. His fingertips glided over the cool, smooth surface of the ancient slabs of Roman stone the cathedral was composed of. Its weathered texture was a testament to the centuries it had lasted—it was the only building originally on this site, each of the others having been purpose-built around it.

Somewhere nearby, a bird squawked, interrupting Auri's unusual near-silence. Julien quickened his pace. Who knew how much longer he had, before Elliot arrived with the cavalry?

It happened so quickly. One moment he was taking hurried steps towards the rift in the ground, eager to see it up close, and the next, a hand was over his mouth, and many arms were restraining him.

"Hmmhmmph!"

Julien's teeth searched for flesh to bite, but instead found thick leather. His shoulders strained against the firm grip of his opponent. Blood pounded through his ears as he readied to reach for motes. If these two assailants thought it would be that easy, they had another thing coming.

"Wait! That's Julien Montaigne." A man's voice. Deep. One he didn't recognise. Julien tried to turn his head, but someone's forearm pressed against his neck.

A pause.

Was his name about to work in his favour, or against him? These people would despise his father, who'd actively spoken out against AP. Yet, they may have counted Béatrice Montaigne as one of their own.

"Montaigne?" said the other at last. A woman. "So he's... Why are you here, Julien Montaigne?"

The pressure on his neck slightly lessened. "Why are you here?" Julien spat, as he gulped a lungful of air.

The man grunted. "That's it. I'm knocking him out. We don't have time for this."

He'd like to see the man try. But Julien also had more important things to be doing. "I came to see if you were who I think you are."

"Yeah?" said the woman.

Again Julien tried to twist his head to see her, and again he was rewarded with a sharp jab to his neck.

"And who do you think we are?"

"Arcane Purifiers."

There was a subtle shift in the grip of the man restraining him.

Julien was correct.

"And what business do you have with them?"

Breaking and entering the Institute, for one.

"I need to talk to them. To someone, at least. About... about my sister."

Julien's mouth dried as their silent pause stretched. After an age of tension, the man finally spoke. "Let's take him to L. They might want to see him."

Abruptly, they dropped their hold on Julien, and he half stumbled forwards before catching himself. He spun around, eager to put faces to the voices, to find them both wearing white cloth masks underneath their dark hoods, only a sliver of a gap for their eyes.

"This way," the man grunted, moving forward without him. "Hurry."

AP's two guard dogs weren't far at all from the rest of the group, by the jagged crack. It was easily two metres wide, now that he was near enough to assess it properly. Some of the cloaked figures were wrapping up whatever they had been doing—stuffing things back in bags, gathering in groups, gesturing towards the barrier.

Those who noticed Julien's presence paused to stare.

"L!"

The woman attracted the attention of someone peering down into the depths of the fissure. Thin metal wire dangled from a coil in their hand.

'L' set down the wire before turning to them. They too wore the mask—it likely concealed a scowl, if their body language was anything to go by. Crossing their arms, they marched towards Julien and his two new friends.

"What's going on? Who's this?" the androgynous voice demanded.

Julien froze, his mind scrambling for words. Why hadn't he rehearsed his opening lines on the short journey here? This was his one shot at finding out about Béatrice's involvement in AP. He couldn't fuck this up.

"I'm not here to cause any trouble," he began. *Please, please, Elliot, don't come yet.* It would certainly reflect poorly on Julien if he suddenly burst into this scene. "I'm Julien Montaigne. I'm here to ask you about my sister, Béatrice."

Brown, inquisitive eyes appraised him, gaze raking over his blond hair, pale face, and grey irises the exact same shade as Béatrice's had been. "Leave us," L commanded, and two pairs of footsteps trailed away behind him.

"I know that she was working with you," Julien hedged. It was something he didn't want to believe to be true for many reasons, but denial would get him nowhere.

"And how do you know that?" L asked, voice perfectly light and pleasant.

Without even a flinch, Julien said, "She told me."

"Liar."

The gut punch the words caused was unexpected. How did this L person know so much about what Béatrice had and hadn't shared with him, her own brother? Were she and L close? They must have been.

Closer than you and Béatrice.

Julien bit his nails into his palms to control the tempest gathering speed within him. "Someone fucked with her locket. That's how she died. I want to know who murdered her, and why."

Was this new information to L? It was hard to tell. They took a second to absorb his words, tilting their head slightly. "It certainly wasn't us, if that's what you think. Béatrice was an extremely valuable asset to our cause." L's voice softened to add, "And a good friend of mine."

"Okay, fine. But what was she doing for AP that got her killed? Did you ever investigate it? Do you even care that you're the reason she's dead?"

Julien bit into his tongue, the pain refocussing him. The last question had slipped out before he could tamp it down, and now L was taking a step back, shaking their head.

Putain. He'd gone too far, his temper ruining his chance for more information.

"Of course we care," L retorted, their eyes narrowing to slits. "If you want to find her killer, I suggest you start by looking a little closer to home."

Julien blinked at L, thrown off course. Before he could open his mouth to reply, a low whistle shot through the air, starting low and ending high.

"Let's go!" barked L, and within seconds, the dozen cloaked figures were mobile, moving towards Caelum Hall.

Non!

Julien stepped into L's path. "Wait! If you really were her friend, help me."

"Look at this," L said, gesturing to the crack. "Look at what we're doing to the planet. How many people will have to die, innocent people who have no knowledge and do not benefit from the world of motecraft, before the consortium takes note? Before your father takes action?"

Julien raised his palms. "You don't need to lecture me. I am not my father, believe me."

They were alone now, the rest of AP was already out of sight.

L closed the space between them, grabbed Julien's arm, and whispered a single name before passing him, to disappear into the shadows.

A single name.

"Eleanor Sinclair."

Julien made no attempt to follow, remaining rooted to the spot.

Eleanor Sinclair.

Non. Julien laughed to himself, hollow and mirthless. L was mistaken. His mind refused to accept it.

He drifted towards the earth fissure, sinking to his knees to peer into the abyss of the jagged scar the quake had made upon the ground. The cool darkness of the gaping chasm, a touch larger than his arm, spun, beckoned him. Julien ran his finger over the edge of the crack, dislodging some dirt that tumbled to its demise. He peered into the depths, where darkness seemed to swallow the light, hinting at the size of the drop.

The crack ran all the way through Auri, and continued on for some length towards Talwacht.

The raw power of it pulsed through him. Followed by a sobering reflection.

Were AP right? Were motes—and the moteblessed that utilised them, *relied* on them—really responsible for the increasing number of catastrophic disasters that were indeed killing people? The fact that this latest wave had hit many of the larger moteblessed hubs was surely not a coincidence.

"Julien?"

When he looked up, he almost fell into the crack.

"*Eleanor?*" It came out with a croak. What were the chances?

The lines on her forehead deepened as she adjusted her glasses. "What are you doing here? The Institute is locked down."

Pounding footsteps approached. Elliot, plus six uniformed gendarmes, one of whom was their chief, Salvatore Gallo. The stout, burly Italian ran a hand through his short grey beard, nodding to Eleanor. "Madame. Pérez sounded the alarm that there had been a breach in the barrier."

Eleanor frowned at Julien. Weighing up the cost of lying, he explained that they'd seen a group of suspected AP members break in and head to the fissure, but they'd been gone by the time he'd reached it himself. Throughout his tale, he couldn't keep his eyes from boring into Eleanor. It was as if L had conjured her by saying her name. Was it possible L had sensed her coming, and that was the reason they'd said her name? Now he was being ridiculous. Julien shook his head, clearing it of nonsensical thoughts.

Salvatore Gallo unleashed rapid-fire instructions into a radio as his men fanned out, baton-shaped weapons at the ready, disappearing down various paths to locate AP members who had likely long since made their escape.

"Why are you here?" Julien asked Eleanor. "If nobody is meant to be here?"

Behind her, Elliot's eyes widened at his blatant rudeness.

"The consortium all took the Baths to attend an emergency conference in New York, ordering the Institute be locked down for twenty-four hours. I had a few things to do first. I was on my way to the Baths when I saw you."

Julien fought every instinct not to squirm under Eleanor's continuing close observation of him. A friend to both of his parents, the woman had known him since he was a child. She definitely knew he was holding something back. But would she call him out on it?

"Well," she started, pursing her lips. "I'm now late. But I will catch up with you, Julien, when I return tomorrow."

Why did that sound so much like a threat?

Eleanor had taken only a handful of steps before Darcy and Cinn appeared, stopping dead when they saw her. The color drained from Darcy's already pale face. Eleanor laughed, then shook her head in dismay. "Gallo, escort them all out for me, would you?"

Once she was out of earshot, Elliot said, "I'm fine to do that, sir," and Gallo waved his hand in agreement, already turning his attention back to listening to incoming reports on his radio.

Julien rounded on Darcy. "Why are you two here?"

She smiled in response. It was not a nice smile. "Well, since AP left, running right past us—weak, defenceless us—awaiting your return at the barrier, we figured we might be *allowed* to follow after you."

Julien's gaze flicked to Cinn's very much unsmiling face. He'd almost forgotten that he'd pissed him off earlier. Now it looked like he was going to suffer the consequences.

Physically pushing them, Elliot led them away, hissing, "What the hell?" into Julien's ear.

A guilty shrug was Julien's reply. He tugged Elliot away from the other two, who seemed quite content to march ahead without them, likely fuelled by their anti-Julien agenda.

"What time does your shift finish later?"

Elliot shot him a slanted, wary glance. "Eleven p.m. Why?"

"I need your help with something. Can you meet me back here? Midnight?"

"*Here*? Julien…"

Cinn spun around, narrow eyes combing over them both. "Well? What happened? Was it really AP, then?"

Julien lifted his finger to his lips. A gendarme could round the corner at any moment. "Let's talk in the car."

This answer did not seem to improve Cinn's mood.

The four of them walked towards the broken barrier in silence.

Two officers now flanked the access point, one of them leaning on the metal pole. Adjusting the collar of his uniform, he winked at Julien and shot him a beaming, wide-toothed grin before raking his gaze over him with a smirk. It took a further moment of studying his—admittedly attractive—face before the memory of hooking up with him last year resurfaced in full-detailed glory. A summer solstice party, if he recalled correctly. Toned thighs for days, if he recalled correctly.

Of course, the gendarme's attention was not lost on Cinn. He shot daggers at Julien, a completely undeserved scathing glare, considering he hadn't even acknowledged the guy. Or returned his smile.

"Cinn," Julien called, reaching for him, but he was already storming up the hill towards where Maz was parked.

The rock in Julien's stomach was becoming heavier by the second.

Once they'd reached the car, Julien drove while filling them in on his entire conversation with the enigmatic 'L', holding back no details.

Elliot whistled. "Well, at least we've heard it straight from the horse's mouth now. Fuck." Julien glanced in the rear-view mirror to see him run a hand through his corkscrew curls, a morose grimace on his face. "I can't believe she kept this from us. Seems like she was in deep too, from what you heard. Full membership, loyalty card and all."

A hand squeezed Julien's arm from the backseat. "Don't let what this *L* said cloud your judgement. They're coming to this with their own agenda," Darcy said.

"Judgement of what?" Julien replied, to make her say it.

"You know, Eleanor and the 'looking closer to home' stuff."

Julien scoffed, turning up the radio music to end the conversation. His brain quickly latched on to more pressing problems as his eyes constantly flicked against his will to a silent, brooding Cinn who stared out the window. Just how much trouble was Julien in now? He pulled up at the cottage to drop Elliot and Darcy off, giving Elliot the most subtle of raised eyebrows to accompany his casual, "See you later."

Then Julien continued driving, allowing silence for a beat or two, before he said quietly, "I can drop you off and then head back to Darcy's."

Cinn's head snapped towards him so quickly, it almost gave *Julien* whiplash. "Why would you do that?"

"You're angry at me. I figured you might have changed your mind about me staying over until my building is repaired."

"Christ, Julien, you're impossible." Cinn groaned, raising his foot onto his seat to rest his forehead on his knee. "Of course, I still want you to stay. It'd be a bit pathetic if I didn't."

Julien couldn't help the smile that tugged at the corner of his lips as sweet, sweet relief washed over him. Cinn's offer that morning, following an uncomfortable night's sleep on Darcy's living-room floor, of temporarily housing Julien was one he was so greedy for, he didn't know what he'd do if it was ripped away from him. Perhaps he could somehow delay the repair of his glass wall indefinitely, if it meant guaranteeing waking up to Cinn in his arms every day...

"You're a nightmare, you know that?"

"Who, me? I don't know what you're talking about."

Cinn snorted, lightly shoving Julien's arm. Julien captured his hand, interlacing their fingers to place them on Cinn's thigh, where they rested for the remainder of the journey.

Cinn's little maisonette had always looked adorable from the outside, but was positively quaint on the inside.

"Why have we been hanging out at mine when we could have been experiencing these delights?" Julien said, nodding to the framed watercolour of a kitten catching a butterfly that hung in the living room.

"Just to be clear, none of this is mine," Cinn said, folding his arms. "Figured you'd prefer your ivory tower to granny chic. But, for the record, I like that kitten."

"Come here." Julien threw himself onto the sofa and held his arms out. To his surprise, Cinn didn't hesitate before joining him, pulling his legs up to lay his head on Julien's lap. "So, are you done being mad at me now?"

"Depends. Are you done treating me like a defenceless kid and charging off into danger on your own? It's so selfish."

Julien smoothed the deep creases on Cinn's forehead with his thumb. "Selfish?"

"Yes. It's fucking selfish when you could get yourself killed." The lines only deepened, accompanied by a scowl so fierce Julien had to fight back a laugh.

"So, would you miss me or something if I died?"

"For fuck's sake, Julien, this isn't funny." Cinn swatted his hand away. "Just... promise me there'll be at least a bit more discussion next time, before you charge off without a plan or backup."

"Okay," Julien lied, gazing into Cinn's golden-amber eyes before pressing a kiss to his pretty head. His pretty head that he'd do anything to protect. "I promise."

"You don't need to baby me, alright? I can hold my own."

You looked pretty fucking spooked when we took down Heino Richter in that warehouse, but fine.

"How are you feeling about the whole Béatrice thing now, really?" Cinn asked, his eyes fixed on Béatrice's locket, which Julien idly twisted around his finger.

Julien's heart lurched at Béatrice's name, his shutter guards flying up lightning fast. This was the last thing he wanted to think about. He'd been busy pushing those thoughts down. Down, down, *down*. He closed his eyes in a pathetic attempt to block out Cinn's question.

Knuckles brushed across his cheekbone. "It's okay to be mad at her for keeping this secret from you."

"I'm not."

Another lie. He wasn't merely *mad*. He was fucking furious. So angry he could punch something, relish feeling the stinging bite against his fist. So angry he could scream until his throat was hoarse.

He and Béatrice had been an inseparable duo for as long as he could remember. From the moment she'd crawled over to him as a toddler, looking up at him so trustingly with big grey eyes, reaching up to tug on his hair.

Béatrice was always a single step away from Julien's shadow.

Always there whenever he needed her.

Always there to keep him in line.

Other siblings fought. But he and Béatrice fought to survive, together, those horrendous few years preceding his mother's death, and then the indescribable ones after.

When she'd followed Julien, Elliot, and Darcy to Auri after graduating a year after them, he'd felt complete again.

He'd known everything about her. Or so he'd thought.

This cosmic shift in the understanding of their shared universe was one he couldn't begin to fathom, let alone put into words.

And now, her final damning act—she'd returned as a shadow cat that refused to come anywhere near him.

Without conscious thought, he unclasped the locket. The silver chain spooled into the palm of his hand. He closed his fist over it, then slipped it into his pocket.

"Okay..." Cinn began, his voice trailing off as he watched the locket disappear. "Well. I'm here if you want to talk about it."

The sincere statement, so heartfelt and genuine, caused a healthy jolt of guilt to shoot through Julien.

"Thank you," Julien whispered, ghosting his lips over his cheekbone before kissing the soft lips already slightly parted for him. "I appreciate that." *You help me so much just by being here, right now, like this.*

Julien would happily spend the rest of the day like this, entwined around Cinn's warm body, but alas, life had other plans. "I need to drive back to mine and see if they'll let me at least access my flat. Get clothes and such." *Enough belongings to stay forever.* "And the paperwork I need for work." And the equipment that would come in handy for his midnight rendezvous. Though Cinn didn't need to know that part.

"That's fine. I'm planning to send some Christmas cards back to England anyway. Darcy mentioned that the post office on the outskirts of town is still open, unlike the one in the town centre, which is just a pile of rubble."

Julien made a retching sound. "Stop saying the C word. You're doing it just to annoy me."

"Once you try my secret-recipe roast potatoes, you'll come around. You'll see."

"Only you would have a secret recipe for a fucking potato."

Four

JULIEN

Julien didn't bother to arrive at the meeting spot until fifteen minutes past midnight. It was a good thing too—it was pushing half past when Elliot rocked up on his Yamaha, the rumbling engine cutting through the peace of the night's still air. He hopped off, his usually spotless navy-blue gendarmerie uniform covered in ashy grey. At least he hadn't changed out of it—they may well need its authority.

Waiting outside, leaning on Maz, Julien said, "What time do you call this?"

"I call it 'the time I should be sleeping rather than risking my career on some sort of crackpot plan my best friend has cooked up.' Sound familiar?"

"I think I've heard of it once or twice before."

Julien flashed Elliot a grin. Elliot would wait a moment, then flash one back, because Elliot loved these sorts of escapades too, even if he'd never admit it.

"Did Cinn not want to come?" Elliot asked, for the sole purpose of being an ass, because of course he knew Cinn had no idea Julien was here.

For a moment, it had been touch and go as to whether Cinn would fall asleep in time for Julien to sneak out. He'd cooked them dinner, wittering on about all the new equipment he'd bought and the rare spices he'd found at the market, while Julien pretended to listen rather than admire how cute he looked in the apron he wore. Trying not to daydream about taking it off him.

Then Cinn had gone and rendered him speechless by showing him his small stockpile of 'French wine' he'd gathered. Julien didn't have the heart to tell him most of it wasn't French, and would be considered battery acid by his father's standards.

They'd cuddled together on the sofa again, and then, only one glass of red later—with Cinn pretending to enjoy it, and Julien relentlessly teasing him—the toll of the past couple of days caught up with him, and the arm that was holding Julien had gone limp, his breaths heavy.

Surviving an earthquake will do that to you.

With all the motetech Julien had installed in her, Maz could almost drive herself at this point, but he needed a clear head for the task ahead, regardless.

"He was too tired."

Elliot snorted. "What if he wakes up and finds you gone?"

Unlikely. Cinn had appeared dead to the world even after Julien transferred him to his bed. He was a remarkably heavy sleeper—Julien's previous attempts to gently rouse him with a suggestive stroking of limbs had sadly failed.

"In that unlikely event, you rang Cinn's phone after your shift, begging me for a lift as your bike broke down."

It was okay. He'd make all this up to Cinn in the morning. He could think of at least five ways to do so, none of which required Cinn to even leave his bed.

"Right. Incredibly kind of you to help me. Shall we? I do actually need to sleep at some point."

Elliot gestured down the valley to where a quiet, darkened Auri lay waiting for them. Usually a sea of twinkling lights after sunset, not even the lumenmote lanterns cast their orange glow tonight. The only source of light came from the red glowing barrier, now fully intact.

As they half walked, half slipped down the hill, Elliot sighed before asking, "What's the plan, then? Can I let you through the barrier and wait outside?"

"Now where would the fun be in that? But yes, part one involves you getting us through the barrier."

"I figured that was why I'm here."

"Hey! Breaking and entering should never be a solo expedition. If you weren't here, I'd have nobody to send around the corner ahead of me."

A firm shove from Elliot had Julien flying down the grassy bank, almost tripping on a rock as he laughed, the warmth of it combatting the chilled air. When they approached the red barrier, Julien sobered. He reached out his hand, allowing the light to cast dark crimson hues on his skin. It was so tempting to touch it, even knowing full well it would jolt his body with a burst of electricity, while repelling him backwards several metres to land on his ass. It had been one of the first projects Julien had worked on years ago as a MEET intern. His colleagues had taken it in turns to test its efficiency. Tech guys really know a good time when they see one.

From the chest pocket of his uniform, Elliot removed the small, golden coinesque object the gendarmerie carried in lieu of plastic badges. He pressed it against the nearest metal pole that created the framework for the fence. The shimmery red light that passed between it and the next pole flickered, then faded, allowing them to pass through.

Walking through a deserted Auri in the daytime had been strange, but wandering through it at nighttime was downright eerie. The lack of any light, bar fleeting glimpses of moonlight, put Julien on edge, and a palpable chill shot down his spine. Julien reached for Elliot's arm to still him before rummaging in Elliot's pocket.

Elliot cocked his head to one side. "What?"

Julien's thumb passed over the cool metal of his lighter. He brought it out, flicking his thumb over the spark wheel to produce a small flame that danced gently in the mild breeze. Now he had the light source—*lu-menmotes* source—that he needed. Slowly, so as to not extinguish the flame, he drew upon the motes. There weren't many, as the flame was tiny, but Julien's best talent—aside from the one he didn't like to think about—back when he'd channelled, had always been amplifying the innate power of motes more than anyone else his age could.

Soon, a large glowing ball of light hovered a few centimetres above his palm. He raised it above their heads before walking on, its light casting upon Elliot's face to reveal his slow grin.

"You little shit. Always were a show-off." Elliot shoved his chest. "You're going to constantly show me up again now, aren't you, just like when we were kids?"

Julien brought one shoulder up in an exaggerated shrug. "You can't fight pure talent, baby."

The snort that Elliot produced echoed loudly off the tunnel created by the stone brick walls of Caelum Hall and the Echelon Quarters. Julien raised a finger to his lips. "Shh."

"Where are we even going, anyway?"

"Eleanor's office."

Elliot stopped so abruptly, Julien banged into his shoulder.

"You're joking," Elliot snapped, but his calculating eyes made it clear that he knew Julien wasn't. "You're really buying AP's bullshit? Why would Eleanor want to hurt Béatrice? And what do you think you're going to find in there, some sort of evil-mastermind cork board with photos and maps and string?"

Julien marched ahead in reply.

"And besides, her office is in Ivory Tower. The other side of the crack!"

Spinning on his heels, Julien continued to walk backwards. "Good thing you bragged earlier about being able to 'jump over it blindfolded' then."

If the look on his face was anything to go by, Elliot did *not* find him funny.

The fissure was hard to spot with limited light. If Julien hadn't been there a handful of hours ago, he might have stumbled right into it, to his imminent death. As Elliot neared it, he reached out to slow him, approaching it with the reverence he felt it deserved, after his little moment with it earlier.

"We can definitely jump it," insisted Elliot.

"With a little help, *oui*."

Julien took a few steps back, sending the lumenmote ball floating high above the crack. After bouncing on his knees for a few beats, he sprinted forward, launching himself into the air while channelling the wisps of windmotes the breeze offered to create a tremendous current of air that propelled him across the gaping crevice, and then some.

Landing with a side roll, and a flourish mainly for Elliot's amusement, a smile spread across Julien's face as he looked up at the night sky. It was as close as you could get to flying, using windmotes in that way. It had been so long since he'd done it. His current adrenaline-fuelled rush was accentuated by the elation his muscles tingled with, relishing the pleasure of channelling again.

A thud sounded, followed by a hand reaching for his. "Having fun?" Elliot asked, as he stood straight and smoothed his clothes.

A handful of twists and turns down cobblestone paths later, they stood facing the Nexus Towers, two symmetrical structures built using deep obsidian stone, silver threads of marble slithering through them like veins.

The grand glass entrance to Ebony Tower reflected their images back to them as they approached, a judgemental warning against their intrusion.

One slide of Elliot's authentication coin against the metal strip of the door later, the entrance quietly opened, allowing them into the uncannily empty lobby. Every step they made on the tiled floor resonated like a thunderclap. Julien took a half step towards the elevators that obviously weren't turned on before sighing and heading for the staircase. Many floors later, they finally reached Eleanor's.

"You know my badge won't get you through her office door, right?" Elliot whispered when they arrived. "We're lucky MEET hasn't installed any sort of tracking in these yet." He spun the coin in his fingers. "Right? *Right?*"

Julien raised one deliberate eyebrow. "Do you take me for an idiot?" He allowed his rucksack to slide onto the floor before his hand sank into it, fingers quickly grasping a smooth, cold, tube-shaped object.

"You and your bag of tricks," Elliot muttered.

Julien brought the floating ball of light close to the barrel lock on Eleanor's door. He pressed the palm-sized cylinder over the keyhole. He'd tinkered around with this design himself, initially just for fun, or perhaps to break into the kitchen cupboard Darcy sometimes locked her good snacks behind. Its maiden voyage into the *real* world of crime took place earlier this year, when Julien broke into the morgue to steal Béatrice's necklace back.

The weight of the metal in his hand vibrated as the motetech device activated, sending malleable metal through the keyhole to work its magic.

He'd forgotten the horrendously loud noise it made.

CLACK CLACK CLICK CLACK CLACK

"Turn it off!"

"There's nobody here, pipe down. You're making more noise than it!"

After several more clicks and even more clacks, the device sibilated a hiss.

Julien tried the door handle. It allowed itself to be pressed firmly down, opening the door. He crept into Eleanor's office. "Mission accomplished."

"Alright, James Bond. Five minutes, then we're out."

Moonlight shone through the large glass window, illuminating the wall. Alongside Eleanor's small collection of Rothko paintings hung a portrait of a girl, by an expressionist artist Julien had never heard of. The young blonde child stared at him suspiciously as he opened drawer after drawer, cupboard after cupboard. Boring administration paperwork and broken staplers were his only prizes.

If Julien were Eleanor, where would he keep the fun stuff?

"Time's up."

Julien almost got up from crawling underneath her desk, but then the memory of L's voice snarling, 'Eleanor Sinclair' ricocheted through him.

"*Non,* not yet." If they'd been betrayed by the woman Julien had grown up respecting, had grown up *trusting*—

He needed to know.

Think, Julien, think!

Something was niggling at the back of Julien's brain. Itching it. Tickling it.

Hold on... that girl in the portrait... an expressionist artist Julien had never heard of? Impossible! He tore across the room to gape up at the canvas of the child.

Girl, Concealed by Céleste Margaux Leclerc.

Who?

Julien studied the portrait, which depicted a young girl with large, haunting eyes, her form partially obscured by swirling, shadowy brush-strokes and a veil-like pattern. If Darcy were here, they'd dissect how the artist was trying to convey both a physical and metaphorical hidden depth, but Elliot wouldn't appreciate his insight.

Julien whistled. He ran his fingers across the painting's ornate golden frame.

"We're not here to steal Madame Sinclair's art!" Elliot scowled, tearing an exasperated hand through his curls.

"Why did your mind jump to that?"

Julien's hands travelled across to grip both corners. Instinctively, he squeezed, pressing the metal inwards. When the painting crumpled like tissue paper, he had to hold back a gasp of surprise.

A subtle hum filled the room as the thin canvas warped into a piece of flimsy cloth.

"What sort of motetech is this?" hissed Elliot.

Somewhat taken aback, Julien stared between the pile of material on the floor and the large metal safe installed within Eleanor's wall. "I'm... not sure."

A safe, yet no visible lock.

It was likely that it had some sort of detection system that would register anyone attempting to access it. Possibly, it could be traced right back to him.

Fuck it.

Julien yanked on the handle with some force.

"Yay, more files."

"Files hidden behind a secret painting, Elliot. You think they're going to be grocery lists? Or maybe her Christmas cards?"

Numerous folders were stuffed inside the safe, a plethora of coloured tabs and chunky paperclips poking out of many of them. With Elliot's patience wearing thin, Julien had to adopt the most efficient search strategy possible. Without further ado, he yanked on the bottom folder, hard, sending the entire contents scattering onto the floor by their feet.

Julien awaited a verbal reprimand from Elliot, but he simply threw up his hands before dropping to the floor.

What Eleanor actually did all day had never been entirely clear, her job title vaguely linked to HR and foreign relations. As Julien poured through the files, helped by the light of his lumenmote ball, he became no more enlightened, as the files were meaningless to him. A fair few of them were in languages Julien had no knowledge of—Arabic? Japanese?

Others appeared to be invoices, rows and columns of senseless numerals. His attention was briefly caught by a document listing a series of coordinates. He studied them, anticipating his brain magically inferring some meaning. Nothing.

Julien tossed the folder back on the pile, a sobering sensation of failure curling up in his stomach. This was useless. He didn't even know what he was looking for. Elliot was exhausted and Cinn was back at home, expecting to find Julien in his bed if he woke.

"Let's—"

A low hiss from Elliot. "This one is personnel files!" He withdrew a pile of paper from the fat manilla folder, flapping it in the air. A photograph of a man's face was clipped to the front of a bunch of papers.

Julien snatched it. "This isn't Béatrice," he muttered, scanning the lines of handwritten information about the German man.

"No, but this one is."

Julien's head shot up. Elliot held up a similar file, this time with his sister's pale face filling the frame. Her Auri intake ID photograph. "Let me see." Julien reached towards it.

Elliot stilled, cocking his head. "Shh... Do you hear that?"

"What?" Julien snapped, trying to tug Béatrice's file from his grip.

Elliot's wide eyes and shushing sound forced him to pay attention. Footsteps. Heavy ones, coming from the floor below them. Whoever else was in the building with them in the middle of the night, it couldn't be good news.

"Let's just take it and get out of here," hissed Elliot, jumping to his feet and stuffing the rest of the files back into the safe at random.

"*Non*, we have to photocopy it. Else she might spot it missing. Though, I think your reorganisation of her secret filing cabinet might have given the game away anyway," snapped Julien, glaring at the pigsty Elliot had made of the safe's interior.

"And which one of us tipped them all on the floor, you twat?" A thud below them, followed by a creak. Elliot sighed. "Fine, give me her file, quick. I saw a photocopier back near the bathroom."

Julien stared down at the manilla folder Béatrice's file had come out of, tossed to the floor with its innards spilling out. If Eleanor had a file on Béatrice... "Wait a second."

"*What*? Give it to me!"

Ignoring him, Julien wedged Béatrice under his armpit and flicked through the rest of the files at the speed of light.

Which was not fast enough for Elliot.

"Julien!"

"Just *one second*!"

His eyes cast over men and women of all ages, some of their files thick, others a single sheet of paper. He'd have loved to take them all home with him, to unravel the mystery of why each was important enough for Eleanor—and therefore the consortium—to have a file on them, but he only had time for one in particular.

There.

A wave of shock pulsed through Julien at finding what he was seeking, as Cinn's unsmiling face glowered at him. A police photograph from his arrest. Cinn appeared so pissed off Julien almost laughed. He turned it around to flash it to Elliot.

"How did you... never mind, stay here and tidy up."

Elliot grabbed the two files, and Julien set about making the safe's interior look less like a bomb had exploded in it. The loud whirring of the photocopier drifted down the hall. Was the sound audible to their friend downstairs?

After an eternity of anxiety-inducing noises, Elliot returned with the originals to put back in the safe.

For a moment Julien feared *Girl, Concealed* would remain *Girl, Crumpled Mess on the Floor*, but the canvas thickened when he stretched it, and easily slotted back into its golden frame.

It really was an impressive work of motetech. One he planned on thoroughly investigating at a later time.

Hovering by the door, Elliot stage-whispered Julien's name. They slipped out into the quiet corridor but Elliot stopped them, placing a finger on his lips and pointing towards the staircase at the far end.

Those damned footsteps, getting increasingly louder, were rhythmically marching up the tiled steps, not making any attempt to be quiet.

Which meant, whoever they were, they were supposed to be here. Unlike them.

"*Putain*," hissed Julien, glancing down the other end of the corridor, which offered no escape.

"You don't say." Elliot grabbed his wrist and pulled him into the bathroom, sending the door crashing into the wall with a bang. They both groaned at the noise. "And this is how my career goes down the toilet," he said, voice deadpan, opening a stall door so they could both squeeze inside.

The humour did nothing to help the guilt quickly rising in Julien. Perhaps he could claim Elliot was there under duress? He could even rough Elliot up a little—a black eye might do the trick.

At the same time as Julien slid the stall lock shut, the bathroom door opened with another bang. Elliot pulled Julien up to stand with him on the toilet, wobbling with him on the small space.

"Who's in there?" a voice demanded. Young, female. "Only gendarmerie have access to the Institute this evening. Identify yourself."

They offered no reply, and for a stretching moment, the only sound was Julien's blood rushing through his temple.

The woman rattled the stall door.

Julien shrugged off his long black coat. "Use this to cover your uniform. Pull the hood up and get ready to run," he said in his quietest whisper.

"I can hear you!"

Elliot's mouth formed a grim line. "What's our plan?"

"I'm sorry if she's your friend." Julien squatted lower, holding on to Elliot to steady himself.

"What the fuck are you doing?"

Julien lifted the lid off the top of the cistern and sent it clattering to the ground, the heavy ceramic creating the most almighty of crashes.

As predicted, the female gendarme dropped to the floor, the cuff of her navy uniform poking under the door.

All they had now was the element of surprise.

Before her face could follow, Julien reached for the watermotes between the molecules of the modest amount of water in the cistern. Without pausing to second-guess his plan, he channelled a forceful stream of—not entirely clean-looking—water directly into the woman's face just as it popped under the crack.

She shrieked in surprise.

Before she had time to react, Julien grabbed Elliot's sleeve, then flung them at the stall door, flicking the lock open, jumping over the lady being pummelled in the face by the relentless jet stream of toilet water.

They pounded down the narrow corridor. Julien was dripping wet himself from the splash back, but he couldn't really complain, he supposed.

Down the stairs.

They took them two at a time, then three. Then, out into the cool night. In their absence, the air had swollen with drizzle, light yet instantly drenching. At least it would wash the toilet off him.

"That was Kayla. We're lucky she's a cocky bastard who never bothers calling for backup." Elliot threw Julien's coat back to him.

"Cocky Kayla. Got it. Let's get out of here before she recovers from her drowning."

By the time they'd reached the Verdant Conservatory, the light rain had rapidly transformed into large droplets pelting down on them.

"Are the files okay?" Devastation would be the word if they risked so much to be left with a soggy, illegible mess.

"Depends how waterproof this jacket is."

A sudden flash of light. *Flashlights,* in fact, two of them, over near the barrier.

Elliot cursed as Julien pressed himself against the wall, then nodded towards the entrance to the conservatory.

Surprisingly, his device wasn't required to open the door this time—apparently the perceived risk of people stealing mote-enhanced plants and flowers was very low.

A few footsteps inside, and the patter of drizzle on the crystal-clear domed glass of the conservatory came to a trickling halt. A few stars revealed themselves. Julien meandered up the chunky cobblestone path, brushing his fingers across the soft petals of bioluminescent orchids, glowing softly in shades of gold.

Well, while they were here...

"Where are you off to?" hissed Elliot, hot on his trail.

"To find mistletoe."

"What? Why?"

"It's Christmas."

"You hate Christmas."

Christmas. It had been a November, when *Mère* had died. They'd spent that holiday season in silent grief, with Béatrice refusing to come out of her room on Christmas Day. Julien passed the day spending his time picking out pine needles from the tree, arranging the spiky leaves in abstract patterns across the floor and meeting any interaction from his father with silence. Each year since, Julien worked to ignore the jovial festivities. Hard, when people erected giant inflatable eyesores of creepy looking Santas on every other road, but he did his best.

They finally located the mistletoe, growing in the far right of the maze-like conservatory, high in the branches of a lone tree.

Instead of only white berries, it boasted waxy clusters of crimson-red and dark green fruit. The leaves had a slight shimmer to them, promising the plant was infused with everglaze, and would appear as fresh as the day they were picked for months.

Standing on tiptoes, Julien ripped a bunch from the tree.

"I don't think you need mistletoe to get Cinn to kiss you."

Julien studied Elliot's expression. He wore a light, amused smile that seemed held in place for Julien's scrutiny. Whether it was all a facade or not, he'd take it. The two of them avoided the topic of Julien's dating life like the plague, since Elliot had bravely made his feelings clear many years ago. Julien was lucky Cinn was so instantly likeable, as it would have been hard for Elliot to hold on to any animosity.

"So, are you *together* now?" Elliot asked, further surprising Julien with the probing questioning.

Together. Julien marvelled at the word—it had never before applied to him. He hesitated for a moment, slanting another look at Elliot. "We haven't said as much, but, *oui*?"

"Don't worry. He's clearly smitten." Elliot rolled and unrolled an elliptical black leaf into a tube, eyes firmly glued to it. "But I suggest you stop pissing him off. You can't count on flowers to save you every time he catches you out in your web of lies."

Web of lies seemed a little extreme, but Julien let it slide, lest he spoil Elliot's remarkably happy acceptance of his relationship.

They walked in silence back to the entrance of the conservatory, opening the door a tentative crack. There was no sign of the gendarmerie, so they resumed their creeping journey through Auri, making it past the barrier and back to their vehicles without issue.

Elliot handed Julien the now tragically damp files before grabbing his motorcycle helmet from the saddlebag. He paused. "Are you going to show him this?"

"Of course!" It was true. Well, after he'd looked over it himself, alone, first. In case there were any nasty surprises.

"Why is it so important, anyway?"

"To see what she has on him. And to see if Eleanor has any information about his mother in there. Cinn said he was sad he'd lost contact with her."

Did he say that? Sort of?

"I was going to hire a PI, check her out a bit. Decide if Cinn seeing her again would be good for him. But this"—he wiggled the file in the air—"could make it far quicker and easier."

Elliot groaned. "You're not listening to me. Dude, he's barely forgiven you for the last ridiculous thing you did."

"What? How is this ridiculous?" What *would* be ridiculous was allowing Cinn to get hurt by his mother again.

With a single shake of his head, Elliot tugged on his helmet and sped away from Julien before he had a chance to defend himself, leaving him alone with a cloud of exhaust fumes and a bitter taste in his mouth.

Julien slipped into Maz's interior, wondering how quiet he'd have to be when he snuck back inside Cinn's house. A cool chill seeped through him that had nothing to do with the frigid air. Was Elliot right? Was he one step away from fucking it up again? Had he just tumbled the house of cards down? Well, it was too late now. He'd have to beg forgiveness. He was getting far too practised at that.

Five

CINN

"**G**ood morning, *mon amour*."

The lack of bright light creeping through his paisley curtains told Cinn it was nowhere near enough morning for his liking. Making a noise of clear dissent, he pulled the covers up over his face, only to have them ripped away from him.

An onslaught of wet, squelchy kisses assaulted Cinn's face.

This was it. The final straw of their incompatibility. Because Cinn wouldn't compromise when it came to sleep. He groaned loudly, squeezing his eyes shut as if it would magic Julien back to sleep at this ungodly hour.

More peppering of kisses followed, with Julien undoubtedly making deliberately ridiculous lip-smacking noises to accompany them. Shoving Julien off him with all his might only prompted him to cackle.

"You've got awful morning breath."

"Liar. I just brushed my teeth."

Cinn peeled his eyes open. Julien lay sprawled across the bed, smirking, one hand resting on his jeans, the dark denim ones that did great things for his ass. But why was he fully dressed so early? In fact, why was he *up* so early? Cinn squinted at him. Julien rarely looked anything but infuriatingly perfect, but today a purple tinge coloured faint bags under his eyes. Was it Cinn's imagination, or was his hair slightly damp, the tips clumped together in tiny spikes?

"Wh—"

His question was knocked out of him by Julien climbing on top of him while simultaneously throwing the duvet off the bed in a rather melodramatic way. Cinn wore only his pyjamas, a pair of ancient track-suit bottoms featuring several stylish holes, and the chill of the air caused a cascade of goosebumps to prickle his skin.

Cinn brought out his best scowl. "I'm cold."

"Don't worry." Julien pressed gentle lips to just shy of Cinn's Adam's apple, sending his pulse skyrocketing in anticipation. He trailed soft butterfly kisses up the column of his neck to finally meet his mouth. "I'll keep you warm."

Julien ground himself into Cinn as their mouths connected in another long, languid kiss.

Cinn broke away to smirk at Julien, saying, "I'm too tired." Then he gave an exaggerated yawn.

Julien pouted. "What if I spoke French to you?"

"Won't make the blindest bit of difference."

A slow grin arranged itself on Julien's face, dimples deepening threat-eningly. "Oh, really?" Julien dropped his low tone down to a seductive purr. "Have I told you how much *j'aime la courbe de ton cou*?" Julien's lips brushed against his neck, and the electrifying tingles he elicited had Cinn closing his eyes. The next press of Julien's mouth came against the tattoo on his rib. "*Tes tatouages si séduisants?*"

Cinn had to bite back a moan. *For fuck's sake.* How was he succumb-ing to Julien so damned easily?

"*Ton menton?*" Julien kissed the very tip of his chin, drawing a small laugh out of Cinn against his will. "*Comme j'aime tes joues?*" Julien drew the flesh of his cheek into his mouth with his teeth. For a tantalising sec-ond, Cinn prepared for him to bite down hard. But Julien only scraped along the skin before releasing him, to place his mouth over the silver bar through Cinn's eyebrow. "*Ton piercing de mec rebelle?*"

Why did Cinn get the feeling Julien had just insulted him?

"Nope. This isn't doing anything to me," Cinn got out, on a gasp, as Julien flicked his tongue over the metal bar. "Nothing at all." His cock twitched in angry protest of the lie.

"Not even if I tell you…" Julien shuffled down the bed to press his mouth against the tip of Cinn's cock, the pressure so glorious he could cry. "*Combien j'aime… ça?*"

Although Cinn wanted to keep the game up for a bit longer—because really, he shouldn't make it *too* easy for Julien—he couldn't help the low rumble of approval that hummed out of him when Julien mouthed along the length of his dick, then followed that up with a firm squeeze from his hand.

And if Cinn had something important he had wanted to ask Julien, it had long since left his head, forced out by the heavy weight of him pressing Cinn deep into his soft mattress. Cinn ran his hands up Julien's back, then down again, landing on his ass to pull Julien further into him, relishing the feel of his hard cock against his own, albeit through too many layers of clothing.

Julien must've had a similar thought, as his fingers came up to hook around the waistband of his tracksuit bottoms, running the back of his hand all the way across his stomach. Left, right—a slow, tantalising trace that had Cinn's back arching up, desperate for his hand to slip lower.

Heat already pooled in the pit of his stomach—there was no way Cinn had the patience for Julien's teasing this morning, especially after all of that sultry French. He made to yank his trousers off himself, and succeeded in tugging them down an inch or two before his hands were captured by long, strong piano fingers closing over them.

Julien tutted.

Releasing Cinn's hands, Julien pulled the bottoms back up, allowing his hand to brush against his poor cock, now straining against the material, creating an impressive tent that Julien was *somehow* able to resist. *Rude.*

"For fuck's sake, Julien!"

"*Pardon*, do I hear a complaint?" Julien shuffled down the bed, before crawling between Cinn's legs and trailing teasing light touches around to cup the back of his knees. His fingers found a hole in the cotton, and Julien kneaded his fingertips into the soft flesh, flashing Cinn an infuriating grin that he ought to punch from his face. Shame Cinn needed his mouth intact.

"I think you need new pyjamas."

Cinn opened his mouth to tell him to jog on—

Riiiiiiiiiiiiiiip

Julien had torn the thinning material in two, all the way from his knee to the waistband. He completed his mission by using both hands to continue to split the grey cotton, fisting two handfuls in opposite directions and yanking hard, completely ruining the garment.

"*Oui*. You *definitely* need new ones." Julien blinked at him, the picture of innocence.

"You little shit."

They were Cinn's only sleepwear, and they had seen him through thick and thin over the years, but he had no time to mourn their loss. Julien's hands, done with ruining perfectly good items of clothing, soon found Cinn's thick trail of hair, his fingers threading through it.

Cinn's neglected dick, now bare to the world thanks to his refusal to wear underwear to bed, now throbbed. *Ached*. Cinn just managed to swallow down a stream of pleading demands that threatened to slip out of him. He wouldn't give Julien the satisfaction. Not yet, anyway.

But then Julien tested that resolve in earnest—kissing up one raised thigh and swiping his tongue against the hollow of his hip, flicking it again and again, *so* close yet never close enough.

"Well?"

Cinn groaned. If Julien didn't take his tortured dick into his mouth right now he might perish. "Urg, I hate you so much," he spat.

"Just keep telling yourself that, *mon joli*."

But Julien must have decided to take pity on him, as finally—*fucking finally*—his hot tongue found the base of his cock, and began a slow, wet, savouring slide all the way to its head, mapping his length.

The shaky exhale of Cinn's breath was met by a small hum from Julien, as he licked a bead of precum waiting for him as if it was the most delicious dessert, swirling the tip of Cinn's dick around his tongue with exquisite pressure.

Then, enveloping Cinn with his mouth, Julien lightly squeezed the base of Cinn's cock. The brightening morning sun fought its way through the gap in the curtains, hitting Julien's face and lighting up flinty grey eyes, alight with hunger.

God, how Cinn could drown in those eyes.

Julien allowed a beat of stillness between them. Then, gripping Cinn's hips with both hands, Julien wrapped tight lips around Cinn, gliding his mouth downwards to take most of his cock into his mouth in one fell swoop.

It only took seconds for Julien to turn him into a writhing mess.

Cinn's hips snapped up to meet the rhythmic pace Julien set, and both of his hands shot straight to Julien's head, communicating his pleasure with the force with which he pulled Julien's hair, instead of the babble of praise that circled around his head like a turntable: *you're a fucking god, nobody else's mouth could ever compare, you make me come undone with just the way you look at me.*

But Julien's name slipped out of Cinn's mouth regardless, and he knew its cadence spoke volumes, a breathy neediness that almost certainly gave any game away.

"Julien," he whimpered again, his entire body a shaking mess, and Julien's free hand grabbed his, squeezing their fingers together, *hard,* hard to the point of pain.

Julien swallowed around his head.

Every muscle tensed as one for a dizzying moment as Cinn's orgasm crashed into him, flooding through him in a flash, and he erupted into Julien. His lover drank him down, swallowing three times more, and Cinn continued to thrust into Julien's deliciously warm mouth, riding wave after wave of pleasure.

Cinn only had time to see two dots of pink flush on Julien's pale cheeks before he melted into the mattress, eyes rolling straight back into his head. As Julien finished him off with the tiniest of gentle kitten licks, he shut his eyes and surrendered to the fuzziness around the edge of his consciousness.

He came around to the sound of Julien spitting.

Propping himself up, he blinked rapidly at the sight of Julien, who'd shed his jeans and underwear, leaving him only in his simple loose white shirt. He kneeled above Cinn, his glorious, long, slender cock in one hand, furiously stroking himself with a glistening mix of cum and saliva.

Julien stared down at Cinn, fierce, primal, possessive.

Cinn made one weak attempt to reach for Julien's dick, but found his hand being batted away with force.

The sight of Julien towering above him, fisting himself with such vigour, was intoxicating to the point of feeling drugged.

As dawn broke, light further filled the room, throwing a spotlight onto Julien, who shimmered in Cinn's dreamy haze.

Dressed in white, his golden-haired boy became an angel. A beautiful angel, who became more and more beautiful every time Cinn pulled a layer off him. Each one exposed new depths, a gradual unveiling of a masterpiece hidden beneath layers of paint.

Yes, his princeling was an angel, and this was Cinn's baptism.

Each wave of his pleasure was a prayer, each cry a hymn of devotion.

"Look at you," his angel said. "So perfect for me."

Then, although it was Julien who was bathing his body with thick ropes of warm cum, it was Cinn who unleashed a series of breathy moans and cries as each one hit his torso. Every place Julien's glory touched his skin anointed him with ecstasy, holy water purifying him.

The bed shifted as Julien climbed up his body, hovering an inch above him to smile at him, smug but softly so. Cinn only had time to blink before Julien swiped his thumb across the sticky mess of Cinn's chest, then brought it to his mouth, caressing his bottom lip with it. Cinn darted his tongue out to trace its path, then brought Julien's thumb into his mouth, sucking it once, then reached for Julien's head, wanting to kiss him again, *needing* to kiss him again.

The kiss was a frenzy—a smash of mouths, tongues enacting a desperate dance, hands seizing hair. Once they were breathless, Julien pulled away, draping his weight over Cinn, blanketing him.

"I think... you just took me to heaven," Cinn may have muttered into a pillow, or may have not.

A pause. "What?"

Yes, definitely out loud.

He took a moment to ride out the last of the blissful high, listening to the sound of his breathing calming. Then, he required a different sort of high.

Wrapping a blanket around him, he hopped over several trip hazards on the way to throw open the window. A flick of a lighter later, he was inhaling his first sweet drag, savouring the familiar rush.

He gestured the cigarette towards Julien, who wrinkled his nose. From his position starfishing on the bed, he eyed Cinn with disdain. "Must you smoke inside?"

The cheek!

To make a point, Cinn turned himself away from the window, cigarette in one hand, allowing the smoke to curl around him. "I'm sorry, whose house is this?"

"Auri's, the last time I checked. Unless it's Eleanor's, but I doubt that with those curtains."

Cinn scoffed, but because he wasn't a totally inconsiderate ass, resumed his position of leaning over the windowsill. Drizzle dampened his hand. Another rainy day ahead. "So, what's the plan today?" he asked, because there was no possibility that his agenda—of spending the day alone together, preferably predominantly in this very room—could be manifested.

"Breakfast. Coffee. Darcy's. I've got something to share."

Of course you do.

Cinn opened his mouth, but Julien raised his hand. "*Non.* First, I have some more very important things to do, involving your lips." He leaned up on one side, patting the empty space next to him on the bed. "So get that cute butt of yours back over here..."

The suspense over Julien's 'announcement'—or whatever it was—grew to infuriating levels by the time they'd reached Darcy's cottage, and began the wait for Elliot to arrive. A mere fifty minutes later, the creak of the front door preceded a cold draft sweeping through Darcy's living room, flickering the flames of her fire.

Darcy sat cross-legged on the rug, because Cinn had snagged the armchair that was surely his now, anyway. She greeted Elliot with a wave. "Your tea is cold, and you're not getting another."

In response, Elliot shook his hair like a dog wet from the rain spraying Darcy with water.

She shrieked.

Elliot stretched himself across Darcy's sofa, looking at Cinn with hopeful eyes. "Got any cookies, at least?"

"Sorry mate, no time."

"Anyway," said Julien loudly, then trailed off, mouth slightly parting as he stared into the corridor.

Béatrice lingered near the door, tail undulating like a wisp of smoke. The shadow cat glanced tentatively between them, bobbing its eyeless head, before scampering past Elliot, Darcy, and Julien without a second thought. The oddly weightless creature jumped onto Cinn's lap, curling up on it with a demanding squeak.

"You know what? I'm getting less and less convinced that is Béatrice, you know."

Cinn shot Julien his most smug smirk as he scratched the cat's ears. Funnily enough, he'd never been one for animals, but it was hard to resist this one when she liked *him* the best.

"Well, Julien? What is it?" Darcy said. "I have other stuff to do today."

"I present..." Julien slammed a pile of creased, battered-looking papers onto the coffee table. "A file documenting Béatrice's every move. Found in none other than our friend Madame Sinclair's office."

Cinn's hand stilled its movements across the cat's knobbly spine. *What?*

"How on earth did you get that?" Darcy echoed Cinn's thoughts. She snatched the papers from Julien, laying the collection flat across the surface. The first page had Béatrice Montaigne printed at the top in big bold letters, and a professional photo of her attached to it, her blonde hair tied up. A quick scan of the first page offered a list of her basic information—birthday, birthplace, et cetera.

"These are her university transcripts." Elliot thumbed through documents, frowning. "And this one... a bank statement? Is it all random crap?"

Cinn grabbed another sheet from the pile, brushing his hand over the crinkled paper. "Why do these all look like they've been fished out of a puddle?"

The slight side-eye Elliot gave Julien did not escape Cinn's notice.

"What's that one there, Cinn?" asked Darcy.

"Addresses." Cinn trailed his finger down the list. "This address, listed as her home address. A Paris address... Julien's father's? Then the next one is Julien's flat in Talwacht, I think."

"Places she frequented?"

"And... I don't recognise this last one."

Darcy plucked the paper from Cinn's grasp. Her eyes narrowed. "Some other address in France. I don't know it either."

"France? I didn't see that earlier." Julien yanked it away before studying it, frown lines across his forehead slowly deepening. Recognition flashed across his face, then a sudden burst of shock that was swiftly replaced by a mask of controlled calm.

"Where is it then?" Cinn asked.

Julien pretended not to hear him, placing it down on the table.

Darcy drummed her fingers against it. "Well, this is all riveting stuff so far."

"God, you're impatient. Keep going." Julien pushed the final few unread sheets towards her.

It was only a second later that she gasped. Elliot leaned over her shoulder and Cinn copied him, dragging himself onto the rug next to Darcy—the large block of text looked daunting.

Béatrice Montaigne (BM) is a verified member of the Arcane Purifier organisation. While it is indicated that she holds a relatively low rank within the group, BM remains on our high-priority watch list. This status stems from substantial evidence suggesting she was personally recruited by L (Category A), a founding member and the chief coordinator of recent lobbying efforts. It is believed that BM's recruitment is linked to her familial connections, particularly her father, Lucien Étienne Montaigne. Lucien Mon-

ntaigne is the CEO of HorizonTech Enterprises and a prominent member of the AAIoES consortium.

Over the past decade, Lucien Montaigne has faced increasing scrutiny due to HorizonTech's acquisition of an estimated ninety per cent of new motetech patents. In addition to his role at HorizonTech, Montaigne holds board positions in six other companies. With HorizonTech's annual turnover exceeding ten million F, Montaigne is often accused of monopolising the industry.

The exact objectives of the Arcane Purifier organisation in utilising BM to gain information about Montaigne remain unconfirmed. Consequently, a specialised team has been assigned to monitor and document BM's activities.

Cinn touched the mysterious blacked-out sign off. Underneath, another lengthy paragraph awaited him.

Darcy tapped her finger next to it. "This one is dated a week or so after she died."

Béatrice Montaigne's central personnel file records that she died in Cagayan Valley, Philippines, while serving voluntarily for AAIoES's branch of WorldAid. At the time of her death, she was allegedly alone, her body discovered five hours later. The autopsy report indicated unusual tissue damage, suggesting her flesh had been exposed to extremely high temperatures. The remaining skin exhibited evidence of umbraphage lacerations. Additionally, a silver necklace found attached to her neck bore tiny traces of mote residue, indicating the object functioned as an amplifier.

Elliot unleashed a long, low hiss. "Fuck. You said, Cinn, that Béatrice told you there was an umbraphage there, before her locket amplified her mote channelling or whatever. But I didn't want to believe you."

Cinn leaned away from the table, folding his arms uncomfortably. *I told you so* seemed inappropriate.

Across his shirt, Elliot's fingers traced the path of the wound on his chest, gifted to him by a single strike of umbraphage tentacles when he'd stepped in to save Cinn. Guilt burrowed through Cinn. He'd never even properly thanked Elliot.

"I hope she went quickly," Elliot said, voice thick with emotion. "Because if she felt double the pain I did..."

The sick feeling in the pit of Cinn's stomach grew. When he was attacked at the lantern parade, the umbraphage picked him up and shook him like a doll. But it hadn't actually hurt him...

Aside from rendering him unconscious and locking him in the shadowrealm, of course.

"There are another couple of lines on the other side," said Julien.

Due to BM's suspected homicide, an investigation has been commissioned to determine her death's connection to the Arcane Purifiers.

"So..." Cinn turned to Julien. "Everyone told you her death was an accident, even though some people at least knew it wasn't?"

Julien didn't look away from staring into the fire. "Eleanor lied to my face. Multiple times."

Julien's voice shook with so much tightly wound rage, Cinn's breath caught in his throat. He gripped the edge of his armchair, as if any sudden movement might shatter the fragile tension hanging in the air.

After an age, Darcy coughed. "Is there any more, Julien? The results of the investigation?"

"No."

"Nothing?"

"*Non.*"

With a single sweep of his arm, Julien collected every sheet of paper, then flicked through them like a flipbook, staring at them like he could force them to reveal more secrets.

The haunted look on Julien's face made Cinn ache for him. If the other two weren't there, he'd cross the room, scoop him up against his chest and hold him close. Press kisses against his neck until he put the paper down and walked away from it all. However, Cinn wasn't quite sure what the rules were in front of his friends—*their* friends—and this certainly wasn't the time to test anything.

"But, if Madame Sinclair prepared this file, and *was,* for some unknown reason, responsible for her murder, why would she write evidence of a suspected homicide?" Darcy waved a hysterical hand in the air. "This makes little sense. Who did she prepare it for, anyway? The consortium? But it doesn't talk favourably about your father..."

"I don't know, Darcy," Julien replied through gritted teeth. "I'm sorry. But months later we're still going round in circles and I'm sick of it!" He threw the papers to the floor, where they scattered dramatically across the rug.

Darcy raised one expectant eyebrow, looking between Julien and the mess he'd made.

Julien picked them up.

After a tired stretch, Elliot leaned back, throwing his feet up onto the sofa. "We also don't know *she* wrote any of this, Julien, before you march up to her shaking your fist. This could easily have been prepared by someone else and given to her."

"Regardless, she still lied."

"I just can't see Madame Sinclair being involved in all this. I really can't," said Darcy.

Julien gave her a vicious shake of his head. "Stop being naïve, Darce."

It was clear Julien was reaching his limit. "Didn't you say in the car you had two things to share, Julien?" Cinn asked.

For some reason, Cinn's attempt at saving Julien only caused deeper crevices across his forehead.

"*Oui*. On to other matters." He slid another bunch of papers out of his shoulder bag. Then Julien's gaze seared into Cinn, whose skin immediately prickled. Behind him, Elliot wore a slightly guilty look, glancing down at the floor. *Odd*. "Or should I say, other files."

An unpleasant rush of heat surged through Cinn. He removed his beanie, fanning his face with it.

Julien placed the documents on the coffee table.

Cinn made no attempt to stop his jaw from dropping as he openly gaped at Julien. "What... what's that?" he heard himself say distantly, though he knew full well what Julien was holding—his own mug shot was glaring at him from across the room. He sucked in a deep breath, forcing his voice steady. "Why do you have that?"

Darcy leaned over the papers, wearing a confused frown.

Though she certainly wasn't as confused as Cinn was.

That morning they'd spent a lazy hour together—Cinn cooking spectacular mushroom omelettes for breakfast, Julien whining about his instant coffee—and all the while Julien had some sort of top secret file on *him* waiting in his pocket? Why the fuck had he waited until now? Because of the misguided notion that Cinn wouldn't explode at him in front of the others?

If so, he was in for a shock.

Cinn glared at Julien. "How did you say you got these files again?"

Come to think of it, Julien hadn't actually answered Darcy's same question earlier.

Before Julien could reply—taking his sweet time deciding what to say, sipping from a mug Cinn wasn't convinced still had tea in it—Cinn added, "And *why* do you have it?"

Julien set his cup down. His gaze turned tender, contemplative.

"After you mentioned your mother, I thought it might be a good place to start. Just to see what Eleanor had, if anything. And it does have information!" He fanned out the papers across the table. "A bit. There's an address, and a work address—she's employed at a hospital." The words tumbled out of Julien as if the faster he got them out, the sooner Cinn would move past his annoyance. "Good to know, *oui*?"

For fuck's sake.

Cinn tilted his head back as every drop of energy drained out of him like water through a sieve. How could he explain to Julien that he had no desire to reconnect with his mother? Especially as he was sure Julien would do anything to spend one more day with his. But it was better to hold on to the few positive memories he had of his mum without risking the pain of opening old wounds that he'd just finished stitching up.

"Look Julien, I'm sure you had... good intentions or whatever, but I think you misunderstood me the other day."

"But that's not all."

Cinn pressed two fingers to his temple. "Julien."

"There's information about—"

"I don't want to know!"

"—your father."

Six

Cinn

S ilence plummeted in a suffocating wave around Cinn, sucking all the oxygen out of the air.

Cinn stared at Julien. His face was about to burst into laughter, any second now. Because Julien was surely joking, though this was hardly funny.

But Julien gave away nothing more, his expression remaining one of controlled neutrality as he patiently waited for Cinn to react.

This wasn't a joke.

"Well, fuck me," muttered Elliot.

"My... my what?" Cinn said weakly, slumping back in the armchair.

His father. A man he had no living memory of.

It had bothered him a handful of times in recent years, how remarkably little his mother had mentioned his father, back when he lived with her.

He knew his father was dead without knowing precisely *how* he knew. He'd certainly got none of the infamous lies of single-mother households. There was no 'he was a famous rockstar killed in a tragic car crash', and no 'his submarine got lost in the Mariana Trench'.

The only thing his mother did share about his father was his taste in music. A song would come on the radio, and she'd say, 'your dad loved this band', and then get that sad look in her eyes that invited no questions.

Apart from that, Cinn's father was only a blank space in the tapestry of his past, a ghost without a story. A blank space. Apart from... There *was* that one photograph on the bookshelf, a framed portrait of a man under a weeping willow tree. Had he actually been explicitly told by his mother that the photo was of his father, or had he simply connected the dots himself?

In the photo, the man's face was obscured, lost in the shadow of the cascading branches, leaving his features forever a mystery. The man's arms were bare, revealing a skin tone strikingly similar to Cinn's own, and it was this fact that squashed his persistent theory that he was just a random man his mum had cut out of a magazine. But he wouldn't put it past her.

"Give me that." Cinn reached out to grab the file, clutching it to his chest.

The first bunch of pages were similar to Béatrice's—basic information. They'd somehow collated a list of every address he'd ever lived at, including all ten of his foster homes. Next was a detailed police report of his first arrest as a teenager, which he quickly flipped over—no need to relive *that* right now.

Another police report, another bad memory—the quadruple homicide that triggered Auri's involvement with Cinn. Even looking at the photographs from the CCTV made a sour taste rise in the back of his mouth, and his warding band heated slightly.

Then, a transcript of a telephone conversation between Viktor Sturmhart and Eleanor, ordering her to go and collect him from England.

A photocopy of a letter to the chief of the gendarmerie, Salvatore Gallo from Eleanor, stating that he might be a flight risk and she may need his officers to help contain him within the Auri boundaries.

His mood plummeted further. He'd never been the biggest fan of Eleanor and this wasn't helping.

Turning the page, Cinn saw Noir's name at the top, heart sinking at the notion of the old codger spilling the beans about their tutorial-come-therapy sessions. However, after an explanation of his visits to Noir, the rest of the page was filled with a single line—*session records confidential.* Cinn laughed, the image of the grumpy bastard refusing to contribute entertaining him greatly. Or, equally likely, Noir couldn't be bothered to type up his notes from his leather notebook.

"The information about your parents is next," said Julien, peering at him from across the room.

Cinn shot him a look that he hoped said, *shut the fuck up,* before studying the documents.

First up, his mother. Just the sight of her name, Esme Saunders, had his heart leaping into his throat. There was no photograph. It had been so many years since he'd seen her—would he even recognise her? Underneath her current residential address—a part of London he didn't recognise, a fancier postcode than he'd grown up in for sure—there was indeed a work address at a hospital.

That was it, aside from a note stating that Cinn left her custody in July nineteen eighty-five. The phrase 'voluntarily relinquished custody to state' wasn't *quite* how Cinn remembered it.

"Alright?" asked Darcy quietly.

Cinn grunted in reply, moving onto the final piece of paper.

A black and white headshot of a man in his twenties filled a corner of the page. Cinn crumpled the corner of the sheet in his shock.

"He has your hair, right?" said Julien.

"I've got my mum's hair," Cinn shot straight back.

But he couldn't deny the similarities between him and this man. His father. The stranger possessed a slightly sharper nose, slightly narrower eyes, but the comparison was indisputable.

A trickle of sweat made its way down the back of Cinn's neck. It was difficult to breathe. He removed his hoodie, but the room was still *so goddamn warm.*

With his file in hand, Cinn stood, swept his rucksack up from the floor and headed out into the corridor, avoiding the three pairs of silent eyes that followed his path.

For reasons unbeknown to him, his feet took him to Béatrice's room, rarely ever entered. But one look at that black bundle of wool on her desk—the knitted scarf she'd never finish—had him pivoting on his heel, dashing through the kitchen to fling open the back door.

He inhaled a large gulp of crisp air, the chill of it hitting his throat like an icy shock.

It took several more breaths for the tightness in his throat to relax.

He headed to the bench, headphones at the ready. Cinn needed something that would blast his anxiety out of his head but his rucksack offered a limited selection of cassettes. He reached for his favourite—*Doolittle* by the Pixies—to remember that it had jammed while he was rewinding it yesterday, and now tangled lengths of black tape spilled out of the cassette like entrails. He picked it up regardless, giving its surface a sad stroke.

It had been the soundtrack to countless lonely nights, and had prevented him from slipping countless times, back when music was his only defence. He twisted his gold warding band before popping his next best option into his Walkman—The Cranberries's *No Need to Argue,* fast forwarding to "Zombie".

Headphones on, cigarette lit, he was finally ready to look at the photograph again.

His father stared up at him, wide-eyed, a startled smile on his face as if the camera had caught him unaware.

Although Cinn could see echoes of himself in the curve of the stranger's lips, the crinkle of his eyes, he couldn't reconcile the image with the man he'd sometimes allowed himself to imagine.

Neon pink leg warmers appeared in his peripheral vision. He hadn't heard Darcy approach over the deafening chorus of the song. He slid his headphones off as she sat down beside him.

"Julien tried to follow you out, but I sent him and Elliot to the shop for milk."

"Cheers."

"I also asked him to pick up some *verjus*. He'll have no idea what it is, so that should slow him down."

Whatever *verjus* was, Cinn didn't have the faintest clue. He nodded along in conspiratorial agreement.

"So, did you have any idea? About him being a shadowslipper?"

Cinn's head snapped to Darcy's. "*You what?*" He stared at her, letting out a hollow laugh that filled the garden.

Darcy's face twisted. "Your dad? Julien just told us that he was also a shadowslipper?" She nodded down to the file Cinn hadn't actually finished reading yet.

"You're fucking with me."

Her guilty, worried grimace suggested otherwise.

"Bloody hell." Cinn leaned back on the bench, watching the clouds in their slow drift for a count of ten. Then he dragged his eyes to the paper.

Nikolas Mavros
Born in Thessaloniki, Greece, 1950.
Deceased 10th March 1976.
Father, Ioannis Mavros. Mother, Eleni Mavros.

Grandparents. Now there was something Cinn had never considered before.

"Why don't I have his name?" Cinn murmured. "I don't think I even knew he was Greek…"

It was one thing to know his father was dead, but entirely another to *know*, know, seeing the word and date on the page.

Cinn glanced at the text below, the spark of a headache already igniting and he hadn't even attempted to read it yet. Béatrice's write up was bad enough, and this looked worse. He rooted around in his rucksack, moving mints and empty lighters aside to locate the yellow overlay Julien had gifted him. Once placed on the first line, the letters forwent their usual wiggling dance.

Fifteen at the time of the Calamities of 1965, Nikolas Mavros was a first generation moteblessed, and confirmed shadowslipper. His abilities allowed him to traverse back and forth to what is often referred to as 'the shadowrealm', or 'the other place', a phenomenon known to challenge the boundaries of reality and perception.

Arriving at AAIoES in late 1975, Mavros presented with severe psychosis, a condition exacerbated by his unique abilities. Medical professionals endeavoured to treat his condition, yet his mental state remained precarious. During periods of lucidity, Mavros offered intricate accounts of his shadowslipping experiences, initially misconstrued as symptoms of schizophrenia. As his illness progressed, he became increasingly unable to differentiate between his experiences in the shadowrealm and the tangible world.

In January 1976, Mavros lapsed into a persistent comatose state, defying all efforts at revival. His tragic case continues to intrigue researchers, highlighting the profound impact of shadowslipping abilities on the human psyche.

Notably, Mavros gained significant attention due to his claims of being able to bring 'spirits' and objects back from the shad-

owrealm into our world. However, it should be emphasised that this aspect of his ability was never conclusively verified. To date, this remains the sole documented potential instance of such a phenomenon occurring.

"Noir talked about him in one of our sessions. He said there was only one other shadowslipper that had brought anything back before. He didn't fucking tell me it was my father, though."

Cinn's earlier wave of fondness for the old man crashed and burned. His gaze combed over the photo of the father he had no memories of, the one he seemingly had to thank for the affliction that he'd once felt ruined his life.

"Before you explode at him in your next session, I have a sense that Julien may not have obtained these files using the most legal of methods. Just a hunch. So you might want to hold back."

Cinn dug the heel of his trainer into the ground, drawing a pattern in the dirt. "I'm not seeing him again until January, anyway."

The sun disappeared behind a grey cloud, removing the sliver of warmth it was offering.

"Come on."

Darcy led the way back into the kitchen to make another round of tea. By the time the leaves in the teapot had brewed, the front door clicked open and noisy footsteps echoed through the cottage.

Cinn didn't hold back his groan. He'd been rather enjoying his and Darcy's silent solitude.

Julien slid a bottle of *verjus* across the kitchen countertop, its glass surface gliding smoothly until it hit Darcy's hand.

"You found it then." She wiggled the small, green-tinted bottle in the air.

"Piece of cake. We asked the shopkeeper," said Elliot.

An awkward pause settled in the room. Cinn added a third spoon of sugar to his tea in order to keep staring down at it.

"So—"

"I think I need to go to London."

The words were out of Cinn's mouth before he even had a chance to understand why he was saying them. He ripped his eyes upward to meet Julien's piercing gaze.

"Really? You want to go see her?"

Cinn gave him a single decisive nod before he could change his mind. His head spun. This morning he barely knew whether his mother was even alive, and now he had an address, questions, and a plan. Well, a plan of sorts.

"I was hoping you'd say that," said Darcy, attracting everyone's attention. "My parents are flying to London for Christmas, but I didn't want to leave you alone this year, Julien, with how much you hate Christmas and such."

"Why does everyone keep telling me how much I hate Christmas?" Julien mumbled.

"Last year you begged me to burn down that obnoxiously large Christmas tree in the town square when it was still there on the second of January," said Elliot.

"And *I* caught you pulling down all the tinsel in the library study room," said Darcy.

"It's a place to work, not a winter wonderland," snapped Julien.

"Anyway, now we can all spend it with my parents."

Sounded like hell, but Cinn could hardly refuse Darcy's kind hospitality. "Okay," he replied weakly.

"I'll go give them a ring from the living room. Elliot?"

Darcy looked pointedly at Elliot, who shot her a baffled look back before a flash of understanding flickered over his face. He followed her out of the kitchen, leaving Cinn and Julien alone.

Julien teetered on the balls of his feet. He wrung his hands together, gaze scrutinising Cinn's face.

Cinn took a small sip of his tea, then set it back down. He leaned casually against the fridge. His gaze bore into Julien as he waited, and waited. He was prepared to wait all day for Julien to speak first.

The chasm between them grew wider with each passing second until it created an unbearable distance that threatened to engulf them.

Cinn cracked.

"You could've at least asked before digging up secret files on me," he said in a rush, folding his arms.

Julien stepped towards him. "I didn't seek it out. Béatrice's was the objective. Yours was a lucky bonus."

Cinn huffed. Nothing felt particularly *lucky* about his current situation. "You could've asked my permission to read it, then."

"I wanted to read it first, just in case." A guilty frown tugged at the corners of Julien's mouth. He closed the space between them, standing so close vulnerability was visible in grey eyes that begged for understanding.

"In case of what?"

Soft fingers slid between both sets of Cinn's. Julien tugged Cinn's arms from their fold, then he interlaced their hands, bringing one to his lips to press a feather-light kiss against it.

Julien dropped his voice to a whisper. "In case you needed protecting from any bad things."

Cinn must have been going mad, because his brain stopped fighting Julien's twisted logic. Or perhaps all rational thoughts were being manipulated by Julien's cologne—he was wearing Cinn's favourite one, the one that carried a hint of cinnamon that made him smell deliciously divine.

Julien pressed his thigh against Cinn's, dropped one of his hands to press it against the fridge, caging Cinn in.

"Let me protect you from the bad things," Julien breathed into Cinn's ear before brushing his lips across its shell, and Cinn leaned back further against the cool metal to stop himself from losing control.

"I don't need your protection," Cinn tried to snap, but it came out as a low, soft whisper.

Julien pulled back to look him in the eye. He cupped Cinn's cheek. "*Oui*, you do, *mon amour*. Just like I need yours."

Goddamn it. Those fucking eyes. Those fucking dimples alongside that sad fucking smile. It was enough to convince Cinn, at least for a moment.

Cinn pressed their lips together, feeling the warm exhalation of Julien's relieved sigh as it ghosted across his cheek. Their bodies shifted, slotting into an alignment that felt as natural as breathing. The kiss deepened as Julien's eager lips sought, and Cinn's responded. The weight of the fridge toppled backwards slightly as Julien pinned Cinn against its cool surface, sliding his leg against Cinn's as he held his chin in place, moulding their mouths together.

Cinn pulled away, breathless. "It's cheating when you use your French on me," he grumbled.

The gleam in Julien's eyes radiated both amusement and desire. He leaned forward once more—

A cough, and what was possibly a retching sound from the doorway. Their heads shot around to see Darcy hovering under the arch, unimpressed, with Elliot behind her, mouth twitching in... *suppressed laughter?*

"We left you so you could talk, not topple over my fridge."

When Julien relinquished Cinn by stepping back, the appliance lurched forward, landing on the tiles with a soft thud.

Oh dear.

Cinn's gaze roamed over to Elliot, stomach tensing. Surely he hadn't liked seeing Julien with his tongue down Cinn's throat? But Julien's oldest friend seemed only entertained.

Darcy moved into the middle of the kitchen, spotlit by her wrought-iron hanging light. "Now that you two have clearly lost all self-control around each other... Julien, I want to restate the fact that, in the event of divorce, Cinn gets custody of me."

Cinn's cheeks burned, but it was his heart that felt the warmest of all.

"And me," said Elliot, slouched against the archway. "Sorry, Julien. I just can't live without his cookies. I'm sure you understand."

Making friends had never come easily to Cinn. Back in his school days, he'd always been conscious of how much quieter he was than his classmates. It wasn't that he was shy *per se*, it was just that the other children were louder, always shouting over him, whenever he tried to speak. Eventually, he stopped trying. Then, it had seemed pointless bothering to connect with others in his numerous foster homes, like trying to plant roots in shifting sand.

Cinn swallowed down the thick lump in his throat, moving to the sink to busy himself with the dishes.

"We'll come for Christmas," Julien declared, raising his voice. "But just because we're in England does not mean I'll do any of your silly traditions. I'm not doing the hideous jumper thing. Or the song thing. And I'm certainly not eating *Christmas pudding*," he spat, as if the words were acid on his tongue.

"Any other demands, your highness?" asked Darcy. "Let me get my notepad."

Cinn snorted, placing the last china mug on the drying rack, stacking it exactly how Darcy liked.

"Why, yes!" Julien clapped his hands together in mock delight. "Please write down that we must have *foie gras*."

Elliot made a disgusted sound, which Cinn concurred with—he'd never had any desire to try the overfed goose liver on bread that only rich snobs ordered.

"Absolutely not. It's barbaric," Darcy replied.

"Oh, and for my final condition—Cinn has to make *la bûche* for dessert."

At Cinn's blank look, Darcy supplied, "It's only a chocolate log. They're obsessed with them in France."

"I'm no baker," Cinn said. "I'll do the potatoes for everyone, but that's as far as it goes."

Julien pouted at him, eyes pleading. "*S'il te plaît?* For me?"

Cinn opened his mouth, quite possibly to give in and agree, but Elliot saved him by whacking Julien on the arm. "That won't work on Cinn. He's immune to your bullshit."

If Cinn was immune, his brain certainly didn't know that.

"You're coming, right mate?" Cinn asked Elliot.

"There's family stuff happening back in the states. But I haven't been personally invited to anything, so I guess you guys win."

Darcy beamed at him.

The festive twinkle in everyone's eyes was infectious. Cinn's mouth pulled up into a smile. The conversation had drifted miles from his initial statement of needing to see his mother. But that was okay—getting lost in the warmth of the moment was exactly the distraction he needed. He couldn't quite believe his luck in getting to spend Christmas with the three of them, but he'd certainly take it.

Seven

JULIEN

It was the morning of the twenty-third, otherwise known as Christmas Eve Eve, according to Cinn. But his childish obsession with Christmas was *not* going to rub off on Julien.

Their flights—business class, naturally—were booked for late that evening.

But first, Julien had lunch plans.

Lunch plans with his father.

When he had informed his father of his holiday plans, the telephone line had fallen deathly silent. Julien had almost felt a shred of remorse for abandoning his only living relative at such late notice—he usually dropped in to his father's estate in Paris around Christmas for a couple of hours at least—but the tone of his father's '*I see*' knocked those feelings right out of his mind.

Then the tragedy occurred—his father announced that he was 'making a flying visit' to Auri for business purposes and would have to 'somehow slot Julien in' to his busy schedule. *How inconvenient for him.* When Julien questioned why on earth he was having meetings during the holiday, his father laughed, and said, "Holidays are for those who can afford to take time off, not for those who run the world, my son."

Julien had covered the mouthpiece with his hand to hide his exasperated sigh.

His father wanted to go to any of the fine dining restaurants in Talwacht. Julien insisted that Auri's Curio Café Collective would do nicely. Not only were many businesses still repairing structural damage since the quake, he wanted to make the lunch as short as possible. Perhaps it would turn into simply coffee. Perhaps he could throw back a double espresso at the bar then immediately call it a day.

The image put a smile on his face, one that was snuffed out like a candle flame when he saw his father in the distance, hovering outside the Solstice Atrium. He was wearing his standard—a tailored dark suit with a crisp white shirt, and a hideous silk paisley cravat. Since marrying his second wife Carrie, his fashion sense had steadily worsened.

Standing with him were two other grey-haired men, and the probable candidates for his business meeting: Jonathan Steele, Julien's boss who'd *still* not accepted his application for a promotion, and the Auri bigwig himself, Viktor Sturmhart.

Julien slowed his footsteps as he approached the trio of decrepit relics. He was supposed to meet his father at the café—was it too late to change paths?

The decision was removed from his hands as soon as his father clocked him.

"Julien!" he called out. With an internal eye roll, Julien made an elaborate show of pretending he'd just noticed them.

He dragged himself over to the three men. Jonathan gave him a friendly nod, whereas Viktor looked right through him, before checking his watch.

"We'll have to call it a day, Lucien." Viktor's thick German accent rumbled through the air. At events, Viktor usually insisted on talking to Julien and his father in butchered French. Today he spoke English, perhaps for Jonathan's benefit. "But we must meet again right after Christmas. Time is very important."

Without waiting for a reply, Viktor pressed stern lips together, turned away, and marched off.

What had put a bee in his beret that morning?

Jonathan Steele clapped Julien on the back, then said some waffle about what the following year had in store for MEET. Julien politely smiled along until Jonathan left him and his father to walk to the café. Julien resisted asking what their meeting was about—he didn't want to give his father the satisfaction of his curiosity. So instead, they discussed how busy the Displacement Baths were, and of course, the cold weather. Riveting stuff.

The café was quiet, like Auri in general—every sane person was home for the holiday. Scanning the space, Julien lamented his choice. The staff had done exactly the same as last year—that silly gimmick where they'd dusted each table with never-melting snow. Did they not understand that people came into their establishment to get *away* from ice?

After ordering sandwiches, they sat down with drinks, Julien holding his so the snow didn't immediately cool it.

"I had expected young Cinnamon Saunders to join us today, as I had proposed."

Here we go. Off to a stellar start.

"Contrary to your belief, father, you do not run the world."

There was no way in hell Julien could put Cinn through another round of their tense exchanges and live to tell the tale. So Julien had deposited him en route, safe and snug in their library study room, to be collected when the coast was clear.

His father's cool grimace tightened with restrained irritation.

Play nice, Julien. One lunch, then you've got three days in London with Cinn, and no Père for at least half a year, he promised himself.

"He had some errands to run," Julien said. "Apparently, one pack of ten Christmas cards wasn't enough." He shuddered.

"How is he? I heard he was hospitalised after the attack, unconscious for nearly a week."

"Mmmm." Julien sipped the heavenly coffee. He was restricted to instant at Cinn's house and was barely functioning because of it.

"He was reportedly seen suspended in mid-air, enveloped almost entirely by an umbraphage."

"Yes."

"But he had no visible wounds, no lacerations to speak of. He wasn't infected with any contaminant? Am I correct?"

Julien studied his father.

This was a lot of questions about Cinn's health, coming from a man who barely cared when Béatrice broke her arm.

"The team surrounding him, including Albert Noir, were prepared for him never to awaken. Yet, miraculously, he did. His vitals made a full recovery mere hours later." His father seemed more animated than usual, leaning forward as if Julien were on the precipice of revealing some great secret.

"How did you get access to his confidential medical records?"

His father blinked and took a moment, running a hand through his neatly trimmed grey beard. "No, no, this is all mere gossip, of course," he dismissed with a wave of his hand. "Just hearsay, circulating through the grapevine and such."

"Right."

"But you two are still quite close, aren't you? You certainly seemed so during my birthday weekend."

Julien suppressed a smirk. *If only you knew.*

His father appeared to choose his words carefully, maintaining eye contact as he inquired, "Would he be interested in assisting with a little project of mine? Of course, we would highly compensate him for his time."

"What? What project? Why *Cinn*?" The words came out sharp, laced with obvious suspicion.

"Something that Jonathan Steele is personally overseeing."

Julien shook his head. "I work for MEET. I have a broad overview of each and every project and product."

"Not this one."

They locked eyes in a silent battle.

The sandwiches arrived, giving Julien precious seconds to measure his words. Something was afoot, and he needed the information. "How could Cinn possibly be of assistance?"

Every muscle in his body tensed as his father's eyes crinkled in a calculated smile.

"I would be delighted to share all the details with you. However, I do require some assurances first."

Julien's stomach clenched into a ball of ice, chilling him to the core. "What sort of assurances?"

"Assurances that we're aligned in our understanding, you and I. While you may be my son, I harbour no illusions that we share the same perspective. We haven't enjoyed a traditional familial bond in many years, and I'm not always convinced we see eye to eye."

There was no love lost between the pair of them, from Julien's perspective, but it still oddly stung to hear it laid out like that. For as long as Julien could remember, he'd detested his father. His cruel, abusive tendencies hadn't stopped when his mother died, and he and Béatrice had escaped from their family home without looking back. Julien's policy of bare minimum contact with him had allowed him to distance himself from the man without causing trouble for himself.

With effort, Julien schooled his face into a neutral expression. He refused to give his father any satisfaction.

"You don't only look like your mother, Julien, but you have her sensibilities, much like your sister did."

Julien drained the last of his coffee. The bitter residue clung to his tongue.

"Your mother had a good heart, Julien. Sometimes, I wonder if you've inherited too much of it. Whether you'll be prepared to do *what must be done*."

His father's gaze bore into him, so intense Julien found himself speechless.

"I wonder where your loyalty will lie when the scales tip," he mused, his voice filled with contemplation. He stirred a teaspoon around his empty mug, causing a grating, metallic scrape. "Whether it will be with us... or them."

His father nodded to the floor, where a scrunched up piece of paper lay. Julien didn't need to pick it up to know what it was—it was one of the thousands of posters the Arcane Purifiers had bombed Auri with after the umbraphage attack. Their logo, and the words, *Ignorance will lead to certain peril'*. The propaganda had been cleaned up, for the most part, leaving just a few scattered here and there. For a group concerned about saving the planet, they certainly didn't mind wasting paper.

"Like Béatrice was?" Julien said, taking a gamble. But there was no way Béatrice was on record as an AP member and *Père* didn't know about it.

Surprise coloured his father's face. It was rare Julien caught him off-guard.

"Have you stopped to consider that they might have a point? People are dying. Not just from the umbraphages. Cities are being destroyed. Half of Talwacht is under rubble! *I* almost died in the earthquake!" Sort of. It had been close for half a second. "If AP is right, then we can't bury our heads in the sand and keep using motes while the world burns around us."

His father leaned forward. "Lower your volume!" he hissed. "Other solutions must be explored. We depend on motetech now. Not just us moteblessed, but you'd be hard pressed to find a single person alive who doesn't benefit from it in some small way."

Julien brushed his hand across the table, scooping up the icy-cold snow. He sprinkled it onto the floor. "Yes, we're really doing great things with it."

"You're not considering the lives *saved*, Julien. The fire-resistant materials being supplied to developing countries? The work our Asian cousins have been doing to develop motetech water purification systems? Not to mention the teams of gendarmerie dispatched worldwide to help in times of crisis."

Julien shook his head. It was always the same with his father—making out he was the saviour of the masses when really it was all about financial gain. Power. Control.

"I know we've grown further and further apart over the years. I shoulder some of the blame for that. And I know you haven't been the same since Béatrice died. Losing her, and your mother—it must be lonely for you. But *I* am still here."

Julien's breath caught in his throat, his father's rare sentimentality knocking him off kilter.

"You and I could be an unstoppable team. Jonathan Steele and I were discussing how we could accelerate your path to senior executive of MEET within five years. With your ideas, alongside your fresh perspective, HorizonTech will have a brighter future." The building excitement in his voice was palpable.

Julien could see it now—the roadmap of his life, as laid out by Lord Lucien Montaigne. Free rein of MEET, numerous development teams at his disposal. All those designs in his sketchbook could finally be materialised. He'd have a seat at the table. Maybe he'd even be in the consortium himself one day, if he played his cards right.

"Your mother would be so proud of you."

There. That was it. The thing that brought Julien firmly back down to earth.

His father was a fool. A fool who clearly had no concept of what the woman he abused would have thought.

His mother would not be *proud* to see him as his father's pawn.

He may have been able to manipulate her into staying with him through his monstrous behaviour, but Julien wouldn't let history repeat itself.

"She *would* be proud of me." Julien even almost believed it. "She would be proud that everything I achieve has been from my own merit. She'd be proud I know my own mind, and stick to it. So, thank you, but I have no plans to join HorizonTech. You can keep your empire, and I'll build my own."

His father leaned back in his chair, blinking at him like he was patiently waiting for a toddler to cease their tantrum. It was infuriating.

"And as for your little *secret project*, you and Jonathan Steele can do what you like, but there's no way Cinn is going anywhere near it."

Something behind Julien caught his father's attention.

"Why don't we ask him that himself, hmm?"

Julien twisted in his chair.

Putain.

There was a figure fumbling about at the café's cash register. One wearing a grey hoodie and green beanie. Holding up the line by counting out dozens of small coins to pay for his order.

Cinn eventually cleared the counter, then headed towards them with a takeaway cup and paper bag in hand. Seeing Julien shooting daggers at him only enticed him over to their table rather than repelling him out the door.

"What are you doing here?" fell out of Julien's mouth before he could stop it. "You were supposed to wait at the library."

Cinn shrugged. "I got bored. They do good cakes here." He held up his brownie before taking a large bite, covering his top lip with chocolate. Cinn shot a courtesy, artificial smile at Julien's father before asking, "You almost done?"

"*Oui.*" Julien sent his chair flying backwards. "*Père.* I hope you and Carrie have a wonderful Christmas," he said, allowing sarcasm to ooze through.

His father only looked amused.

Julien pushed Cinn towards the exit while his father relayed his festive good wishes.

"What's your deal?" hissed Cinn.

Leading the way back to Maz, Julien checked over his shoulder that they were out of earshot. "I had the most intense conversation with him. About you. Him and the director of MEET apparently need your help on some sort of 'project'."

"*Me?*"

"He wouldn't tell me what it was. But I don't have a good feeling about it. I told him you weren't interested."

"I could play along for a bit, to see what's what?"

Julien's steps faltered. "*Non!* Are you mad? If necessary, once the office reopens in January, I can dig around. But you're not going anywhere near either of them."

Cinn's attention was diverted by a tiny robin perching on a branch. He reached his hand out.

"Cinn, listen to me. Promise me you'll keep your guard up. If he or Jonathan tries to talk to you... fuck it, if *anyone* tries to talk to you—"

"Yeaph shurre shurre," Cinn mumbled, mouth full of brownie.

"*Excusez-moi?*"

Cinn swallowed. "I'll be careful. Don't worry so much."

"I'm sorry. But I can't take you seriously right now. You've got chocolate literally all over your face."

"Kiss it off then." Cinn stepped towards him, puckering his lips.

Don't tempt me.

Julien pushed him away. "You're not treating this situation with the gravity it deserves!"

Cinn held up the last chunk of brownie to Julien's lips. Julien opened his mouth, allowing him to feed it to him. He only chewed the overly rich dessert once before Cinn followed it up with his lips.

They exchanged chocolate kisses until the taste of cocoa was a distant memory, replaced with a lingering warm sweetness that made Julien wrap his arms around Cinn's waist, lest he have any notion of moving away.

"I've got the message," Cinn said, nuzzling into the hair near his ear. "If your dad comes near me, I'll drop-kick him."

"And if he kicks you back?"

"I'll spit in his face. It worked for me once before, remember?"

"Apparently so. But refrain from reminding me I'm dating a feral animal."

Cinn pulled back, his eyebrows furrowed. "Oh? I didn't know we were dating. Don't remember being taken on any dates."

"What about all those times you've cooked food for me and I've showered you in compliments?"

"Sounds pretty much like working in a restaurant."

"You feed all your customers by hand?"

Cinn shot Julien a wicked smile. "Only if I know where their tongues have been."

They walked in companionable silence. When they were sitting in Maz, Cinn turned to him, bottom lip caught between his teeth. He seemed even more awkward than he usually was about asking something.

"Hey, you know tomorrow? Christmas Eve?"

"Hmm? I've heard of no such thing."

Cinn scratched the back of his neck, gaze flicking between Julien and the windscreen. "Well, my mum and I used to have this tradition. We'd use the leftover wrapping paper, and make Christmas hats with them. You know, the crown ones." He mimed a zig-zag pattern in the air. "It's not like we didn't have crackers," he added quickly. "But the wrapping paper hats were cool. I thought we could do it this year."

Hats out of wrapping paper?! Did Cinn's obsession with Christmas have no limits? What was next, making snowmen out of mashed potatoes?

Julien opened his mouth, preparing several retorts like, *"You really expect me to wear a Christmas hat?"* and, *"You want to ruin perfectly good wrapping paper?"* but swiftly pressed his lips together.

How could he possibly dampen that adorable sparkle of childish excitement, clear as day, on Cinn's face? The puppy-dog eyes that seemed prepared for him to say no, while desperately longing for him to say yes?

Julien had hated every holiday season since his mother died. Cinn likely had equally terrible memories of Christmases past—who knew what they were like with his mother, and Julien couldn't imagine them being a joyful affair in foster care, either.

So if Cinn wanted to make up for all those shitty, lost years? He'd let him.

In fact, if he'd allow him to, Julien would give Cinn the best Christmas ever, every year from now on.

If he wanted that disturbingly dry fruit pudding, he'd get it. If he wanted a tree, Julien would find the biggest one that would fit in his living room. If he wanted their own sickeningly cute Christmas traditions, he'd have them, ten times over. Julien would even go as far as allowing him to put a spot of tinsel over the mantelpiece. As long as it was silver. Definitely not red, or green.

Realising he'd left Cinn hanging in silence, he lurched forward, grabbing the nape of Cinn's neck with one hand and holding his face with the other.

"We'll make a hundred crowns," Julien said, pressing his lips to Cinn's. "A thousand." He pulled Cinn against his chest, ignoring the bite of the gear box digging into his flesh.

Cinn rumbled a laugh against his chest. "I mean, I was thinking more like ten max, but whatever."

Eight

Cinn

Flying was never going to be Cinn's favourite thing, but his journey to London was comparatively non traumatic.

What *was* traumatic was waiting for the bus to Darcy's family's holiday rental in a torrential downpour. The freezing rain pounded relentlessly, soaking through Cinn's hoodie within seconds. Each gust of wind sent stabs of icy needles into his small patches of exposed skin. The final straw was the red bus that sped past, drenching them with a wave of grimy water as it splashed through a puddle.

So he didn't get blamed if the four of them caught pneumonia, Cinn relented and allowed Julien to call a black cab. The drive was gloriously warm and dry all the way to Belgravia, a snobbish, posh area of London Cinn had never set foot in before. The pristine streets were lined with grand, white-stucco townhouses, and luxury cars were parked in front of undoubtedly overpriced boutiques and art galleries, which caught Julien's attention.

Everyone arrived damp, but it was only Julien who arrived hungry, as he refused to eat the aeroplane food, despite it being the fanciest Beef Wellington Cinn had ever seen. It was way past midnight, but Alexander and Fiona Beaumont greeted them with an infectious festive cheer in their Scottish accents, far stronger than Darcy's. The couple pulled them all in for unsolicited hugs one by one.

The townhouse the Beaumonts had rented was even more fancy on the inside. The living room, with its velvet drapes and meticulously arranged antique furniture, had the feel of a museum exhibit.

Cinn perched awkwardly on the edge of a plush, overstuffed sofa. Darcy's mother immediately started bombarding him with questions that deepened his exhaustion, though he couldn't be rude, not when her smile was so genuine and bright.

Darcy winked at him. "Cinn is tired, Mum. How's Dad, anyway?" she said, dropping to a low voice, adding an extra layer of meaning to the question. Cinn subtly glanced towards the other half of the room, where Darcy's dad appeared to be reeling off questions about Elliot's motorcycle.

Fiona sighed. "I didn't want to dampen the celebrations, but he keeled over again this mornin'."

"Any luck bringing forward the final clinical trials?"

"I'm afraid not, my dear."

Cinn shuffled slightly away from them to give them space, but Darcy turned to him.

"Do you remember that motetech pacemaker my parents are directing a medical trial of, Cinn?"

He hadn't the foggiest what she was on about.

"We spoke a little about it at Lucien's party?"

"Right." Cinn nodded like he remembered.

"Well, my dad has ventricular fibrillation. The condition where the heart's lower chambers don't pump blood properly?" She inhaled one deep, shaky breath. "It's life threatening."

"Oh." Cinn couldn't help but look again at Alexander, who'd been so welcoming when he'd met him earlier that year. Though at first glance he hadn't *appeared* ill, now Cinn noticed subtle weariness in his eyes, a slight shortness of breath to his jolly laugh.

"My parents have been developing medical mote-powered devices for many years, anyway. But for the past two years, they've been exploring how to improve treatment of cardiac conditions like Dad's. They're almost at the finish line of this enhanced pacemaker. It's equipped with specialised receptors that capture and convert ambient mote energy to regulate and stabilise the heart's electrical impulses. As it uses a motecell as a power source, it'll mean continuous operation without the need for frequent replacements."

It was all gibberish to him, but Darcy's voice buzzed with pride that made Cinn smile. He settled back into the sofa to sit back and listen. Just when he'd worked up the courage to announce he was going to bed, Mr. Beaumont pressed mugs of hot chocolate into everyone's hands. Rich, creamy, brimming with marshmallows. Julien gobbled his own down before fishing out Cinn's with his fingers until Cinn told him to fuck off.

The conversation quickly turned, as usual, to the earthquake and the Arcane Purifiers. Cinn's eyelids grew even heavier, each blink lasting a fraction longer as exhaustion seeped through him. When Cinn eventually gave up and slumped against Julien, he found himself ushered into a dimly lit bedroom.

The second they were alone, Julien started sending Cinn odd glances, opening and twisting his mouth as he fiddled about, unpacking a few bits from his suitcase.

The weighted pressure of the silence became too much.

"What is it?" Cinn said with a bite, then yawned loudly. He had no energy left for any massive dramas, like Julien having forgotten the cucumber moisturising cream he applied religiously every night.

"Are you going to see Tyler while we're here?"

"What?" said Cinn, as his brain processed the question. "Oh. Right. Yeah, I should really."

Neither of them had mentioned Tyler in days, so it was jarring to suddenly hear his name on Julien's lips. Cinn tensed as he awaited Julien's delayed reaction. Well, if he got into a fuss about it, that was his issue. Cinn had made the situation crystal clear.

"Good," said Julien, his voice just a touch too bright. He suddenly became very interested in inspecting the bristles of his toothbrush. "*Oui. That's good.*"

A bubble of laughter burst out of Cinn before he could contain it. Julien raised a confused eyebrow.

"Nice effort, there."

If he did swing by to see Tyler, would he mention him and Julien? It felt dishonest to hide it, but he didn't think Tyler needed to hear the words explicitly stated. Especially with the challenge of staying sober around Christmas. Especially while he was still recovering from his broken ribs.

A problem for tomorrow's Cinn.

"Look," Julien said brightly. He was pointing at some strangely coloured mistletoe balanced on the mantelpiece.

"Hmm?"

"I just put it there." Julien was looking at him expectantly. "I brought it from Auri."

"Oh."

What did Julien want, a gold medal?

There was a stretched moment, then Julien slipped away into the en suite, just as Cinn was realising Julien might have wanted a kiss for his efforts.

Ah.

Cinn reached down to unzip his duffle bag. Hand outstretched, he froze.

The bag had *moved*. Just an inch. But it had nudged itself towards the wall.

A tiny electrical zip shot through him, similar to his body's reaction to shadowmotes landing on him in the shadowrealm.

Something was in there.

Or... had he finally reached a new level of exhaustion?

Yes, that was it.

Cinn gripped the zip, unzipped it partway. He paused again. No, something *was* in there. The bag wasn't moving. He couldn't hear anything. But he could *feel* it. An invisible pressure was emanating from the bag. His skin prickled. Every hair on the back of his neck raised.

"What the fuck?" he mumbled. He opened his mouth again, to explain the sensation to Julien, but lacked the words.

Slowly, *ever so slowly*, he continued to unzip the duffle bag, the sound of the zipper teeth separating the only sound in the tense silence. His hands trembled slightly as the gap widened, revealing the contents.

Hoodies. Batteries. Three lighters. Christmas presents wrapped so badly, parts of them were poking out of the paper.

He untensed his shoulders. *You bloody moron.*

Cinn's sea of grey hoodies shifted, a slow, unsettling ripple that sent a shiver down his spine. *Fuck.*

"Julien..."

"Hmm?" Julien emerged from the en-suite bathroom, toothbrush in mouth.

"There's something moving... I can *feel* something..." Cinn pointed to the duffle.

Julien produced a confused scoff, gesturing 'what?' to the bag with his free hand.

Then, he kicked it.

The contents erupted in a chaotic burst. A flying lighter hit a crystal vase, sending a sharp clink reverberating through the air. A spare battery for his Walkman landed squarely in the middle of Julien's forehead.

Colourful Christmas present paper fluttered gently down around them like confetti.

"What the...?"

Because he had his priorities in order, Cinn quickly swept up all the unwrapped presents and stuffed them into a drawer while Julien was distracted with the bag.

"This must be a joke!" Julien said.

Cinn spun to see a pair of black, shadowy ears poking out of the duffle. His terror dissipated, heart rate slowing to a steady thud of cautious relief.

"Béatrice!"

The cat ignored Julien and went straight for Cinn, weaving through his legs repeatedly with a determined persistence. Her grizzly, demonic purr was oddly soothing. As Cinn ran his hands over the knobs of her spine, a strange warmth spread from her into him, starting at his fingertips and cascading throughout his limbs. Simultaneously, he became aware, for the very first time, of her heartbeat—a rapid, steady drumming, a primal rhythm far faster than his own. Though, as he narrowed his focus, the pace of his heartbeat gradually increased—or did the cat's decrease?—until their heartbeats synchronised, aligning in a soothing, grounding rhythm.

"Hello," he whispered, and Béatrice replied with a hum that he didn't so much hear as feel.

"*Cinn*?!" Julien shouted, deafening him. He'd possibly been shouting Cinn's name for a while.

He dragged his eyes away from the cat to Julien, sitting on the bed, arms crossed.

"I said, what the hell are you doing? You've been staring into each other's eyes for the last five minutes."

He sounded quite cross.

Cinn shrugged. "But she doesn't even have eyes!"

"Exactly!"

A ripple of energy shot through Béatrice, flowing seamlessly into Cinn like a gentle stream merging with a larger river.

It should have been terrifying. Instead, it was... invigorating. Whereas before he'd been so tired, he now possessed a surge of alertness. A thrum of power. Power he'd never felt outside the shadowrealm before.

"We're like... connecting or some shit," Cinn tried to explain. This wasn't going to do Julien's jealousy over Cinn's relationship with his dead sister come demon cat any good, was it?

"Oh?" Julien unfolded, then refolded his arms. "Are you now?" He paused, shaking his head. "Of course you are. She won't even sniff me and yet she's happy to fawn all over you."

At the sad look in Julien's eyes he failed to hide, Cinn scooped up the shadow cat. The way she felt had changed—previously his hands glided through her like smoke, but now he could feel the tension in her muscles. "Here we go." He placed her gently on Julien's lap. "Be nice."

The cat hissed lowly. She emitted a low, discontented growl, her form shifting. Before Cinn could react, the cat sprung off Julien, then darted into the shadows in the corner of the dark room, disappearing with a flicker of movement.

She was out of sight, but not out of presence; Cinn could still feel the subtle tether of their connection lingering.

What the fuck was that all about? He wasn't convinced he needed some psychic cosmic connection with a cat made of shadows complicating his life.

"Well then," said Julien. "I guess I shouldn't interfere with your *special bond* again."

Cinn gave him a playful push, nudging him further back onto the bed. "Don't be sad. I'll cuddle you instead."

Julien's huff ghosted across his cheek as Cinn rested his weight on top of him, sliding his hand across Julien's thighs through his pyjama bottoms, the silky ones Cinn loved feeling against his skin in bed.

"I suppose there's significantly less risk of you scratching and biting me." Julien's playful grin was just evident in the dim light. His eyes roamed across Cinn's face, landing on his lips.

Cinn let out a low laugh. "That's normally your job. But anyway, we better put your nice mistletoe to use, right?"

In answer, Julien captured the skin of his neck with his teeth, teetering on that thin ledge between pleasure and pain that he knew how to navigate so well. Julien's tongue pressed against his pulse point, and Cinn pushed himself down to grind against him, to let him know exactly how hard Julien had made him so easily. He wasn't surprised by it—Cinn's body was quickly becoming conditioned to Julien's touch. Every time they fucked, the experience somehow grew with intensity. Intimacy with Julien was becoming a visceral need, an addiction he was all too happy to crave and feed.

Though, behind it was that tiny seed of doubt that sometimes reared its ugly head—what if their unlikely connection was nothing more than a fleeting spark destined to burn out?

The shred of fear ignited into a wildfire of panic, and Cinn brought Julien's lips up to him to kiss him deeply, allowing the heat and passion behind it to overwhelm his senses, burn the negative thoughts away.

Julien's tongue slowed, and he pushed up on Cinn's chest. He stared up at Cinn, face a soft mask of affection.

"What?"

"I just wanted to see your beautiful eyes for a second, *mon amour*," he said, in the softest whisper of breath, mouth curving up into a gentle, vulnerable smile that nestled itself into Cinn's mind, making a home there.

Cinn swallowed.

No, theirs was a flame that would endure the fiercest storm that tried to extinguish it. Cinn would make sure of it.

Because life without his infuriating princeling by his side would be very dull and very dim.

Abruptly, Julien's muscles tensed.

He flicked his eyes to the left. "Is she still watching us?"

"No doubt about it," Cinn replied.

Julien groaned, picking up a pillow and throwing it into the dark corner where Béatrice had intertwined herself with the shadows.

"Yep. That will do it."

Nine

CINN

If someone had told Cinn a week ago that he'd be seeing his mother on Christmas Eve, he'd have died laughing.

But there he was, travelling in a crowded, noisy London Underground tube carriage, his nose pressed into a stranger's armpit, on the way to see her.

There had been no telephone number in Madame Sinclair's file. Only a home address, and a work address. Their first port of call had been her house. A new one—not the one of Cinn's childhood, although it was only a twenty-minute bus journey or so between this and their old digs in Croydon.

When the moment came to walk up to the ground-floor flat, Cinn's legs trembled uncontrollably. Every step felt heavier and heavier, as if the gravity of the past was pulling him back. What if his mum slammed the door in his face? Or didn't even recognise him? Sweat dampened his forehead by the time they reached the door.

The old lady who answered informed them Esme Saunders had moved last month.

Cinn almost cried in relief.

Well. That's that, then. It isn't to be. Not this time. Oh well.

But no such luck. The others insisted they go to the hospital where she worked to see if they could source her current address.

"She might even be on shift," Elliot said cheerfully, and just like that, Cinn's nausea returned in full swing.

After the fun and games of Cinn's family reunion, they were supposed to be catching the afternoon matinee of a pantomime with Darcy's parents, so Darcy and Elliot were tagging along for the ride. While it was nice to travel all together, the amount of moral support was actually making Cinn's nerves even worse. He certainly didn't think he'd be up for a pantomime afterwards, but it had all been too much to explain to Mrs. Beaumont when she'd handed out the tickets that morning.

Maybe he could hang out at the theatre bar. He'd likely need the drinks.

The trek up to Westminster on the Northern Line to St. Thomas's Hospital passed quicker than Cinn wanted, even with the number of sticky bodies pressing against him in the carriage.

Before he knew it, he was dragging himself towards the hospital entrance. A fine mist drizzled down on them. Seemed like an ominous sign.

"Hold on." Darcy pulled his arm back. "There's a library on the other side of the street. Elliot and I can see if she's in the White Pages phonebook."

Agreeing to reconvene by the fountain, Cinn found himself fixated on the black lettering of the hospital sign as it loomed over him. How was it even possible that *his mother* worked here? She'd never shown any interest in medicine before, let alone caring for the community or shit like that. In fact, she'd ignored their neighbours and given him paper towels in lieu of plasters. One time she'd even tried to cure his cold with boiled water and the 'Italian mixed herbs' they used in every dish.

He was getting himself worked up, and that wouldn't do. He wasn't looking to meet her to resolve his childhood trauma. No, he was here for answers, and answers only.

"If we *do* track her down, there are some ground rules you'll have to follow if you want to be there."

Julien's eyes widened. Had he expected Cinn to say he wanted to meet her alone?

Well, newsflash, he was way too chicken-shit for that.

Julien may be a fucking nightmare, but he was Cinn's fucking nightmare, and he needed the layer of armour that his presence offered him.

"Rules you say? We both know how much I love following them."

"Shut up and listen. Don't get on at her for stuff that happened back then. It's all in the past now. Alright? Else you're not coming."

He met Julien's gaze fiercely, jaw set. But Cinn's sharp tone clashed with what his eyes undoubtedly communicated—*please don't make me do this alone.*

"*Oui,*" he said softly. "I understand."

Yes, Julien understood him completely.

The hospital lobby was bustling, the low hum of conversation and the overpowering scent of disinfectant surrounding them as they joined a lengthy queue, to inch closer to the receptionist's desk at a snail's pace.

The wait was torturous. Cinn rehearsed possible lines in his head.

Two people in front of him, then one.

He fiddled with the cuff of his beanie.

"Want me to talk?" asked Julien.

Cinn shook his head. He was perfectly capable of this basic task.

The man in front of him walked away from the desk, muttering obscenities under his breath.

"Next," a burly woman called, her eyebrows so thick and bushy they were like two fat grey slugs. "Next! How can I help?"

Cinn jolted himself forward, Julien sliding in alongside him.

He opened his mouth. "I was wondering if you could help me with something. I'm looking for the address of one of your employees. At least, I think she works here..."

"We can't give out personal information."

"I know, but she's my... my... mother?" The word felt dry and sticky on Cinn's tongue. "Her name is Esme Saunders."

The receptionist gave no flicker of recognition, only pierced him with beady eyes.

Damn it, why hadn't he thought to bring his passport along? He could have used it to prove they shared a surname.

"Are you listed as an emergency contact?"

Very unlikely. He shook his head.

The receptionist raised a large, sceptical eyebrow, which Cinn couldn't help but fixate on. "Is there some sort of emergency?"

"Umm, no," said Cinn.

"Yes, there is," said Julien.

Cinn stepped on his foot.

Another lady, who'd been busy filing paperwork in cabinets, suddenly stepped forward to join the receptionist. She narrowed her eyes at Cinn and Julien, her withered face further wrinkling in distaste. "Esme Saunders? What are you two playing at? She doesn't have a son."

The entire hospital seemed to hold its breath. The distant beeping of monitors and murmurs of staff faded into a weighted silence as a thousand pinpricks stabbed into Cinn's heart.

Obviously, she wouldn't be going around shouting about the son taken away from her. Even so, the words still stung. *'Yes, she fucking does!'* he wanted to shout. Instead, he strained his facial muscles to lift his heavy cheeks into a neutral expression.

Julien pressed a firm hand into the small of his back, using his thumb to rub small circles into it.

The receptionist glanced behind them at the growing queue. "I'm sorry, but I'm going to have to ask you to move along."

An ear-splitting shriek ripped through the hospital lobby.

Spinning on his heels, Cinn quickly found the source of the commotion. An elderly man was shaking his leg, which was soaked with coffee, if the empty paper cup and brown splatter on the tiled floor was anything to go by. The man shook a furious fist at a female nurse in turquoise scrubs standing next to him.

Cinn gawked at the woman.

The woman with her hands over her mouth.

The woman with the chestnut-brown curls twirled into a tight bun.

The woman who he'd recognise anywhere, even after a decade apart.

Bringing her hands down, she mouthed more than said his name—'Cinnamon'—rolling it around on her tongue, tasting its flavour for the first time in aeons.

Then, his mother stood frozen, disbelief etched into her features as she stared at him, as if seeing a ghost. She wrung trembling hands together, a slight quiver in her lips. Was she going to cry? *Oh God, please don't let her cry.*

Without another word, she dropped to her knees, hastily trying to mop up the puddle of coffee with napkins from her purse, her movements frantic and uncoordinated. "So clumsy of me!" she gasped.

Julien's head flicked to Cinn, clearly waiting for him to make the next move. But now it was Cinn's turn to freeze. His throat was unbearably tight, so tight he couldn't breathe.

Battalions of conflicting emotions warred within him.

Shock that they'd actually managed to find her.

The raw ache of abandonment.

Relief that he'd never have to wonder *what if*.

Julien nudged him gently with his elbow. His mum had finished cleaning the floor and stared again like a deer caught in headlights.

One deep breath in. Cinn took a hesitant step forward. "Hi."

An awkward silence followed, and Cinn had to resist the temptation to close his eyes and wait for the ground to swallow him up.

Julien extended his hand. For a moment his mother stared at it, then grabbed onto it to shake it with vigour, a drowning person offered a life raft.

"It's a pleasure to meet you. I'm Julien," Julien said, ever so calm, ever so casual.

The effect was like a drug, the tension instantly evaporating. The tightness in Cinn's throat lessened as his mum beamed at Julien.

"Shall we go and replace your coffee?" Julien continued. He nodded to the café across the lobby. "Is it any good here?"

"Yes!" Her eyes drifted back to Cinn. Her voice softened. "Yes. Let's go there. I've got twenty minutes left of my break." She checked the fob watch attached to her uniform.

Cinn still couldn't believe it. His mum, a *nurse*. That felt like the most unbelievable thing out of everything.

She led the way to the café, walking slightly too quickly.

"You're not complaining to the barista if it's not up to your standards," he hissed to Julien, to dispel the tension in his gut.

"No promises."

Julien ushered them to a quiet table in the furthest corner, then insisted he'd get the coffees. Cinn couldn't help but watch Julien's back as he left Cinn alone with the stranger opposite him. He wasn't ready to face her. He needed more time.

"So..." his mother started.

Cinn dug his nails into his palm. "So you're a nurse now?" he blurted out. It just seemed like such a strange choice for someone who'd spent his childhood treating fevers with crystals.

"Yes." The proud edge to her voice softened him. "For several years."

"That's cool. You have to work Christmas Eve, though. That's not as cool."

Stop rambling.

Smiling, his mother replied, "Someone has to. And the other staff have young children."

"Speaking of Christmas Eve…" Heart pounding, Cinn unzipped his rucksack. They'd spent a good half an hour that morning making them, and now he may as well hand it over.

He held up a crown made of wrapping paper. Green with shiny red foil swirls. Sharp, jagged points, as even as he could make them. Of course, the ones Julien made looked like masterpieces, but his own looked rather professional, if he did say so himself.

"This is for you."

Her eyes filled with tears that spilled down her cheeks, unwiped. It was like she'd been holding back, and now a dam had burst.

Cinn was still holding the hat in mid-air when Julien set the tray down. "Should I…" he started, looking back towards the hospital lobby, but Cinn grabbed his jacket and yanked him down into the seat next to him.

With gentle, reverent hands, his mother took the hat from Cinn. "Thank you. It's lovely. I can't believe you still do this."

Had his mother's voice changed, or was it simply that he didn't remember it properly?

"It's so good to see you," she said softly, tucking a stray strand of hair behind her ear. "You look… well. All grown up. Are you doing alright?" Before Cinn could respond, she continued, "I tried to contact you, you know."

"What?" This was news to Cinn. "When?"

"It was also around Christmas time. You must have been seventeen."

He'd spent that Christmas behind bars, but if she didn't know that part, he wasn't going to tell her.

"But that stupid social worker! She just made everything so difficult. So you didn't get my letter, then? I gave it to her to forward to you."

"No," Cinn whispered, his eyes falling to his drink. The room went fuzzy at the edges of his consciousness. The lump in his throat came back with a vengeance.

He'd thought about his mother every day at Feltham Young Offenders. Sometimes, he became melancholic, missing her warm laugh and the way they'd dance around the kitchen, remembering their life together through an idealised lens. Other times, he'd worked himself up to fucking furious, angry enough he'd punched walls. Because if she'd had her shit together, he'd never have gotten involved with the crowd one of his foster brothers introduced him to. He'd never have been on that forged-banknotes job. He'd never have been hiding with them in a garden shed, with the police knocking on the door.

Yes, it had been far easier to blame her for his landing in jail than to accept responsibility.

To hear now that she hadn't completely abandoned him, erased him from her mind like he'd never existed, and had even tried to contact him? It was too much.

The walls of the café closed in further. His breath grew shallow. The coffee cup blurred as the world tilted.

The gold band around his wrist heated, almost to the point of pain. *Calm the fuck down.*

His mother carried on talking, but the words were just noise. He pointedly focussed on the bubbles, slowly dissipating within the foam in his coffee. Then, his mother's reaction be damned, his hand slipped off the table, fingers reaching out for Julien's. He needed an anchor.

Julien's hand clamped around his like a vise. Within a heartbeat, he was grounded. The chaos in his mind settled, replaced by a soothing calmness radiating from Julien all the way through him. Every stroke of Julien's thumb over the back of his hand had his pulse falling steadier and steadier.

"I actually came to talk to you about something," he spat out, interrupting her. He couldn't bear any more conversation that skirted too close to his battle wounds. Not today, not this time.

"Oh?" His mum blinked in surprise. "What is it?"

Without any fanfare, he got straight to the point. "My dad."

"Oh?" she said again, face falling like a house of cards. "*Oh.*"

"So…" Cinn began. He really should have prepared for this bit. "I sort of live in Switzerland now. In this"—*oh, God*—"special place. And I found out that my dad was there, too? Just before he died?"

For a moment he held his breath, fearing that he'd got it wrong and she didn't know his father was dead. But his mother only looked confused.

"Switzerland…" She rolled the word around on her tongue. "What on earth was he doing there?"

"I also found out that we've got something in common. That we share the same… ability."

His mother's face revealed nothing. In fact, her eyebrows knitted even tighter together.

"You know…" Cinn shifted uncomfortably. *Did* she know? "I don't know what he would have called it back then. How he would have explained it. He wouldn't have had the right words for it until he got to Auri, just like me. But sometimes I… leave this world, and visit another. And sometimes, I see dead people there."

There. The words were out. Now he only had to deal with the consequences. Maybe she'd march him up to the psych ward and lock him up.

"Remember after that car crash? When you thought I'd passed out from shock?"

Very slowly, his mother shook her head. "This has always happened to you?"

"Falling in the river set it off. After that, it only happened a few times before I… moved out."

The loaded silence sat between them.

Julien squeezed his hand tighter.

"I thought…" his mother eventually said, pressing one hand to her mouth, and running the other through her ponytail. "Oh, my God. I thought he was sick." She squeezed her eyes shut. "He told me the same thing. *Exactly* the same thing. Oh my God," she repeated, as more tears cascaded down her cheeks.

Fuck. He didn't want *this*. Should he do something? Hug her?

"I told him he needed to get help," she whispered. "I'm the reason he left us. I'm the reason you... you..."

Julien passed her a silk handkerchief that Cinn had never seen before, materialising it from thin air.

"He was acting so crazy," she continued, an edge to her voice, a plea to understand her. "It just got worse and worse and I just couldn't cope any more. Not between looking after you *and* him." She paused to blow her dripping nose. "We had you so young. I always thought, if only we'd been just a couple of years older, then everything would have been different. I thought the stress of having to provide for us drove him to madness."

Cinn searched for words that didn't come.

"Sometime after he left, someone phoned me," she said slowly, as if forming connections. "I don't think they said Switzerland, but they sounded foreign. They told me he'd died. And that was that."

"Don't blame yourself," Cinn blurted out.

Now he knew all this, there would be a tiny part of him that would blame her, of course. He wouldn't be able to help it. But there wasn't any point in her beating herself up over it. Not over twenty years later. Not now, when they'd just reconnected, when they had the rest of their lives to try to forge *something* together out of the rubble they'd been left with.

"There's no way you could have known. It sounds bonkers, even to my own ears." Cinn managed a meek smile he hoped would comfort her.

His mum offered him a watery smile. "That's kind, honey."

The rain outside pelted the café window with a suddenly increased vigour, reaching deafening decibels. "Did he ever bring anyone or anything back, though?" he shouted, battling against the noise.

"What?" she shouted back, eyeing the rivulets of water streaming down the glass.

"Did my dad ever return back from one of his... *visits* with something from that realm?" *Murderous ghosts? Demon cats? Nope, just me?*

Her mouth opened in surprise. "I don't think so." Her eyes narrowed. "Well, there was one time..."

Cinn leaned forward. "Yeah?"

"He was in the bedroom, talking to someone, even though there was no phone in there. I tried to open the door, but he'd locked it. He screamed at me to go away, like a mad man. This was right at the end, just before he left. I didn't even bother to question him about it, I don't think. I was just... getting through it all, back then."

This is fucking horrific.

No wonder Cinn's poor mother had cracked. He pictured her back then—young, poor, a demanding baby to care for, and a partner slowly descending into madness.

"I have to go," she said, glancing at her fob watch. "I'm so sorry... but my patients need me." She stood up.

"Mum?"

She held his gaze, eyes wide. It was the first time he'd called her that today. A name she hadn't heard in a decade.

"I'm proud of you. For... you know." Cinn gestured to the hospital, hoping she would glean, 'for sorting your shit out, for becoming a fucking *nurse*,' out of it.

His mum nodded, pressed her hand to her mouth like she was suppressing a sob. She reached into her bag and brought out her set of keys. Her fingers quickly found what she was looking for.

She flashed Cinn some sort of coin. It was green with a gold triangle in the middle, with the numeral V dead in the centre.

The shock of what she was showing him delayed his reply.

"Five years?" he said, his voice choking. His mum, who'd had at least one drink every day of his childhood that he could remember, had been clean for *five years*?

He jumped to his feet and threw his arms around her. Her soft gasp of surprise tickled his ear as he clutched her tight. He was taller than her now, but he hugged her like a child, clinging to her like he never wanted to let go.

But he did.

He stepped back, blinking back the hot prickles behind his own eyes.

Rummaging around in her bag again, she brought out a scrap of paper and scribbled a phone number on it. "You'll have to come round before you go back. And your... *friend,* of course. Julien, wasn't it?" She beamed at Julien, the smile a touch too bright, proving something.

Julien had been the quietest Cinn had ever known him to be in the history of their entire existence together. It was unsettling. Creepy, in fact.

He could only imagine how much it was paining him.

An overwhelming urge to kiss him, fiercely, struck Cinn. But he tucked it away for later.

Cinn's mother turned her smile back towards him. It was at once both heartbreakingly familiar and strangely foreign, as if time had reshaped it into something different. Something new.

"It was so good—"

An intense wail sounded from just outside the café. Next came gasps of shock, then a flurry of hushed, concerned murmurs.

They stepped back into the lobby, stopping dead at the sight that was causing the commotion: three people staggering towards the reception desk, surrounded by a growing audience that had cleared a wide semi-circle around them. A young woman clutched her side, her fingers slick with blood from a deep wound, while an older man limped beside her, his arm hanging at an unnatural angle. The third, a teenage boy, had a gash across his face, his eyes wide with terror as he stumbled forward.

He looked towards the hospital staff. "Help!"

The less-than-helpful receptionist from earlier stood up from her desk. "The emergency department is—"

"Help," the teenager repeated, falling to both knees and clutching his stomach. Blood pooled around his fingers.

"I'll go see who I can find," Cinn's mother said, disappearing into the crowd.

Julien snaked an arm around Cinn's, tugging him to close the space between them.

A knot formed in Cinn's stomach, one that grew tighter with every passing second.

"Hey!" Darcy's face, with Elliot standing close behind, appeared beside them. "We saw these three from across the road. The old man was screaming about invisible demons throwing people about. Pretty loudly."

Elliot pushed past the throng, beelining straight towards the teenager who'd now half-collapsed sideways onto the floor. He knelt down, gently moving his hands away from the wound.

A female doctor shoved Elliot away with force. "What are you doing?" she snapped, before barking orders to several staff just behind them. Three stretchers were placed on the floor. The receptionist barked that the crowd 'move along please', giving Cinn in particular a pointed look. He had a new enemy for life, apparently.

Wild-eyed, Elliot lowered his voice to hiss, "I knew it. His wound has umbra contaminant in it."

"What?" asked Cinn, but as he said it, his mind flickered back to the umbraphage attack they'd witnessed in Seville—the blackened veins of the officer who'd been treated by the paramedics, the tiny flecks of black ink that looked like they were swimming in his blood. Madame Sinclair had said that it made the wounds difficult to close, poisoned them, and often gave their victims terrifying hallucinations and delusions.

The teenager let out a harrowing wail as a team of doctors marched him down a corridor, out of sight. Was this poor boy about to experience such a thing? Cinn was lucky his own encounter hadn't resulted in that outcome. Then again, he had been imprisoned in some hellish version of the shadowrealm...

"Which direction did they come from?" Julien snapped, eyes darting to the hospital entrance, where the torrential downpour was intensifying—sheets of rain pounded the pavement, obscuring visibility and sending pedestrians scurrying for cover.

"The old guy was shouting about Westminster Bridge." Water dripped from Elliot's soaking wet curls. He hesitated. "I'm sure the alarm is sounding back at HQ, but it'll take a while for them to get through the Baths. It's Christmas Eve—skeleton staff only. Plus, we've got bare minimum gendarmes on shift, with the rest on call. Fuck!" He slammed his fist into a nearby column.

Cinn winced. This was an Elliot he'd never seen before—frantic, a raw, urgent energy dictating his actions.

Conflict passed over his troubled expression. "Look," Elliot said, "I *have* to go. Swore an oath, in fact. But as for you three..."

"Don't be ridiculous," Julien snapped. "As if I'd let you go alone. That's quite frankly insulting."

Before Julien even considered ordering him and Darcy to stay put, Cinn caught her eye and suggested, "Darcy and I will come but stay way back."

"That way, we can brief the gendarmerie as soon as they arrive," Darcy added.

Julien's lips curled into a thin line. He and Cinn entered a staring match, a silent battle of wills that Cinn refused to back down on.

"Fine," Julien said through gritted teeth, storming towards the entrance. "Let's go, then."

The sky was an ominous, murky grey, the light levels so dim it felt almost like nighttime.

Westminster Bridge might have been only round the corner, but the rain turned the trek into a marathon. As they sprinted across slick pavement that was more puddle than concrete, a squall brought more water lashing down upon them with relentless fury, drenching them to the bone and blurring the cityscape into a watery haze.

Elliot, leading the charge, jogged backwards, shouting, "The Baths for this side of London are close to here—underneath Waterloo Station, hidden in the Leake Street Arches. So it shouldn't be *too* long until they arrive."

But that would only be the handful of officers actually at Auri today. Most of the gendarmerie would be at home enjoying Christmas Eve, relaxing with their families. How quickly could they possibly get here?

For every two steps they took, a howling, wildly strong wind pushed them back.

"This isn't normal weather!" Darcy might have shouted over the deafening gale, followed by something about a hurricane.

London was in chaos: umbrellas turned inside out, people darting for cover, other people shouting and pointing in the direction of the bridge. Sirens wailed in the distance.

Cinn attempted to regulate his erratic breathing. He only had moments left to prepare for what was to come. He was about to encounter an unknown number of umbraphages. His previous two experiences with them hadn't been pleasant. The sensible thing would be to *run*, run like the wind in the other direction and keep running. That's what any sane person would do.

But Cinn wasn't a sane person. Never had been. And he wasn't about to go and cower in some corner when the lives of the people he cared most about were on the line.

More injured people staggered past them, haunted looks of terror plain on their faces. One middle-aged woman caught sight of the four of them running *towards* the danger. She was wearing a yellow mackintosh, raindrops washing off traces of blood. She gave them several violent shakes of her head, throwing her arm out to block their path.

"What are you doing?" she screamed in Elliot's face as he tried to push her out of the way.

Darting around her, they increased their pace.

A blood-curdling scream pierced the air, followed by a thunderous crash.

Mere metres from them, an enormous truck had overturned in the middle of the road, its twisted metal frame skidding across the rain-soaked tarmac and blocking off access to the road leading to the bridge.

"*Putain*! That's all we need!"

A woman in St. Thomas's hospital scrubs darted towards the truck, closely followed by more staff.

Cinn couldn't take his eyes off the truck's driver, the sound and sight of the accident taking him back a decade to the only other car crash he'd witnessed. As if sharing in his memory, the warding band warmed.

Julien grabbed Cinn's arm. Yanked hard. "Come on!"

Thunderclaps. Mighty splashes of puddles as their footsteps pounded. Shouts and cries of pure panic, muffled by the ruthless, incessant downpour.

Then, in the near distance, through the haze, the bridge came into view.

And so did two dead bodies.

Forms illuminated by the dim glow of streetlights, they lay sprawled across the wet pavement, motionless, the chaotic scene around them a chilling contrast to their stillness.

Cinn found his eyes drawn to Julien's as he ran alongside him, his own fear reflecting back at him. Shielding his head from the rain with his hand, Julien's eyes, as grey as the stormy sky above them, grew wide, his expression tender as he reached for Cinn's hand.

"Cinn—"

Cinn cut him off with a brief press of his lips against Julien's. "Later," he promised, directly into his ear. Because there *would* be a later. There had to be.

Westminster Bridge now loomed ahead, a hint of its Gothic arches and ornate lamp posts visible through sheets of rain. A flash of lightning split open the stormy sky, casting fleeting glimpses of *something* far onto the bridge. Something dark. Something shadowy. Something that shot an instant jolt of terror through Cinn's every limb, slowing him down.

Two? Three? It was impossible to tell how many umbraphages hovered threateningly in the air, the amorphous entities writhing their tentacle-like appendages in the air amidst the swirling rain.

"There's still people over there!"

Indeed, there was a sprinkle of blurry figures attempting to dash across the bridge.

"What the fuck are they doing running towards them? Why are they being so stupid?" shouted Cinn.

A shadowy limb snatched up one runner, to shake them in the air like a rag doll.

Darcy threw him a quick, confused look. "They can't see them, Cinn. They have no idea what's going on!"

"What?!"

The information didn't have time to sink in—they were there, at the entrance to the bridge. It seemed like they'd reached the heart of the storm, because here the wind was even more vicious, ripping against Cinn's skin. His beanie flew off his head, to be caught by Elliot. Cinn stuffed it into his rucksack.

A colossal *whomp* reverberated through the air, followed by the sound of rushing water. A tidal wave rose out of the Thames, a wall of muddy grey froth rising as tall as the bridge's central arch.

Cinn pressed a hand to his mouth to suppress a scream. "Holy shit!"

The wave crashed into the bridge with a thunderous roar, a *smack* against the tarmac. Shrieking was just audible over the din. Cinn's heart lurched. The poor people still on the bridge—he couldn't help imagining the crunch of their fragile bones as they were crushed against the parapet.

"Over there!"

Elliot motioned over to the right, where the bridge's entrance was flanked by a lion statue. It towered above them, its silent, wise gaze cautioning them not to proceed. Elliot ushered them all into the statue's weak shadow, then grabbed both Darcy's and Cinn's arms. "You two stay here and keep an eye out for the gendarmerie's arrival, and keep back any idiot who's running in the wrong direction."

Julien and Elliot wore identical grimaces as they readied themselves, Elliot rolling on the heels of his feet.

A coldness flooded through Cinn, not just from the icy rain. A tightening chokehold of panic began to grip him. Horrific images of the two bloodied dead bodies from earlier, now wearing Julien and Elliot's faces, flashed through his mind. This plan was a bad idea. He couldn't lose them, not either of them, not when he'd just found them. It simply wasn't an option. They should all stay together, right here, and await the assistance surely on the way.

Reaching an arm forward, he opened his mouth to tell Julien just that.

Nothing came out. He tried again. His tongue felt heavy in his mouth, a lead weight anchored to the bottom.

His outstretched hand fell. His face slackened, as if drugged. He stumbled backwards, falling against the hard stone plinth, his skin scraping against it.

Three concerned faces swam before him.

WE SEE YOU, SHADOW

The layered, deep, booming voice came from directly inside his head.

A cold, creeping sensation began to crawl through his limbs. What started as pins and needles soon grew into a fiery, aching burn, numbing his muscles and seizing control of his body.

No, no, no!

His body's instinctive reaction was to reach for Julien, but his arm remained petrified by his side.

He lurched sideways, stumbling through Elliot and Darcy. His vision blurred and darkened at the edges, a dark haze clouding his sight.

COME TO US, SHADOW

He felt his legs move, not by his own will, but pulled by a puppet master, propelling him forward, step by step, towards the bridge. His fading mind screamed in protest, but his body betrayed him, marching steadily into the heart of the storm.

Ten

Julien

I t took longer than Julien would care to admit to react to Cinn's peculiar behaviour. When Cinn first stumbled back, he'd thought he was simply knocked back by the wind, or exhausted perhaps.

It was only when Cinn pushed past them, face expressionless, eyes lifeless, to walk jerkily towards Westminster Bridge that he finally realised something was wrong. Something was very wrong.

Julien screamed Cinn's name—once, in confusion, and then again, a strangled, desperate sound, dampened by the pounding rain.

It was to no avail.

Cinn kept walking straight forward, magnetised to the damn bridge, where the umbraphages seemed to be expanding, their dark forms whipping this way and that.

Putain! Putain! Putain!

Sheer panic rooted him to the spot. Distantly, he knew his brain should be kicking into overdrive, weighing up which plan of many options was best. Instead, he was frozen, feeling a little more lost with each step Cinn took away from him.

"Quickly!" Elliot yelled.

Blinking, Julien followed Elliot's command, finally moving. Julien squeezed Elliot's arm as he joined him. It was okay. Elliot was here. He wouldn't let anything happen to any of them.

Darcy made to follow him and Elliot. Julien gave her a firm shove, praying she got the message, then pivoted sharply and ran.

It took only a few precious moments to catch up with Cinn. Elliot restrained his left arm while Julien grabbed his right. Their efforts ceased his movements, Cinn's taut muscles straining against Julien's tight grip. Cinn's hoodie was entirely soaked through, and rain ran down his body in rivulets, his brown curls plastered to his forehead.

Julien pushed the soggy strands out of Cinn's eyes, dull and blank. "Cinn! *Mon amour!*"

There wasn't even the slightest flicker of recognition in Cinn's clouded expression. He only grunted as he once again attempted to overpower them to continue on his path, a train on invisible tracks.

The wind picked up. *Non*, that wasn't the right expression, because suddenly it grew to an almost sentient, furious roar. It whipped around them. Like it was stealing the very air from their lungs, every breath becoming a struggle.

All around them, debris was surging towards the bridge, pushed by a wind tunnel. A chaotic urban cyclone—coffee cups, a stray bike tyre, newspapers. Several items slammed into them, the force of the wind growing with every passing second.

One of Julien's feet slipped. Knocked off balance, his grip slackened and Cinn surged a step forward.

Unable to find the breath to even shout, Julien caught Elliot's eye. Elliot shook his head wildly.

It would be a futile effort, but he had to try. Julien reached for the windmotes—the air charged with an unlimited supply, a buzzing energetic frenzy of them. He brought an unfathomably high quantity of them under his control, reaching out as far as possible, squeezing his eyes shut for a second for that extra sliver of concentration—

No sooner than he'd begun to channel them—to propel them *against* the tempest that was sucking them towards imminent doom—they slipped out of his control. The sensation was like holding onto a slippery fish. Julien was channelling but a drop in the ocean compared to the maelstrom of energy the gale possessed.

Elliot let out a loud roar of frustration, setting his face in a grim line and repositioning himself to push his entire body weight into Cinn.

Julien's aching muscles strained to the point of shaking, the burn in them something unreal. His heart gave a painful squeeze when he shouted, "It's no use!"

A powerful surge knocked them forwards, once, then again, even though Julien pushed against Cinn with all his might, clutching his grey hoodie like it was the only thing tethering him to the earth.

How have you let this happen? You only just saved him, and now you've marched him straight back into mortal danger.

If this kills him...

A few hot, frustrated tears made their home amongst the rain dripping down Julien's face.

A wobble of his left knee. His leg gave way, slipping past Cinn's and landing with a painful smack on the tarmac. Elliot shouted his name—without Julien's support, Cinn flew forward out of his grip.

Non!

Using the last dregs of his energy, Julien pushed himself forwards, fingertips brushing against the fabric of Cinn's coat before it was wrenched out of his hand.

Julien stared at his empty palm.

This was it. The moment they lost the battle.

And now, it was better to face the enemy head on than bury their heads in the sand.

Julien gave up resisting, allowing himself to be pulled deeper into the bridge. He grabbed Cinn's hand, wrapping it firmly around his own. If they were going down, they'd go down together.

With Elliot on one side of Cinn, and Julien on the other, they fastened their gaze ahead of them, to the middle of the bridge, to face their fate.

Three umbraphages, wildly whipping their tendrils of black in every direction. Their shape and space expanded horrifically wide, creating a wall of darkness that stretched the entire width of the bridge. Several cars lay misshapen on their sides, haphazardly strewn across the ground, flung like toys by the hurricane. Even they were being dragged by the powerful tempest, scraping along the ground.

A fork of bright white lightning tore the dark sky in half.

A murmur of thunder smothered Julien's anguished groan as he stared into the black pit created by the umbraphages, a hungry maw awaiting its prey.

In a handful of seconds, it would all be over.

Then—

A flicker of *something* in the corner of Julien's eye. He spun. Embedded in the parapet was a trio of dim orange lamps on a single post, their weak light stuttering. The lamppost cast a weak shadow onto the bridge's pavement. A shadow that moved.

It grew darker, darker still, until an ebony black puddle of darkness writhed on the ground.

Their ugly, demented demon pet sprung up from the surface, fleshing out its three-dimensional body with a very catlike shake of its non-fur. It cast its eyeless head about, gaze passing straight over Julien—of course—to find its one true love, Cinn.

A molecule of hope reared its head within Julien, which he quickly shot down—what was one measly shadow cat going to do against a wall of pure evil darkness?

The cat launched itself towards them, leaping like a tiger over an abandoned motorcycle to land by Cinn's feet. It screeched. An animalistic piercing warble, frenetic in tone. Then it dashed between Cinn's legs, pausing in his shadow. Dissolving like sugar in coffee, it melted into the ground.

"What the—" Elliot began.

The wind seemed to lessen, like the umbraphages had paused their efforts to watch with them. Cinn slowed his jerky movements, then stilled.

The darkness in the centre of Cinn's shadow spread outward like an ink spill, clambering to fill every inch of his shape.

In one abrupt movement, Cinn stumbled forward, landing on his hands and knees and taking Julien down to the concrete with him. Smashed glass littered the road, a mosaic of shimmering shards that swiftly pierced Julien's thigh.

He pushed the sharp pain to the back of his mind. It wasn't important. It didn't exist.

Cinn pushed himself up to kneel, staring down at his palms, bloodied with razor-thin cuts that created a small pool of crimson under them, quickly diluted by the rain.

"Cinn!"

Julien closed the small space between them, embedding yet more glass into his flesh. He bit the side of his cheek to distract himself, a burst of copper exploding in his mouth. He grabbed Cinn's hands, plucking out one particularly large chunk of glass from near his left thumb.

"Ouch!" snapped Cinn, pulling his hand away.

Ignoring Cinn's glare, Julien held his face with both hands, brought his lips to Cinn's, pressing them together with bruising force. Cinn made a small noise of shock before he responded in turn. Impossibly, Cinn's lips were even colder than Julien's own. He kissed them again and again, breathing heat into them, his relief melting into the kiss. He devoured every warm exhalation of Cinn's like it was his only substance. And in a way, that was true.

"Julien!" Elliot shouted, not sounding pleased for some reason. "We're kind of in the middle of something here."

He had a point, so Julien clambered to his feet, pulling Cinn up with him. Cinn gingerly rubbed at his left knee. His jeans were shredded and blood soaked, and seeing the glass embedded in his flesh caused Julien's thigh to throb in sympathy.

The torrent of wind streaming through the bridge had desisted. Instead, water from the Thames churned upward around them, forming a circular vortex that encapsulated them in a surreal bubble of swirling fog and turbulent currents.

They were in the eye of the storm.

The air was eerily calm, ominously tranquil.

Elliot tipped his head back, assessing. "There's fuck all lumen-motes, and we normally have at least twenty of us for a light net, but we'll have to try. Unless you want to…"

Julien didn't need Elliot to finish his sentence. He was asking if Julien would draw upon *his* motes. The illicit ones. They were, as usual, just within reach, their low hum his ever-present companion, begging to be channelled. As tempting as it was, the last time he'd used them, shadowrealm aside, he'd reduced a church to rubble. He had no desire to do the same to Westminster Bridge.

Regret slashed through him like a knife, closely followed by self-loathing, due to the pleading look in Elliot's eye that he felt said, *come on, save us.*

"Woah! Wha—"

Julien's head snapped to the object of Elliot's sudden shock: Cinn's shadow. Where before the cat had simply darkened it, when it had climbed inside or whatever the fuck it had done, now the silhouette stretched and undulated, edges trembling with an unsettling flicker. It pulsed and swelled, a monster being fed, growing larger with each heavy thump of Julien's heartbeat.

"Cinn," Julien croaked, a single chill running down his spine, as he remained transfixed by the shadow's unnatural movement. He pointed behind Cinn.

Cinn spun, flinching at the sight. He raised one arm, and the shadow responded, stretching further along the ground like an oil spill. "Holy fuck."

HELLO, SHADOW

How had Julien almost forgotten they were about to be devoured by three lethal beings from another realm? Apparently, they'd remembered how to talk.

Cinn stepped forward. "Hello."

Alarmed at the unmistakable note of confidence in Cinn's voice, Julien blocked him. "What are you doing? Don't engage," Julien hissed.

Ignoring him, Cinn moved around Julien. "I'm here. What do you want?" he hollered up at them.

"What the fuck, dude!" Elliot threw out his arms, as if ready to defend against any retort from the umbraphages.

Julien yanked on Cinn's shoulder. "Have you gone quite mad? Don't provoke them!"

Cinn spun, piercing him with his glare.

His black-eyed glare.

His gorgeous golden orbs were gone, now replaced with obsidian depths that reflected Julien's stunned face. Only a tiny sliver of white remained. Behind Cinn, his shadow reared up, twisting like a dark serpent preparing to strike.

Julien's hand fell away.

"Well?" Cinn screamed at them, with a stamp of his foot. "You want me? Come and get me then!"

Yes, indeed, Cinn had gone quite mad. Certifiably insane.

The umbrages erupted in response: their amorphous forms writhed and contorted violently, tendrils lashing out in every direction with chaotic fury.

YOU ARE SHADOW

What?

Julien was out of time to talk Cinn down. Before he could react further, Cinn—and his shadow—surged forward, charging towards the umbraphages with an alarming ferocity. As he tore down the bridge, his shadow widened, *deepened,* darkened impossibly.

The three foes rose, merging as one to become a singular, colossal entity.

The air crackled, a volatile energy that charged the swirling foggy mist. Then, it struck at Cinn.

A dark tendril whipped out from the umbraphages, racing towards Cinn's tiny body, standing alone in the middle of the wide bridge. As fast as the lightning flashes above them, Cinn's shadow expanded, its form shifting and morphing with a life of its own, to counter the strike with a swift, fluid movement.

The sight was mesmerising. Really, Julien ought to be screaming after him, terrified for his safety. Instead, he stood back, watching on in stunned awe.

Cinn threw his hands out in a position identical to the one young moteblessed channellers were encouraged to adopt when they first began. Julien could hear it now: *Arms out, chest forward, eyes closed,* feel *the motes. Let them come to you.*

The umbraphages hissed and recoiled, their countless shadowy tentacles flailing wildly—in shock?—before once again attempting to overpower the sentient darkness that was Cinn's shadow.

With a sweeping gesture, his shadow morphed into a massive, clawed appendage, swiping at the umbraphages with a force that sent them reeling. The creatures retaliated, lashing out with their own tendrils, but Cinn's shadow somehow managed to absorb the blows, its form rippling like water.

The two creatures of darkness clashed again and again, the umbraphages twisting and coiling their malleable limbs to avoid and deflect Cinn's attacks.

Knees bent, Cinn's legs were visibly shaking as he clearly pushed his body far over its limit. Julien ran to him. His eyes, now even deeper pits of blackness, looked straight through Julien, unseeing.

"Cinn!" Julien lightly slapped his cheeks.

"Leave him!" Elliot snapped.

"*Non*! It's too much!"

The street lights flickered and dimmed, taking with them the remnants of daylight. The air around them grew cold and oppressive. Every clash of shadows sent a tremble through the bridge.

"Look!"

The umbraphages twisted and undulated, their movements erratic and unpredictable. In a swift, decisive motion, Cinn's shadow entirely engulfed one of their number, its form dissipating into wisps of dark mist.

Elliot cheered. Warm pride exploded through Julien like a sudden burst of sunlight. It apparently took twenty gendarmes to take down an umbraphage. Twenty gendarmes, or one Cinn.

His Cinn.

Taking on the umbraphages by himself, while he and Elliot stood back and watched.

But there was no time for celebration. There were still two left, and they were pissed—rearing up, ready to strike.

While his shadow defended against an incoming blow to the right, an inky, fluid tentacle lashed towards Cinn's left, curling around his forearm. Heart skipping several beats, Julien braced, preparing to see Cinn lifted into the air and torn in two.

The umbraphage released him with a flick.

Julien hissed through his teeth. He stared at Cinn's arm, ready to observe the flesh torn to shreds, or worse—swimming with the contaminant—but instead, he witnessed Cinn's metal band shattering into a million pieces.

The gold fragments fell to the floor like sparkling confetti.

The umbraphages made a low rumbling noise—of satisfaction? Of *amusement*?

Anger flared through Julien. Just what were they playing at, toying with them like this?

They don't want to hurt him.

They... want him.

A horrible sinking feeling took root in Julien's stomach.

Something was changing. A seismic shift. What started as a vibration under their feet soon rose to shake the very air. Cinn still stood, shadow at the ready, eyes black as the night, but the umbraphages ceased their attacks. An eerie, guttural hum emanated from them.

The sinking feeling grew like a weed, climbing up through him to squeeze his heart, then further up to wrap around his brain, choking it. An unmistakable sensation of melancholy washed over him. It was as if it drained away all of his colour, all of *himself*, leaving only an empty vessel.

His one remaining thought—that he held onto with absolute clarity—was that nothing mattered anymore. Not his never-ending mission for answers. Not this fight on the bridge. Certainly not his own survival.

The last fragment of light faded further, plunging them towards near darkness. The umbraphages expanded and expanded, their shadowy forms coalescing into an inky mass that surged forward, enveloping everything in its path: pavement, cars, lampposts, bodies, all swallowed into oblivion.

Elliot shouted curses and prayers. Julien felt him draw upon the weak supply of lumenmotes. A last-ditch attempt at defence.

Cinn's shadow wavered, shrinking in on itself. His hands were by his sides, fisting the cuff of his hoodie's sleeves in that childlike way he did when he was nervous.

Or scared.

Only moments left now—the impenetrable wall of darkness closing in with relentless certainty.

Cinn turned his head to meet Julien's, fear etched into every line.

Some small part of Julien forced himself to react.

Julien dove towards Cinn, wrapping himself around him as the world became a swirl of darkness and dread.

Eleven

JULIEN

Julien lay flat on his back, the rough surface beneath him pressing uncomfortably against his spine.

But that was okay, because the horrible feeling was gone.

It had only plagued him for a minute at most, but it had been the sort of minute where the threat of it continuing made an eternity of time pass. The absence of the empty dread was like an oppressive weight being lifted, and he breathed in one heavy, grateful breath.

Oui, the feeling had gone, the rain had stopped, the sky was red, and all was well again.

Red?

Julien shot straight up. A single glance informed him the weight pressing on his left leg was Cinn, who was also sprawled on his back. Cinn was groaning, stretching, and very much *alive*.

For now.

A few shakes of Cinn's body, and his eyes opened—thankfully the blackness had left them, bringing back the soft shade of golden hazel Julien could never help spending too long secretly admiring.

But now, those eyes drifted past Julien to perform a sweeping glance across the horizon.

"Back again, huh?" Cinn said.

Julien nodded, then joined him in surveying the shadowrealm. The odd, perpetual twilight from Julien's last visit here remained, as did the fractured moon hanging low in the sky.

They were still on Westminster Bridge, that was for sure—but now it was a warped, sad reflection of its former self. The iconic lampposts were now gnarled and twisted, casting no light into the thick, red-tinged haze that surrounded them. The outlines of Big Ben and the Houses of Parliament loomed ominously through the gloom, their facades now ravaged by those crimson ivy vines, disturbingly large, eerily alien. A large portion of the Palace of Westminster had crumbled to the ground, leaving gaping holes where walls once stood, the ruins overtaken by the pulsating, grotesque vines that seemed to feed off the destruction.

"You clearly can't keep away," Julien eventually retorted.

They walked over to the parapet, leaning across for a better view of what remained of the River Thames: a desolate riverbed, a vast expanse of cracked, parched earth, streaked with the remnants of dark, stagnant pools that had long since dried up.

Cinn pulled away, hanging on to the railing and leaning back, gazing up at the sky. He wrinkled his nose. "How come you're here?"

"That isn't entirely the response I was hoping for. I'll go, shall I?"

"You know what I mean." Cinn picked at a crimson vine wrapped tightly around the bars. It resisted at first, then its thick, sinewy strands gave way, leaving behind a rust-coloured imprint. "You were only able to come here last time because of the Mortalisfade."

Julien gazed down the length of the bridge. "I've not the faintest clue," he said. "Just before we came here, I felt this… horrible emptiness. It was awful. Like nothing mattered." Julien swallowed; he could still taste the despair lingering on his tongue. "Then I looked at you and was reminded that it did. You matter."

Cinn closed the space between them to press their foreheads together, grasping the nape of Julien's neck. "Let's get out of here. I'm so done with this shit."

As if on cue, a blackness flickered behind Cinn. Not his shadow—that was Cinn-shaped again. The umbraphages had rejoined them.

Julien pulled Cinn behind him so fast he let out a gasp of air.

SHADOW

Cinn mumbled something like 'for fuck's sake' before shouting, "What do you want?"

TO TALK WITH YOU

YOU AND HIM

That explained Julien's invitation. He stepped forward, tipping his head back to fully take in the umbraphages and their immense size. "Talk then!"

WHAT DO YOU KNOW OF THIS WORLD

Cinn frowned—the question had surprised him, too. "I don't know… it's the *shadowrealm*?"

THIS IS YOUR WORLD

AND IT IS NOT YOUR WORLD

"Yeah?" snapped Cinn. "Real helpful."

IT COULD BE YOUR WORLD

Was it as they'd theorised? A prophetic glimpse into the planet's destiny?

"Like, the future?"

WHAT YOU CALL THE SHADOWREALM CAN BE OF PAST AND OF FUTURE

There were three separate umbraphages writhing in the red, hazy sky. The one Cinn banished had returned, or perhaps a new one had joined them—Julien couldn't recognise one from another and he didn't care to learn.

WE ARE HERE TO WARN

THE SANDS OF TIME SLIP AWAY

Cinn scoffed. "Why should we listen to you? All you do is go around murdering people and causing earthquakes and tidal waves and whatever the fuck you do!"

NOT US

MOTHER EARTH IS UNBALANCED

SHE HURTS

SHE CRIES

WE ONLY COME TO WARN

"There's about ten dead bodies on Westminster Bridge!" said Julien, dripping incredulity into his voice. "That, my friends, is not only coming to warn."

HUMANS RESPOND BEST TO VIOLENCE

Did the umbraphages sound puzzled by Julien's comment?

THE POWER YOU CALL MOTE IS UNBALANCING MOTHER

God, if only the Arcane Purifiers were here. They'd be frothing at the mouth to hear all this.

But it was one thing hearing the idea abstractly, and another from the horse's mouth.

Were the umbraphages really saying that they needed to stop all use of motes? It would be nigh on impossible for moteblessed channellers—the need to channel was built into their very DNA. The years Julien had resisted had carved scars into him that would never heal. Not to mention the motetech embedded in millions of materials and objects all over the world.

THE POWER WAS A GIFT

A GIFT TO CHERISH

A GIFT TO PROVIDE

NOT TO BE MISUSED FOR HUMAN GREED

"Why are you telling *us* all this?"

Impatience spiking, Julien reached out with his sixth sense, feeling the air around him for the elusive motes he knew would be there. His skin prickled as he made contact with the tiny, pulsating specks of energy. Without conscious effort, he tugged on a few, the warm, comforting thrum resonating through his body like a soothing balm. The motes responded, vibrating with promises of untapped potential.

STOP

YOU WILL LISTEN

They sounded pissed. He sent a pulse of energy towards the umbraphages, the motes surging forward, crackling with intense, barely contained power that shimmered in the air.

A rumbling growl reverberated through the bridge, shaking the entire structure. Glass from a close-by lamppost rained to the ground.

"We don't want to fuck with them!" hissed Cinn, digging his nails into Julien's arm.

Then, Julien felt it again. That horrible sensation. The nothingness. The dread. He felt more than heard a low groan tumble out of his lips. A palpable wave of despair washed over Julien, coiling around his bones like the vine's insidious grip on the city.

"*Arrête!*" Julien eventually spat out, the word dragging itself out of him through a mire of thick, suffocating tar. "*Je t'en prie!*"

To his astonishment, they obeyed, the oppressive atmosphere receding as the umbraphages halted their assault.

Cinn was staring at him with concern, as if he'd gone mad. Evidently the umbraphages only wanted to torture him.

Julien regained his breath, his composure. His sanity.

"But what do you think *we* can do about it?" Julien ran his hand through his damp hair to resist folding his arms. "Tell all this to Auri's consortium!"

JULIEN MONTAIGNE

Julien flinched at the sound of his own name in the booming, inhuman voice.

A sharp intake of breath. Cinn gazed down at the floor, where the shadow cat slid out from between his legs. It angled its eyeless sockets towards Julien while its wispy tail flickered metronomically.

YOU ARE NOT THE FIRST MONTAIGNE WE ATTEMPTED TO TALK TO

Béatrice's document flashed in his mind: *The remaining skin exhibited evidence of umbraphage lacerations.*

"You hurt her!" Julien cried.

Cinn pressed his hand against Julien's back, but it did nothing to calm the storm that thundered within him.

IT WAS NOT OUR INTENT

WE APPEARED TO HER

SHE WAS SCARED

THE LOCKET KILLED HER

WE ONLY TOUCHED HER TO MAKE HER SHADOW

Julien's gaze fell to the cat. *Maybe she didn't want to be shadow!* "So this really is her then?" he asked them in a flat tone. It wasn't lost on him that if an umbraphage hadn't 'appeared' to her at the top of that mountain, she wouldn't have channelled, and the locket wouldn't have killed her. But this line of reasoning would be lost on the umbraphages, of this he was sure.

"Why did you appear to her?" asked Cinn.

WE WERE BOTH OF THE SAME INTENTIONS, US AND SHE

HER AND HER ARCANE PURIFIERS

WE WANTED TO HELP

SHE WENT TO HIM, JUST LIKE YOUR MOTHER DID

The ground vanished beneath Julien. His mother? His breath caught in his throat as the weight of the words crushed into him with the force of a hundred thunderclaps.

"What? Who?" he whispered.

PÈRE GÉRARD

"Father Gérard?"

Hearing the recognition in Julien's voice, Cinn slid him a look. *Père Gérard.* Now there was a name he never expected to hear. But this wasn't the first time he'd thought about the kindly old priest in so many days. Although he'd kept it from the others, he'd recognised the address of

Father Gérard's church in Béatrice's file—the mysterious location in France that he'd pretended to the others he didn't recognise.

"Why did she go there?" Julien shouted at the umbraphage, while glaring at the cat between Cinn's legs.

YOU DO NOT TRUST US

BUT YOU TRUST HIM

HE IS OF OUR CAUSE

HER CAUSE

YOUR CAUSE

A pause.

THE MACHINA TENEBRIS MUST BE DESTROYED

"The what?" muttered Cinn. "Do they think they're clever, talking like this?"

The air was growing hazier with each passing shouted exchange. The red mist swirled around them, wrapping them in a serpentine embrace, obscuring the umbraphages.

"Wait," Cinn shouted, threading his fingers through the fog as if he could sweep it away. "Why did you keep me here last time? And none of that *shadow* crap."

YOU ARE SHADOW

Their cadence changed slightly—the umbraphages sounded confused. Julien snorted. Reasoning with them was clearly a hopeless endeavour.

MUST PROTECT SHADOW

"You're the ones I need protection from!" Cinn snarled. "You won't fucking leave me alone!"

MUST PROTECT SHADOW FROM HIM

Julien felt the umbraphages gaze turn to him, which was ridiculous, because they didn't have eyes, and Cinn wasn't in any danger from *him* for Christ's sake.

The accusation rekindled his hot fury. Without a second thought, he reached for the motes—

Twelve

ELLIOT

The very second that Julien and Cinn fell to the ground like puppets with their strings cut, the storm stopped. The clouds didn't miraculously clear, but the punishing rain stopped pelting Westminster, and the cyclonic wind ceased.

And when Elliot looked up from the lifeless bodies of his best friends, he found the umbraphages had vanished.

He allowed himself one large breath to steady the tempest that still raged inside him, then leapt into action. Wasting not a second more, he charged over to his fallen comrades, dropping to his knees to snatch up Julien's wrist. Elliot's trembling fingers sought the telltale flutter of his pulse. It was there.

"Thank Christ," Elliot muttered.

Though—did it feel weak? Elliot was no doctor.

"DARCY!" Elliot bellowed at the top of his lungs, using his palms to cup his mouth.

Her small frame soon sprinted towards him, auburn hair a wet, bedraggled mess. "What happened?" she gasped, looking between the two slumped forms and Elliot, still with Julien's wrist under his fingers.

"The umbraphages fucked off at the same time they hit the ground. They're both unconscious. Do you think they've—"

"—gone to the shadowrealm," Darcy finished, falling to the ground to join them. "Ouch!"

She pointed at Cinn's shin, shredded from the glass. Blood pooled out from the wounds, staining the blue denim of his jeans. Julien's thigh was a similar story. Elliot himself must have been covered in bruises—he felt like he'd been thrown down ten flights of stairs. Every muscle ached, a deep throbbing pain that pulsed in time with his heartbeat, but there was no time to think about himself when his friends' unconscious bodies were bleeding. Sirens sounded, growing increasingly louder.

"A couple of gendarmes have arrived, but they're outnumbered by paramedics. We can't let them have these two like this."

"What?" Elliot blinked at her, exhausted mind running on empty fumes.

"We can't have them interfering with their bodies if they're in the shadowrealm," she snapped at him. "We need to move them out of the way, then see to their wounds."

Elliot dragged himself to his feet.

Darcy looked between the heavy bodies and Elliot. "Do you need me to—"

"No."

For a delusional second, Elliot considered lifting each of them over a shoulder to carry them both at once, then laughed at himself. He picked up Cinn first. He looked heavier—best to get the worst of it over with.

Elliot heaved Cinn's limp body up, staggering under the weight as he adjusted his grip to place him in a fireman's carry. He was even heavier than expected, his solid frame dead weight in Elliot's arms. Every tired muscle screamed in protest, but he ignored them, gritting his teeth and marching down Westminster Bridge.

The rain-soaked pavement slick beneath his boots, Elliot splashed in puddles as he pushed forward. Reaching the lion statue, he ducked around it, out of sight from the prying eyes of the paramedics. Two ambulances had pulled up near the bridge, sirens casting blue light that flickered across the wet streets like flashes of lightning. The paramedics moved swiftly, urgent shouts cutting through the already chaotic scene.

Ever so gently, he lowered Cinn down to the ground, placing him on his side, and trying not to look at his bleeding leg wound. Then, he turned, jogging all the way back to Julien.

Darcy helped lift Julien off the ground this time. It was a good thing she did—Elliot was quickly running out of emergency energy reserves. He threw Julien over his shoulder.

"I'll run ahead to see what I can find." Darcy sprinted off before Elliot could agree.

"Come on then," he murmured to Julien. The bridge stretched out ahead like a marathon, the towering statue of the lion his finish line.

As he dragged one foot in front of another, Elliot's gaze fell on Julien's expressionless face. The usual spark in his eyes, that quick wit always dancing at the corners of his lips—gone. His face was eerily still, a mask devoid of life, pale beneath the wet strands of blond hair plastered to his skin. Panic clawed its way into Elliot's chest, his heart pounding as blood rushed through his ears.

"Don't you dare," he whispered, voice tight with fear. "You need to come back, you hear me?"

Julien's body remained limp, unresponsive, the weight of it pressing heavier on Elliot's mind than his shoulders.

Ten years. That's how long it had been since that life-changing moment when he'd met Julien, on the first day of summer camp. Yet, he could remember it like it was yesterday—the long bus journey from Barcelona airport.

Elliot hadn't wanted to be sent away at the age of fourteen to spend his summer in Europe, to hone his channelling skills. Yet there he was, last to arrive at the designated bus stop—late, after a slight detour to the shop to buy some candy. He'd spent too long choosing between the fruity gummies or chocolate-covered peanuts. After all, it was incredibly important that he got this decision right—how would he possibly make friends if he couldn't bribe them?

When he'd finally paid using strange coins, he sprinted to the bus, where the angry face of the bus driver greeted him as he ticked Elliot off on his clipboard. Elliot swallowed down a thick lump in his throat, cursing his parents once again for forcing him to travel alone to another continent, sending him away for an entire month of his summer.

The driver stowed his luggage, shouting at him in Spanish and gesturing to the door.

Elliot only managed to take three shaky steps down the aisle of the bus before the driver accelerated, sending Elliot flying forward onto his knees.

The thirty-or-so passengers, all around his age, burst into raucous laughter that echoed off the walls of the bus, filling the tight space with a wave of mocking glee. Elliot's cheeks burned with embarrassment as he scrambled to his feet, trying to gather what little dignity he had left. The sound felt like it went on forever, each snicker and chuckle twisting his stomach in knots.

Before Elliot could fully right himself, a pale arm shot out from one of the seats and yanked him sideways. He stumbled into the empty spot, heart still racing. Glancing over, he found a boy with tousled blond hair and a lazy smirk, his grey eyes gleaming with something like amusement, but not mockery. An open sketchpad lay on his lap, but the boy snapped it shut.

"Do you want to be friends?" the boy asked, his English thickly accented.

Elliot stared at him, blinking rapidly. How was this his luck? He hadn't even brought the fruit gummies out of his pocket yet!

"Well?" the boy asked impatiently. He wasn't smiling. "I'm only going to make you this offer once. It's now, or don't bother talking to me again."

Realising his mouth hung open, Elliot snapped it shut, but not before a nervous laugh slipped out. He studied the odd boy—the slight tremor in his hands as they rested on the sketchpad, the way his foot tapped anxiously against the floor. Beneath the bravado, there was a flicker of vulnerability in his eyes that mirrored Elliot's own fears.

Elliot held out his hand.

The boy eyed it. "Do you promise to stick with me?" It sounded more like a threat than an offer.

Elliot nodded, and the boy took his hand.

In that moment, Elliot felt a sudden, visceral connection with the stranger. Where their hands locked, a jolt of electricity passed through. His breath was stolen, and the boy finally flashed him a dimpled smile, that brilliant, beautiful smile. And so began the theft of his heart.

By the end of that summer, Elliot was deeply and irrevocably in love with Julien.

Behind the lion statue, Elliot lowered the body of his best friend down to the ground. He couldn't resist gently brushing Julien's hair away from his face.

Elliot had been Julien's shadow for that entire summer, and the one after that, and so on.

Then he'd followed him to Paris for college.

By the time Julien announced his plans to move to Auri, there was no question about where Elliot would go. He'd go wherever Julien—and Darcy, by that point—went.

Julien's chest rose and fell shallowly.

Fuck. What if—

Panic surged through him, and his breath quickened as the world around him began to blur. Logic slipped from his grasp with every heartbeat, and all he could think about was Julien slipping away beneath his hands.

No!

Elliot shook Julien. Gently, at first, then more violently, shaking his entire body. "Wake up!" he said, voice cracking. "You don't get to leave me! Remember our promise!"

"Elliot!"

A hand behind him squeezed his shoulder. He turned to find Cinn, still half-slumped on the floor, but awake. Alive. Alive, but alarmed. "Hey! Calm down!"

Relief coursed through Elliot, but it was the tidal wave of guilt that knocked the breath from his lungs. Partially because he'd just shaken Julien like a rag doll. Partially because he'd completely ignored Cinn's equally lifeless form. But the largest source of his guilt was—

Fuck, Cinn had just heard the raw desperation in his voice as he cradled Julien, and Elliot had been trying so, so hard to show Cinn how much he supported their relationship.

Hot prickles behind Elliot's eyes blurred the world. "Here," he croaked, passing Julien to Cinn. "Take him." A look of alarm crossed Cinn's face as he reached out to grab him.

He rounded the statue, tipping his head back to rest on the cool stone plinth.

Cinn was awake. That meant Julien would surely soon be too. Any second now.

Chill the fuck down, Elliot urged himself, but it was difficult in the chaotic environment. Medical personnel and police flooded the road and pavement. The blue light of several ambulances spun dizzying patterns across the wet ground, illuminating the tumultuous scene as people dashed around.

He fixed his eyes on a stone on the pavement, willing his horrible, confused feelings away. He'd count to ten, then return to Cinn and pretend nothing had happened.

Darcy's boots materialised. "I've got bandages."

"Cinn's awake."

"Oh, thank God! Julien?"

Elliot sighed. "Let's go see."

He braced himself as he rounded the corner, plastering on a neutral expression.

There, on the ground, Cinn was holding Julien with a fierce tenderness that made the world around them fade into the background. Cinn's lips were pulled into a wide smile as his gaze locked onto Julien, his eyes wide with a mixture of relief and intense emotion, as if he were afraid to blink lest this fragile moment shatter.

Julien reached up, fingers visibly trembling, and brushed against Cinn's cheek.

Elliot swallowed. The air between Julien and Cinn shimmered with unspoken words, and he almost took a step backwards, until Darcy shoved him forwards.

Cinn's head snapped up to lock eyes with Elliot, and Elliot tensed, prepared for any mixture of distrust, annoyance, *hatred* even to be shot at him.

But instead, he only saw concern on Cinn's face.

"Well, you're awake now, so I guess you should go see the paramedics," said Darcy, still clutching the bandages, sounding put out by the whole thing. "Probably sooner rather than later. Though they're pretty swamped."

"Give us one more minute." Cinn reached for the bandages, but Darcy crouched in the puddle to press a bundle of them to his leg, tossing some to Elliot for Julien.

Julien hissed in pain when Elliot compressed his wad of fabric against the torn, bloodied material on his thigh, quickly taking it from him to do it himself.

"What happened then?" asked Elliot. "The umbraphage disappeared and you two fell to the ground."

Julien shuffled, sitting himself up higher. "Well," he started, before launching into the tale.

Elliot only interrupted when they reached a name he didn't recognise. "Father Gérard? Who's that?"

Julien tipped his head back and sighed. "He's the priest of the church my mother frequented, in the village outside Paris where she grew up."

Darcy caught Elliot's eye.

"*Oui*," Julien snapped. "The church where..."

Elliot could see the sentence running through Julien's head: *The church where I killed her.*

"The church where she died," Elliot, supplied for him, tone firm.

Julien shook his head almost imperceptibly, lips pursing together. Elliot's heart ached for him, and he was a fraction of a moment away from stepping towards him, stopping himself only when Cinn squeezed Julien's shoulder, tilting his head in concern.

"Well, apparently Béatrice was dropping in for coffee with the priest, completely unbeknown to us!" Julien glared between Elliot and Darcy as if they were co-conspirators—projecting his own self-loathing. "Can you believe it? *When?*"

Elliot's heart gave another painful squeeze. He could see right through Julien. How he wished Eleanor would miraculously tell him Béatrice's file was all a misunderstanding. How much he wanted the sister he knew back, living on in his memories, untainted and pure.

Elliot gently fell to the ground to press Julien's hand more firmly against the blood flow. The bandages were quickly soaking through. "I get it. No, I can't believe it, and I'm hurt by it too. But look, you're not in this alone. Let's get through Christmas, then we'll get to the bottom of it all."

Elliot's eyes were glued to where his hand was on top of Julien's. His face warmed, his brain imagining Cinn glaring at him, despite the unlikeness of that. It was Elliot who'd been jealous of Cinn, initially. Cinn had been nothing but friendly. Elliot forced his head up. Cinn was indeed looking at them, but there was a soft smile on his face, warm and understanding, as if he saw through Elliot's hesitation and felt no threat, only kindness.

Darcy let out a random, abrupt squeak, attracting everyone's attention. "Okay, so don't get cross, I was just about to get to this—"

She didn't bother finishing her sentence.

A face Elliot didn't expect to see was marching towards them.

Eleanor Sinclair.

True, upon reflection, it should have been obvious that she'd come to the crisis, even on Christmas Eve, which Julien mentioned she usually spent with her sister in Norway. She'd taken the Baths—her glasses were missing, and she wore the grey baggy clothes the service provided.

Julien started climbing unsteadily to his feet, with Cinn following close behind. Elliot reached out to grab Julien's arm, hauling him up so Julien could continue pressing against his leg.

"Julien!" she said, by way of greeting. She eyed him expectantly, completely ignoring Elliot and the others. When Julien only stared back, she continued, "Darcy told me some insane tale about the three of you marching onto the bridge to play heroes."

Elliot snorted before he could stop himself, then chuckled at Darcy's wide-eyed look of horror.

"I'm sorry, are you joking? This is your response? Without even asking how we are? Without a thank you for the fact we chose to help, on behalf of Auri, when we easily could have run home to hide?" replied Julien.

"Do you have a death wish I should be aware of? You are not invincible, Julien Montaigne!"

Ignoring her, Julien continued, sweetening his tone to say, "Thank you so much for attempting to save innocent Londoners, Julien, Elliot, and Cinn. On behalf of the consortium, let me extend our most gracious thanks for your valiant efforts. It was truly noble of you to risk your lives, and we will now forever be in your debt."

Pure fury flashed on Eleanor's face, her lips curling into a sneer as she opened her mouth to retort.

"*Non!*" shouted Julien, startling Darcy, who flinched. "I'm not going to stand here for one more second and listen—"

Elliot shifted restlessly on the balls of his feet, a knot of anxiety tightening in his stomach. This was the last thing they all needed, especially Julien.

He'd have to intervene, to calm Julien down. He'd—

Cinn grabbed Julien's shoulders, swiftly twisting him so they faced each other. "Hey," Cinn said, pressing a hand—covered in small, bleeding lacerations that really ought to be looked at sometime soon—against Julien's cheek. "Let's leave it. It's not worth getting worked up over."

Julien's jaw clenched. "But—"

"Nope." Cinn's other hand snaked around Julien's waist, drawing him closer.

Elliot held his breath. Half of him almost expected Julien to throw Cinn off, turn back to Eleanor, and continue to give her a piece of his mind.

Then Cinn's bloody hand tangled in the mess of Julien's hair, brushing it out of the way to lean in and whisper something softly to him. Julien melted into him, and soon they formed a bubble of just the two of them while they all looked on from the outside. Julien and Cinn against the world.

A traitorous hot, thick lump formed in Elliot's throat as his heart tied itself in a knot. *Look at them,* he forced himself to think. *Look how easily Cinn talked Julien down off the ledge. Look how perfect they are together.*

You're happy for them. You are.

Elliot didn't realise Darcy had moved behind Eleanor to stand next to him until her small hand slipped into his and squeezed. He squeezed it back without looking at her.

Eleanor cleared her throat. "Clearly, it's been a long and difficult day for everyone," she managed, sucking her lips into her teeth until they disappeared. "Quickly recount to me what happened here, then we can all be on our way. We can debrief fully after the holidays."

Eleanor directed the question at Elliot, evidently acknowledging Julien was a lost cause.

Elliot licked his lips. If they'd never found Eleanor's secret files, this would be so much easier.

A deep frown fragmented Eleanor's forehead. "Well? By the time Salvatore Gallo had arrived with the small number of gendarmerie he could pull together, the hurricane was barely a breeze, and the umbraphages had vanished of their own will? Unless you're about to tell me that Julien..."

Eleanor redirected her gaze to pierce Julien meaningfully with her beady glare. Elliot knew what she was asking him—did Julien tap into his enigmatic motes? As far as Elliot knew, Julien's mother had confided in her, back when she and Julien were attempting to figure out his inexplicable abilities together.

Elliot was sure Eleanor would be delighted if Julien announced that he was the solution to their biggest problem.

But that wasn't going to happen.

"They simply vanished," Julien said, smiling at her.

Eleanor sighed, pressing two fingers to her temple. For once, she almost looked her age. Elliot forced himself to squash down the tiniest shred of remorse.

But Eleanor was the closest thing Julien had to a parent he actually had a relationship with, and she'd been deceiving him for months. Was possibly involved in killing his sister, even. So Elliot's sympathy for the moment was short-lived.

A *tsk* from Eleanor, then a single shake of her head before she spun on her heel and stormed off, swallowed instantly into the crowd.

"Are you okay?" Cinn hadn't released Julien, the two of them still interlocked. A complete unit. The connection between them undeniable, two halves of a whole.

"Absolutely fine," Julien said, sounding almost delirious.

Cinn looked over Julien's shoulder to Elliot. "What about you, mate? Are you alright? Sorry we left you on the bridge."

Elliot shrugged. "Don't worry about me." *I was absolutely fine, not on the verge of a breakdown at all.*

Cinn untangled one arm from Julien and reached out for Elliot. When Elliot didn't immediately move closer, Cinn leaned over and tugged on his coat sleeve, pulling him into the embrace. Julien sagged against him, his weight pressing onto Elliot's shoulder with a groan. Cinn, still holding Julien, seemed to wait for Elliot to meet his gaze, offering a subtle, deliberate smile when he did.

The tension that had been gripping Elliot's chest like an iron vice finally began to ease. Elliot mirrored Cinn's smile with a grin of his own, warmth flooding through him. If he believed in lucky stars, he'd be thanking them a thousand times over for bringing Cinn into his life. Into all of their lives.

"Fuck, Eleanor was just a real piece of work," said Elliot, before he started crying or something.

"A complete bitch," declared Darcy, earning the three shocked heads snapping towards her.

Elliot made a hooting noise, filling the air with laughter. "Are you finally over your girl crush on her?"

A beat of silence.

"Fuck you."

The look on Darcy's face was so utterly serious, so fiercely resolute, that Cinn started snickering, joining in with Elliot, and then Julien finally cracked, joining in with his own laughter—his genuine, loud, cackling laughter Elliot treasured so much.

Darcy managed all of five seconds before her stern scowl twitched, her face splitting into a smile as bright as the sun.

"You're all idiots," she said at last. "But yes, Elliot, I am very much over my girl crush."

Thirteen

CINN

There wasn't even a hint of dawn outside the kitchen window, yet Cinn was wide awake.

Where's the goddamn cocoa powder?

He rummaged through the unfamiliar drawers and cabinets, his frustration mounting with each search of the holiday home's sparsely stocked cupboards. Honestly, it was a miracle he'd found a whisk earlier.

Footsteps crept on the old creaky floorboards. Cinn frantically surveyed the countertops. Various ingredients spilled across the counters, several egg shells had somehow managed to fall on the granite tiles, and a trail of sugar led to the half-opened pantry door. A small puddle of batter glistened near the sink.

This is why he didn't cook in other people's kitchens.

The door opened slowly. Messy auburn hair poked around it, and for a moment his brain screamed Darcy, even though the figure in the doorway was a foot taller than her, and male.

Heart plummeting, he lunged for a dishcloth, and held it up. "Hi. I'm just about to clean it all up."

Alexander laughed, a booming chuckle that somehow carried his Scottish twang. "Ye're alright, lad. Sorry to startle ye. I couldn't sleep."

"Me neither," Cinn heard himself say, as if insomnia was a good excuse for destroying a kitchen.

"Can I give ye a hand?"

"No, no. Well... I can't find your cocoa powder. Figured you had some around, since you made us hot chocolate yesterday..." He probably should have said please and also thank you for all the ingredients he'd already stolen. *Oops.*

Alexander crossed the kitchen. "Ah. I put it behind the cereal boxes so I'd remember where it was, after Fiona crammed all the groceries in." He passed Cinn the small cylinder, thankfully still heavy—he'd need a fair bit of it.

Cinn tipped in the powder, eyeing Alexander while he stirred the mixing bowl. The man seemed set to linger, leaning against a counter, stretching. Cinn didn't really have the time or inclination for company right now.

"I'm gonna pop out for a cig." Cinn swiped his packet of cigarettes off the counter near the back door, which led to a dingy alley.

"Oh aye," Alexander said brightly. "I'll join ye."

For fuck's sake. But Cinn could hardly be rude, not when the man had invited them to stay in this posh house for free.

They slipped out back into the frigid night air. Cinn offered him the carton and lighter, and soon they were blowing dual streams of smoke into a dark, starless sky.

Did Cinn need to make conversation? Surely they could just be two blokes enjoying a silent smoke in the early hours of the morning?

"She speaks so highly of ye, ye know, Darcy does. All the time, lad."

"Yeah?"

Alexander hummed on an exhalation of smoke. "I think she struggled after their friend Béatrice died, being left with those two numpties. She's never said anything, mind."

Cinn snorted at Julien and Elliot being labelled numpties. It was a fitting description.

"But since ye came, she's been much happier."

The smoke from his cigarette was blowing into Cinn's eyes. Yes, that was the reason for the hot prickle behind his eyelids.

"They were both dicks to me at first. But she wasn't." Well, she'd used that Frostbite shit on him within minutes of meeting him, but it was smooth sailing after that. "She's got a heart of gold."

"Aye, that she does!" Alexander chuckled on a drag of smoke. "Takes after her mother."

The light streaming into the alley from the kitchen flickered.

"Oh, bloody hell!"

As the back door flew open, Alexander dropped his cigarette, smashing the glowing ember with his heel.

"Dad!"

It was hard to take Darcy's angry tone and furious face seriously, thanks to her outlandishly fluffy pink dressing gown.

"You promised!" she almost shrieked. "You said you'd stop!"

No wonder Alexander had been so keen to join Cinn for a smoke.

"I didn't know!" Cinn threw up his hands, dropping his own offensive cigarette for good measure.

Darcy clucked her tongue, glaring at her father. "Every doctor has told him it's not good for his heart condition."

Alexander chuckled. "Aye, lass. It was just a wee cheeky one for Christmas." He shivered, then slipped behind her. "I'll catch up wi' ye two at a more decent hour."

"Sorry, Darce," Cinn said, following her back into the kitchen.

"You weren't to know. He's such a pain."

Darcy scanned the kitchen, as if seeing it for the first time. Her frown deepened.

Cinn shuffled uneasily on the spot, feeling rather like she'd discovered him in the act of a crime.

Surely Darcy wouldn't click—

"No," she said, a gasp of pure horror. Darcy rubbed Cinn's cheek, with her thumb, then held it up to the light to present cocoa powder. "You did *not* wake up at four a.m. to make Julien that chocolate log he rudely demanded. Tell me this isn't true."

Heat rushed across Cinn's cheeks. He broke eye contact, dropping to his knees to pick up the scattered egg shells.

"No," Cinn muttered. "This is just a backup dessert. The Christmas pudding your mum bought looked a bit small."

In actuality, it served twelve, but they were going to be tiny portions, he could tell.

"There's no rolling pin for the sponge," Cinn said too quickly.

Darcy crossed the kitchen to the wine rack, tucked neatly between two cupboards. She passed him a bottle of red.

Why hadn't Cinn thought of that? He'd been too spoiled using Darcy's cottage kitchen.

"You'll want to—"

But he was already reaching for the parchment paper, to wrap it around the bottle.

Darcy rested both of her elbows on the counter, watching him closely. She laughed. "He does not deserve you, you know."

Cinn hummed in reply.

"Are you always this nauseatingly cute in relationships, or has Julien put you under a spell?"

This was only his second proper relationship, but it was definitely the latter of Darcy's two options.

"I'm nice to everyone!" It sounded weak to his own ears.

Cinn reached for the chocolate ganache he'd cobbled together earlier, again mourning the lack of vanilla extract. He spread an even layer of the filling across the sponge.

"What about you?" Cinn shot back at her. If Darcy wanted to interrogate him about his love life, she would get a taste of her own medicine.

She scrunched up her face.

"What are you like in a relationship?" Cinn asked.

Darcy was oddly quiet about such things, come to think of it. She dropped her gaze, toying with the belt of her dressing gown.

Immediate guilt coursed through Cinn. "Don't worry," he said in a rush, laser-focussing on rolling the sponge into a tight spiral, ensuring the creamy filling stayed perfectly swirled inside.

"No, it's fine. I guess I find it more difficult to connect with people in that way, especially compared to other people."

Cinn tensed, praying she didn't start on about Julien's 'many, *many*' again.

"So I'm not sure what I'm like." She shrugged. "Maybe one of these days."

He nodded, offering her the bowl with the tiniest amount of ganache left, to scrape off with her finger.

She immediately obliged.

"Mmm. You've nailed it, as usual."

Cinn scoffed. Darcy was being generous, but he happily absorbed the praise. It always felt good to excel at cooking something. He didn't have many talents, newfound part-time shadow abilities aside.

"But thank you." Darcy caught Cinn's arm. "Lord knows you need the patience of a saint to put up with Julien. You're so good for him. You're helping him more than you know. And this cake is so sweet of you. Sorry for teasing."

"This isn't for Julien," Cinn protested. "I would have made it, anyway." An outright lie—he valued his sleep far more than a variety of dessert options.

"Right. Of course." Darcy winked at him.

The chocolate log was in the oven, the dishes were at least *near* the sink. Time for a well-deserved thirty minute power nap.

Fourteen

CINN

The Beaumonts were supposed to go to Darcy's cousins' in Kensington for most of Christmas Day, but Alexander had experienced two dizzy spells the day prior. Between that and the umbraphage attack, they decided it was best to stay put in the townhouse.

The Westminster incident certainly put a dampener on yesterday evening's festivities. Their living room housed a tiny television, which everyone crowded around to watch the news. The catastrophic weather event had spanned across the whole of London, causing flooding in several boroughs.

Even though the unblessed couldn't see the umbraphages—which Cinn was still processing—he'd maintained that there must have been some sort of footage of *something*. However, Darcy informed him Viktor Sturmhart had moteblessed positioned in every large media company and every government department. The handful of deaths were blamed on the hurricane, and then the news moved on to a celebrity dressed up as Santa caught passed out drunk on the street. Classy.

"We'll have more fun staying with you four today, anyway," Fiona said at the breakfast table, once everyone had made it out of bed.

The Buck's Fizz was already being served liberally. Christmas with Cinn's mum had always started this way too—the difference being that she'd play cheesy Christmas songs, whereas Julien had somehow found a radio station playing smooth jazz instrumental Christmas classics. Though Julien was already wearing the paper crown Cinn had made for him—a swirl of red and silver to accentuate the shades of gold in his hair—so he couldn't moan too much.

Was his mum wearing the one he'd given her yesterday? Did she have people to spend the day with? The alternative made him unbearably sad. Surely she'd have friends, maybe even a new partner. There were so many questions he wished he'd thought to ask.

Next time.

The Beaumonts insisted on cooking the Christmas lunch without any assistance, despite Cinn's credentials of being a former semi-professional chef. They obviously didn't trust him with such an important task.

So Cinn found himself in the living room, lit only by soft fairy lights, sprawled across the sofa with Julien. It wasn't quite a Christmas jumper, but Julien was wearing a thick, patterned cardigan, and Cinn's gaze kept hitching on it. Julien looked different in it. Looked nice in it. Looked softer, like the wool it was made from. Squishable.

He'd accidentally grabbed on to it, because now Julien was grinning at him.

"Mince pie crumbs," mumbled Cinn, patting it down.

Julien pulled Cinn's legs onto his lap, his hands drifting at once to the three stitches installed just under Cinn's knee, gliding his fingers over them gently.

Cinn shot him a glare; he looked like he was about to repeat the same bullshit he'd spewed last night, after he'd kissed each of his wounds in turn. Julien had a similar number of stitches himself, but he wouldn't shut up about how awful he felt, and how next time Cinn wasn't going within ten miles of the danger. Cinn told him to shut the fuck up, considering Cinn had been way more useful on the bridge than Julien, anyway.

Julien grabbed his face, turning it into the light. "Just checking your eyes are still normal. They were so black. You looked terrifying. Like a demon."

"I think it was a one-time thing," Cinn muttered. His thoughts churned as he replayed the events at Westminster for the umpteenth time.

When he'd lost control of his own body, it had been horrific in a surreal, distant way. Like being trapped in a dream, aware but powerless to change anything, as his own limbs moved without him.

Then, Béatrice had climbed inside his shadow—or whatever had happened—and he'd felt an unsettling mix of exhilaration and unease. The sensation of wielding the shadow like an extra limb felt like a searing current running through his veins, both electrifying and unnervingly invasive. Even once it had vanished, a disquieting sense remained—that this... *shadow* was now a part of him in ways he couldn't yet grasp. It felt like a heavy, intrusive guest in his mind, its dark tendrils still clinging to his consciousness.

Something whacked him on the nose—a bauble from the overdressed Christmas tree. "Why are you so glum?" asked Elliot. "Are you still upset they wouldn't even let you cook the potatoes?"

"It's just a bit weird today," said Cinn. "Like yesterday didn't happen. Like those people didn't die. The world has just gone on."

The world would go on. Until it didn't, according to the umbraphage.

Darcy came over to wrap her arms around Cinn. He tensed for a fraction of a moment, then relaxed into her.

"You're allowed to forget about that today. It'll still all be there tomorrow. Presents?" Darcy said brightly, then scampered over to the tree like an excited puppy, sorting gifts into piles. "Come on then," she said, patting the floor.

Cinn fetched his gifts from the bedroom. He'd spent a fair bit of time yesterday patching up the paper after Béatrice's handiwork had destroyed the perfectly adequate wrapping he'd been proud of. When he returned, the others were sitting around the tree, and Darcy had arranged gifts in a pile for him.

It wasn't like Cinn hadn't ever got a Christmas present before. He had a treasured refillable silver lighter from Tyler somewhere in the bottom of his rucksack, his initials engraved on it. And Bradley usually bought him his favourite chocolate, a Cadbury's Spira.

But this pile of gifts, small in size, was monumental in significance. He fought with a lump in his throat, mumbling his thanks, eyes downcast.

For some reason, the protocol seemed to be watching each other open the gifts in a round robin, rather than being normal and everyone quickly opening them all at once.

Darcy suppressed a laugh when she held up her present from Cinn, a lopsidedly wrapped gift adorned with mismatched tape and crooked folds. She unwrapped it in milliseconds, revealing a squashed, battered box.

"Tea!"

She was at least pretending to be enthusiastic, which was kind. As usual, Cinn had been on a very limited budget.

"Vanilla Rooibos. The guy said it was kinda similar to chai."

She beamed at him, and Cinn shuffled on the floor, averting his gaze. He wasn't sure he could stand all this for long. Perhaps he could escape to the kitchen and outright insist he did the potatoes. It would only be polite.

Thankfully, Elliot disembowelled his presents at the speed of light, turning the floor into a sea of shiny foil.

Out of the corner of his eye, Cinn's gaze caught on something in the dark shadow of the Christmas tree. A slinky, sinewy tail, flicking around the crimson tree stand. Was this all entertaining Béatrice? She could come out and apologise for Cinn's wrapping, if she liked.

"Your turn!"

Three pairs of expectant eyes turned to Cinn.

Inwardly sighing, he began.

Darcy's parcel contained two tiny jars—one containing the delicate pyramid-shaped crystals of Maldon sea salt, and one containing saffron threads. She informed him he also had some kitchen knives waiting back at home that wouldn't have made it through the airport security.

Elliot gave him a guilty smirk as Cinn unwrapped his rectangular present to find *Decadent Delights: The Ultimate Dessert Collection for the Pro-Baker*, of which he'd gone through and sticky tabbed his favourites. *So kind.*

Cinn groaned, pressing the book to his forehead. "For the last time, I'm a chef, not a baker." Then he flashed a warm smile at Elliot to show his appreciation.

It did not surprise Cinn in the least to find Julien's presents meticulously wrapped, crisp folds and red bows that bordered on origami-level skill.

"Are we safe to watch you two open each other's presents, or will I throw up from cuteness overload?" asked Darcy, scrutinising Julien with wariness.

"You're welcome to leave the room," Julien retorted.

Cinn hesitated for a moment, pulling his face into a neutral expression. Then, one tug of red ribbon later, a pair of silk pyjama bottoms fell into Cinn's lap.

He laughed.

The label, a French brand Cinn didn't recognise, informed him they were crafted from the finest mulberry silk. The fabric had a subtle sheen that caught the flashing Christmas lights, highlighting their rich, deep olive-green colour that was remarkably similar to his beanie.

"I hear they're rip proof," Julien said, in a completely casual voice that did nothing to stop Cinn's cheeks from burning as his eyes traitorously glanced between Darcy and Elliot.

"Let's hope," Cinn muttered.

"There's another one," said Julien, eyes twinkling with an excitement that caused Cinn's anxiety to return with fresh vigour.

"Darcy owes me a fiver," announced Elliot, then sniggered. "Because she insisted you'd have got him at least three."

"You two have no lives," Julien retorted. He may then have mumbled something about another four presents back at Auri that Cinn ignored.

Desperate to move the spotlight along from him, he opened the next present far too quickly, sending a pile of cassettes scattering across the wooden floorboards, chased after by a dozen AA batteries that rolled in every direction. Cinn reached for the tapes, fearing Julien had decided to 'educate' him with some blues or jazz, but found instead some of the Pearl Jam albums he didn't own, and something by a newish band named Wu-Tang Clan. Julien nudged the final cassette towards him with his foot, but it was one he'd recognise from a mile away—*Doolittle* by the Pixies.

What?

For a moment, he thought it was his own copy, the one that ended up royally fucked from years of relentless rewinding. However, this cassette was in a plastic wrap, brand new.

"How did you—"

"I found the remnants of it in the bin the other day. What did you do to it, use it as a chew toy?"

Cinn peeled off the wrap, and popped out the tape, running his fingers over its immaculate shiny surface, ready for him to undoubtedly scratch and dent again.

Julien looked rather proud of himself, preening for praise.

Ordinarily he'd give him shit for it, or at least attempt to, but today the fuzziness in his chest softened any sarcasm on the tip of his tongue.

"Thank you," fell out as a whisper as he locked eyes with Julien, who was smiling at Cinn in a different sort of way. No smirk, no edge of wickedness, only a gentle upwards tilt of the lips, a gleam of white teeth, a melting of grey eyes. It was possibly the most genuine smile he'd ever seen from Julien. He wanted more. He'd collect them like gems, store them in the crevices of his mind to brighten the darkest days.

"Right, let's get this over with," Darcy interjected. "We're not spending all Christmas Day swooning over you two. Give Julien his present, Cinn."

Elliot cackled. "This is top-tier entertainment, Darce. What else could you possibly want to be doing right now?"

Cinn's stomach clenched as he handed over Julien's. He'd wanted to give it to him in private. Alas, no such luck.

The paper practically fell apart in Julien's hands, and Cinn cringed. "I ran out of tape to fix your one." He became uncomfortably aware of the increasing rate of his heartbeat as Julien held up the black mass of wool that was vaguely scarf-shaped.

"It's... wonderful," Julien said.

The style of the scarf drastically changed halfway through—neat rows of tightly interwoven yarn descended into an erratic, uneven pattern with loose, tangled strands that Cinn wouldn't want to test.

"It's fucking awful, don't lie. Half of it looks like a cat attacked it," Cinn said, wincing, then held his breath, waiting to see if Julien would even understand what he was looking at exactly.

Julien carded his fingers through the professionally knitted half of the black scarf, recollection dawning on his face.

Finally.

"Wait. Is this... the scarf that Béatrice was halfway through knitting for me? The one on her desk?"

It hadn't escaped Cinn's notice that Julien hadn't put Béatrice's locket back on since the day he'd taken it off.

If Julien didn't want to wear that, would he even want this scarf?

Cinn unclenched his fists which had formed tight balls in his lap. "Yeah. Don't be pissed that I fucked up her work, okay? I tried to make

Darcy help me, but she had no clue either." He shot Darcy a scowl, like the end result was all her fault. "I tried. Knitting's hard. I stabbed myself about eight times. There's probably blood all over it."

With a slap of her legs, Darcy jumped to her feet. "Right, I've hit my limit. Elliot, let's crack open the mulled wine."

They disappeared, closing the living-room door behind them.

Alone, the room stilled, and an age stretched out before Julien finally declared, "I love it," a rough edge of *something* in his voice. "It's my new favourite thing."

"I don't actually expect you to wear it or anything." Cinn bit into his lip, tearing his eyes from the scarf to stare into a large red bauble hanging on the tree. "But I kept thinking about how she'd never finish it, and how it would just lie on her desk, unfinished, forever. I thought she'd want me to finish it. And you got me this hat, so now we're even."

"Cinn."

"What?"

Julien shuffled across the hardwood floor to cup Cinn's cheek, forcing him to look at him. He stroked his thumb over Cinn's cheekbone, and Cinn's breath audibly hitched.

"Don't you dare tell me you spent hours learning how to knit so we can be *even*."

Pinned in place and rendered speechless by the intensity behind Julien's gaze, Cinn could only swallow.

Julien's voice dropped to a soft hush. "Because I won't believe you."

Cinn must have bit into his lip again, because Julien was tugging it free, tipping his chin upwards.

"Well, yeah, like I said, I did it for Béatrice mainly." And Cinn rather liked the idea of Julien walking around wearing a piece of him, in some small way. "And you look good in black stuff," Cinn added begrudgingly. Hopefully Julien would leave it at that.

"*Oui*, that is true." Julien wrapped the scarf around his neck, then pouted like a catwalk model, his dimples flashing like twinkling stars.

At that moment, Darcy burst back into the room, holding the largest jug of steaming mulled wine Cinn had ever seen. "Who's ready to get sloshed?" she shouted, sounding well on her way already.

Christmas dinner was a surprisingly lavish affair.

Fiona dressed the table of the townhouse's modest dining room to Michelin Star standards, complete with napkin swans and crystal wine glasses.

Once they were all seated, Alexander placed a large white taper candle in the middle of the table. "I thought we would light this for Béatrice," he said, looking to Julien, whose mouth fell open.

"*Merci*," Julien replied at last. "That's so thoughtful of you."

"She was such a lovely lass." Alexander sat down, his hand slipping into Fiona's open palm.

Fuck. Cinn hadn't even properly considered this would be Julien's first Christmas without her. Not that he'd ever enjoyed the holiday, apparently, but still...

He eyed the shadows in the room's corners. Was Béatrice here, lurking? Perhaps she'd appreciate some meat scraps in addition to the candle...

Mountains of food were delivered to their plates. Cinn had to admit it—the Beaumonts' Christmas dinner turned out delicious without his assistance. Although, the roast potatoes weren't *quite* as crispy as he would have made them, using goose fat and extra salt.

Darcy sat wedged between her two parents, and Cinn's attention kept snagging on the three of them. How they were such a tight family unit. How Fiona knew Darcy would want extra gravy. How Alexander groaned when Darcy reminded him to take his medicine.

It wasn't like he'd spent the last decade feeling sorry for himself for being parentless. But the glimpse into their 'normal' family dynamic stirred up the tiniest bit of unexpected longing within him.

When the time came for dessert, mortification about the chocolate log he'd made much earlier froze Cinn in his seat, pretending he didn't notice Darcy's meaningful glances. Perhaps he could just slide it into the bin later.

"Oh, for goodness sake," Darcy eventually snapped, leaping up from the dining table with a loud scrape. She appeared a minute later with the cake in tow. It looked a bit haphazard from its time hiding at the back of the fridge, but its rich chocolatey exterior still gleamed under the dining-room lights. It wasn't half bad, considering Cinn's limited resources.

"*La bûche!*" Julien immediately exclaimed, and Cinn wanted to crawl under the table.

Cinn begged Darcy with his eyes, but it was a lost cause. There was no way she'd pass up on the free show.

Darcy threw the log down unceremoniously right in front of Julien. "The poor slave you guilted into making this for you was up at midnight preparing it. It took him hours, so you best pretend this is the most delicious chocolate log of your life."

Elliot was quietly laughing to himself while Fiona and Alexander looked upon the scene with a fair bit of confusion.

Cinn groaned. "That's a bit of an exaggeration. It was four a.m., not midnight. And for the last time, I—"

"You made this for me?" Julien asked softly, voice brimming with marvel.

Every single pair of eyes bored into Cinn, who was surely scarlet by now. He glared at Darcy. *I'm going to fucking kill you.*

"Of course he did. What did you expect, after your tantrum about it?" she continued, regardless of Cinn's death stare.

Julien turned to him, genuinely surprised in a way Cinn hadn't seen before, eyes wide as saucers. Possibly on the verge of tears.

Why on earth did his past self think this was a good idea? Especially after the scarf, as well. He may as well scream his tragically hopeless adoration from the rooftops at this rate.

"No! Not exactly. It's a thing people have at Christmas, right? Everyone likes it." Cinn cringed at the volume his voice had reached.

Fiona coughed. "I'll certainly have some, if it isn't all for Julien."

Cinn shut his eyes, leaned back in the chair, and prayed for the ground to swallow him whole.

Elliot saved him by redirecting attention, reading out every joke from their crackers in a monotonous deadpan voice. But Julien seemed not to listen, only wanting to stare at Cinn between mouthfuls of cake, his stormy grey eyes glowing with a soft warmth that spoke volumes.

"Stop it," Cinn hissed. "It was only a bloody chocolate log."

But Julien's smug cat-got-the-cream grin remained in place until it was time to clear the table, with Cinn jumping up to do the dishes before anyone else had a chance to offer.

They retired to the living room, where Julien played several rounds of Scrabble in French with Alexander. Julien won every time, which made sense, with how Alexander barely seemed to know the language.

Cinn and Elliot had much more fun. Fiona took off her pair of reindeer antlers, and they took turns wearing them while the other threw rings fashioned out of tin foil onto them for points.

Darcy mocked the game, then ultimately mediated it, shouting at Elliot for cheating using windmotes to knock the rings on course, completely unbeknownst to Cinn.

Before long, the room was bathed in the soft glow of lamplight, and the festive energy mellowed into a cosy calm as the day drew to a close.

True, there wasn't stiff competition, but it had easily been Cinn's favourite Christmas ever. Maybe even one of his favourite days, full stop.

"See," Cinn whispered, tugging on the black woollen scarf Julien insisted on wearing for the entire day despite the fifty degree heat from the roaring fire. "Christmas isn't so bad, right?"

Julien leaned towards him, bringing the smell of the mulled wine he'd had countless glasses of. "Nothing could ever be *bad* if you're there with me," he said, slightly slurring. He kissed the bulge of Cinn's cheek, the smile he'd created. "But..."

Julien kissed the corner of Cinn's mouth, and it was all Cinn could do not to grab Julien's neck, pull him into the kiss he wanted to give him, one inappropriate for the eyes of others. The taste of wine was a whole different experience from Julien's mouth.

"Maybe if you agree to make me *la bûche* every year, I'll come to love it."

Every year.

The words were doing weird things to his insides. Warm things. Fuzzy things.

Cinn opened his mouth to give Julien shit. "I—"

Two twin shouts of alarm erupted from the other side of the living room. Alexander, sitting in an aged rocking chair next to the fire, had dropped his drink, sending a cascade of mulled wine splashing across the floorboards, shattered glass scattering in all directions. His hand clutched at his chest, eyes wide with pain and panic, as he gasped for breath.

Cinn sprang to his feet, lurched towards the man, then rocked back on the balls of his feet—Darcy and Fiona were already crowding him. Elliot spluttered something about ringing for an ambulance and dashed out of the room, leaving Cinn to turn to Julien, whose face mirrored his own fear as Darcy's father began to make laboured, wheezing sounds.

"Julien, get my luggage bag!" Darcy yelled. "Bring the entire thing!"

Julien narrowed his eyes, pursed his lips in his telltale sign he was about to argue, then disappeared without a word.

Lingering uselessly on the periphery, Cinn steadily retreated until he had his back against the curtains, well out of the way. The urgent flurry around him was a dreamlike bubble that he was very much on the outside of.

Keeping remarkably calm, Darcy and Fiona tried to keep Alexander conscious, speaking to him in soothing tones. When Alexander's head lolled to one side, however, Fiona let out a small cry, composure cracking.

Cinn found himself clutching the curtain, the fabric crumpling tightly in his grip as he fought to keep his own rising panic at bay. Was he about to watch Darcy's father die, right before his eyes? The man who'd spent thirty minutes with him in the middle of the night, helping him drag out baking ingredients? Who was so clearly adored by his wife and daughter?

Cinn's own breathing became unsteady as the corners of his vision swam.

No. Not now!

Instinctively, he glanced down at his wrist, where his warding band was conspicuously absent, smashed to pieces by the umbraphage yesterday.

The last thing everyone needed currently was for Cinn to shadowslip, and become another unconscious body, causing a scene. His headphones were in the other room. He could go get them. Though, what would it look like if he started listening to music through all this?

Julien burst back into the room, sending Darcy's small blue suitcase sliding across the wood towards her. She kneeled, her hands shooting straight to the seam where the zipper would be, her fingers fumbling desperately to find it, her entire arms visibly shaking.

One moment, Cinn was clutching the curtains, then the next, his knees were hitting the floor alongside Darcy, pushing her hands out of the way to swiftly unzip the bag. She offered him the quickest flash of a smile before she tipped the contents onto the floor, immediately sighting her target: a transparent organiser stuffed with tiny pots and vials.

"The ambulance will be another twenty," Elliot said from the doorway. "I tried telling them it was an emergency, and they gave me lip back."

All eyes drifted back to Alexander. Had his breathing grown even shallower? His face was certainly paling as he lay slumped in the chair, his eyes fluttering weakly. He was trying to say something—Fiona's name?

His wife took his pulse with two fingers against his neck. Then her gaze levelled with Darcy's, who was holding a vial containing a clear liquid. Fiona gave her one decisive nod, though she didn't look happy about it.

"What is that?" Cinn asked Julien quietly. "Do you know?"

"Something Darcy and her friend cooked up the other day. It's perfectly safe. Probably. Worst-case scenario, it doesn't do much. Hopefully. It's some sort of blend of mote-enhanced extracts, to stimulate cardiac function."

Fiona produced a syringe, needle, and tourniquet. Darcy passed her the vial.

"It should temporarily improve blood circulation. She's just trying to buy time."

From the other side of the wall, Elliot's voice rose even higher, still arguing with the emergency dispatcher.

"Someone take this," said Fiona, holding up the used needle.

Cinn's arm shot out to grab it. He wrapped it in a piece of bubble wrap being kicked around before placing it in the small waste bin. His light-headedness had completely cleared—if anything, his senses had sharpened.

"They're a minute away now," shouted Elliot. "I threatened them," he added proudly.

They allowed Elliot to pretend his demands had been met.

Cinn moved closer to Alexander's rocking chair. "Is he doing any better?"

Taking her father's pulse again, Darcy made a non-committal sound.

The minute passed quickly. The paramedics let themselves in, strapping Alexander to their cart in seconds. Fiona relayed information about his condition as they wheeled him outside. A small argument erupted about Darcy travelling in the ambulance as well as Fiona, her voice getting increasingly insistent until they gave in. They said a speedy goodbye to her tear-streaked face as she climbed into the vehicle.

"He's stable for now," Darcy reassured the three of them. "Stay here."

Once the noise of the siren faded along with the blue lights, Cinn, Julien and Elliot went inside to a starkly quiet kitchen.

"I need another drink." Julien poured out the dregs from the mulled wine jug.

Although Cinn had never felt so sober, he had no desire to numb the sharp sting of reality. He slid down the wall to slump on the cold tiles, resting his head against the fridge.

Elliot wound a piece of confetti string from a cracker around his finger. "They really need that pacemaker to go through, huh? Can't you tap up your MEET connections, Julien?"

Julien took several large gulps of wine. "Medical stuff takes ages. They don't want to kill people and such."

It seemed like Alexander would die without it, but what did Cinn know about the bureaucracy of motetech?

"God, has it been a couple of days." After draining the last of his glass, Julien threw himself down next to Cinn. He leaned his head on Cinn's shoulder, nudging into the crook of his neck. Julien's breath was warm against his skin, sending pleasant tingles dancing across it.

Julien had never been more correct—it'd been two roller-coasters of days, complete with dizzying loop-de-loops Cinn could have done without. He was entirely drained of every last inch of energy. Humming in agreement, he traced the outline of Julien's knee through his corduroy trousers.

If Elliot weren't in the room, he'd pull Julien into his lap, tangle his fingers up in his hair, kiss him until they forgot everything else and went back to talking about how great Christmas was. But he settled for a hand on Julien's thigh, squeezing it tightly to communicate what he wanted to say in words: *I'm here. The world might be falling apart around us, but I'm here. I'm not going anywhere.*

Elliot busied himself with delivering glassware to the sink. They were making him uncomfortable. The feel of Julien pressed up against him was everything Cinn needed just then, but not at the expense of Elliot. Cinn began gently prying Julien off him by nudging him away. He paused when Julien reached out a sudden hand towards Elliot.

For a lengthy moment, Elliot looked unsure, blinking at Julien's outstretched hand in mild confusion. Eventually, moving very slowly, he sank to the tiles to join them, wedging Julien in the middle. Julien nuzzled his head further into him and Cinn smiled against his hair.

Then, dragging both Elliot's and Cinn's hands onto his lap, Julien made a small, satisfied noise, and promptly fell silent, his breaths swiftly becoming deeper and deeper until it was apparent he'd somehow managed to fall asleep in the awkward position.

A soft laugh came from Elliot. "This idiot. Think we can move him so we can go smoke?"

Cinn gently tried to slip his hand free, but Julien let out a low, disgruntled sound that rumbled against Cinn's neck, and tightened his grip, holding his hand with surprising firmness.

"I think we're prisoners." Cinn whispered.

Elliot chuckled quietly, shaking his head. "We'll give our captor a pass, just this once."

Humming in agreement, Cinn shifted slightly, repositioning Julien so his head rested more securely against his chest, allowing Elliot to stretch out a little more beside them.

Cinn looked down at Julien's peaceful face. With his free hand, he ran a finger over the bridge of his nose. He loved the rare moments he got to watch Julien sleep. It was the only time Cinn ever saw Julien truly relax. "Right now, this feels like exactly where we need to be."

Christmas Shopping List

Doolittle – Pixies

MUST FIND!

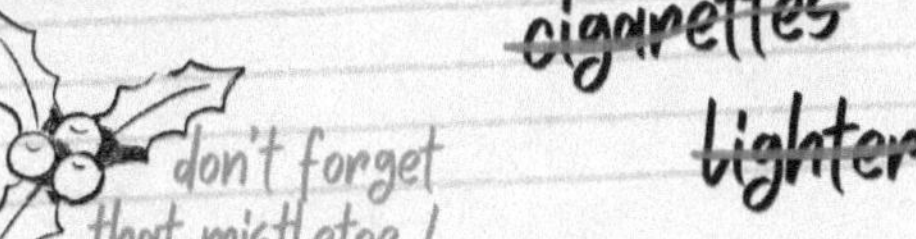

a sh*t ton of batteries

(find out what type Cinn's
(walkman needs)

Christian Dior?

↳ fancy silk pyjamas

(hopefully in olive green!)

~~a hoodie that isn't grey~~

~~cigarettes~~

don't forget
that mistletoe !

~~lighters~~

Xmas List for Julien

- ~~expensive wine???~~
- ~~another stupid jazz vinyl?~~
- ~~a framed photograph of Maz?~~

- black wool
- knitting needles
- how to knit for dummies book
- plasters (lots)

Fifteen

JULIEN

It wasn't fair. Julien's hangover was thoroughly undeserved.

He'd only had ten or so glasses of mulled wine, for Christ's sake. Nothing to warrant this horrendous drilling sensation throbbing through his temple. He kept the covers firmly over his head for as long as possible, enjoying the warmth of Cinn's thighs between his. He'd happily have spent a good few hours like that, but then Cinn spoiled it by insisting he had to leave Julien and get out of bed.

They were flying home late that evening, and Cinn was going to ring his mother's phone number to see if she'd be up for a quick visit. Then, pulling on his clothes facing away from Julien, Cinn hastily mumbled something about swinging by to see Tyler.

Naturally, Julien put on a massive show about *what a great idea* that was.

Cinn rolled his eyes, falling back onto the bed, fully dressed. He hooked his leg around Julien's hip, dragging him over to him. With gentle, caressing strokes, Cinn shifted Julien's hair away from his face.

"There's mixed messages going on right now," Julien informed him. "You can't put *on* clothes, then do this to me."

"Don't worry, I won't be gone too long," Cinn said, his face only an inch from Julien's on the pillow. His eyes sought out Julien's, locking onto them to say, "I already can't wait to get back to you."

The statement was said in a whisper, but Cinn may as well have screamed it, as far as Julien's brain was concerned. It clung on to the sentiment like a child with their favourite toy, wrapping it around himself like a blanket.

He already can't wait to get back to me.

Cinn shouldn't have to placate him with such things, Julien knew that. He'd only said it so that Julien wouldn't sit around moping all day. But regardless, it had sounded authentic, and Julien would treasure the words.

"I already can't wait for you to get back, too," Julien replied, kissing the smile on Cinn's lips. "Go then, quickly, before I start taking your clothes back off."

Cinn shuffled to perch on the edge of the bed. He appeared to be weighing something in his mind. After a long stretch of silence, he yanked his grey hoodie up and over his head in one rapid movement.

Julien couldn't believe his luck—he hadn't even been *that* persuasive.

Cinn's hoodie hit him square in the face.

"You can borrow this while I'm gone. Wear it or whatever. If you want."

There weren't many moments of his life where Julien had been shocked into silence, but this was one of them. Julien's mouth refused to move, and he openly gaped at Cinn, who'd flushed red.

"Or not," Cinn mumbled, looking anywhere but Julien. Then he reached over to take the hoodie back.

"*Non*! It's mine now." Julien gripped the fabric tighter than he'd ever held anything before. "You're not getting it back." *Ever* was the unspoken word.

Was it normal to have heart palpitations over a hoodie? To feel like you were standing on the edge of a cliff, exhilarated and terrified all at once?

"Fine then," Cinn said, tugging on his green beanie.

He turned to leave.

"Wait," said Julien.

Cinn froze.

"One more kiss. On my forehead. For my headache."

Cinn pressed his lips between Julien's brows, one quick, firm kiss while his hand brushed over the mess of Julien's hair.

When Cinn closed the bedroom door with a soft click, Julien expected his heart to sink, but it stayed firmly put, lodged securely in its place by Cinn's words and the hoodie Julien put straight on. It was baggy on Cinn, even larger on Julien's more slender frame.

He nestled straight back under the duvet, lulled back to sleep by the faint smell of Cinn on the sweatshirt. Ignoring the lingering smell of cigarettes, he focussed on cocoa powder and lemon shampoo.

It was way past noon when Julien stumbled into the kitchen in search of painkillers.

"Darcy!" Julien's shock at her sudden return gave way to delight.

Hair damp from the shower, Darcy gave him a tired smile. "He's okay. Up and walking and everything. They're organising for him to fly home to Scotland later."

Julien scooped her up into a hug, pressing her tightly against his chest. She was warm, and her woollen dress was soft.

"It's all fine for now. Thank God." She sighed into his shoulder. "One of these days it's not going to be fine though, is it?" Darcy pulled away, red rimming her eyes.

A true pessimist at heart, Julien always struggled to comfort others. But he tried. "He's doing better. Hold on to that for now," he replied, switching on the kettle and reaching for the new tea Cinn bought her. "Shall I—" Facing the wall, he grimaced. "I could see if my father can do anything to speed up the pacemaker. He's got to be good for something, right?"

Darcy scrunched up her nose. "After that last conversation with him, when he was weird about wanting Cinn? No thanks. My mum has people on it, anyway."

Julien nodded, relieved. His father would have absolutely *loved* it if Julien came begging at his door.

"Hey." Darcy plucked at the sleeve of Cinn's hoodie. "Your current outfit reminds me I have a bone to pick with you." Her gaze narrowed, spelling trouble.

"What could I have possibly done now?" Julien groaned.

"When we were all tidying up in the kitchen, without you—"

"I don't like this accusation."

"No, shut up. My mum was talking to Cinn, and referred to you as his boyfriend."

This was certainly going in an odd direction. "Okay..." Julien said slowly.

"Well, he just about had a breakdown over the word. Almost died trying to correct her, getting completely tongue-tied. At the time I was wetting myself in the background, then I realised the poor sod was genuinely worried."

"What? Why was he trying to correct her?"

"Exactly, Julien! Why, indeed?"

Her tone had reached frenzied levels. Julien passed her some tea to calm her down.

"That's very strange. I'm hurt that he doesn't want to use that word."

Darcy pierced him to shreds with her icy gaze. "Are you fucking joking with me right now? Are you actually trying to convince me that you're not at fault here?"

"He knows he's my..." Julien waved his hand. He couldn't quite truthfully say the word, could he? "Whatever... or whatever..." he finished lamely.

"So you haven't had that conversation?"

"What conversation?" he pretended, because turning Darcy grey was brightening today's dull mood.

Darcy only offered him a deadpan look in response.

"Look, we don't *need*—"

"No, *you* look, I know this is your first time having actual romantic human emotions towards another human being, so I'm going easy on you—"

"Hey, you don't have any more experience of such conversations than I do—"

"Yet I'm emotionally intelligent enough to know that it's not only warranted, it's *expected* of you. You promised me you weren't going to fuck this up!"

That one hurt. Julien wasn't fucking it up at all. He'd never been happier. Aside from all the other crap they were dealing with, of course. But being with Cinn, even in the mundane moments—*non, especially* in the mundane moments—filled him with a contented warmth he'd never understood was possible. Looking back, most of Julien's time used to be underscored with a subtle anxiety, an edge of loneliness that constantly buzzed away in the background, unnamed. Now, when he woke up each morning, he got to turn over to find Cinn waiting for him, ready to tell him to *go the fuck back to sleep* as he nuzzled Julien into his arms.

Cinn was what he'd been missing all these years.

And he certainly wasn't going to fuck it up, *merci bien*.

"And before you say 'Cinn hasn't asked me either,'"—Darcy's whiny mock impression of Julien was truly ridiculous, quite frankly—"Cinn is likely terrified you'll turn around and say you thought you two were casually dating or something."

A sharp shard pierced his heart. Darcy was completely wrong—there was no way Cinn would think that. Julien had been crystal clear with his affections towards him, right? *Right?*

"Okay, okay. Message received. I've already got something planned out."

Darcy *clinked* her mug down on the counter, eyes as fiery as her hair. "Good," she said, far too aggressively. "Good."

Sixteen

CINN

"Think that Noir will have another warding band lying around for you, then?"

"Who knows, mate, but I've told him I need one."

Cinn and Elliot were two of the first to arrive at Auri that morning—the sound of their boots crunching through snow, the only interruption to serene silence. The sun had recently risen, casting a soft, golden light over the white-blanketed valley. Neither of them were here at this ungodly hour by choice—Elliot was on the first shift at work and Cinn had a meeting scheduled with Noir, who evidently hadn't listened when Cinn had said afternoons were better for him.

Though most of Auri was yet to return, the holiday buzz was well and truly over. They'd all seen in the new year with Eric and his group of friends—Julien's suggestion, surprisingly. Curio Café had hosted a party, a party involving many drinks, and the end result had Cinn swearing off tequila for life. At least he hadn't embarrassed himself as much as Elliot—his attempt to chat up some guy had ended in him vomiting on the poor fellow's shoes.

Now, the reality of January in Switzerland was in full swing—the sky was a pale grey, heavy with the promise of more snow to come, and the air was crisp, biting any tiny patch of skin that dared to be exposed. Winters in London had been cold, but this was a whole other level. The only upside was that Cinn didn't pay his own energy bill any more. Instead of sitting around in coats and gloves indoors, he whacked the heating on around the clock, feeling smug every time he hit the button.

"So, apparently Tyler is going to go to some rehab facility now it's the new year?"

"Julien told you that?" Cinn snorted. "Yeah, that's true. What else did he say?" he asked, curious.

"Not much, but I could tell he was pleased. He still feels bad over that whole... money incident."

"Yeah..." Julien needed to move past it now, though Cinn knew his initial reaction was partly to blame. But as Cinn had reassured him plenty of times now, although Julien had *enabled* Tyler to act like an idiot, it was Tyler's choices that ultimately got him injured. Though Tyler had been in great spirits when Cinn met him—he'd almost fully physically recovered and seemed genuinely committed to his rehab plan.

"Psst," Elliot said quietly, right into Cinn's ear. "Don't make it obvious, but we're being watched."

Cinn immediately darted his eyes across the landscape.

Elliot elbowed him in the ribs. "Stop that!"

Cinn glowered at him. Elliot was the one practically shouting in his loud American accent.

"Three o'clock. Sitting in the pavilion. They're being careful, but they're glancing through the gaps."

Far more casually now, Cinn turned his head as if interested in a passing bird's path. He caught the person Elliot meant. They didn't look particularly suspicious, but he trusted Elliot's judgement. And the more he observed the person, the more evident it became that Elliot *was* correct—the figure kept darting their head towards them. The angle made it hard to make them out, but they were tall, almost certainly male, with very dark hair.

"Hey!" shouted Elliot, abruptly shifting gears and heading towards the wooden structure. So much for being subtle. "You alright there?"

The person's head whipped away from the pavilion's wall, their darkly dressed form slipping out the other side, where they could easily disappear out of sight down the side of a building.

Elliot came to a halt, grunting in annoyance. "I really didn't like the feel of that."

That felt a little extreme. The guy was only peeking through some wood. "Maybe they're shy," suggested Cinn.

They continued on, Cinn's path soon diverging from Elliot's, to take him to the Ebony Tower. He forwent the so-called elevators for the thigh-aching staircases. He fancied his breakfast should stay in his stomach, thank you very much. The tower was almost deserted—its usual traffic not having picked up yet from the holidays.

Noir had his silver pipe lit already as Cinn took a seat opposite him, taking one of the twin armchairs in the corner of his cluttered office. His wild grey hair and thick beard looked even more unkempt than usual, though the black cloak-like coat he wore was unwrinkled.

Usually the old codger initiated their conversations, but today Noir only nodded, taking a contemplative puff from his pipe.

"Umm... good Christmas?" asked Cinn at last.

"It was certainly a lot quieter than yours," Noir said, then chuckled warmly. "I must say, I've never seen Eleanor Sinclair quite so fired up as when she was talking about Westminster Bridge the other day. I think you added a couple hundred more grey hairs."

If only he could tell Noir about Béatrice. About her climbing into his shadow, about the raw power he'd felt on the bridge, holding his own against the umbraphage at last. He would bet Noir would have several thoughts on the matter.

But, alas, Noir had betrayed his trust, and it was a very different conversation that needed to happen today.

When Cinn had rehearsed this moment in his head last night, he'd imagined himself stony-faced, furious, giving Noir a good piece of his mind.

Instead, now he was sitting with the man, watching the smoke curl lazily from Noir's pipe, he found he really didn't have the energy or the inclination. He'd simply lay down his cards.

He cleared his throat. Looked Noir in the eye. Made his tone as level as possible.

"In London, I met up with my mum for the first time in a decade. We talked about my dad. She told me about some things that happened back then, stuff she put down to mental issues. Then she said she got a call after he died, from a foreign number. Was that Auri? Did my dad come here after he left her?"

Cinn could only hope he'd worded all that in a way where it wasn't obvious they'd obtained Eleanor's stash of secret files. What Cinn had failed to do, however, plain to his own ears, was keep the disappointment out of his voice. In a way, Cinn had grown quite fond of Noir during their sessions together. There was no denying it—to learn that Noir had kept this from him hurt.

Noir took a long, slow draw from his pipe, exhaling thoughtfully before he spoke. "Yes, your father came here."

Cinn stared at him. Was that really all Noir was going to say? "And... you didn't think I might have wanted to know that?"

"It wasn't my decision to withhold that from you."

Cinn didn't bother to ask if it was Eleanor's. Frankly, he didn't care. "Why?" he shot back.

The man sighed, running wrinkled hands through his scraggly beard. "By the time your father came here, he'd gone quite mad. Some would say he was haunted by his frequent encounters with the shadowrealm, which were far more numerous than yours ever were. You described a visit a month perhaps, but his plight was a daily occurrence."

The way Noir was speaking about him...

"Did *you* meet him?"

Another sigh. "Ah, Nikolas Mavros. Yes, I met your father, Cinn. He was a kind man. But as I said, extremely troubled by the time we became aware of him."

"So you've lied to me this whole time," Cinn stated, flat-toned.

"I wouldn't say that. You've never explicitly asked before."

Cinn's fingernails bit into his palm. He forced his jaw to unclench. "We did discuss him, though. You told me there was only one other shadowslipper that had brought spirits back from the shadowrealm. That was him, right?"

Noir pierced him with heavy, beady eyes. Likely, Cinn was revealing too much, but he needed answers.

"When you first arrived, Cinn, you spoke very negatively about your 'affliction,' as you put it. We talked at length about how challenging it made your life, even before the accident with the four deaths."

Cinn flinched, blindsided by the reminder of the innocent lives he would never not feel responsible for taking.

"Imagine if I'd told you back then that the father you don't even remember became so traumatised by his ability, that he became clinically insane, then eventually slipped and did not return. What would your reaction have been? Hmm?"

Not a very good one.

Cinn didn't reply, looking past Noir to a spot of peeling wallpaper.

"Would that have improved your already low mood?"

Still avoiding Noir's eye, Cinn snapped, "Can I just get the new band and go?" Then added, "Please," because his mother raised him right.

"Between that and the pressure on you to assist in the fight against the umbraphage—withholding it made sense, Cinn. But I would have gotten to it, eventually." Noir's voice dropped softer. "You saw your mother? How was that?"

Goddammit. What was it about Noir that made Cinn want to open up?

"It was nice," he admitted, his eyes sliding over a stuffed bookcase to land back on Noir's face. "It was really nice. She's sorted herself out. Five years sober. I went to her house and everything. She has a dog. A beagle." He swallowed to remove the crack in his voice. "We're going to keep in touch from now on."

"I'm so pleased to hear that, Cinn."

Noir leaned over to squeeze his knee. Cinn didn't completely hate it.

"And are you doing alright, since the bridge? Eleanor said you were mostly unharmed, physically, but it must have been terrifying, considering what happened last time."

It had been terrifying. He'd lost control of his own body, watching from within himself as he marched onto the bridge...

Cinn nodded. "Just a few scratches."

Noir wasn't fooled. But he stood up, slow movements deliberate and measured, lines on his face deepening with the effort. It was only a short time ago Noir was sprinting across Auri with Cinn, rushing to the building that had been under attack, but now he paused for a moment to steady himself before crossing the small space to slide his desk drawer open.

He collapsed in his desk chair, then tossed Cinn a gold band identical to his old one.

"Hello old friend," he murmured as he slipped it on. Relief surged through him like a tide, washing away days of tension from living without the warding band. Living like he did before he arrived at Auri, in constant fear of slipping.

The band wouldn't slip off, but Cinn tested it anyway, flicking his wrist. He grinned at Noir. "Cheers."

Stuffing yet more of that unknown substance into his pipe, Noir said, "You know I'm here to talk about anything at any time, don't you, Cinn? I hope this little bump in the road won't set us back."

Cinn really *should* hold his grudge for a tad longer, but.... "Sure," he said, and meant it.

When he left Noir's office a while later, it felt like a ten-tonne weight had been lifted. He navigated his way through the maze of corridors. He had ages until he was due to meet Julien. Perhaps he could—

A prickle of unease crept up his spine, the sensation of unseen eyes.

He glanced over his shoulder, but the empty hallway revealed nothing. Walking quicker, he reached the tower's grand spiral staircase. The wrought-iron railing curled gracefully downwards, the steps winding like a coiled serpent. The soft light from above cast intricate shadows on the walls.

Just my shadow. My normal shadow.

As Cinn descended, the feeling persisted, each echoing footstep sounding like a phantom companion. It didn't matter how many times he spun around, the sense of being followed down the staircase clung to him—someone was silently mirroring his descent, just out of sight.

It shouldn't have bothered him, not with his trips to the shadowrealm and the defeat of an umbraphage under his belt. But it did.

With a surge of panic, Cinn pounded down the staircase, the sound of his footsteps thundering loudly in the empty tower. He reached the bottom, staring up at the winding staircase. Nobody was there.

You're being stupid.

Cinn left the tower, the shock of the icy air a harsh slap in the face. He picked a direction at random, walking around the perimeter of the glass-domed Solstice Atrium. The skeletal branches of the bare trees were etched against the pale sky, creating a serene, fractured landscape mirrored in the Atrium's smooth glass surface. The quiet beauty of the reflection finally calmed his beating heart.

See. You were being paranoid. It's all good.

A sudden, sharp yelp cut through the stillness, followed by someone mumbling curses.

Lightning quick, Cinn spun, eyes *finally* catching something. Someone. Someone hovering back near the building's entrance. Dark skin, long black coat, thick, ebony black hair...

That same guy from earlier, the one watching them from the courtyard pavilion.

His pursuer's eyes opened saucer-wide, and for a moment the two of them remained stone-still, eyes locked.

Then he dove into the Solstice Atrium, a flash of black trench coat there one second, gone the next.

Cinn stared at the spot where he'd been.

This fancy building was only for consortium members to meet in. Cinn would potentially be risking trouble by following.

Now he'd seen the scrawny-looking guy, Cinn wasn't the slightest bit scared of him. But he *was* curious as to why the stranger was following him. It hadn't been his imagination earlier, in Noir's tower. What if this prick had been listening at the door?

Without a second more hesitation, Cinn dove towards the Atrium's entrance.

Seventeen

Julien

Julien's work day was quickly turning out to be long and boring. Each time he checked his watch, he expected it to be close to noon, but no such luck.

He'd barely gotten any work done so far today. His first distraction occurred when Elliot dropped into his office cubicle at MEET, with some strange tale about some creepy guy who had been watching him and Cinn, which was slightly alarming, to say the least.

Then, he'd poured over pages and pages of numerical data about MEET's new motecell line they had in the pipeline for production later that year. Julien stared and stared, but no matter how many times he adjusted his reading glasses, they weren't adding up.

His back creaked when he got to his feet. Time for a stretch anyway, he meandered through the corridor to Jonathan Steele's office, on the very top floor, and the very end of the corridor. The director of MEET enjoyed being undisturbed as much as possible.

Jonathan's assistant, who usually manned the desk outside his office, wasn't in her usual seat. Looking closer, there was a note pinned to her tidy tray that read, *on extended holidays.*

Nice for some people.

His knuckles raised, Julien prepared to knock briskly on Jonathan's door. He paused. Jonathan's door was slightly ajar. *Strange.* Jonathan kept his door firmly closed, always locking it if he wasn't in.

Pushing gently on the wood, the door swung open, and Julien stepped inside.

He was alone. In Jonathan's office. For how long, he didn't know. What he did know was that he couldn't pass up the chance for any scrap of information he could find about the elusive project Julien's father had mentioned.

Julien flew across the room at breakneck speed. The desk was vacant, aside from a single shiny ballpoint pen. Three options to search next—the filing cabinet, the bookshelves, the computer terminal.

He launched himself towards the filing cabinet. Locked. Every single drawer.

Obviously, Julien.

Even if he had his unlocker on him, that would be a step too far should anyone enter while he was using it.

The computer was switched off, which wasn't promising, so he moved quickly to inspect the bookshelf.

Lined with classics he suspected were simply for show, Julien's fingers danced along the spines, pausing on titles that seemed suspicious: *The Purloined Letter* by Edgar Allan Poe, *The Double* by Fyodor Dostoevsky.

He pulled them from the shelf one by one, thumbing through their pages, but each was hollow and empty—no hidden notes, no secret compartments. Just empty volumes pretending to be profound. Well, his boss never did have a sense of humour.

Sighing heavily, Julien took a moment to enjoy Jonathan's desk chair. Its leather creaked luxuriously as he leaned back, the chair swivelling slightly beneath him. It was absurdly comfortable, like sitting on a cloud of authority.

Imagining Jonathan's face if he caught him like this, Julien dragged himself up and headed for the door. He'd wasted enough time.

As he reached for the handle, the door swung open with a sudden force, and he collided headlong into Jonathan, who was clutching a steaming mug of coffee and a thick stack of papers. The coffee sloshed over the rim as the papers flew out of Jonathan's grip, fluttering to the floor like a burst of startled birds. Anger flashed across his face before his eyes narrowed as they locked onto Julien. "What are you doing here?"

"I just came in. Your door was ajar."

Jonathan's jaw twitched. "I always lock my door."

"Not this time," Julien said smoothly. Coffee dripped down onto the scattered papers. One caught his eye—handwritten, on lined paper. The only phrase visible was, 'this third version of the attachment device'. Julien dropped to his knees. "Let me help you."

"No!" Jonathan snapped so violently Julien flinched.

"Okay..."

Julien took several steps backward until he hit the desk.

His boss gathered the papers, arranging them in a particular order. "I apologise," he said stiffly. "There are confidential documents in here." For a moment, Jonathan eyed him, as if he were about to say more. Then he moved to his desk, unlocking the top drawer, to slide the papers away. "How can I help you?"

For a horrible second, Julien forgot why he came. "Uhh— I just had a question about the proposal paperwork, for the fourth generation motecells. Thirty percent improved efficiency? That's insane. I don't see how we could produce them at the rate suggested. We wouldn't have the raw energy for that. I wondered if there were errors in the numbers."

"*We* don't produce them, Julien. We only design. You don't need to worry about that. Though I'm sure you don't need me to outline the role of lead project coordinator to you."

Julien's heart stopped. He took several moments to process the words. "So... my application was finally accepted?"

Finally, a hint of a smile from Jonathan. "I was going to tell you later before I announced it in our afternoon briefing. But we'll have to catch up shortly. I have a meeting in five."

Taking the hint, Julien nodded, and slipped out of the room. Walking back to his own office, he should have felt euphoric. On cloud nine, in fact. He'd worked tirelessly over the last few years, doing the lion's share of the work under arrogant supervisors, for little credit on paper. In this new role, he'd possibly be able to bring some of his creations lying around in various sketchbooks to life.

But the whole thing was now poisoned. Overshadowed by his father and Jonathan's little club, and whatever they were up to. Had he only gained the promotion as part of their twisted plan? *Non*. He deserved it, through and through. His application was exceptional.

His part of the office was quiet when he returned. Julien stood next to the wide window, and gazed out at Auri's skyline, tracing the outline with his finger against the glass. It would make for a fantastic line drawing. Maybe he would slack off on his next task—specifications for an improved version of their security barrier—and do a quick sketch of Auri, instead. The glittering glass dome of Solstice Atrium captured his attention, a sudden ray of sun piercing through the clouds to highlight it like a beacon.

His eyes drifted downwards, to land on a very familiar green beanie hat. One that instantly caused his heart to squeeze, even though he'd only said goodbye to its occupant a handful of hours ago, after Cinn had cooked him breakfast. It was developing into a regular routine, which Julien was very much encouraging.

Julien caught himself smiling at the window, then chided himself. He was acting like a lovesick teenager when his colleagues could return any second. As he was about to pull away, he paused. A figure shuffled ten or so paces behind Cinn, at the exact same pace. Something about the *way* he was moving bothered Julien. A tension in his shoulders. Then, the unknown person appeared to stumble on something—they flew forward, catching themselves at the last second.

Cinn spun around to face them, body language hostile.

Was this... the person Elliot was talking about earlier?

But what would this random guy have to gain from stalking Cinn?

Cool fury seeped through Julien, quickly followed by a possessive urge to go and smack that man, to let him know exactly what he was in for, no matter what his intentions were.

The figure lurched to the side, disappearing inside the Atrium. After a stretched moment, Cinn shot forward to follow him.

Julien yanked his coat off the hook.

It seemed like his work *would* have to wait, after all.

Eighteen

CINN

Cinn launched himself forward, reaching the Atrium's entrance in seconds. The sleek, polished steel doors glided open effortlessly, granting him access to an antechamber boasting a polished marble floor, sparkling in the natural light.

It was fancy in here indeed, and Cinn had just traipsed muddy footprints in. *Oh dear.*

Cinn was momentarily distracted by the sun streaming through the glass panels around him, refracting the light into a dazzling array of colours, which scattered across several marble busts set into alcoves.

All very lovely, but there was no time to admire the surrounding beauty. He had a spy to catch.

Cinn took the far door that led deeper into the Atrium. He stepped into a vast chamber with tiered seating, sleek lines forming a semi-circle around a podium. An auditorium. This must be where the consortium heard presentations. The sheer size of it left him momentarily awestruck.

Cinn's feet slowly took him down the staircase towards the stage. The silence amplified every squeak of his boots. He tiptoed down the last few steps.

A faint murmur of voices *just* reached his ears. The source was hard to place, but there was definitely *something*. He moved quickly—climbing the stage's stairs two at a time to slip behind heavy curtains, pressing himself into the folds.

He strained his hearing. Yes, definitely voices. Two, one far higher pitched. For one confusing moment, his brain struggled to pinpoint where it was coming from. Then it clicked. The voices were *under* him. Under the stage.

He was about to drop to the floor and press his ear to the polished wood when a creaking sound, then a scuffle, froze him still. The conversation became abruptly more audible as the pair moved out from under him.

"This is the very definition of careless!" a stern voice said.

Cinn knew that voice.

It was extremely tempting to peek his head out of the curtains to confirm it.

The second voice, the deeper one, sounded almost amused. "But they were totally clueless up until now, Madame Sinclair."

Score.

Cinn would've fist-pumped the air if he wasn't wrapped up like a burrito.

"I don't want to hear it. Listen to me. You're off this job. Honestly, how was it possible to fuck up twice within a few hours? What part of 'from a distance' do you not understand?"

Madame Sinclair had often shown her temper in front of Cinn, but this was on a new level: venomous, filled with a seething intensity. He almost felt sorry for the guy.

His mind reeled. This must be their pursuer. Though, what possible reason did Eleanor have to make this random guy follow them?

"If I could—"

"No," Eleanor snarled. "Stop talking. I've never seen such incompetence. I should have known you weren't capable of this." She unleashed a frustrated growl. "I'll need a new plan now. After this, they'll be constantly vigilant." Footsteps sounded on the staircase leading out of the auditorium. Eleanor's voice became fainter. "Go, lie low and wait for further instructions."

The heavy doors on the far side banged shut, the sound echoing off the glass dome and leaving Cinn with only the sound of his racing heartbeat. He remained in the curtains, the risk of one of them returning too great. He counted until he grew bored at fifty-two. That would have to do. He'd sneak around the side, and duck if he heard something. His fingers twitched towards the curtain—

The fabric was wrenched to one side.

"What the hell are you doing, *vraiment*?"

Cinn flinched so violently he nearly fell backward, fumbling around for a fistful of material to steady himself.

Julien was there. Standing on the stage. Wearing those ridiculous suspenders of his again, in addition to his puzzled expression.

Cinn glowered at him, folding his arms. "How did you know I was here?"

Julien pointed at Cinn's boots. "Your shoes were poking out."

"But... how did you know I was *here*, here?" Cinn gestured to the glass-domed ceiling.

"I was watching you from a window at MEET."

"Well, that's not fucking creepy as hell."

"Not as creepy as you having a stalker!" Julien raised his voice, and Cinn shushed him. "Elliot swung by to tell me about it. So I assume you followed that guy in here because you recognised him from earlier? Because any other reason would be weird, obviously."

Cinn scowled at Julien. "Obviously." He then recounted his curtain experience to Julien, whose shock radiated from him in palpable waves when he learned who their stalker met. When he'd finished, Cinn waited for Julien to explode, predicting a stream of curses from him alongside Eleanor's name. Instead, Julien silently grappled with his frustration, eyes darkening before he dropped his gaze to fiddle with the cuff of his coat.

"So you didn't get a good look at that guy?"

"No. It kind of sounded like he had an American accent? Not like Elliot's, though."

"That doesn't narrow it down. Americans constantly invade Auri. Come on." Julien nodded downwards. "Let's see what's there."

When they flung open the narrow door by the stage stairs, Cinn braced, ready for a hidden room filled with suspicious equipment that would surely reveal the full extent of Eleanor's operation.

Nothing.

Absolutely nothing.

Deflating like a balloon, Cinn dragged his feet into the starkly bare, cramped space beneath the stage. "Well," he said. "This was fun."

The door clicked shut, Julien plunging them into darkness except for a shred of light seeping through the crack.

"Now," Julien said, crowding into Cinn's space. "I don't know *your* definition of fun, *mon amour.*"

Back hitting the wall, the warmth of Julien's body pressed into Cinn. His hand sought the shape of Julien's face. "You know, you've really messed up my whole solo covert-operation thing I had going on. I was just about to track down that guy and give him a taste of his own medicine."

Under the knuckles Cinn was gliding over his face, Julien's cheek twitched. "*Oui?* What would that involve?"

Cinn reached underneath Julien's heavy coat, found both his suspenders, and yanked them. He leaned forward, teeth seeking Julien's ear. A surprised, appreciative sound rumbled out of Julien, and Cinn smiled against his hair. Catching Julien off guard was no easy feat. Cinn scraped his teeth over the shell of Julien's ear, and whispered, "Roughing him up a little," attempting a seductive purr and succeeding, if the firm bulge now pressing into Cinn's thigh was anything to go by.

"Rough you say? How rough?"

A sudden yank of Cinn's hair made him gasp, his body arching instinctively closer to Julien. He pulled Cinn's hair again, the sharp tingle of pain making him shiver. "Because I might need to do something about that. There's only one person you're allowed to be *roughing up*."

Cinn opened his mouth to ask Julien what he was going to do about it, but only managed the first word before Julien's mouth claimed his in a fierce kiss. The intensity of it stole his breath, knocked their conversation out of his head. Julien's hands roamed possessively over his waist, his thighs, his ass.

Then Julien pulled back, his hands moving to Cinn's shoulders, gripping them tightly, holding him in place against the wall.

Cinn's eyes had adjusted to the dark; the determined set of Julien's jaw did not escape him.

"Come with me to Paris," Julien said in a rush. "I know we've only just got back from London, but I need to go to that church. Talk to Father Gérard. It's our only lead. Who knows what Eleanor is playing at, but we need answers, and quickly. And I know you won't want to fly again, so I thought we could take Maz, and drive all the way. We'll need her to drive to the church anyhow. It's an hour outside the city." Julien took a breath, eyes flashing as he reached to squeeze Cinn's hand. "It'll just be us this time. We won't stay at my father's, of course, so don't worry about that. We'll get a nice hotel, over looking the Seine."

It took Cinn the entire length of Julien's rambling to notice the subtle undertone of anxiety in Julien's voice. He was trying to persuade Cinn. He thought there was a chance Cinn would say no.

As if Cinn would deny him anything.

"Julien," Cinn said, when he seemed poised to continue. "You had me at *come with me*."

If Julien heard him, he couldn't tell.

"Or maybe even the *Hôtel de Crillon*, overlooking the *Place de la Concorde*. But then again—"

"Julien!" Cinn pressed his palm over Julien's mouth. "You had me at *come with me*," he repeated, forcefully hammering each word home.

Julien removed his hand. "You didn't give me a chance to get to the fun bit yet."

"What?" Cinn shook his head.

Julien's hands squeezed tightly on his shoulders.

"I want to take you on a date."

Heart racing, a warm glow spread through Cinn. Though Julien looked far too proud of the suggestion for Cinn's liking.

"A what?"

Julien's forehead crinkled. "A date."

"Huh? What's that?" Cinn cocked his head to one side, adopting a blank look.

Julien tipped his head back. "*Dieu donne-moi la force*," he muttered.

"I'm serious," Cinn protested, suppressing bubbles of laughter. "You're going to have to say it one more time, because I thought you said 'date'. But that can't be right."

Julien pressed his forehead against Cinn's, continuing to curse under his breath.

"Well?" Cinn asked.

Pulling away from him, Julien's frustration melted into his wolfish grin, dimples flashing. "Right then. Challenge accepted. If you truly don't know what a date is, prepare to be educated."

"In the meantime..." Cinn yanked on the clasp on Julien's belt. Despite the meandering conversation, his dick hadn't forgotten Julien had locked him in a small dark room to push him up against a wall.

"Mmm," Julien hummed. "That would be nice, but I have to go now."

"You're joking." Cinn snatched up Julien's hand, and pressed it against his tented trousers. "You can't leave me here like this!"

"I'm afraid I'm too busy. Mind-blowing dates to plan. You'll have to wait." Julien squeezed Cinn's cock, sending more blood rushing south.

"What? Until when?" There was a frantic, desperate edge to Cinn's tone, and he pawed at Julien's suspenders. "*Paris?* Fuck off!"

Julien leaned in to whisper into Cinn's ears. "Don't worry, *mon amour*. You know I'll make it worth the wait."

Laughing in a way that bordered on manic, Julien slowly backed out of the cramped space, shutting the door behind him and leaving Cinn alone in the darkness to curse the day he met Julien.

Nineteen

CINN

As much as Cinn hated flying, spending over ten hours in a car wasn't particularly appealing, either. Thankfully, Maz was the fanciest car he'd been in—not that he'd travelled in many fancy cars—with a luxurious leather interior and motetech enhancements that heated the car in seconds, besides making the suspension ultra smooth.

They hit traffic on the way out of Talwacht. Julien clucked his tongue, then drummed out a tune on the wheel, humming.

"Hey!" Cinn could barely contain his excitement. Julien, singing one of his *silly hip-hop songs?* "That's a song from the Wu-Tang Clan cassette you got me!"

Julien's fingers immediately ceased their tapping. "No, it isn't."

Cinn cackled gleefully. "Don't lie. I saw you miming the lyrics the other day."

"Only because your headphones leak so much sound that I can't help but hear when you're blasting your music," Julien shot back.

His defence was futile—Cinn was already taking the cassette out of his bag to pop it into Maz's sound system.

"*Non!*" Julien screeched, though a wide smile broke across his face. "Don't torture me so!" His arm batted out to stop Cinn, but he failed, collapsing into laughter when the opening track came on.

Julien continued to moan for the duration of the album, but Cinn wasn't fooled. And although it took much more persuasion, Julien eventually relented on his 'no food in the car' rule, to allow for Cinn's chocolate-chip cookies he'd now perfected. The version of them with larger chunks, of course.

"Wait," said Cinn, after six hours. "I just realised I've never seen you put fuel in Maz."

Julien only shook his head and laughed, as if the idea was too outrageous to consider.

"You really don't need petrol?"

"I do use some. But I only top her up a couple of times a year. The engine is a sophisticated design that converts ambient motes into energy."

"But that's great!" Cinn cried. "Isn't that so much better for air pollution? Why haven't we put this motetech or whatever into every car?"

Julien glanced at him. "It's not quite that simple. There isn't an infinite supply of motepower. It has to be converted before it can be utilised for technology. The conversion process is complex and requires a lot of specialised equipment. There are a fair few factories around Europe that create all the motetech products we use." Julien drummed on Maz's wheel. "My father now owns most of the companies," he added, sourly. "Anyway, their output is still a drop in the ocean compared to the car manufacturing industry, for example. There simply aren't enough resources."

"Right," Cinn said slowly.

"One thing that's helped this past decade is the invention of motecells. I've told you about them before. You know, a bit like a battery for motetech? Far more advanced, of course. They're everywhere now. They power the majority of motetech."

"Oh, yeah?" Cinn stared out of the window, watching as the fields and sky blurred into an endless, seamless haze. He'd never get completely used to living outside of a city.

"They can be tiny, like the ones in my gold mugs at my flat. Or they can be bigger, like the size of your hand even, for more complex things. They're crucial for maintaining efficiency and extending the range of motetech applications, but even then, their production is limited. So, while they've made a difference, it's still a balancing act with the resources we have." Julien's eyes suddenly slid over to him. "What?"

Cinn flinched. He'd switched from staring at the view to staring over at Julien, a grin aching his face.

"Sorry, I wasn't actually listening to half of that. I was just enjoying listening to you nerd out." Cinn lightly punched Julien's arm. He scowled. "Sounds like you know what you're talking about. You'll be running MEET in no time."

After a scoff, Julien paused for a long moment. "I love the design side of things," he said. The last time they'd gone to Paris, Cinn had flipped through an old sketchbook of Julien's, and had been extremely impressed. "But I can't continue to work under Jonathan Steele if he's aligned himself fully with *Père*."

Julien shifted the gearbox with violent force, then rested his hand on the gearstick, knuckles going white. Cinn gently pulled it onto his lap, rubbing the tension from Julien's fingers and interlacing them with his own.

"Don't think about him right now," Cinn murmured, squeezing his hand tightly.

The warmth of the car lulled him to sleep for the rest of the journey. Julien gently woke him at the France–Switzerland border so they could flash their passports. Then, the next thing Cinn knew, he was rubbing bleary eyes, to see more clearly the industrial sprawl of Paris's outskirts.

"Will you get annoyed at me if I tell you I booked the most expensive suite at the hotel?"

Cinn pressed his head back against the headrest. "We talked about this!"

"I know we did. And I stand by what I said—the towels alone are worth the price."

"Just don't tell me how much it cost so I can't convert it into months of groceries."

When Julien pulled Maz up to the grand entrance of the hotel, Cinn wanted to punch him. It was simply the most outlandish building he'd ever seen—an elegant facade adorned with intricate stonework and twinkling lights—easily passable as a fairytale palace.

Inside, the lobby was a blend of marble floors, glittering lights, and ritzy seating. They moved past the check-in desk, their footsteps hushed by the opulent carpet, and took the elevator up to their room.

When the suite door swung open, Cinn's jaw nearly dropped. Julien's apartment back in Talwacht was one thing, but this was a whole other universe of opulence. Its sheer extravagance was overwhelming: floor-to-ceiling windows offered a dazzling view of Paris, while crystal chandeliers cast a soft glow over the plush furniture. The living area boasted a piano grander than Julien's own, and a lavishly stocked bar. The bathroom—complete with a jacuzzi and a rain shower—was practically the size of the entire ground floor of his house.

It was absurd, luxurious, and completely over the top. "Julien, this is... wow."

There was no reply. He turned and found Julien sitting on the piano stool, his fingers gliding over the keys, as he played a soft, melodious tune.

"Right." Julien sprang up from the piano stool with a sudden burst of energy, like the music had inspired him. "Let's go."

"Don't you need to rest? You've just driven all day." While Cinn slept like a baby.

"What? No. Paris awaits. And I've told you, Maz drives herself." Julien wrapped that awful scarf around his neck. He'd kept his promise, wearing it almost every day, to Cinn's mild horror, as it really didn't go with his sleek, tailored wool overcoat, with its deep navy hue and sophisticated cut.

Julien held out his hand. "Ready for the best date of your life?"

Cinn's bar for dates had historically been set fairly low—six-packs shared between two on a park bench low—but Julien didn't need to know that.

The streets of Paris buzzed with late afternoon hustle, the crisp January air carrying all the big city sounds Cinn often missed—honking horns, chatter from sidewalk cafés, and the rhythmic clatter of footsteps on cobblestones. Shop windows glowed warmly against the gathering twilight, their displays a riot of colour amidst the swirl of passers-by wrapped in dark scarves and overcoats.

They walked for an age by the riverbank, the low winter sun casting long shadows and shimmering off the Seine's cold, rippling surface, before heading to *Rue de Rivoli*. Julien led the way, reeling off facts about historic monuments that were difficult to study when Julien's serious tour-guide face was far more amusing. And attractive.

Julien slowed the walk by giving extortionate amounts of money to any busker they came across, especially the terrible ones, but eventually they wandered over to a cluster of shoe shops where a stark white pair of trainers caught Cinn's eye.

"Penny for your thoughts?"

A memory was resurfacing from the depths of Cinn's childhood. He pressed his fingers against the impeccably clean glass.

"When I was about twelve, all the kids on my street had these trainers. Not these exact ones, but close. They were bloody expensive, some new brand everyone was mad about. I kept asking my mum for them, and she'd always say no." A pang of guilt hit him; as a kid, he hadn't understood that if you couldn't afford brand-name cereal, you definitely couldn't afford brand-name trainers. "She got really pissed off whenever I brought it up. Then, one day, I came home, and there they were, just sitting on the kitchen counter."

"New shoes on the table?" Julien pretended to shiver. "Well... that was nice of her."

"Six months later, she told me she'd sold my grandmother's amethyst bracelet to pay for them." It had been brutal—she'd thrown it in his face during a heated argument, but he didn't want Julien to know that part. "I couldn't even look at the trainers after that, let alone wear them."

Julien took a moment, his gaze drifting thoughtfully as he carefully chose his words. His voice was gentle when he finally spoke. "Well. She evidently cared deeply about you, and that meant making difficult choices." He caught both of Cinn's hands, warming them between his. "But now you can start to make new memories with her, when we go visit again."

"*We?*" Cinn teased.

"She loved me, couldn't you tell?"

"You only said about five words to her. It was some sort of Christmas miracle."

Julien lightly shoved him before walking on.

Cinn's stomach growled loudly—it had been hours since the cookies. "Not to complain, but any chance there's food on this date at some point?"

Julien sent him a bemused sidelong glance. Five seconds later, they turned a corner, and the air turned thick with tantalising aromas of sizzling meats, fresh spices, and sweet pastries. The lively chatter and clamour of the crowd meant they could barely hear each other. Stalls lined the street, each one bursting with things so delicious Cinn would happily try them all.

He settled for three items. By the time they escaped the market, he was almost done with the second one.

"Ice cream?" Julien said, even though Cinn was still chewing his spicy chorizo taco. It had just the right amount of smokiness to it.

"No way," Cinn replied through a mouthful. "Jog on. It's already fucking freezing."

"*S'il te plaît?*"

Cinn shook his head. "I'm genuinely immune to your French now."

Julien pouted. "But I know this hidden gem of a place. Béatrice and I would go there every time."

Dead-sister card played, they weaved through several back alleys, and joined the long queue for the wooden hatch, where it almost appeared like someone was selling ice cream from their own kitchen.

"We used to eat so much, we'd almost throw up," Julien remarked.

Cinn studied Julien. This was the first time he'd brought up Béatrice's name casually since he took off her locket. Sometimes he'd see Julien reach for it, only for his fingers to meet empty air.

Whenever Cinn thought of Béatrice, he would meticulously examine the shadows for her looming presence. But she hadn't decided to join them in this dingy alley, even for ice cream.

"Oh, really?" Cinn nudged Julien with his hip. "I'm having a hard time imagining you going that wild." Then, with a sudden burst of courage, he added, "So, how are you feeling about all the Béatrice stuff now, anyway?"

A visible stiffness crept into Julien's posture, his smile faltering slightly. "Fine," he said curtly. "There's nothing to say on it, really."

Cinn rolled his eyes, but there wasn't any point pushing Julien, so he turned the conversation to ice-cream flavours. It was exceedingly tricky, but Cinn managed the feat of paying for their two tubs before Julien could, and they walked away with two lavender-flavoured ice creams sculpted into rose shapes. Almost too pretty to eat. Perching in a shop alcove, they watched the world go by as they inflicted brain freeze upon themselves on a glacial January night.

Cinn was definitely in charge of planning the next date.

"Right," said Julien, getting to his feet before dragging Cinn up. "I hope that sugar has given you suitable energy, because next up, we're about to do a lot of climbing. Over five hundred steps, in fact."

Cinn blinked at him, then his gaze drifted past Julien to the looming silhouette of the Eiffel Tower against the night sky. Surely Julien didn't mean...?

"I thought you said you'd never go near that so-called 'metal-beam monstrosity?'"

"*Oui*, I did, so you better be very impressed that I'm putting myself through this just for you."

"Totally." Cinn's voice dripped with sarcasm, but beneath it, warmth spread through his chest.

"Come on. Let's get this over and done with before I change my mind."

They continued walking through the quieting Paris streets, the city's lights casting a warm glow on the cobblestones. As they crossed the *Champ de Mars*, the tower's massive structure rose above them, reflecting in the nearby ponds and framed by the lush greenery.

They approached the tower's base.

The base, with its darkened ticket booths and very much closed gates...

"It's shut." Cinn fought to keep the disappointment out of his voice. Of course it was closed—it was almost eleven at night. He tipped his head back to take in as much of the golden glow of the tower as possible. "It's still cool to see it up close."

A sigh from Julien, like Cinn had disappointed him. "Ye of little faith. There was no way we were coming here during visiting hours. The time wasted queuing would be one thing, and then there would have been all those *people.*" He shuddered. "But fear not, we're still climbing up the stupid thing."

Was Julien really suggesting what Cinn thought he was suggesting?

"No." Cinn shook his head. "We are not breaking into the Eiffel Tower. That's mental. Absolutely not."

Surveying him, Julien said, "Darling, I'm hurt that you would expect anything less."

He held out his hand.

Cinn took it.

Thoughts of 'how is this my life' and 'he's insane, he's absolutely insane' circulated through Cinn's head as Julien catapulted them towards a security gate.

"But what about the—"

"CCTV?" Julien finished.

A sudden pop sounded from above them, followed by several more, further away. It took a few seconds for Cinn to locate the security cameras... now with a wisp of smoke curling from their housing.

"Aren't there guards or some shit?"

Julien shrugged, leading them to a service entrance. He swung his rucksack off his back and grabbed the strange device that allowed him to unlock anything he wanted, seemingly.

An image of Madame Sinclair arriving at a Parisian jail to bail them out plagued Cinn.

"Julien, I'm really not sure about this."

Julien's standard infuriating smile plastered itself on his face. "You wanted a date, remember? I'm giving you a date. The most memorable date of your life, *mon amour*."

It would certainly be memorable when they got arrested, he'd give Julien that.

Cinn followed Julien inside, the interior dimly lit by emergency lights. The steel beams and industrial feel of the tower's underbelly were starkly different from its glowing exterior.

"We take the stairs." Julien dropped his voice. "Elevators are too risky. I hope you're ready for your thighs to ache. And not in a fun way." With a single wink, Julien left Cinn to begin a swift march.

Cinn had to exert himself to catch up, the metal stairs clanging softly under his feet. It wasn't long before his breath came in quiet gasps. "How far up are we going?"

"All the way to the top, obviously."

After an age of climbing, with every step feeling heavier than the last, they finally reached the final platform.

First to reach the railing, Julien leaned backwards, throwing his arms out, looking pleased. "See? Worth every step."

For a long moment, Cinn froze, unable to move past the sight of Julien, bathed in the golden glow of the city lights. That single image—his blond hair catching the light, his high cheekbones casting delicate shadows, and his smile radiating warmth against the backdrop of Paris. If he had any air left in his lungs, Julien's beauty would have stolen it away.

Julien reached out, taking Cinn by the arm and guiding him to the railing, finally getting him to move. The striking panorama of the city of Paris spread out below them. For a timeless moment, they stood silently, gazing at the city lights shimmering like a thousand stars beneath them, a sea of twinkling lights.

"Ah, the perfect view of Paris—one that doesn't feature this ugly blight of steel." Julien sighed dramatically, clutching his heart. "So, while we're here..."

Trailing off, Julien pressed his other hand to Cinn's chest, kicking his heart into overdrive.

It was the look in Julien's eye that sent Cinn into a spiralling panic.

"Don't do it," Cinn warned.

"Do what?"

"A dramatic declaration of... whatever. If you're about to do that, I'll throw you off this tower." Cinn attempted to sound stern despite the heat creeping into his cheeks.

"What? I was only about to comment on the glorious nighttime view we're both enjoying." Julien threw his arms out wide.

"Oh, really?"

A mischievous grin danced across Julien's face. "*Oui*, and the way it makes your eyes look like molten gold flecked with emerald, shimmering with an ethereal light that could only be captured in the most poetic of sonnets."

Cinn rolled his entire head, nudging his elbow into Julien's ribs. "Move over, Shakespeare."

"You know what?" Julien pushed himself against Cinn, the cold bars of the railing digging into his back. "I think you secretly love all this mushy stuff."

"No way." Cinn shifted uncomfortably, ignoring the flutter of butterflies in his stomach that certainly didn't exist.

"Oh, come on. You mean you don't melt at the idea of us as star-crossed lovers, defying the odds under a blanket of shimmering Parisian lights?"

Cinn groaned and covered his ears. An involuntary twitch cracked the edges of his mouth. "Please stop."

Julien moved away from him, folding his arms. "I guess I'll save my question for when we're on the bus later, then. Sitting next to the old lady who smells like cats."

Cinn studied Julien, but he gave nothing away.

"What question?"

"*Non*, it's fine. I'll save it for when we're down there, near the trash bins."

Groaning, Cinn pushed against Julien's chest. "I don't even believe you have a question."

A silent stillness took hold of them, which stretched into the night. Cinn waited for Julien to say something else, but something was wrong with him. He opened and shut his mouth, and kept glancing over Cinn's shoulder. Was he... nervous?

"My question is..."

Cinn waited. And waited.

What the hell? Was something lodged in Julien's throat?

"I…"

Another pause.

"Oh, stop," Cinn said, whacking Julien and making to turn away.

"Hold on!" Julien clutched his arm, a flash of desperation in his wide eyes. "Fine." He took a deep breath. "As we've come to this apparently romantic location, I should ask you if you want to be my boyfriend."

Cinn almost choked on his own spit. He couldn't have said why, but that was the last thing he expected. A dozen snarky comments lined themselves up on Cinn's lips—*did that word burn your tongue?*—but he swallowed them down.

"Well?" Julien demanded, his face displaying a soft vulnerability Cinn had never seen before, his fingers tightening nervously around the railing. "I guess that's a no, then?"

Cinn did his best not to laugh. "For fuck's sake, Julien. Obviously yes. You didn't need to bring me up the metal-beam monstrosity to ask me that."

"But how else could I wax poetic about the shape of your face compared to the moon? Ever so shiny, ever so round?" Julien poked Cinn's cheek. "It's not my fault you demanded a date."

"Julien, if this was meant to be a special moment, you're spoiling it. Shut your mouth."

"*Non.* But now, seriously."

Julien caught his chin, tipping his face up. In this light, his grey eyes were the colour of moonstone. Moonstone that reflected the twinkling stars.

The volume of Julien's voice dropped low to say, "I don't know if I believe in destiny, but you are the most compelling case for it I've ever seen."

Cinn's heart skipped all the beats. Every single one.

It was a sentence he never expected to hear aloud, even though it was the exact one Julien had written at the bottom of the letter he'd written to him.

Cinn had always believed love was something you made work, not something that was written in the stars. But here, in the quiet glow of Paris, Julien's words felt like the universe's own whisper. Like the moment was... predetermined? Like they were always meant to find each other.

"You're biting your lip again," Julien said, nudging his thumb against Cinn's lip. "What are you so worried about?"

"How much I like you."

The honesty spilled from his mouth before he had a chance to censor it. If Julien was hurt by the statement, he concealed it.

Julien brushed his knuckles against the edge of Cinn's chin. "That's one thing you don't need to worry about. But you don't need to take my word for it." He pressed his lips against Cinn's. "I plan to spend every day proving it to you."

As their lips met, time paused, the world around them fading into a velvety blur.

Slow. Tender. Exploratory. The kiss was like the first light of dawn breaking through after a long night. It was a slow dance in the quiet of their secluded spot, a melding of breaths and hearts in the gentle illumination of the tower's lights. Julien worked his way under Cinn's hoodie to press a cold hand against his spine, but the cool touch heightened the warmth being shared between their mouths. Each touch of their lips was a promise, an exchange of unspoken dreams of the future. It was their own brand of communication, their kisses brimming with everything they hadn't said out loud.

But... if Julien had been brave enough to ask his question, surely Cinn could be brave too?

Breaking the kiss, Cinn pulled away, gaze steady as he searched for the exact right words, a surge of emotion pressing at the edge of his resolve. He started to speak, but just as the first syllable left his lips, Julien's hand gently cupped the back of his neck, pulling him closer, making the moment stretch into a quiet, charged pause.

Cinn's heart raced with a mix of exhilaration and sheer terror, his breath catching in his throat as the weight of unspoken words pressed heavily on his chest.

He had to say it. He wanted Julien to know.

Fuck, why was he shaking this much? It was just one tiny sentence!

A deep breath.

He took the plunge.

"Julien, I—"

A sudden, harsh voice came from behind them.

A figure emerged from the shadows, wearing a sharply pressed uniform, a handheld radio transceiver clipped to his belt.

His flashlight swept over them, revealing a stern expression as he barked, "*Restez où vous êtes, la police arrive!*"

Twenty

CINN

Cinn's gaze shot straight back to Julien. Surely his maverick new boyfriend would have some sort of cunning plan up his sleeve for this very scenario. Some sort of elaborate lie. Or a hefty bribe.

"Run!"

Julien snatched Cinn's arm and yanked him towards the other staircase, swift and decisive. The guard let out a startled yelp, and from the corner of his eye, Cinn saw the walkie-talkie short-circuiting, sparks flying.

Without missing a beat, their feet pounded on the spiral staircase, their footsteps creating a loud rhythmic clatter as they flew down it so fast it felt like flying. Each step blurred into the next as they plunged into the darkness, Cinn's breath coming in ragged gasps. The distant hum of the city below grew louder. Where the fuck was the bottom?

Julien's grip tightened on Cinn's hand, pulling him along with an urgency that matched the drumming of his heart. As they rounded a corner, the faint sound of footsteps and shouts from the guard echoed throughout the spiral of the staircase.

"Quick, quick, quick!" hissed Julien, who, unbelievably, was grinning. It really was unfair that Cinn was the convicted criminal of the pair of them.

The last few steps came into view. Bursting through a side exit, they sprinted back towards the *Champ de Mars*, the open expanse of grass and the nearby pond a welcome sight. Julien pulled Cinn into the cover of a nearby grove of trees, their chests heaving as they caught their breath.

No sign of the guard.

Cinn exhaled a long, shaky breath. "Well, that was fun. Where should we break into next?"

Julien, panting from the marathon they'd just run, eventually got out, "Anywhere... on... ground... level..." between gulps of air.

Then he burst into laughter, light and infectious. Cinn cracked, joining in. Their combined laughter collided in the cool night air, mingling with the distant hum of the city. Cinn's heart slowed, the adrenaline rush dissipating like the mist from their breath.

The tower rose up behind Julien, perfectly aligned, the golden glow bathing him in glorious light. The brightest star in the Parisian night sky. Cinn reached out to brush Julien's dishevelled hair away from his face, then captured his chin.

"Hey," Cinn said, and for some reason, that one word alone was enough to make Julien smile as wide as the horizon. Cinn pressed gentle lips to each of his dimples in turn, his skin cold, wind-bitten. Cinn tightened the black wool scarf around Julien's neck before slipping his hand underneath Julien's coat to pull his suspenders. "Let's go back to the hotel."

Julien hummed against his cheek. "There's one more stop on your date. But don't worry"—Julien slid a hand down Cinn's thigh—"we'll be back in our room soon enough."

Protesting seemed ungrateful, so Cinn bit back his remarks about needing to rip Julien's clothes off him in the next five minutes or he'd die.

They walked along the riverbank, hand-in-hand. There weren't many people left out on the street this late to show their unwanted judgement, not that Cinn ever cared about that.

"Where are we off to, then?"

"A little place on the bank called Café Crescendo."

Something about the name registered a ping deep in his memories.

"Wait... isn't that the jazz bar you're always banging on about?"

"It might be."

Cinn didn't hold back his groan.

"I think you'll like it if you give it a chance! It's a minute away from our hotel. And they do nice cocktails."

Cinn had already given jazz lots of chances, mostly recently for hours at a time in his own house, but fine. "Fine."

The temperature plummeted further, rendering Cinn frozen by the time they arrived at Café Crescendo, where the warm glow of street lamps reflected off the frosted windows, and soft strains of jazz seeped through an old brick facade.

The bar was comparatively boiling hot when they entered, so Cinn's coat and hoodie went straight into the cloakroom. The attendant gave them an odd look when they aggressively refused his offer to check in the beanie hat and black scarf.

With no vacant tables, they had to stake a claim standing next to a column. On the stage, a tight-knit ensemble played upbeat jazz, the saxophonist, pianist, and bassist appearing lost in the music.

"Well?" said Julien.

"It's... not bad," Cinn managed. It was the truth. It wasn't *bad*, it just wasn't good.

The crowd was enraptured, eyes fixed on the stage, bodies swaying in time with the music. He may never enjoy the music, but jazz bars seemed to be an appropriate date setting. Couples sat close together, sharing whispered words between melodies, and the soft, amber lighting created an intimate ambiance that seemed to wrap around each pair like a warm embrace.

"Come on. My heart bleeds, but I won't torture you." Julien hooked his arm around Cinn's, guiding him towards the small staircase in the room's corner.

The top floor of the bar was completely empty, a quiet oasis of calm compared to the bustle of downstairs, though the jazz was still audible. A cosy, semicircular alcove tucked into one corner beckoned them, offering further seclusion.

A single cocktail menu lay on the table.

"This lighting is awful," Julien murmured, slipping on his reading glasses. The thin goldenwire frames caught the dim glow, creating soft halos around his eyes.

And there went Cinn's heart, momentarily forgetting how to function.

Not the glasses.

Every time these damn glasses made an appearance, Cinn struggled to keep his eyes off Julien, let alone his hands. Between those, his tousled, windswept hair, and his crisp white shirt showing off a delicious amount of collarbone, it was a lost cause.

Cinn's faded Red Hot Chilli Peppers band shirt suddenly seemed comically out of place in comparison.

The cocktails had stupid names like 'Midnight Serenade' and 'Parisian Passion,' so Cinn allowed Julien to choose. When it became apparent nobody was going to serve them up on this floor, Julien went to the bar, returning with two glasses of 'Moonlit Rendezvous,' so dark blue they were almost black.

Sliding back into the leather-lined booth, Julien went to remove his glasses. Cinn's hand wrapped itself around Julien's wrist before he knew what he was doing.

"No, keep them on."

Behind the frames, Julien's eyes widened, sparkling in the low light. "Do my glasses turn you on or something?" He smiled like the cat who got the fucking cream.

"No." Cinn folded his arms on the table.

"Come here." Julien patted the space next to him. For half a second, Cinn considered refusing, lest he feed further the smug princeling he now had before him. Inevitably, he gave in to the subtle commanding edge of Julien's tone, and slid over.

As soon as their thighs touched, Julien climbed onto his lap, resting his knees on either side of Cinn's hips.

Cinn's pulse skyrocketed, the rhythm of his heart matching the increasingly rapid beats of the jazz music below.

Julien untied his scarf with one hand, removed Cinn's beanie with the other, then scratched his nails in circles across Cinn's scalp, coaxing ripples of pleasure to shiver through him.

Cinn leaned forward, taking Julien's bottom lip between his teeth, opening his mouth to send his tongue gliding over his. A tight hand soon squeezed the nape of Cinn's neck as Julien took control of the kiss, deepening it to devour Cinn as he ground his full weight against Cinn's groin. The jazz bar around them blurred and vanished, leaving only Julien's heat on top of him, and the rush of their shared breaths.

Breathlessness finally had them breaking apart.

Cinn panted, pressing his forehead against Julien's. "I told you we should have gone back to the hotel." As much as he was enjoying the background music, there were many things he'd enjoy even more.

Julien nuzzled against Cinn's face, then made an 'mmm' noise against his neck before pressing open-mouthed kisses down the column of his throat. "Plenty of time for the hotel later."

"Someone could come up any second," Cinn hissed. Though he wasn't a prude, he had some dignity. "They'll see us."

"Not if we turn the lights off."

Above them, the vintage-style pendant lights flickered, producing a crackling sound.

"Stop!" Cinn pushed a hand against Julien's chest. "Don't break them, you dick. Some poor sod will have to change them."

Against his palm, Julien shook with laughter. "See, this is why we balance each other out." Julien smoothed out the frown on Cinn's forehead. "You're too good for this world. Lucky for me, I get to keep you."

Just as Cinn was about to tell him that not making more work for people in shitty service jobs was basic human decency and didn't make Cinn a saint, Julien mouthed a spot on his neck. *That* spot. The one he could never resist returning to, after he marked it their first night together.

Cinn moaned loudly before stuffing his hand in his mouth. *For fuck's sake.* Julien hadn't even touched his dick yet, and he was already losing control.

Julien's tongue licked against his collarbone, making Cinn swallow down a gasp. "You know, there's a hot tub back in our hotel room. With four walls of privacy," Cinn hissed.

"Oh, we'll definitely be getting use out of that, don't worry," Julien's voice rasped as he unbuckled Cinn's belt. "Now pull these down."

Cinn could have told Julien no, but by now Julien's hand was tracing the outline of his hardening bulge over his jeans. Every stroke sent fire racing through his veins, and it was all he could do not to grab Julien's hand and shove it directly onto his dick.

Yes, his fate was sealed.

Sliding his jeans down to below his knees, Cinn lay flat against the plush, tufted-velvet sofa they were very potentially about to ruin. He grabbed Julien's shoulders and pulled him down with him.

"You've changed your tune," Julien murmured into his ear, before his mouth captured Cinn's and his hand closed over the length of Cinn's cock, and moved.

Cinn cried out, his noise silenced by Julien's mouth as he dove in once again, matching the slides of his tongue with firm strokes of his hand. His rhythm soon grew faster and faster—Cinn had seemingly bypassed Julien's torturous teasing that he considered foreplay and Cinn considered cruel. It was a good thing too—Cinn already shivered all over with surging need.

When Julien abruptly stopped, pulling away slightly, a small, desperate sound escaped Cinn.

"Do you trust me?"

Julien's usual question.

"Not in the slightest."

Cinn's go-to response.

A chuckle was Julien's only reply, as he shuffled down his corduroy trousers, then guided Cinn's body to the edge of the seat.

As if in a trance, Cinn felt himself slide to the floor, where cool tiles awaited. A whimper escaped him as he did so, his rock-hard dick agreeing with him that this was a poor turn of events. Though he knew in the depths of his mind, after plenty of first-hand experiences, that following Julien's instructions led to greater rewards.

And it had to be said that he never minded having Julien's rather lovely dick in his mouth, so he happily crawled over to settle between Julien's knees, his eager fingers tracing the firm length of him. Julien watched his every move with an intensity that only stoked the flames of Cinn's desire.

Cinn had barely touched Julien, yet the tip of him was already slick in anticipation. He offered Julien his best devilish smirk before lowering his head to trail kisses down his shaft.

"You're driving me crazy," Julien gasped, his voice barely audible.

Cinn looked up, meeting Julien's feverish gaze through those damn glasses, the tension between them palpable, a tangible force that filled the room with an almost electric charge. "Just giving you a taste of your own medicine, love," he said, before lowering his head once again.

One hand cupped Julien's balls with a gentle caress, eliciting a small gasp from Julien's lips. Then, when Cinn's mouth finally reached the tip of Julien's cock, the soft moan escaping his own lips mingled with the sounds of the jazz music filtering up from below. Slow licks and the pulsing heat of his breath melded with each note, rising and falling with the saxophone's melody. He ran his tongue up and down Julien's cock, feeling it stiffen further beneath his touch, while his hand softly squeezed the base.

Julien's soft gasps descended into impatient whines as Cinn's gaze raked over him. His face was a canvas of sheer ecstasy: head tipped back, eyes half-closed. "Cinn..." he pleaded, the single soft word a desperate prayer. Julien's fingers tangled deep into Cinn's hair, pressing him closer, urging him to continue. Cinn obliged, his other hand massaging Julien's inner thighs, feeling the muscles tense and release under his touch.

He took Julien deeper, his lips stretching around his hard length, the velvety skin sliding against his tongue. He relished Julien's groans, the muttered curses, the grip on his hair tightening with each bob of his head. The jazz music below seemed to pulse in time with his ministrations, each note echoing the rhythm of his mouth. Julien's body tensed under him, his thighs quivering as Cinn's tongue traced the veins of his cock. Julien's breath came in short, sharp gasps, betraying the pleasure he was trying so desperately to contain. But Cinn wasn't interested in containment. He wanted to unravel Julien, to feel him lose control under his touch. He wanted to hear his name on Julien's lips again, and again, and again.

Julien's hand pressed against Cinn's cheek, the movement causing a surge of heat to race through him. "Cinn." Julien's voice was so gravelly it was like *he* was the one whose throat had just been thoroughly abused. "I'm going to come in your mouth. Do not swallow."

The command had an edge of threat to it, like Cinn would be sorry if he did. Julien's gaze brimmed with desire and anticipation. The sight of him, lost in the throes of pleasure Cinn created, was almost enough to send him over the edge himself, his dick throbbing with jealousy.

Then, with a final low growl, Julien came. Cinn's lips tightened around him, feeling the warm rush of cum fill his mouth. There was so much he had to fight back the urge to swallow. Instead, he savoured the taste of Julien, the *feel* of him still pulsing in his mouth as he wrung every last drop out of him.

Finally, Julien's grip on his hair loosened, and he pulled away. Cinn breathed in through his nose, chest heaving, dick aching. Julien looked down at him, his face a mask of pure satisfaction.

"Open," he instructed, on a breath. Cinn complied, opening his mouth wide, allowing Julien to see his prize.

Julien held out his palm, and Cinn stared at it in a sex-fuelled daze for far too long before he realised Julien wanted him to spit into it. He did so, the viscous fluid pooling in Julien's hand.

Julien's gaze darkened, his eyes fixated on Cinn's mouth. Reaching out, he traced the curve of Cinn's jaw, a soft smile playing on his lips. "Good," he murmured, the praise going straight to Cinn's dick. "So good. On the sofa, now."

Cinn didn't need to be told twice. With never-seen-before swiftness, he was up, his jeans falling to his ankles as he climbed onto the plush velvet sofa. Julien slid on top of him, his weight pressing Cinn into the soft cushions. His lips found that spot again, on Cinn's neck, nipping it to the point of pain before soothing the skin with the flat expanse of his tongue. Cinn groaned, baring his neck to give Julien better access. The wet heat of Julien's cum-slick fingers traced circles around his entrance. He squirmed, desperate for more, heart lurching at the thought of Julien dragging this out in retaliation of Cinn's earlier teasing.

Not this time—Julien's finger slipped straight in, the sudden intrusion eliciting a sharp gasp from Cinn. His body tensed. Julien's tongue immediately sought Cinn's mouth, giving him slow, encouraging kisses that pleasantly distracted him from the sharp sting.

As Cinn relaxed, Julien began to slide his finger inside him, bringing it nearly all the way out before gliding it home again. Groaning, Cinn's body arched off the sofa as Julien found his prostate, the sweet pressure of his touch sending waves of pleasure coursing through him.

If the jazz was still playing, Cinn couldn't hear it, so lost in the blissful sensations Julien was eliciting. Cinn's moans were now the only music, his body writhing beneath Julien's as he increased his pace. He could feel his orgasm building, his body trembling on the edge.

When Julien added another, Cinn's arm flew out, connecting with the glass of one of their cocktails they'd ignored in favour of actual cock. The smash of glass against the floor reminded him painfully of where they were.

"Julien," Cinn hissed. "What if someone comes up?"

"If someone comes up? Then they'll see my fingers fucking you while your eyes beg me for more," Julien replied, voice low, rough. "They'll see you losing yourself in the pleasure that only I can give you, your body trembling for me and only me. They'll see every roll of your hips against me. They'll fucking *wish* they were me, feeling your tightness and knowing it's mine. But don't worry, *mon amour*," he hissed, aggressive, possessive. "They'll never get to touch you like this."

Cinn's breath hitched in his throat as Julien spoke, his heart pounding in his chest. He could feel his cheeks burning with a mixture of embarrassment and desire. He couldn't deny it—the thrill of being caught had become *slightly* more appealing.

Julien leaned down, his lips brushing against Cinn's ear. "Would you like that?" he murmured, his breath hot against Cinn's skin. "Would you like them to see you like this, to know that you're mine?"

Cinn whimpered in response, entirely incapable of speech.

A low, dangerous chuckle. "I thought so." Julien's fingers still moved inside Cinn, making it extremely difficult to think about anything else.

"Now, you're going to come for me so I can take you back to the hotel room and fuck you properly."

Cinn's body responded to Julien's words, wanting desperately to please him, warmth pooling at the base of his spine.

"Touch me," Cinn finally got out between ragged gasps, his urgent plea hanging in the air.

For a moment, Julien paused, his fingers still buried deep within Cinn, the pressure on his prostate keeping him at the edge of a precipice he longed to fall from.

Cinn braced for Julien's refusal, for him to insist he come untouched.

Then, fingers still curled inside him, Julien slid down the sofa, his mouth engulfing the entirety of Cinn's length in one swift movement that caused hot tears of relief. Cinn watched through hooded eyes as Julien took him in, his lips stretching around his dick. The sight, the feel, was too much. His hips bucked upwards, unable to control the desperate urge to thrust. Julien's hot mouth, the swirl of his tongue, consumed him, and the tightly coiled spring of his orgasm exploded, every single nerve in his body igniting as he came with a roaring cry, Julien popping him out of his mouth, and his cum painting his stomach in hot streaks.

Julien didn't stop, his finger continuing its relentless assault on his prostate, drawing out his orgasm until he was nothing but a quivering, panting mess beneath him.

A sudden, unexpected sound from near the door.

The music had stopped. When had the music stopped?

Cinn jolted unpleasantly back to reality.

A reality where they were horrifically naked on the sofa of a jazz bar, covered in cum. Would this crime carry a longer prison sentence than breaking into the Eiffel Tower?

Cinn dragged himself up, peeking his head over the sofa. A figure in a navy blue uniform stood in the doorway, clutching a dishcloth to their chest. "This is not... a room!" she gasped, voice a mixture of flustered horror and confusion. "Get out!" Her eyes took in more of the scene before she sharply pivoted to thunder down the stairs.

They both jumped to their feet, to a floor sticky with spilled cocktail. Julien was visibly shaking with laughter as he pulled up his trousers.

"This isn't funny," snapped Cinn. Visions of the bar staff watching them do a very unique walk of shame had him groaning softly. "We're going to have to walk right by them all now. I told you—"

Julien clamped a hand over Cinn's mouth, his eyes sparkling with delight. "You worry too much. Come."

He led Cinn to a window, the cool night air hitting them as they lifted it open. A back alley greeted them, a fair drop down.

"This isn't a movie!" Cinn cried, visualising his bones shattering as they hit the concrete.

"How much longer do I have to wait until you blindly trust me?" Julien asked. "Because this is getting old."

Cinn shoved Julien's chest, finding his hands captured by Julien's. He dragged Cinn further towards the window. "I'll break our fall," he said, kissing Cinn's temple. "I promise."

"*What?!*"

"I can hear them coming," Julien warned, nodding towards the staircase.

The thought of dealing with a mob of angry staff pushed Cinn over the edge. Quite literally, as he and Julien jumped from the window into the night.

Firm fingers clutched his forearm. Cinn prepared for the sudden drop, bringing his legs up into a crouch. However, he didn't plummet to his death as expected—with a loud roar, the air below them came alive, bursting upwards and slowing their descent. The wind cushioned their fall to the point Cinn was a leaf gliding down to earth on a gentle breeze.

I'm flying. Sort of. The closest he'd ever get, and he had to admit—it was pretty incredible.

Regardless, Cinn's heart still pounded as his feet hit the ground, fear coursing through his veins as he continued to grip Julien's forearm.

Julien chuckled to himself in a way that was about to get him punched before sliding his hand into Cinn's, tugging him into a sprint. Cinn could barely think straight, barely understood where they were going until the hotel came back into view, just around the corner, as Julien had promised.

The journey to their room was a daze, Cinn's mind scrambled from the several back-to-back adrenaline rushes he'd just endured. Before he knew it, the pair of them were in their room's extravagant bathroom, Julien had turned on the tap for the tub, and then returned his attention back to Cinn in an instant, to share frantic kisses as intense as their escape had been.

Cinn stumbled back, his legs hitting an upholstered chair, of all things to have in a bathroom.

Julien cupped Cinn's cheek, one hand sliding around his waist. "If you're not entirely naked by the time I get back in ten seconds, I'm going to make you beg for hours," he whispered into his ear. "You know I mean that."

Then he was gone, disappearing out of the bathroom like the rising steam from the tub.

Cinn wasted a full two seconds staring after him, before shedding every inch of clothing like his life depended on it—which it very much did, because the thought of Julien's threat...

When Julien returned, he'd somehow managed to unclothe himself en route from his mission to grab the small bottle of lube. Impressive.

Julien stared at Cinn as he crossed the bathroom, eyes dark with desire as they roamed over his body.

The light in the bathroom was too bright, and although Cinn had been naked more times than he could count now, he'd rather not feel *quite* so exposed. He flicked the light switch off, leaving them with light seeping in from the main room.

"But I like seeing you," Julien whispered, running his hand over the Fleetwood Mac lyric inked across one rib. "Let me light the candles, at least."

Reaching into the pocket of Cinn's crumpled jeans, Julien retrieved his lighter. But instead of using it to light the candles, he used the small flame to do his crazy mote channelling shit, weaving small bursts of fire through the air to light the tea lights. The flames flickered, casting shadows across the bathroom that danced like fleeting moments.

"Show-off."

"Admit it. You're a little bit impressed."

"Never."

Julien tutted, locking firm fingers around Cinn's chin. "I'd be careful with that attitude if I were you," he warned.

"Yeah?" Cinn's arms slid around Julien's waist before he pulled him flush against his body. Both their dicks were already semi-erect again. Cinn wrapped a hand around Julien's length. "Sometimes you forget which one of us is the strongest here." He dug his fingers into the flesh around Julien's hip.

Julien's eyes narrowed, a smile playing at his lips. "You think so, *mon amour*? We'll see who's the strongest after I take you apart." His fingers traced the sensitive curve of Cinn's hip. "Piece by piece."

Then Julien's hands were on him, spinning him around and pressing his front against the cold, tiled wall. Julien's body moulded against his back, a solid, unyielding heat. His hand slid down the length of Cinn's spine, then the press of Julien against him vanished, Julien falling to the floor, pulling his thighs apart.

Julien bit into the flesh of his ass.

"Ouch!"

His tormentor laughed against his skin, lightly slapping the other cheek. Then Julien trailed his mouth lower, licking a soft path all the way to circle around Cinn's entrance.

Cinn rolled his forehead against the tiles, groaning softly. Julien spread his cheeks wide before flicking his warm, wet tongue against him, and Cinn's knees grew weak.

The *click* of the lube opening, then Julien climbed to his feet, pressing his body against Cinn's again. He nuzzled into his hair. "Are you okay to go again? If I'm gentle?"

You, gentle? "It's all good." Cinn tipped his head back to rest it on Julien's shoulder. "Go on."

Cinn gasped as Julien drenched his crack in the cool liquid. He slowly slipped a finger inside, the stretch stinging slightly.

With far more tenderness than in the jazz club, Julien slid his finger all the way in, then out.

In, out.

In, out.

Cinn shut his eyes, leaned his whole weight against Julien. Somehow, these new slow, soft strokes were more intense, his legs soon trembling.

Another finger, stretching him as it twisted and curled, then Julien whispered promises into the crook of his neck. "Hot tub." On a heavy breath, he removed his fingers to take Cinn's arm, guiding him over to the bubbling water.

The water enveloped them, warm and inviting. Cinn sighed, any inch of tension melting away as he floated for a moment, enjoying the sensation. Then, he faced the side of the tub, the marble cool against his skin. Julien's hands mapped Cinn's body as if he was discovering every inch of it for the first time. Cinn moaned, his head tipping forward to rest on the edge of the hot tub as Julien's lips found the nape of his neck.

"Turn around," Julien murmured. "I'm missing your face."

Cinn pretended to protest, as if it were a great hardship. He spun in the water, his legs floating upwards to find Julien's thighs, locking around them.

Julien smiled at him. Cinn smiled back.

"Relax for me." Julien's finger breached Cinn for a few moments more, before it was replaced by the tip of his cock nudging against him. "Okay?"

Nodding against Julien's shoulder, Cinn tightened his legs around him. Julien's length pushed inside, inch by heavenly inch, deep and all-consuming, stretching him in the most exquisite way. Cinn's back arched, a low moan leaving his lips as Julien's hands gripped his hips, guiding him downwards.

Julien's fingertips dug in tightly, and Cinn gasped. The hot water lapped gently at their skin, bubbles popping and fizzing around them.

Cinn's arms came around Julien's shoulders, his body entirely supported by him now. His eyes fluttered shut.

Julien pulled out before sliding home again, both of them groaning in unison.

And holy fuck, why had he never had hot-tub sex before? The way their bodies glided together, the slickness, the glorious heat...

Julien's thrusts were slow, measured, as if he was savouring the feeling. Cinn's legs tightened around his waist, urging him deeper, as his own dick became harder, aching between their bodies.

It was at once everything, yet not enough.

Cinn rocked himself, using Julien's shoulders as leverage. "Julien..." Rough with desire, his voice cracked.

"You want more?" Julien asked, his voice a dangerous whisper.

Cinn's mind a haze of pleasure, he could only nod and whimper in agreement.

Julien's pace increased, filling Cinn over and over with sure, urgent thrusts. He smashed his tongue violently against Cinn's lips, forcing them open, then fucked his mouth in time with his cock.

Jolts of pleasure zipped through Cinn's own dick, the warmth of the hot tub only intensifying the delight, and the familiar pressure coiled in the base of Cinn's stomach.

Julien pulled away, inhaling a gasp of air. "You're so tight. So fucking beautiful like this."

With one hand resting against the edge of the tub, Julien grasped Cinn's hair with the other, then pulled his head back.

Julien wanted to see Cinn's eyes. He always wanted to see them as he came.

Cinn almost couldn't meet Julien's gaze, the sensations burning through him overwhelming him. He forced himself to stare into Julien's dark eyes, pupils blown wide, flickers of candle flame reflected in their depths.

That look. The look of *wanting* in Julien's eyes.

Like Cinn was the only man in the world.

It made him feel high, more intoxicated than any drug could offer.

Julien reached for his hand, entwining their fingers.

Two more slides against his prostate, two more incredible flashes of pleasure. Beautiful wet friction against his cock.

He came again, the full-body orgasm wrecking him in waves, the immense pleasure threatening to drown him. Julien held him securely as he thrashed around in the water, continuing to thrust inside him as Cinn screamed his name, and dug his fingernails into the flesh of his shoulder blades.

The world blurred, Cinn's brain short-circuiting. He welcomed the blissful abyss. There was only Cinn, Julien, and the warm water cocooning them in this rapturous bubble. The room darkened, like the candles had been extinguished.

Cinn almost closed his eyes, fighting the instinct at the last second to continue the eye contact that had him in a chokehold.

He was soon rewarded by a rush of warmth filling him as Julien's dick pulsed deeply inside of him. But he didn't stop, Julien fucking and kissing him through his orgasm, extending Cinn's own as his walls seized around Julien.

Julien cried out softly, squeezing Cinn tightly to him as he continued to pound into him, albeit slower, more erratic.

In the end, Cinn had no choice but to beg Julien to stop, his own voice sounding distant, tinny. Julien slid out, continuing to hold him, running wet fingers through Cinn's tangled hair.

Julien murmured sweet French into his ear, but Cinn was unable to articulate any reply—he trembled head to toe with relentless aftershocks, consumed by the rush of oxytocin.

For a while, they simply floated together, Julien against the side, Cinn's back pressed into Julien's chest. Wandering hands continued to explore soft skin under the water.

Exhaustion hit him. Running around Paris all night and two mind-blowing sex sessions would do that to a guy.

Julien pressed a kiss to Cinn's shoulder blade, where his spiderweb tattoo—his prison tattoo—was inked across his skin. "I think this is my favourite one," he said. "Don't get me wrong, the ink work is shocking, but... it's messy but proudly so. Like beautiful chaos. It kind of reminds me of that night we met."

Still in his blissed-out state, Cinn found himself being guided out of the tub, towel dried and helped to dress in his new pyjamas before being led to the king-sized bed.

They slid back together like puzzle pieces under the sheets. Julien burrowed his back into Cinn, reaching for Cinn's arm to pull it across him before pressing their threaded fingers against his chest.

Why on earth then, he'd never know, but a sudden thought occurred to Cinn. "Fuck! Our coats are still in the cloakroom!"

Julien burst out laughing. "I'll go get it all back tomorrow before the church. You can wait outside."

The staff had probably binned or stolen their stuff in revenge, knowing their luck.

It wasn't until Julien was snoring in his arms, blissfully warm, blissfully *his* to hold, that Cinn remembered his earlier mission, the words interrupted by the arrival of the Eiffel Tower security.

"I'm pretty sure that I love you," he whispered into Julien's hair, still damp from the water. "Even though you're a fucking nightmare."

There. He'd said it.

It felt good to say it aloud, the weight of the words against his chest partially lifted, at least.

Hopefully, it sweetened Julien's dreams.

For a while, Cinn lay there, on the precipice of sleep, his thoughts drifting like leaves on a slow river, enjoying the warmth of Julien's body against his, and the rhythm of their combined breaths.

It was pitch black, and Cinn couldn't breathe.

A hand clamped tightly over his mouth, silencing any attempt to scream. Abruptly, a cloth was stuffed into Cinn's mouth, its rough texture smothering him as a strange powder filled his nostrils. He had no choice but to inhale, his panic only intensifying as the substance invaded his lungs. His heart pounded wildly in his chest. Fear surged through him as he was yanked from the bed, the sudden loss of Julien's warmth replaced by cold dread.

His limbs flailed in a desperate struggle, kicking with all his strength in any direction he could.

Then they slowed.

Seized up, locked solid.

The sensation was horrific—paralysed from head to toe, a cold numbness spreading through his body being dragged across the floor. Unable to cry out, as his throat was immobilised.

Though, this wasn't a wholly new experience.

He'd been through all this before.

In that thicket of woods, after his fight with Julien, when Darcy blew that white powder in his face...

Frostbite.

These moteblessed assholes had drugged him.

The vague dark shape of the sofa in the lounge area receded from view.

A cold draught swept across the room. The glass doors of the balcony were open.

His fate was inevitable.

All he could do was stare at his lifeless legs as they slid across the cold floor, to their doom.

Twenty-One

JULIEN

J ulien was having the most delightful dream.

It was summer, a blissfully hot summer's day, and he and Cinn were eating ice cream on the riverbank. Lavender ice cream, shaped into roses. Elliot and Darcy were somewhere nearby, joining them soon. The blue sky stretched out above him, and the intense sun bathed his face in a wave of joyful warmth. The sheer *completeness* of the moment enveloped him, wrapping him in a cocoon of contentment. Contentment that he'd never felt before.

A chill suddenly prickled his skin, slicing through the summer's day like a cold blade. His instincts flared, pulling him from the depths of sleep. The room was unnervingly silent, save for the faintest of clicks, like a door softly creaking. He reached out, searching for the familiar warmth of Cinn beside him, but his hand met only empty sheets. He jolted awake, his heart pounded with a primal sense of dread.

Something was wrong.

Something was terribly wrong.

Julien went to shout Cinn's name, caught himself at the very last second.

Julien slid out of bed, his movements deliberate. He placed his feet on the floor, muscles tense like a coiled spring. With small steps and shallow breaths, he moved slowly, avoiding any hint of noise. In the thick darkness, he padded towards the lounge area, ears straining for any sound of Cinn. The outlines of furniture became clear, and he inched forward with mounting dread.

As he reached the doorway, Julien's pulse stuttered, the sight before him sending a shockwave through his body, freezing him in his tracks.

Two dark figures, dressed in black, dragged Cinn across the floor. Julien's breath caught in his throat, a surge of panic rising as he tried to process what he was seeing. Cinn wasn't resisting, wasn't moving at all. His body hung limp, unnaturally still, as if someone had knocked him unconscious. Or worse. The sight of his lifeless form in their grip sent an icy wave of terror crashing over him.

The glass doors leading to the balcony were open wide, plummeting the room to sub-zero temperatures. Barefoot and in pyjamas, Julien already had the disadvantage.

With a grunt, the duo dropped Cinn like a sack of potatoes, tossing him against the wall. One reached down to grab a huge swath of material—a sack? A body-sized sack?

One assailant reached for Cinn's legs while the other held out the body bag.

Oh, God. If he's dead…

Nausea roiled in Julien.

He'd had precious moments to form a plan, but hadn't, so all he could do was charge into the room.

"Stop!"

Julien threw his hands out, flickering the overhead lights in warning. These men had to be moteblessed—this couldn't be random. They'd see Julien was about to channel. They'd surrender, and back away from Cinn slowly. Then he'd knock them off their feet, knock them out, then knock them around until he got the information he wanted.

Because whoever was responsible for this now had a ticking bomb strapped to their back, fuse lit.

The two men did not surrender.

Both reached for guns previously unseen, moving in unison, mirror images.

The muted clicks as they trained their guns on Julien indicated they had silencers.

The pair looked at each other in silent communication.

One pointed their gun at Cinn.

The world seemed to freeze, the moment stretching into an eternity. Julien's mind raced, a surge of raw panic and fury crashing over him like a tidal wave. That monster had a gun pointed at Cinn—*his* Cinn. His vision narrowed, focussing solely on the assailant's finger tightening on the trigger. The room blurred at the edges, the ticking of his own heart slowing, each beat an agonising thud in his ears.

Without conscious thought, he channelled, reaching for motes. *The* motes. The ones that were always there, waiting for him. Their energy surged through him, and it was like they were singing to him, thrilled to finally be used after a decade of being repressed.

The sheer amount of power almost had Julien reeling backwards.

He was invincible.

Unstoppable.

The men shouted, waving their guns in warning, but Julien wasn't listening. His mind screamed for the guns to be removed, to be gone—*now*. In an instant, the energy built up inside him released, a blinding flash of power ripping through the air. The guns exploded in their hands, the metallic shards bursting outward in a deadly spray.

No time for hesitation—Julien reached for windmotes, channelling the shattered metal towards them.

The two men barely had time to register their shock before the shards tore through them, ripping through flesh and bone with brutal efficiency. Their bodies crumpled to the floor, blood pooling around them, eyes wide with the realisation that they'd just met their end.

Julien released his hold on the motes immediately, falling to his knees and pressing his fist to his mouth. The power coursing through him vanished like a snuffed-out candle, leaving him with two dead bodies.

Putain.

What have you done?

A noise from the balcony had Julien spinning. Another man, frozen still, stared through the open doors, taking in the scene. How much had they seen? Julien's heart lurched as they locked eyes. He'd need to kill them now, too.

In a blink, the figure jumped over the balcony railing, disappearing. Julien took a single step towards it, but then a noise came from Cinn's body, slumped on the floor—a choked cough.

Alive.

Somehow, it wasn't a surprise. Perhaps because Julien couldn't possibly fathom a world without him.

He threw himself down beside Cinn, bringing his heavy head onto his lap. His eyes were wide open, blinking rapidly. Desperately.

Julien ran his fingers through Cinn's hair.

Alive. Awake...

"Cinn?" Julien lightly slapped his cheek.

His fingers grazed over traces of something fine, something granular. A cool sensation seeped across his skin. Julien held his fingers up to the light. Something white...

Ahh.

Julien should kick himself. Of course. They'd drugged Cinn with Frostbite.

He could already feel the effects of the miniscule amount he'd touched numb his fingers. With his sleeve, he brushed the remaining traces from Cinn's cheek.

"Hold on." He delivered a swift promise in the shape of a kiss to Cinn's forehead and was rewarded with some more blinks.

Julien stood and surveyed the bodies. Steeled himself—this was going to take some mental preparation.

The floor was a chaotic tangle of limbs and blood, peppered with small shards of bullets. Julien wasn't squeamish, but this... wasn't pretty.

After a deep breath, Julien crouched, then rolled the closest body over, covering his hands in hot, thick blood. He avoided looking closely at the dead man's face, torn to shreds, clumps of skin hanging loose. It was nobody he recognised, he was sure.

A leather sling bag hung around the man's waist, now partially torn. Julien pulled out its contents, sifting through grimy receipts, small knives, and a few crumpled maps of Paris. Interesting, but his mind was solely fixated on finding the red pellets these two had surely carried—the antidote to Frostbite. Finally, his fingers closed around a small plastic cylinder.

Gotcha.

Without wasting a moment, he grabbed Cinn's chin, yanking it down and forcing the antidote into his mouth. The pellet dissolved almost instantly, fizzing on his tongue.

Julien held Cinn close, his hand gently cradling the back of his head as he waited.

Cinn's chest began to rise and fall with more rhythm, each breath deeper and more deliberate than the last. His arm muscles twitched, an elbow jolting out, jamming painfully into Julien's side.

"Holy fuck," Cinn croaked out.

And then, as they gazed into each other's eyes, reunited after their near-death experience, Cinn said those magic words: "Get me a cigarette?"

Julien dropped his hold on him, sending Cinn sprawling to the floor. It wasn't like he'd expected a gushing thank you for saving his life, or anything. "You're joking."

Cinn wasn't.

But, he *had* almost died, Julien supposed, so he went to fetch the materials before disabling the smoke alarm. Its activation was the last thing they needed right now.

Leaning out of the window, Cinn smoked with a shaky hand, the cigarette's ember glowing softly against the night air. He offered it to Julien, who took one quick drag to steady his still pounding heart.

Grimacing, Cinn made a tsk sound as he brushed his fingers over the arm of his new silk pyjamas, now splattered in blood. "I don't think these are rip proof after all."

"What?" Julien moved Cinn's fingers. The blood on the silk wasn't from the men—it was Cinn's. His blood turned to ice.

What have you done?

"It's just a scratch," Cinn said quickly.

A scratch from a bullet you exploded.

And if that bullet fragment had 'scratched' an artery in Cinn's neck...

"I almost killed you," Julien stated calmly. It was a fact.

"Julien—"

"I didn't think, I just acted, just like last time."

Julien stood, turning away from Cinn to press clenched fists against the wall.

Softer now, Cinn repeated, "Julien," but Julien ignored him, leaving to find something to bandage Cinn's arm.

He returned with a scrap of sheet he'd cut with scissors, then carefully wrapped the makeshift gauze around Cinn's arm, ensuring it was tight enough to stem the bleeding.

"Julien!" Cinn's voice, insistent now, forced Julien to look at him. "Are you okay?"

"Of course I am."

Cinn flicked the butt of his cigarette out of the window, closed it with a slam.

The noise was loud. Had anyone heard all the earlier commotion? The shattering of metal had created a sharp, jarring sound, then a clatter of debris had hit the walls and floor. Hopefully, the other guests slept through it.

"So... these bodies... they're dead," said Cinn, rather unnecessarily. He nudged one body with his bare foot. "Should we... call the police?"

"*Non*." Julien tried not to look exasperated, but *honestly*.

Calling Eleanor was the first idea on the tip of his tongue, before the gut-wrenching knowledge of her betrayal came flooding back to him.

"Alright. No. Course not. So what *are* we going to do?" The panic in Cinn's voice only amplified Julien's own. "Fuck!"

"I'm sorry to say this," Julien said as calmly as he could manage. "You don't quite know how sorry I am. But we're going to have to put them in Maz's boot."

The shock on Cinn's face hammered home to Julien just how horrific the idea was.

"No." Cinn shook his head. "*No!*"

"Well, what else are we going to do with them?" Julien snapped. Then wanted to kick himself, because it was *him* that had just straight up murdered two people, leaving Cinn traumatised at best, arrested again at worst, with no Eleanor to rely on for backup. Overwhelming tidal waves of emotion that he'd so far repressed bubbled to the surface.

What have you done?

"I'm so sorry," Julien croaked out, between the fingers that were now pressed over his mouth. This date was supposed to be perfect, *was* perfect, but now there were dead bodies, and he'd hurt Cinn, and everything was falling apart.

Julien felt his knees hit the floor before Cinn caught him, pulling him onto an armchair and wrapping his arms around him. Cinn pressed Julien's face against his chest. He repeatedly worked his fingers through

Julien's hair, murmuring things like, 'Hey, you saved me,' and 'I would be dead by now if it wasn't for you.'

"There was someone else on the balcony," Julien said. "A third man. I think he saw everything."

Julien untangled himself from Cinn's embrace, because as much as he needed it, he couldn't accept the comfort right now. There were dead bodies to be dealt with and such.

He slipped onto the balcony, looking down into the dark abyss of a side alley. There was no ladder left behind, no rope—only a maze of shadows and the faint echo of distant city sounds. The only sign of life was a stray cat slinking between trash cans, its eyes reflecting the meagre light.

What was their assailants' plan, exactly?

Julien sighed, then went to check over the bodies again. His fingers shook, and acid roiled in his gut, but he forced himself to inspect the bodies of the men he'd murdered. He found no ID cards or any identifying objects on the two men.

Two men, well built, late thirties.

Two men with families they'd never come home to.

They were going to hurt him. And if you had the choice, you'd let it happen all over again. It was the truth. Julien felt it to his core.

But that didn't change the fact that he had blood on his hands.

Again.

His heart sped, racing as though trying to outrun the guilt and the horror of it all.

Julien was spiralling.

He needed help, quickly.

"I'm ringing Darcy," Julien said.

If only she was down the corridor, in another room. The simple act of her being there would have calmed him. Between the pair of them, they would have had it all sorted out in no time. They'd probably still make the hotel breakfast.

Cinn snorted. "*Darcy*? What's Darcy going to do?"

"Tell us how to get blood out of the rug, curtains, and furniture for one."

Julien picked up the phone, input the international code, then dialled the number for her cottage, long since committed to memory.

Darcy answered on the third ring. Julien opened his mouth, the words on the tip of his tongue.

Nothing came out.

"Hello?" Darcy repeated. She sounded far away. So far away.

Cinn gave him *a what are you doing* look.

Again, Julien tried to talk, but produced no sound, his eyes glued to the two bodies, their blood pooling on the floor.

What have you done? was what Béatrice never explicitly said, back in the ruined church, when she'd dragged herself on an injured leg towards him and their dead mother. But Julien said it enough times for the both of them. That day, and almost every day that followed.

The phone was snatched out of his fingers. Cinn pressed it to his ear. "Darce? There's been a bit of a… situation…"

Julien wandered away from him, to sit by the window, staring out at the dark sky that would soon break into dawn.

Their reservation ended today. They had a mere handful of hours to clean up.

Julien didn't hear Cinn end the call, only felt the press of his hand on his shoulder.

"I'm going to the hotel's kitchen. I'll be right back. Will you be okay?"

Cinn must have decided Julien's silence was a good enough response, because the door to their suite opened and closed behind him.

An undetermined amount of time passed, with Julien on the armchair staring blankly out of the window, avoiding the bodies' lifeless eyes, the blood that had now dried in thick clumps, and the smattering of gore across the floor.

A stench already filled the room. Julien's stomach turned at what horrors they'd have to experience next.

When Cinn returned, he tossed a cardboard box full of cleaning supplies down in front of them. "They don't bother locking anything here. The guests must be too posh to knick stuff."

Kneeling down on the floor beside him, Cinn took Julien's hand.

"Look, I know what you're feeling. I went through this last year, remember? Only this time, it was self-defence. It was us or them. They made their choice when they broke into our room and grabbed me."

What Cinn didn't understand, was that this was less about the fact he'd killed two people—he'd kill them all over again in a heartbeat, for Cinn—and more about the fact he'd lost control of himself. Like last time.

"Darcy suggested you channel some water or some shit. Pressure hose style? Then tell housekeeping the tub exploded. Maybe you could blast it or something?"

"I'm not a Power Ranger," Julien bit out.

Instead of glowering at him, Cinn burst into laughter. "How do *you* know about Power Rangers? You'll figure something out. First job, though, is tossing the bodies out the window and stuffing them in Maz before it gets too light. You'll have to go to reception and get the keys back."

Julien stared down at his bare feet, sticky from stepping through puddles of blood.

They'd need another long, hot bath after this.

Maz was many things, but built to transport dead bodies was not one of them. The main issue was that she only had room for one body in her boot, meaning the other had to be laid across the back seat. Every time Julien glanced in his rear-view mirror, the black sack caught his eye, a constant reminder of his extra passengers.

They'd set off an hour before check-out, wanting to be well on their way in case housekeeping wanted to talk to them about their flooded room.

They had left it blood free, for the most part. They'd even cleverly explained to the receptionist the smell of chemicals resulted from their attempt to clean up the hot tub explosion.

The journey to the church was painful. Not only was the traffic heavy on the way out of the city, but Cinn kept asking Julien if he was okay again and again, not seeming to accept, 'I'm fine' as an answer.

They'd swung by the closed jazz club, with Julien breaking in through the back door to retrieve their possessions from the cloakroom. Then they'd visited a hardware store in the city's outskirts, where they'd purchased a shovel, for when they found a pleasant countryside resting place for their extra passengers later, deep in rural France.

But first, it was straight on to Moret-sur-Loing, where the church awaited.

It wasn't ideal attending the house of God with two dead bodies in the back of their car, but really, what were they to do?

Nestled on the edge of the village, they drove Maz up the long, winding road that led to the small building. The church's steeple, slender and graceful, pierced the pale winter sky, and the bare branches of the surrounding trees, outlined against the pale horizon, framed the scene like an old painting.

The church stood serenely against a backdrop of rolling countryside, its ancient stone walls crowned with a steep, slate-tiled roof dusted with the first hints of snowfall. But not each of its four walls looked the same.

Julien glanced at Cinn, waiting for him to comment on the appearance of the church, make the connection between what he knew about his mother's death and what he saw in front of him.

To give the church credit, the rebuilding effort had attempted to match the previous architecture, but the contrast was evident: the new sections, though skillfully done, stood out with a slightly fresher hue and cleaner lines, lacking the centuries-old patina of the rest of the church. The once-smooth walls were now a patchwork of restored sections and ruins, where the newer stonework struggled to blend seamlessly with the weathered, original materials.

"Have you been back here—"

"*Non.*"

Oh, how Julien didn't want to think about that day, especially after what had just happened back at the hotel. It was one big, cosmic joke.

His mother had grown up in this tiny village, Moret-sur-Loing, describing this church as her childhood sanctuary. But it wasn't so much the building that she routinely came back to visit, but its priest, Father Gérard.

After the Calamities of Nineteen Sixty-Five occurred, and a small fraction of the world population became moteblessed, an often-studied phenomenon came to light—some communities emerged with denser percentages of moteblessed than others. The village of Moret-sur-Loing was one such location, with Father Gérard one such individual.

"We're just here to talk to Father Gérard."

No trips down memory lane, *merci bien.*

"I should prepare you. The moteblessed wing of the Christian church believes that being moteblessed is a gift from God."

"I'm guessing that you disagree?"

Julien snorted. "*Mère* was very religious, but I'm not." Not since that day, anyway. What god would allow him to kill his own mother? "And if he offers to bless you with water, heads up that it'll be infused with something."

Julien pulled Maz right up to the building, feeling the car's tyres skid against the gravel as he braked. The quicker this visit was over, the better. Cinn was practically running to keep up with him as Julien marched up to the front door with its scuffed dark wood. He ignored the ornate knocker shaped like a lion's head and pressed on the iron handle.

The door swung open to reveal a dimly lit interior that Julien partially recognised from his handful of visits here. Candlelight danced unevenly across the stone walls, dramatizing the stark contrast between the ancient stone and the newer, lighter materials used in the rebuilt sections. The high, vaulted ceiling arched overhead, but halfway down the nave, the wooden beams and fresh mortar betrayed the point where the old church met the new.

He couldn't help but flinch at the sight, but Julien dragged his gaze away. It wouldn't do to get distracted by memories of that day.

Stepping further inside, the pungent scent of incense immediately filled Julien's nostrils, both overwhelming and familiar. Cedarwood and frankincense. It was exactly as he remembered it from over a decade ago, unchanged despite everything else that had been lost.

Of course, there was one other thing that had survived that day, miraculously unscathed. A true holy miracle.

At the far end of the aisle, near the altar, stood Father Gérard, his hands folded in front of him, eyes solemn as he watched Julien and Cinn approach.

Father Gérard's gaze was calm and steady. He wasn't surprised to see Julien.

"*Père*," Julien said, his voice more clipped than he intended. He nodded towards Cinn, who looked as French as a British tourist in a beret and a striped shirt. "Or rather, Father."

Cinn gave him a nudge with his elbow.

Had he sounded rude? Maybe, but Julien was too damn exhausted to care.

Some days, it felt like Béatrice had died just yesterday; on others, like a lifetime had passed. The weight of it all blurred time, leaving him frayed at the edges. He was all done with this now. He had nothing left in the tank.

"Julien Montaigne! And a new friend," the priest said in thickly accented English.

Father Gérard shook Cinn's hand first, causing him to squirm uncomfortably. Then the old man hobbled over to sit on a pew, his movements slow and deliberate, each step seeming to weigh heavily on his frail frame.

The priest had seemed ancient when Julien was a child, and now he was almost spectral, a fragile remnant of the past Julien wanted to forget.

"I've been waiting for you to pay a visit."

"Have you?" Julien said flatly. "What a surprise."

Father Gérard's face crumpled. Julien cared very little.

"You sound angry, child. Tell me, what is the matter? Tell me your problem."

"My problem?"

Cinn squeezed tightly around Julien's arm in warning.

"My problem is that you were having secret meetings with my dead sister."

A ripple of laughter echoed through the church.

"These were not 'secret meetings,' Julien. We were not meeting by moonlight in disguises. Young Béatrice was lost, and I was acting as shepherd."

"Ah," Julien said. "You were *guiding* her. I see. So I'm guessing you advised her not to continue her involvement with the Arcane Purifiers?"

Father Gérard flinched.

Cinn tugged on Julien's sleeve. "Julien."

Julien ripped his arm from Cinn's grasp.

"Now that—" Father Gérard's words were interrupted by a harsh coughing fit, his frail body trembling with each ragged breath.

Reaching deep within his well of patience, Julien waited.

"No," Father Gérard stated firmly. "I did not encourage her away from the Arcane Purifiers. Our cause is too great. The Lord's plan unfolds beyond our grasp, and we must not falter in our duty."

If this priest dared to suggest that it was Béatrice's path to die, Julien wouldn't be able to control his actions, he knew that for sure.

Then, Father Gérard's words snagged in Julien's mind. *Our cause.*

Julien studied the old man. "What do you mean, Father? Are *you* a member of AP?"

A heavy silence settled over the church, the kind that stretched and thickened.

The priest smoothed a hand over his vestments, his fingers trembling slightly as he sought to compose himself. "I am."

Again, Cinn tugged at Julien's sleeve. Again, he brushed him off.

"You?" Julien spluttered out. This was the last thing he'd expected to learn today.

"Hey! Listen! I feel really weird, like," Cinn hissed into his ear.

Julien spun to face Cinn, who slowly lowered himself down onto another pew. Was he feeling faint? Had this morning's blood loss caught up with him? "What do you mean, weird?"

Cinn stared down at his ever-present gold warding band. Then, after squeezing it tightly, he started to take it off. *What on earth?*

"*Non!* What are you doing?" Julien said, exasperated and oh-so tired. *Not now.* The last thing he needed right now was Cinn disappearing on him.

The priest coughed again. He seemed to have more to say, eyeing Julien with an oddly urgent expression, like he had to get his next words out quickly. "I am. And so was she."

"Béatrice? *Oui*, I've got *that* by now," Julien replied sharply.

Abruptly, Father Gérard stood up, on shaking legs. "No, Julien," the priest said. "I meant, your mother."

What? A cold dread crawled up Julien's spine, louder than any alarm. Was the priest suggesting...

Non. Impossible.

Julien opened his mouth, but nothing came out.

A hand closed around his wrist. Cinn's. He tugged Julien towards him, but his face looked vacant, slipping out of usual expressive form. "She's... calling me," he said. "She needs to talk to me."

Twenty-Two

CINN

C inn had become so familiar with the red city greeting him in the shadowrealm that its absence caught him off guard.

He'd long since given up deciphering the rules for this place, choosing at this point to simply go with the flow. In contrast, Noir was endlessly fascinated by Cinn's experiences—he'd probably go nuts if he ever heard that, for the first time, Cinn had felt summoned, slipping voluntarily rather than landing here as a product of a panic attack.

Cinn was still in the church, with several key differences. A plain window had become stained glass, gleaming with vibrant colours. On the far wall, an old fresco had materialised, depicting the figure of Saint Michael the Archangel, sword raised, triumphing over a twisted, shadowy serpent. The pews had also changed—each one aged and scarred.

It didn't take a genius to work out—Cinn was in the church pre-accident.

He was in a memory.

A light touch on his shoulder had Cinn spinning. Standing before him was a woman with blonde hair and those piercing grey eyes he knew intimately. Julien's mother. He'd seen her in the shadowrealm before, briefly. Now, up close, the resemblance to Béatrice was startling. Her delicate features, the soft curve of her lips, the intensity in her gaze...

"Hello," she said.

Did she know who he was?

"Hello," Cinn replied. He racked his brain for her name... "Isabelle?"

A smile broke out across her face.

A meow sounded from between their feet. Not the soft mew of a cute kitten, but the guttural, raspy yowl of their ugly shadow cat. It jumped into Isabelle's arms.

Leaning over, Cinn scratched Béatrice's flickering ears. The cat leaned into the touch. "And where the hell were you when I was attacked last night?" It seemed rather unfair to give him epic shadow powers, then snatch them away again.

Béatrice gave him no answer, only licked a smoky black paw.

"Why am I here, Isabelle?" Cinn asked. Back in the present day, Julien's temper with the priest was likely fraying even further in Cinn's absence.

Isabelle's smile fell. "To watch," she said simply, then crossed the church to press her back against a brick wall, still stroking the cat. "Come."

An unpleasant knot tightened in Cinn's stomach.

He'd already seen how this story ended—did he really need to see it all unfold? To see the moment Julien's life forever shattered?

Even if he could refuse, he was out of time—Father Gérard entered the nave, slipping into the church through a back door. Although only a decade younger, he seemed a youthful man compared to the elderly gent Cinn had just met. He had a spring in his step as he hummed a hymn to himself, while sorting through a pile of bibles.

Bang.

The heavy oak doors burst open.

Isabelle marched through, closing an umbrella, hair damp from rain. She was the twin of the woman standing next to Cinn, down to her knitted blue jumper. On her heels, two unsmiling, young blonde teenagers shadowed her.

"Stay here, please," Isabelle said, English to Cinn's ears, the words sounding in his mind with a disembodied clarity, as if they were being whispered directly into his consciousness.

Young Julien and Béatrice pulled symmetrical despondent faces at their mother. Had they been dragged from the city against their will? The pair located a secluded pew towards the back of the church, settling into it and lowering their voices to a hushed murmur. They glowered at their mother's receding back.

The Isabelle who stood beside Cinn chuckled lightly. "They were supposed to go to a friend's party that day."

What was so important it required Isabelle to visit Moret-sur-Loing so urgently?

Father Gérard's hymn faltered mid-note, his mouth moving silently as Isabelle strode down the aisle. The stack of bibles he was sorting toppled. "Isabelle."

"Father." Isabelle's hushed tone contained unmistakable fear. "I didn't know where else to come. He's finished it. Against all the warnings. He switched it on yesterday."

"Come," the priest replied, expression grave. "Sit."

The pair perched on the edge of the altar steps, sitting closely together to continue their hushed conversation.

"We've failed. The *Machina Tenebris* project is complete," Isabelle said, her voice cracking, her eyes wide as if the words themselves were a curse.

"The dark machine." The priest wrung his hands together before staring up at the stained-glass window, which depicted Christ the Redeemer with outstretched arms, light pouring down from heaven. He made the sign of the cross, his voice trembling as he said, "Lord, give me strength."

"I tried. I really did. I'm so sorry, Father. I've let everyone down."

"Your husband's choices are not your burden to bear, Isabelle. Marriage does not bind you to his sins."

Isabelle glanced towards Julien and Béatrice, still sulking in the corner. "Now I'm worried, Father," she said, clutching his forearm. "If he finds out what I've been doing, about all the ways I've betrayed him, he'll use my children as leverage against me. You know his ruthlessness doesn't stop at hurting me." She touched her eyebrow, drawing attention to a faint bruise. "I've thought it through, and I need to step back now, before it's too late."

Father Gérard placed a hand over hers. "You've walked a dangerous path, Isabelle. If you must step back, do so, but know that God's light will guide you, even through the darkest shadows. Though, remember why we are concerned. Your children must remain untouched by the darkness he'll create—trust in His mercy, and in your own strength."

"There's something you don't know. It's about Julien. He's... *blessed* you would say. In a unique way. Although, it remains to be seen if his blessing will be a curse. He possesses power like I've never seen, not from any first or second generation moteblessed. He describes these extraordinary motes I've never heard of, and can't even fathom."

The priest took a moment. "Does Lucien know about this?"

"No. Not yet, anyway. I've told Julien to hide it from everyone for now, including his father. He didn't need to be told twice there. But—" Another fearful glance towards her children. "There's been a couple of times where he's almost revealed himself in front of Lucien. Usually, when Lucien has upset him. Or me."

Guilt splashed across Isabelle's face before it crumpled. She threw her arm over her eyes to hide tears. Father Gérard embraced her, patting her back.

Were Julien and Béatrice paying attention to all this?

Yes. Yes, they were.

Julien's gaze latched onto his crying mother, nudging Béatrice with his elbow.

The lull in conversation allowed Cinn to turn to his Isabelle. "*Machina Tenebris* project? I think the umbraphage mentioned that to us. Did Julien's father make it? What is it?"

"Yes. Lucien and his friends." Isabelle's face soured as she ran her fingers through Béatrice's shadowy fur. "It's everything he ever wanted. Unlimited motepower, on tap, controlled by him."

Cinn opened his mouth to ambush her with a dozen more questions, but Isabelle held up her hand. "I'm sorry for what you're about to see," she said softly, nodding towards the church's door.

In all the revelations, Cinn had briefly forgotten Isabelle was going to die today, in this very church.

His stomach tightened with a grim sense of inevitability. The weight of what was about to happen crashed over him, settling into a deep, sorrowful sadness for the woman whom Julien loved.

The heavy oak flew open with a bang. Around six armed officers rushed into the church. Navy blue uniforms, strange weapons that looked familiar... It took Cinn's reeling brain a second to realise who they were—Auri's gendarmerie.

They're all in his pocket, Julien often said. *Everyone is.*

One man stepped forward from the group. "Isabelle Montaigne."

Julien's mother stood, eyes wide and hands trembling, as she instinctively reached for the pew in front of her to steady herself. "No. Not here."

Father Gérard stepped forward, raising a hand as if to ward off the intruders. "This is a house of God," he said, voice steady with conviction. "You cannot bring violence into this sacred place."

"There will be no violence," the officer said, "if Isabelle Montaigne respects our arrest warrant and comes with us."

"On what grounds do you dare to arrest her in this holy place? Isabelle is a good woman, and this is a sanctuary. What charges could possibly justify such a breach of peace?"

The officer's lips curled into a sneer. "That isn't your concern, old man. Step aside before you find yourself in more trouble than you can pray your way out of. Isabelle Montaigne knows exactly why we're here."

A soft noise from the corner of the church. Béatrice held her hand over her mouth, as if muffling herself. Julien stood behind her, fists clenched, face a tornado of anger.

Cinn battled an overwhelming urge to look away, to shield himself from the pain and fury twisting across Julien's face, but he couldn't tear his eyes from the scene unfolding before him.

In unison, the gendarmerie marched down the aisle. Several of them had the motetech batons Cinn had seen around Auri, which doubled as a taser.

Father Gérard rose to place himself in front of Isabelle. She pushed him aside, murmuring something into his ear. He nodded, then swiftly headed towards the door he'd entered through earlier. Was this escape how he survived whatever happened next?

"I will willingly do whatever you wish as soon as I've delivered my children to safety," Isabelle said, clear and calm.

"We'll get them back to Paris, ma'am," a female officer said. "Don't worry about that."

Julien had left the corner to stride down the aisle.

"Julien! Stay back with Béatrice," Isabelle ordered.

Footsteps faltering, Julien paused.

"They're not going back to Paris." Isabelle burrowed her gaze into the female officer's, like she was entrusting her with a secret. "Please, let me get my children to safety."

A wave of confliction passed over the officer's face, and she glanced between her colleagues. Cinn held his breath.

"Our orders are clear," said the man, glowering at the women's exchange. Stepping forward, he grabbed Isabelle's wrists, handcuffs swinging from his other hand. These weren't your average handcuffs that Cinn himself had experienced first-hand—these bulkier cuffs emitted a faint, ominous glow.

"Get off her!" little Julien screeched, wildcat-like.

The rest of the gendarmerie parted like the Red Sea, content to let their leader deal with the tempestuous teenager.

"I said, *get off her*," Julien repeated, his small frame tense, fists clenched at his sides. His stance was defiant, shoulders squared, as if ready to pounce. "Or you'll be sorry!"

The gendarme clutching Isabelle's wrist barked a laugh, a harsh, dismissive sound that echoed through the church.

"Julien!" Isabelle begged. "Do not anger these officers. Go back to Béatrice, now!"

But her son ignored her, eyes only for the man who threatened his mother, staring him down as if to will him to release Isabelle.

The broad man yanked firmly on Isabelle's arm, and a sharp yelp left her lips.

This was it. Cinn could see it in Julien's eyes.

From Cinn's vantage point, the memory unfurled in surreal intensity.

Julien unleashed a primal scream, charging at the officer like a panther.

The boy's scream was more than a cry; it was a force of raw, unfiltered power. The surrounding air shimmered with electric tension. It was undoubtable—he was channelling, accessing those elusive motes, just as Isabelle described. An invisible wave surged outward, rippling through the space with a roar that shook the very foundations of the church.

The shockwave was a violent crescendo, a pulsating blast that struck with the fury of a hurricane. The gendarmerie, taken by surprise, were hurled through the air as if thrown by the divine hand of God. Their bodies, flung against the walls, collided with a sickening clamour of splintering wood and shattering glass. The explosive force shattered the holy atmosphere, sending debris—plaster, stained glass, splinters—raining down from the vaulted ceiling.

The force of Julien's power had cracked the very bones of the church. With an almighty groan, the ceiling buckled under the strain, heavy stones and timbers collapsing in slow-motion—the church itself bowing to Julien's fury.

Cinn watched on, breathless and awestruck. The altar was wrenched from its moorings as Julien transformed the sacred space into a tumultuous battlefield of fallen monuments and smoke. Grey ash filled the air, and that's when Cinn realised he'd reached the part of the journey he'd been on once before, although witnessed through Béatrice's spirit.

Where was Isabelle now? Cinn couldn't make her out through the carnage.

"Over there," the Isabelle beside him said, nodding to the far wall, where her twin lay crumpled, ruined. Deceased.

And there was young Julien, cradling his mother's head on his lap.

Studying the devastation on his face reminded Cinn all too viscerally of *his* Julien's expression, when he'd learned Cinn had seen this fragment of memory.

"My girl," Isabelle murmured, watching her determined daughter cross the wreckage, limping.

Béatrice attempted to throw her arms around a screaming Julien. Cinn braced for what was next—Julien pushing her away, throwing her off. He grimaced anyway, witnessing it again.

"It's all my fault!" Julien's voice boomed through the church, desperate, ragged.

Cinn's heart shattered into a thousand pieces, each fragment piercing his soul with the intensity of Julien's raw anguish. The weight of Julien's guilt and desperation was so palpable that Cinn could almost taste the chasm of grief that stretched infinitely in the face of Julien's self-blame.

The sight of Julien's tortured expression had Cinn drowning in a suffocating wave that left him gasping, closing his eyes.

All sound blurred, then faded, sinking into a distant abyss. All that was left was a hollow silence, punctuated only by Cinn's own breaths. A soft, tentative touch brushed his shoulder—Isabelle's hand, warm and reassuring.

When he finally dared to open his eyes, the church was gone, replaced with darkness. Isabelle stood before him, Béatrice in her arms still, flicking a shadowy tail. The pair both looked at Cinn with a blend of solemnity and sadness.

"Don't worry, love," she said. "He'll be okay."

Cinn was rendered speechless, the weight of her words hanging heavily in the air. Isabelle seemed so certain, but Cinn's Julien was laughably far from *okay*.

"Look after him for me," Isabelle continued, pressing a motherly kiss to his cheek. "And for her."

Darkness encroached on the edges of Cinn's vision, rushing inwards at breakneck speed. "Wait!" he managed to get out, but it was too late, for the void swallowed them whole.

Cinn blinked awake, stomach lurching. He felt like he'd just been spun around on a fairground ride. His eyes quickly adjusted to the dim light of the church.

The thick dust had gone, and so had the screaming. He was back in the present day, but instead of feeling relief, he found he still carried the heavy sadness instilled in him from what he'd just witnessed.

Julien's concerned face, over a decade older than the youth Cinn watched fall apart, soon filled his vision. He pressed a hand either side of Cinn's head. "Finally. I've been so worried. Are you alright?"

No, Cinn wanted to answer. *I'm so far from okay after watching that, it's not even funny.*

Instead, he mumbled, "Sorry," pulling himself upright on the pew. "Did I miss much?" he asked, but as he looked between Julien's tense face and Father Gérard, it became clear that the conversation that had been held in his absence was very likely a rendition of what he'd just witnessed himself.

Observing Julien's cold gaze pierce through the priest, it was impossible not to imagine that Julien harboured a deep-rooted resentment for him. Julien's mother had perished that day, while Father Gérard escaped.

"So you're telling me," Julien said, "that AP has been around since way before my mother's death?"

The priest nodded. "Out of the public eye for many years, but yes. We started as a small group of like-minded individuals with concerns about the wider impact motecraft was having, particularly motetech. You'll know this, Julien, from both your father and your time with MEET"—Julien flinched—"but the late seventies, when AP was established, saw an explosion of motetech. The industry simply couldn't keep up with demand."

"Are we talking about that machine thing?" Cinn interjected. "I just, uhh... saw you talking to Isabelle. On the day she died. About it all." He pointedly focussed on the priest.

"The *Machina Tenebris* project." Father Gérard nodded. "It existed only in the whispers of rumours. Until it did not. As far as my information serves, it is some sort of technology that enables extreme production of harnessed motepower. But at a price."

"And this has been operating all this time?" snapped Julien. "Really?"

"How do you think we suddenly found the energy to power a network of portable Displacement Baths ten years ago using motecells, hmm?"

The fight visibly drained from Julien's face.

The image of the umbraphages shouting at them, their voices filled with urgency, replayed itself in his mind. They'd wanted the machine destroyed. Desperately. "What price?" asked Cinn.

"The Arcane Purifiers believe the price is the end of the world."

A heavy silence followed, the words hanging in the air like a dark cloud.

If the umbraphages's red cities and prophetic warnings were anything to go by, the old priest was correct.

"So what exactly have AP been doing about this? Also, they may have started out however you say, but their actions last November have led most of the community to see them as a terrorist group. People died in the Cerulean Auditorium attack."

Father Gérard nodded gravely, his fingers tracing the edge of his collar. "Yes, that was deeply unfortunate. You must understand, I am very much on the fringe of the Purifiers these days. But I understand that there was some... *division* between different sub-groups operating under the AP banner. If it's any consolation, I assure you the people responsible for the violence are no longer with us—they're under God's judgement now. 'Vengeance is mine; I will repay, saith the Lord.' They have met their end, as all must who stray from His path."

Violence met with violence. Makes sense.

"As for what we're doing? There is a taskforce attempting to verify the existence and location of the machine—"

"Existence?" Julien cried. "You just said it *definitely* exists, and that my father built it. Does it exist, or not?"

"Your mother claimed so. She tried to stop it, stop him—"

Julien slammed his fist against the wooden pew, causing the entire church to echo with the force. His patience had evidently reached its limit. Saying his name, Cinn reached out for Julien, but without another word, he stormed down the aisle.

"Wait!" shouted Father Gérard, lifting a withered hand. "There's one more thing you should know. Someone who can help you far more than—"

The heavy oak doors slammed shut behind Julien with a reverberating crash.

Cinn sighed. This all clearly hadn't done Julien's mood any favours. "Sorry about him. It's all been a bit of a time. I'll go get him back."

Expecting to see Julien by Maz, it was a surprise to find him leaning against the church's wall, knee bent against the stone.

"Don't," Julien warned.

"Don't what?"

"Lecture me for running off."

"I wasn't about to."

Cinn allowed a silence to settle over them, waiting for Julien to be ready to lead the conversation.

"I..." Julien started, eyes high, fixated on the grey sky. "I can't believe it was him. My father. It must have been him who sent the gendarmerie to arrest *Mère* that day."

Something in the way he said the words, laden with resignation, implied Julien had always known this truth, deep down.

"That *bastard*!"

Julien had never sounded quite like this, this raw, guttural eruption of pain and disbelief. The anguish in his voice was so palpable it felt like a physical force, a storm of rage and sorrow.

"I'll kill him." Julien's quiet conviction was alarming, especially when he stepped forward from the wall, as if he were off to do just that.

Cinn threw his palms out. "Hey now—"

Instead of pushing Cinn out of the way, Julien spun, face twisted with fury, and slammed his fist into the brick wall with so much momentum, Cinn's teeth ground together in sympathy for his knuckles.

"I'm going to fucking kill him!" Julien screamed, and made to punch the brick again.

Cinn caught his elbow, wrenching it backwards. "Jul—"

"How *dare* he? How fucking dare he sit there across from me all these years, knowing the whole time?"

"I don't know." Cinn tugged Julien away from the wall, trying to grab both his arms, but Julien broke out of his grip to pace up and down.

"How was I this stupid?" Julien shook his head at himself, genuine confusion written across his face. "*Putain*, how I've been so *stupid*!"

Cinn had been expecting this moment, of course. Julien had been on a collision course for some sort of breakdown since the moment Cinn had met him. But now, wading through the thick of it with him, the depth of Julien's self-critical despair was almost too much to bear, leaving Cinn to drown in a tide of helplessness.

"And—" Julien stopped pacing. "Of course. Yesterday. That was him, as well. I can't believe I didn't see it before."

"The break in?" Cinn rubbed his tired eyes. It already felt like a lifetime ago since those men dragged him out of bed in the early hours of that morning. "You think your dad sent those men?"

Cinn didn't mean for the words to sound so doubtful; he was simply processing it all.

However, Julien's face crumpled in disdain. "But of course it was! It makes complete sense. Remember just before Christmas, when he asked me about you 'helping' him? Well, obviously, he didn't want to take no for an answer. Trust me. I *know* it was him. Why don't you trust me?"

Julien glared at Cinn, daring him to challenge him.

Cinn raised two palms in surrender. "Okay, okay! Just chill out for a second, I'm—"

"Chill out?" Julien shrieked.

—on your side, here.

Inwardly, Cinn groaned. He should have led with that.

"*Chill out*?! How can I possibly chill out when I've just found out that it was my father who sent those men to arrest *Mère*, resulting in me killing her? And that she came here to tell Father Gérard about some sort of..." Julien waved his arm wildly in the air. "Some sort of secret destructive device that's causing the umbraphages and this second wave of calamities."

Again, Cinn attempted to catch hold of Julien, and again, he writhed away, a feral animal in distress.

"And then last night, he fucking sent people to our hotel to snatch you!" At that, Julien finally looked at Cinn, deep wells of horror replacing his eyes. "I almost lost you!" A deep breath. "I almost lost you to *him*! So I'm going to kill him. I'll do it, I swear. Fuck him. And fuck Eleanor for supporting him. I thought I could count on her, of all people. Why was I so trusting?"

Julien's tirade was becoming more rapid, more deranged by the second. Before Cinn could formulate a plan of action, Julien twisted away from him.

Wham.

His fist connected with the unforgiving stone wall again, Cinn's heart absorbing the blow.

Wham.

"And fuck Béatrice!" Julien tipped his head back, shouting towards the heavens now. "My only sister, for lying to me for months, then dying and leaving me alone to deal with all this shit!"

Cinn found himself flattening against the wall of the church as if Julien's words were a strong wind.

"We were meant to be a *team.*" Julien's voice cracked. "We were all we had left. Why didn't she tell me about AP? Why didn't she trust me?"

Julien looked to Cinn for an answer, blinking rapidly.

"Um…" he started, fumbling around for something comforting to say. "I'm sure she had her reasons. Maybe she was trying to protect you? She ended up dead from it, after all."

"Dead…" Julien ran the word over his tongue. Something was ticking over in his brain, and Cinn braced for the next inevitable outburst. Pressing two palms against the brick, Julien slowly shook his head. "I… I think he killed her as well."

"What?"

"I think my father killed Béatrice."

A sharp gust of wind whistled through the bare branches, cutting through the cold air.

"It adds up with his wife acting weird when she saw Béatrice's locket on me at his birthday party." Julien's hands went to his empty neck, where the locket usually lay. "I stole it back from the evidence locker. They probably had the whole thing covered up."

Cinn started to protest, to deny the possibility that Julien's father could have had his own daughter killed, but the conviction in Julien's eyes stopped him cold.

Julien often maintained that Béatrice's relationship with their father was even worse than his own. If Lucien had learned that his daughter had joined the very organisation that threatened his power…

But to kill your own flesh and blood? In such a brutal way?

Cinn hesitated for a moment, mind racing. Looking into Julien's tormented eyes, he realised there was no room for empty reassurances. Instead, he reached out and gently tucked a stray lock of Julien's hair behind his ear, his touch lingering to squeeze the back of his neck. "I believe you," Cinn said softly, lifting Julien's hand to press a tender kiss against his knuckles, scratched and already bruised. "Whatever happens, we'll face it together."

"He killed Béatrice. He's partially responsible for *Mère*—"

"*Entirely* responsible," Cinn insisted, rubbing his thumbs over Julien's swollen hands. "You need to stop blaming yourself. It's not healthy."

"It's the truth! It's fact. It's what happened. You saw it with your own eyes!" Julien cried, trying to free himself from Cinn's grip.

"Yes, exactly." Cinn battled to keep hold of Julien. He wouldn't allow him to punch the wall again. "I saw a terrified child be very brave and try to help his mother."

Julien visibly rolled his eyes.

"Julien, you need to listen to me. Please."

After a beat, Julien stilled, finally meeting Cinn's gaze.

"It. Was. Not. Your. Fault."

Cinn said the words often enough to himself, whenever the memory of the four bodies, bloodied and staring towards him with lifeless eyes, haunted his thoughts. If Cinn could believe them, so could Julien.

"It was his." Cinn brushed his knuckles against Julien's chin. "And if I have to tell you that every day for the rest of time for you to believe it, I will."

Julien opened his mouth, eyebrows drawn in defiant lines.

Cinn pressed a finger to Julien's lips. "No. You're not allowed to say another word except 'you're right.'"

Julien's mouth snapped shut at the touch of Cinn's finger, his defiant expression wavering. For a moment, his eyes flickered with the familiar storm of anger and guilt, but then something softened. He let out a shuddering breath, the tension in his shoulders easing just slightly. His gaze remained locked on Cinn's, searching for any sign of insincerity. Finding none, Julien swallowed hard, the fight slowly draining from him.

A small, bitter smile tugged at the corner of his lips as he finally whispered, "You're right."

Thank God.

A small sense of victory tinged with sorrow settled over Cinn. This was simply one battle in a long war, but seeing the fight leave Julien, if only for a moment, gave him the strength to keep going. Keep filling the cracks in Julien's soul, the ones caused by years of grief and self-blame. And as he stared into Julien's hopeful eyes, and saw the trust so plainly written there, it strengthened Cinn's resolve to stay by his side, no matter how many battles lay ahead.

Then Julien's eyes narrowed, and his smile dropped. "He's taken both of them from me, and now he's trying to take you from me."

"I won't let him." Exactly how Cinn would ensure that was a problem for later.

"But you're not just in danger from him. It's me as well. This morning proved that." Julien ran his hand up the arm of Cinn's hoodie to where the makeshift bandage was. "You can't trust me not to hurt you, Cinn." Julien grabbed Cinn's shoulders. He sobered, lowering his voice to say, "And I know you wish you were back in London," like a confession.

What? Where the hell did this come from?

Reeling, Cinn's mouth fell open in shock.

"So you should go back there, right now. Hide away somewhere." Julien squeezed Cinn's arms, digging in painfully, then stared down at the ground. "I know it's only a matter of time before you leave, anyway."

Me was the unspoken word.

For one, Cinn was pretty sure being in a different country wouldn't protect him, but he moved past that argument.

"Julien," Cinn said through gritted teeth. "Stop."

A flash of defiance crossed Julien's face, his jaw twitching.

Cinn slapped him. Once, lightly, on the cheek.

"Listen, you muppet." Cinn wriggled free from Julien's tight grip and wrapped his arms around Julien's waist, pulling him close. Resting his chin on Julien's shoulder, Cinn spoke softly into his ear. "I'm not going anywhere, you idiot. Do you really think I'd just walk away from all this?"

At Cinn's words, Julien settled slightly into the embrace, holding Cinn in return, trailing a tentative palm across Cinn's back.

"I don't know what you take me for, but I'm in this for the long haul. Why you've got this idea in your head that I'd rather be back in London is beyond me."

Cinn pulled away to clasp Julien's head with both hands, looking deep into the grey eyes that captured his heart the first time they met, even if he didn't know it then.

"There is nowhere, *nowhere* I'd rather be than with you, wherever you are. Do you hear me?"

Julien's Adam's apple bobbed.

"So, I'm sorry, but you're stuck with me. Besides, I just promised your mother's spirit I'll look after you. I've already got Béatrice haunting me. I don't want your mum as well."

Julien's breath caught. "What did she say?"

"Very little. But she didn't need to. I could sense the love for you and Béatrice pouring out of her."

Speaking of love...

"Also..." Cinn inhaled a deep breath to settle the wildfire of nerves igniting in his stomach. "I know this is weird timing, but I tried to say this yesterday, twice, actually."

A puzzled frown from Julien.

"Once at the Eiffel Tower, and then again when you were asleep."

"Cinn—" Julien looked past his shoulder.

"So, just so you know, for the record—"

"Wait—"

"Bloody hell, Julien, can you not just give me one more second to finish!"

The frown deepened. "But—"

"I love you, okay?" Cinn screamed at him, then cringed at his frantic declaration. "Just so you know."

Julien froze, his entire body going rigid. His eyes widened, unblinking, as if he were struggling to comprehend the words that had just been hurled at him. His mouth opened slightly, a mixture of disbelief and confusion etched into his features.

Mortification rolled over Cinn in violent bursts. The sudden urge to run and hide somewhere in the church's graveyard was strong. "Forget it," he mumbled, dropping his hold on Julien.

Why did he think burdening Julien with *that* right now was a good idea? He'd been so desperate to unleash those words, yet now a cold wave of regret crashed over him.

"*Non*," Julien whispered.

"Just forget I said anything," Cinn pleaded, frustration intensifying. Could this day get any worse? "Please! Just forget it. I won't bring it up again."

"*Non*! Stop! Look!" Julien pointed to behind Cinn, voice brimming with urgency.

Cinn turned. A black SUV sped along the long, winding road leading up to the church. It hurtled towards them with alarming speed, its tyres screeching against the gravel.

The car was fast. Fast and loud. Cinn surely would have heard it coming if he hadn't been so absorbed with his crisis. His heart plummeted. Yes, apparently the day *could* get worse.

"That's not good, is it?"

Julien moved towards Maz. "Quick. We need to run." He tossed Cinn the car keys.

Cinn looked down at them in confusion, then back up to Julien.

"You drive, I'll channel and see what I can do to slow them down," Julien said.

"What? Me? I can't drive." Cinn tossed the keys back.

"What? You can't drive *at all*?" Julien shrieked.

"London, mate," Cinn said apologetically.

"Well, Maz practically drives herself." Julien sent the keys flying back, hitting Cinn square in the chest.

"Julien, practically isn't good enough if you want to live!" shouted Cinn, as the SUV was moments away from them. He launched the keys back at Julien.

Julien made a frustrated sound, then dove into the driver's seat.

The moment they slammed Maz's doors shut, the SUV skidded to a halt in front of the church, sending a spray of gravel scattering across the ground.

"Buckle up," said Julien, turning on the ignition. "This is going to be one hell of a ride."

Twenty-Three

JULIEN

Julien's fingers gripped the leather steering wheel, cracked, bleeding knuckles white as he navigated the narrow, winding road that led away from the church. The frosty air clawed at the edges of the windshield, dustings of snow falling onto the glass before the wipers violently cleared them.

Hardly ideal driving conditions for a to-the-death car chase.

Behind him, the SUV loomed large, its headlights glaring through the snow like the eyes of a predator.

"Hold on, Maz," Julien muttered under his breath, urging the car forward, pedal to the metal. The engine roared as she accelerated smoothly, handling the icy corners with a grace no ordinary car could manage. Still, the tension in the air was palpable, the cold seeping through the vehicle's frame and into Julien's bones.

Although Julien's eyes should have been firmly planted on the road, he couldn't help but routinely flick them to Cinn. His body pressed tightly into the seat, fingers digging into the leather. Every twist in the road was punctuated by a short, sharp burst of breath. "They're gaining on us," he said, voice tight with worry. "Can you go any faster?"

Julien was already pushing eighty, an impressive feat considering the conditions. "Now is not the time for back-seat driving!"

A glance in the rear-view mirror revealed the black SUV closing the gap between them. Julien cursed under his breath.

If he wasn't driving, he could've done something—channelled wind-motes to whip up a blinding flurry of snow, or better yet, frozen the tarmac to send the SUV skidding off the road. But with both hands on the wheel and every ounce of concentration focussed on keeping them on the winding road, there was little he could do but push Maz to her limits.

The road twisted through the forest, and they raced past tall, skeletal trees. The headlights caught glimpses of the frosted bark, turning the world into a blur of black and white. Julien's heart pounded in his chest, each beat matching the rhythmic thrum of the engine. The SUV remained dogged in its pursuit, its driver showing no signs of giving up.

Just who exactly was chasing them, and how many in number? Likely, they were good buddies with the two dead bodies in the back. Would it be safest to stop and fight them? What were a couple more murders to his tally at this point?

Tempting, but the memory of bandaging Cinn's arm that morning had Julien aggressively slamming the pedal down. *Non.* However tantalising, Julien's abilities couldn't be trusted, especially in this state of mind. He wouldn't lose anyone else by his own hand. Especially not his boyfriend. His boyfriend, who'd told Julien that he loved him. Loved *him.* It was unbelievable, but Julien would take it.

He'd protect Cinn if it killed him.

They rounded a particularly sharp bend. The body laying across the back seat lurched forward, smacking into the headrests. Julien winced.

The village of Moret-sur-Loing came into view—the cobbled streets were quiet, only a few locals braving the cold to run errands. Julien cursed again. He didn't want to involve innocents in this mess, but he had no choice. The narrow streets of the village, with its sharp turns, were their best chance to lose the tail.

Blaring the horn, which roared like a foghorn with its enhanced volume, Julien gunned the engine, and Maz surged forward into the village.

A couple of pedestrians on the pavement stopped in their tracks, faces alarmed as the black car sped past them. Julien narrowly avoided a cart full of produce, sending apples tumbling into the street. The vendor shouted something that was lost in the carnage.

Cinn craned his neck to look behind them. "They're still there, Julien! We're not losing them."

I have eyes.

Julien's jaw clenched. He swerved around a parked car, barely missing the side mirror. The SUV followed, its tyres screeching as it skidded slightly on the icy road but quickly regained control. They tore through the centre of the village, the ancient buildings a blur on either side.

"Watch out for those kids!"

A group of youths bundled in scarves and hats gawked as they zoomed by. Julien winced. He really would be off to hell if he mowed down a bunch of children.

Rubber burned. Nerves frayed.

Maz blasted through the last stretch of the village, the paved streets giving way to the open countryside, and its dirt tracks. The snow was falling heavier now, the flakes sticking to the ground and making the drive even more treacherous. Maz handled it better than most cars would, the motetech enhancements giving her an edge in the worsening conditions.

But Julien felt her strain as if she were a part of him, the violent billows of fumes trailing behind them acting as a sign of protest. He stroked the steering wheel. "Well done, girl."

"This isn't working." Cinn's voice was edged with panic. "We're not going to shake—holy shit! Look!"

Julien's eyes flicked to the rear-view mirror, heart skipping a beat. The SUV was still on their tail, but now a passenger was leaning out of the window, clutching a sleek, black weapon. It was unmistakably motetech, and Julien's blood ran cold as he recognized the design, tendrils of electric-blue light snaking around the barrel.

Cinn was right to be scared—this wasn't just a chase any longer. They were about to be under attack.

"We can't let them hit us with that," Julien said.

"No shit!"

Julien's mind raced, calculating the success of their very few remaining options. "Hang on tight." He tightened his grip on the wheel.

"What are you—"

Julien yanked the wheel to the right, sending Maz careening off the road and onto a dirt track that cut through a field. The tyres skidded on the loose gravel, and Cinn was thrown against the door.

"*Julien!*"

The SUV followed, barrelling down the narrow track after them. Julien fought to keep control as Maz bounced over the uneven ground, the suspension struggling to compensate. He felt every jolt, every bump, reverberate through his spine. But the SUV was heavier, less agile. They hurtled towards the end of the field, and Julien scanned the horizon, heart hammering. Then, he spotted it—a small gap in the tree line. A Maz-sized gap.

If Julien could make it through there, maybe they'd reach another road, and maybe, just maybe, they'd lose the SUV in the process.

The gap loomed closer. They were moments away now. Julien glanced in the mirror—

The smooth control Julien had over Maz vanished in an instant as the tyres hit a patch of ice. Julien swore, fighting to correct their path, but it was too late. The steering wheel jolted violently in his hands, and the car seemed to float for a heartbeat, weightless and terrifying, as if the ground had simply disappeared beneath them.

"Watch out!" Cinn shrieked pointlessly, because there was nothing Julien could do to stop the car skidding wildly, spinning across the icy ground towards a sharp drop.

A sharp drop which soon revealed itself to be more of a—

Cliff.

They plunged off the edge.

Julien's stomach plummeted as the world tilted violently around him. They tumbled down the steep incline, the rough ground blurring past his vision. Maz's wheels spun futilely, kicking up dirt and rocks as she tilted further to the right. The groaning metal filled his ears, and for a heartbeat, everything seemed to freeze before Maz completely flipped.

Snow.

Sky.

Earth.

Do something. Anythin—

Julien's head smacked into the window, his vision exploding into stars as the impact reverberated through his skull.

Snow.

Sky.

Earth.

Everything became a blur as they tumbled, gravity pulling them in every direction at once.

The crunching metal and shattering glass drowned out Cinn's scream. Julien's hand shot out, grabbing his in a desperate grip, their fingers intertwining as the car continued its chaotic descent. Julien squeezed tighter, holding on with everything he had as Maz rolled over again, then again, each violent jolt threatening to rip them apart.

Was this really how Julien's life ended? Tumbling down a cliff in his wreck of a car, clutching the hand of the boyfriend he'd had for less than twenty-four hours, to meet their shared, tragic fate?

In the madness of it all, their gazes met for a split second—eyes wide with fear, but also with something else, something unspoken. Julien didn't need words to tell Cinn what he was thinking; the silent promise was there in the way they held onto each other, refusing to let go.

The car flipped one last time, finally slamming to a stop with a sickening thud that threw them violently forward. The airbags exploded with a deafening pop, cushioning the impact but not the terror. A tree branch speared through the shattered windshield, narrowly missing them by inches, knocking the breath out of Julien's lungs. The world fell silent, save for the ticking of the cooling engine and the ragged sounds of their breathing. Snowflakes drifted softly onto the fractured glass, a stark contrast to the chaos surrounding them.

Julien's breath came in gasps, his chest aching from the airbag's impact. One hand was still clenched on the wheel while the other squeezed Cinn's incredibly tightly, as if letting go would unravel his fragile grip on reality. Each and every muscle trembled. Eventually, using all of his energy, he relaxed his grip on the wheel to press against where he'd hit his head, his fingers coming away sticky. He blinked, trying to focus, trying to make sense of the world around him.

Please, let him be okay.

"Cinn..." Julien rasped, turning his head slowly. His neck protested the movement, a sharp pain shooting down his spine. "Are you... alright?"

Cinn slumped in his seat, groaning softly. A trickle of blood ran down his forehead. But he was alive. *Alive.* With obvious effort, he twisted slightly to face Julien with unfocussed eyes, then nodded weakly. "Right as rain, mate. You certainly delivered on your whole wild ride promise."

Julien let out an unsteady laugh.

He tipped his head back on the seat, rubbing a hand over his face. Oh, how he wished he could sleep for a week.

Sadly, that definitely wasn't on the menu. Because a plume of smoke was curling up from the crumpled bonnet, thick and black. A strange scent filled the air: chemical, sharp. A rapid, irregular popping noise accompanied it.

Once he realised what was going on, panic surged through Julien as yet another wave of adrenaline seized hold of him, overriding any concussion.

"Out! Now!"

Their hands dove simultaneously for their seatbelt buckles. Julien jammed on the door handle. It miraculously opened enough for him to slide out.

But Cinn wasn't copying him.

"What are you doing?"

He was rooting through the glove compartment, now half-open, a crumpled mess of papers and debris strewn across Maz's interior. Cinn held up their passports, grinning victoriously, as the trickle of blood beaded down his left cheek.

"Get the fuck out of the car, you idiot!" Julien shouted. Why was now the moment for Cinn to develop organisational skills?

They stumbled away from the car, the frigid air hitting their faces as they scrambled to safety. The strange sound of something hissing and sputtering from the engine only intensified their desperation.

Hitting a tree line, Julien slowed, turning back to survey the mangled wreckage from a distance.

Julien's heart stuttered as he took in the horrific sight: his once sleek black Mazda, his beloved pride and joy, was now a crumpled mess of twisted metal and shattered glass. The car was half-buried in snow, its front end smashed against a cluster of gnarled tree trunks, while black smoke now billowed from the broken engine.

There was no further warning.

The black smoke thickened into an ominous cloud, and then, with a thunderous roar, the car exploded in a blinding flash of orange and red. The shockwave rocked Julien back, the heat and debris sending him stumbling as his hand shot out to find Cinn's arm.

They both ended up on their backs on the soggy ground, breathless and disorientated, inhaling air thick with the acrid smell of burning metal.

Julien pushed himself up to stare at Maz, alight with flickering flames. At least she went out in style.

"My poor baby."

Cinn grunted in annoyance. "Yeah, don't worry about me. I'm fine. Just bleeding from my head wound over here."

Julien captured Cinn's face with two icy hands. "My poor, poor baby." He kissed his forehead, his lips meeting the coppery taste of Cinn's blood.

In unison, they turned back to face the hypnotic blaze, flames dancing wildly in hues of orange and crimson. The fire licked greedily at the air, casting flickering shadows that seemed to writhe and twist with a life of their own as it devoured everything inside.

"Well," Julien said. "At least we don't need to worry about burying those bodies any longer."

Cinn let out a sharp, hysterical laugh, the sound echoing strangely in the thicket of trees.

A sudden thought burst into Julien's mind, sending him flying to his feet. "*Putain*! Your Walkman! Your cassettes!"

He took a step towards Maz. Maybe they could still be saved. Maybe he could—

Cinn yanked his arm backwards. "Are you mad? Julien, your car is on fire. *Maz* is on fire. Who cares about a music player?"

Julien wasn't fooled—the strained edge to Cinn's voice was a giveaway, as was the sad look in his eye. "You!" he cried. "You care!"

Cinn smacked him on the arm. "Stop. The only really important thing is standing right here with me."

Julien's heart squeezed itself into a tight ball. "What, your beanie hat?" Julien tugged on it, resulting in another smack.

"You're such a dick." Cinn slid away from Julien to fold his arms. He nodded his chin at what was left of Maz. "Didn't you think to build some sort of anti-explosion device into her?"

"Well, I have to say, I didn't expect to get entangled in a high-speed car chase, resulting in us being driven off the road into a tree. To be honest, I mainly concentrated on the clarity of the sound system, and her ultra-smooth suspension."

"We better get moving. The SUV could still find us here."

"Once we've ripped the number plates off Maz, yes. I'll cool her down with some of this ice once I get my strength back. Though there's something even more important I have to do first."

A small frown split across Cinn's forehead, and Julien smoothed it with his thumb. His other arm snaked around him, drawing him close. The warmth of Cinn's body seeped through the coldness, quickly embedding itself in Julien's bones. As he lifted Cinn's chin, his mouth fell open in a small circle of surprise.

"I think this could probably wait," Cinn muttered, jerking his head towards the billowing plumes of smoke that choked the air.

"*Non!*" Julien declared dramatically, enjoying Cinn's look of alarm as he brushed some of the ash that clung to his cheeks away, marking Cinn with grey war paint. His head pounded, his muscles ached, he'd quite like to lie down on the ground, but goddammit! "It will not be said that I made you wait a second more than I had to."

Confusion and mild annoyance flickered across Cinn's face as he tried to pull away.

"Since you've apparently tried to tell me this three times in total, I'll do the same."

Un. "*Je t'aime.*" Julien kissed Cinn's forehead again.

Deux. "*Je t'aime.*" He trailed his lips down to press them to his cheek.

Trois. "And, in case you still don't understand basic French, which is probable: I love you." Their lips met, tender and slow. Julien closed his eyes, enjoying the soft gasp that Cinn made, that he swallowed with his own mouth.

Tomorrow, and tomorrow, and tomorrow.

Julien pulled back. Cinn's expression was so utterly stunned—dazed eyes, slightly parted lips—that Julien fought to suppress a bubble of delirious laughter.

"Now we're even again. I know how much you like things to be fair."

A smile slowly broke across Cinn's face, his widened eyes softening into something more certain. He attempted to move away, but Julien clasped him against his chest.

"I love you too," Cinn breathed into the crook of Julien's neck. The warmth of his words had his heart bursting full of helium, lifting him skywards. The tether that was his fears and doubts snapped, the gravity of the world relinquishing its grasp on him. If there was one thing right now that Julien knew for certain, it was that this was a moment he'd remember for the rest of time. He pulled Cinn tightly against him, clutching him as though, if he squeezed hard enough, Cinn would stay right there by his side. Always.

The fire had grown so furious that it radiated a fierce, almost unbearable heat, and the thick smoke stung Julien's eyes, but he needed one more kiss before they sprinted through the woods in search of civilization. Something to give him strength.

As their lips met amid the snowfall and swirling ash, he could taste the love pouring out of them and into each other—an unmistakable blend of desperation and devotion. It was their own brand of love, one forged in light and shadow. A gritty, relentless sort of love. The ride-or-die kind.

Us against the world. The tomorrow, and tomorrow, and tomorrow sort of love.

Twenty-Four

ELLIOT

That guy was stalking Elliot again.

That one from the other day—tall, dark skin, velvety black hair. About as stealthy as a neon sign.

Today, he was once again demonstrating a spectacularly poor job of being covert.

Now, to be fair, Elliot had never trailed anyone himself. But he was fairly sure you weren't meant to stand out in plain view, leaning against one of the stone columns that housed lumenmotes in its glass tip, looking like you were waiting for a bus.

To give some credit, the dude was at least pretending to study a crumpled newspaper, but his eyes kept flicking periodically towards Elliot, as if he was trying to memorise his every move while maintaining a facade of casual disinterest.

Right then. That's enough of this shit.

Changing paths, Elliot walked right past the column, the very picture of nonchalance. Then, at the last second, he turned, ready to slam his arm against the guy's neck.

The man stepped to the side, a fluid, swift motion that hinted at him having expected the move.

Elliot gritted his teeth, a frustrated growl escaping him. He reached out, but the guy effortlessly slid backwards. Then he shot Elliot a brief, amused glance before twisting around quickly to sprint down the narrow, winding passageway behind the Lunarium Observatory.

Elliot didn't hesitate.

He plunged into the chase with quick determined strides, his footsteps echoing off the ancient brickwork and worn pavement.

The man ahead of him darted with an agile grace, weaving through narrow alleys and courtyards. His dark coat flared behind him like a cape, his black hair a wild streak against the pale stone walls. Although, he'd soon be no match for Elliot—his own movements were a blur of practised efficiency, each calculated to close the gap. He leaped over a low wall and vaulted onto a narrow ledge, propelling himself into the next alley with precision honed from years of athletic training.

The narrow passageways twisted and turned like a maze, forcing Elliot to navigate sharp corners and sudden drops with barely a moment's notice. His lungs burned as he pushed himself faster, his legs pumping rhythmically over the uneven stone pavement.

The chase spilled into an open courtyard, its flagstone floor lit by the soft glow of street lamps. Several walkers gave a sharp gasp at the sight of them. The stalker skidded around a fountain, water spraying up in an arc.

Elliot saw his chance. A sudden burst of speed saw him leaping over the fountain's edge, landing lightly on the other side and forcing the man to veer off his course.

He darted out of Elliot's grasp, Elliot's fingers closing to make a sad fist, as the fountain splattered him in icy water.

The chase continued, taking them zooming over one of the many temporary metal bridges across the giant crack, then past the Aurelia Library, the guy weaving in between the columns of the portico like he was performing some elaborate dance for Elliot's entertainment.

This fucker is fast. Stupidly fast.

But he *was* tiring, at least—the man's ragged breaths fuelled Elliot's relentless determination, each laboured inhale pushing him to close the distance.

They'd travelled some distance—they were at the far edge of Auri now, with few light sources to illuminate the early evening's darkness. In front of them lay Sylvan Glade, the small garden where the Verdant Conservatory grew some species of plants. Its sizeable pond boasted a grand bridge with high stone railings, and the man's strides became uneven as he stumbled onto it.

Come on, Elliot urged himself. *Get him.*

They neared the end of the bridge. If the man cleared it, he could easily lose Elliot in the thick foliage. Elliot lunged forward with a burst of final, powerful energy. He grabbed the guy by the collar, hard, spinning him around.

The panting man staggered, partially slumping against the stone railing.

Yes!

Elliot wouldn't have lasted much longer at that pace.

Locking the guy in place with an arm against his chest, Elliot had to tilt his head up slightly to address him. Though the man was slightly taller, Elliot could easily overpower his thin, lithe build now that he had him pinned. He was sure of it.

Elliot allowed himself a few breaths. "*You!*"

It seemed as good a start as any.

Elliot appraised the flustered figure in front of him, pushing him firmly into the stone while he hooked a leg around his, lest he get any clever ideas.

Sweat dripped from his captive's forehead. His deep brown eyes were set beneath a strong brow, framed by high cheekbones and a sharp jawline. His dark complexion was complemented by full, expressive lips, which he licked.

Breath coming in ragged gasps still, he took a moment to say, "Elliot. You caught me."

"Damn right I did," snarled Elliot, giving him another push for good measure. He didn't like the way he'd said his name—like he had power over him.

The guy had the audacity to smile.

"You won't be smiling in a minute."

He was unable to take his eyes off the other man's face. His lips in particular.

That smile. It's familiar.

"What's your name?"

"Malik," said the man, with a calm confidence that didn't belong to someone currently being held prisoner.

Malik...

Nope. It didn't ring any bells.

"What's that accent?"

"I grew up out on the West Coast, moved to New York for the hub there a few years back. Then a few months ago, I guess adventure came knocking."

Elliot rarely got homesick for the States, but the tiniest pang shot through him now. The shit Swiss January weather was likely to blame.

"West Coast? Oregon?" Where Elliot himself was from?

"Nah, California."

Why was Elliot making idle chit-chat with this dude? He shook his head, then looked Malik squarely in the eye. Fellow American or not, the guy was trouble. "You've been watching me. Watching *us*."

"Yeah. Sorry about that." Malik didn't look sorry. Didn't look sorry at all.

The strange man wasn't struggling against Elliot's hold on him. Rather, he seemed almost relaxed, as if this confrontation was more of an inconvenience than a threat. A faint smirk played on his lips, and his eyes glinted with amusement. This wasn't how Elliot imagined this would go at all. Unease crept up his spine, and he loosened his grip, just slightly.

"Guess the game's up, huh? Took long enough. You four were all over the place. But hey, it wasn't a bad gig. Definitely helped having some eye candy around."

Elliot scoffed. *This guy.* "I'll be sure to pass along your compliments." He'd meant it sarcastically, but thinking about it, it probably would tickle Julien's ego. More than a bit.

"What?" Malik blinked, then snorted. "Oh, them? Hell no. Julien Montaigne acts like he's got a stick up his ass, and his boyfriend dresses like a hobo. Not my type. I'm more into uniforms." Malik raked his eyes up and down Elliot's gendarmerie's attire. Then winked.

It took an embarrassingly long time for Elliot to realise the guy was attempting to flirt with him.

Likely, he was trying to flirt his way out of Elliot deciding to punch him in the face, but hey, he'd take it. It had been a while.

"But speaking of which—I gotta know—does Cinnamon Saunders own five identical grey hoodies, or does he just never do laundry? These are the real questions that came out of my investigation. Though, Madame Sinclair didn't exactly share my enthusiasm. She actually kicked me off the job."

Elliot schooled his expression. Just what was this guy playing at, revealing so casually that it was Eleanor who was having them tailed? If he was attempting to earn Elliot's trust, he was failing.

"Really?" Elliot eyed Malik carefully. "Probably a good thing, since you were too busy checking us out to bother hiding yourself properly."

"Well, after months of it, I just couldn't be bothered any more, honestly."

"*Months?*"

The word left Elliot's mouth hanging loose. *No way.* It was impossible that this idiot had gone undetected for months.

Nodding, Malik smirked, one corner of his lip twitching up. "My favorite part of your adventures? Watching you three haul those unconscious bodies out of that sketchy warehouse in London."

Time stilled as Elliot tensed. So long had passed since he'd helped take down the maggot of a crime boss who had made Cinn's life hell, he'd long since stopped worrying that it might come back to bite him.

"Eleanor... knows about that?"

"Of course she does. It was all in my report. Great stuff, really. Though Eleanor seemed pretty uninterested in my section about your order at the fish and chip shop..."

Malik babbled on, but Elliot tuned him out, mind spinning. How did Elliot still have his job? Why hadn't Eleanor informed Salvatore Gallo that one of his gendarmes had been gallivanting around London unchecked, taking down gangsters and reducing their minds to mush?

"I... don't understand," was all Elliot could say. He dropped his grip on Malik, who shifted away from him, straightening his coat.

Malik ran a hand through his shaggy dark hair. "Ah, got it. So we're finally getting to the part where I allowed you to catch me this evening."

"*Allowed?* Come on. You were running pretty fast from where I was standing."

"The chase is a part of the fun, don't you think?" Malik gave a low laugh.

Elliot moved away from him, folding his arms. He assessed the man again. "I feel like I've met you, but I can't put my finger on it," he admitted.

"Yeah?" Malik openly grinned at him now, winding Elliot up further. "That's probably because I called it quits on this little game a while back—at that New Year's party." Malik nodded in the vague direction of the Curio Café.

Oh.

Oh, no.

Fuck, no.

Elliot was powerless to repress the look of horror undoubtedly blooming across his face.

"I tried to talk to you, remember?" Malik didn't hide the mischievous sparkle in his eyes. "But you were at least ten shots deep, so I can't blame you if you don't recall."

A horrible, distorted memory tormented Elliot as deep-rooted mortification rolled over him in waves.

"I... Didn't I... Were you the one..." Elliot couldn't bring himself to say it.

"Yes, that's right. You came up to me at closing time and rather crudely propositioned me." Malik pressed a hand against his heart, feigning shock. "I was blushing like a fair maiden. Then you ruined the moment by hurling all over my best shoes."

That's why his smile looked so familiar. He's hot-guy-in-the-tuxedo.

A blurry image of himself pawing at the guy's waist assaulted him. Oh, what Elliot would do for the ground to swallow him whole right about now. "You'd been staring at me all evening!" was his only defence.

"I was patiently waiting for you to stamp my dance card. Unfortunately, you didn't even notice me until you were completely hammered."

Elliot needed to redirect this conversation before it went off the rails. "Let's rewind so I can get this straight. Madame Sinclair had you tailing us, but you've decided to... what, switch sides?"

"Not exactly. But I've gotta admit, for a group that spends most of their time throwing insults at each other, you're surprisingly tight-knit. It made me feel lonely. Got me thinking I'd have way more fun on the inside."

"What do you mean, *not quite*? Look, dude, just tell me what's going on here."

Malik started moving backwards. "Look out for a message tomorrow."

"What?" Elliot snapped. "No, hold on. What do you mean?"

"If I say any more, I'm definitely gonna get lynched this time. But trust me, this will be easier. Just believe me, Elliot."

There he went again, wielding Elliot's name like he owned it. Elliot ground his jaw. He trusted this twat as much as he trusted a rattlesnake in his boot.

With one final, calculated smile, Malik turned and took off into the night.

Allowing himself to unleash a loud, frustrated sigh that filled the quiet garden, Elliot stared at the space where Malik had been moments ago. Elliot could chase him again, but he had a feeling he wouldn't catch him this time.

He also had a feeling he'd be seeing him again soon.

He hated how he didn't completely hate the idea.

Twenty-Five

JULIEN

I t took three hours of brisk walking from the crash site to reach some semblance of civilisation. It took a further two hours to locate a rental car office.

The woman behind the counter gave them a horrified gasp when they staggered through the door. It might have had something to do with their bloodied clothes, or the thick layer of ash that still smothered their faces.

When Julien politely asked if she had any painkillers, she passed them wordlessly over the counter.

Though, shortly later, she was extremely reluctant to hand over the keys for the car Julien selected. Julien himself was reluctant to take the keys from her, because since when did he drive a Renault Clio? *Sacrilège.*

An attendant brought the car around for them. It was a good thing they didn't still have possession of their two dead bodies, because the tiny boot wasn't up to the job of housing even half of one.

Julien slid into the driver's seat. He was already cramped as hell. The tacky plastic interior only added to the insult, and the faint odour of cheap air freshener almost made him gag. He opened his mouth—

"Don't," Cinn warned. "Just drive."

Julien pulled out onto the road with a rough jerk, gritting his teeth at the Clio's attempt at acceleration. "I could pedal faster than this," he muttered.

And so began their very slow journey back to Talwacht. Although he originally intended to drive flat out, no stops, Julien's eyes kept betraying him by fluttering shut. To avoid car crash part two, he pulled over to sleep, although the experience of trying to nap in the hire car was anything but refreshing.

It was mid-morning by the time they reached Darcy's cottage, avoiding Cinn's house, lest any more badly trained assassins pop up. They'd rung Darcy to forewarn her from a payphone before collecting the car. She'd been surprisingly sympathetic about Maz. But then, the car *was* her daily ride to Auri.

Elliot's motorcycle claimed its usual spot outside Darcy's, frost spreading like cracks across its mirrors. When they reached the living room, it was as if they'd never left—Darcy was sprawled out on the worn armchair near the fireplace, one leg draped over the side, a book in hand. Elliot perched on the edge of the sofa, his hands extended towards the flames.

Darcy looked up from her book. "You two look like shit."

"Thanks, Darce."

She turned a page. "Let Cinn have the first shower, else you'll steal all the hot water and his will be cold."

"You know, I'm beginning to wonder why we came here."

"Because you have literally nowhere else to go?"

Darcy grinned at Julien.

He crossed the room to kiss both her cheeks.

Ten minutes later, Cinn returned, looking slightly cleaner, although the gash on his forehead looked more prominent now that his skin was grime free. He scowled when he caught Julien staring at it, tugging his beanie down to hide it. "No, it doesn't need looking at. Neither does my arm."

"So, you guys really took out two people?" Elliot said, then whistled.

That particular delight already felt like a lifetime ago. Julien leaned his head against a bookshelf, his eyes slowly closing.

"He did," Cinn confirmed. The pride in his voice made Julien feel nauseous, the image of the bullets unexpectedly exploding ricocheting around his mind. Cinn could protest that the fragment that hit his arm caused 'just a scratch' all he liked. Julien wouldn't forget it in a hurry.

"So, it wasn't only you two off having all the fun." Darcy closed her book shut with a snap, then leaned forward. "Tell them, Elliot."

"Yeah…" Elliot began. "So I tracked down that dude who was stalking us. The one Cinn overheard Eleanor tearing into. He's been tailing us for months. It was a really weird exchange. He claimed he wanted to be caught. Introduced himself as well. Admitted everything."

"That's weird as fuck. Does he not want to work for Eleanor any more? She sounded proper pissed at him," said Cinn.

"Well, I asked that, but he said some random rubbish I didn't understand. Then he left it by telling me to wait for a message."

Darcy laughed. "But the best bit is—"

A loud cough from Elliot cut her off.

"What?" asked Julien.

The other two side-eyed each other, then kept mute. Without warning, Darcy's fire crackled intensely, sending sparks dancing across the cottage floor. One landed on Julien's trouser leg, singeing it slightly—as if his poor clothes hadn't been through enough.

The flames flickered and danced. A small piece of parchment slowly materialised within the glowing embers, rising from the hearth, pulled from the depths of the fire itself. It drifted gently onto the stone.

Elliot dove from the sofa to snatch it up, knocking Julien rather rudely out of the way.

"Hey!"

Ignoring Julien, Elliot poured over the note, his face falling slightly. "It's not that interesting. Just a location and time."

"How is that not interesting?" Julien seized the paper. The note read: *Midnight. Where the shadows guard the ancient whispers.*

"Oh, come on." Cinn read the note over Julien's shoulder. "What's that supposed to mean? Is he having a laugh?"

"What? It's pretty obvious," said Darcy, in that infuriating know-it-all voice she knew they hated.

Julien refused to ask her, so instead said, "Should we go, though?"

Elliot's head whipped towards him. "What? Why not?"

"Well, Cinn and I have almost died twice in the last two days. This might be a third time unlucky sort of thing."

Cinn frowned. "Elliot said this guy is on our side."

"What? What *side*?" Julien retorted. "Our 'side' is just us wanting to live."

"I agree with Cinn." Elliot claimed the parchment back, to flap it in the air. "We have to see what this is all about."

"Alternatively, let's all pack our bags and do a beach holiday in the Bahamas. I hear it's nice this time of year."

Darcy bopped Julien on the head with her book. "Stop. We're going and that's that. You've got twelve hours to get over it, or you can stay here and sulk."

Julien pouted at Darcy, who sounded confused about how things worked around here. "I thought I was the leader of this ragtag group of merry men."

Darcy let out a laugh so exaggerated and theatrical, it echoed through the room like a villain in a pantomime. "Oh, you do make me laugh!"

"There he is." Elliot jerked his head towards a dark figure leaning against the library's portico. "There's Malik."

Oui, there he was, the mysterious American man who'd apparently had the edge on them for months.

Malik peeled himself away from the column, walking a few paces to greet them. It was a moonless midnight, the street lit only by a pair of lumenmote columns either side of the building. Julien studied the man in the dim light. He hated to admit it, but the guy didn't look the slightest bit familiar.

The four of them stood opposite Malik, a silent impasse.

"Hold on." Cinn screwed up his face, looking between Malik and Elliot, who was hanging back in an odd, hesitant manner. "Aren't you the one from New Year's? The one Elliot chucked up all over?"

Elliot groaned, and Malik grinned at him, a sudden flash of white teeth. "He owes me new shoes."

Julien stared at him again. *Non*, his face definitely didn't ring any bells from that night. But then, by the time Elliot had reached peak drunkenness, Julien was solely focussed on physically restraining Cinn, who kept trying to request songs from the DJ that nobody wanted to hear. Genuinely, nobody.

"What have you been playing at, mate, messing with us like this?" Cinn demanded. "Was that you in Paris yesterday?"

Malik tilted his head to one side. "Yesterday? No, I can't say that it was. I was too busy with Elliot here. Look, if you just follow me, all will become clear."

"Follow you where, into the library?" Julien eyed the dark building dubiously. Maybe he was still bitter that Darcy had deciphered the ridiculous clue.

"No." Malik barked a laugh. "Auri's library would be way too obvious. This was just the meeting spot to see if you'd actually show up."

Malik seemed less of a dangerous assassin about to knife them, and more of an annoying prick, so Julien humoured him.

"Where are we going, then? We don't have all night, and you've already wasted our time dragging us out here," Julien said coolly.

"It's a bit of a drive, I'm afraid," Malik said, then strolled on past them without looking back.

Julien already wanted to punch this guy. He met Elliot's gaze, silently asking him, '*Who is this clown?*' but Elliot only shrugged, not giving Julien a second glance before jogging to catch up with Malik.

Dropping his voice low, Julien fell into step with Darcy. "I don't trust Elliot's judgement on this. This guy has got him bewitched somehow. He barely knows him."

All he received in reply was Darcy's indecipherable look, so Julien shut up and dutifully followed Malik down the path, heading back towards the car park.

When Julien unlocked the rental car, Malik stopped short. "What happened to your nice car? I thought we were riding in that."

Malik sounded so genuinely disappointed, Julien had to laugh.

"You definitely picked the wrong time to stop stalking us. If we'd had some backup yesterday, maybe Maz would have survived."

Malik directed them out of Auri, through the countryside and the town centre, constantly looking behind them to see if they were being followed. Then, they took a convoluted route around the northern residential area.

Cinn tapped on the window. "We're almost back at my house!"

"Yeah. That's not a coincidence."

Quiet for a moment, Cinn then asked, "Have you watched me through my window?" to which Malik violently shook his head in a very unconvincing way.

They drove on. Just when Julien thought they were genuinely heading to Cinn's house of all places, Malik instructed Julien to pull the Clio up to the kerb outside a small grocery shop, complete with grimy windows, faded posters and peeling paint.

"This is us."

Julien turned off the engine, then stared at Malik. What on earth was going on here? He half expected some sort of camera crew to jump out and announce they were all on a prank show.

"This *corner shop*?" Cinn gave a disbelieving huff. "I come here every other day for cigarettes!"

"And that awful store-brand lemon shower gel you love so much," Malik said, wrinkling his nose. "Can't forget that."

"It's shut," Julien informed him.

"Of course it's shut. It's past midnight!" Malik jumped out, slamming his door.

Julien twisted in the driver's seat. "Do we take our leave and run now? I'm sorry, Elliot, I know you two have your little thing going on, but I make a habit of not trusting Americans. I don't fancy murdering him if he's led us to some sort of underground torture dungeon."

"Yes, I'm sure there are whips and chains waiting for us in between the packets of crisps," Darcy deadpanned, before opening her door. "Come on."

Leading the way, Malik took them around the back of the shop, revealing a narrow alleyway cluttered with discarded crates. Stale dampness clung to the air. The shadows tucked a heavy metal door into the brickwork, nearly rendering it invisible. The door had no discernible handle.

Malik paused briefly, glancing back at them with a look that offered no reassurance, before pulling out a small, sleek device from his pocket. Its subtle blue glow alluded to motetech in play. He waved it in front of the door, and with a soft, mechanical click, it swung open.

"Follow me," Malik said, slipping into the darkness.

Julien hesitated, his gaze shifting to Elliot, who nodded firmly before stepping through the doorway. The others followed, with Julien bringing up the rear, feeling the weight of each step as they descended a narrow flight of stairs. The further they went, the darker and cooler it became, the faint hum of hidden mechanisms filling the silence.

Malik moved confidently, leading them down a series of turns that seemed more labyrinthine with each corner.

Each step frayed Julien's wrought nerves. This frustrated him. There was no logical reason to be growing more and more tense. This nut job was probably just going to lead them to a dead end, then laugh at them. The on-the-edge feeling was very likely a continued response to their Paris trauma. Yet knowing that didn't uncoil the tension in his gut or silence the alarm bells ringing in his ears.

"Come on," Cinn hissed, reaching back to grab Julien's arm, as he'd started to lag behind the group.

But he could see another door, this one far more imposing, with a panel beside it.

He knew there was *something* behind it.

Julien had no energy for any more *somethings*.

None, *nada*.

He allowed Cinn to drag him along as Malik placed his palm on the panel. After a brief pause, the door slid open with a quiet hiss, revealing a dimly lit corridor beyond. The atmosphere inside was charged, the air buzzing.

Julien's heart pounded in his chest. He was too tired for this next goose chase. He should have waited in the car.

"We're almost there," Malik tossed over his shoulder, his voice low. "This is the last door."

Malik must've led them about three floors underground, all in all. Your average grocery shop basement, this was not.

"Are you okay?" Cinn murmured into Julien's ear, having possibly realised that no, Julien was, in fact, not okay. He hadn't been okay in a long time. A very long time.

Unable to muster the energy to reply, Julien watched as Malik knelt down to open a wooden trapdoor, of all things. What now? Were they descending into the nine circles of Hell?

Malik sank down into the darkness first, followed by Elliot. Darcy finally had the good sense to look afraid—glancing nervously down at the ladder—so Julien pushed his way past her to go next.

As he climbed down the cold metal rungs of the ladder, the sound of machines whirring softly reached his ears, growing louder the further he descended. A faint blue light pulsed rhythmically from below, casting eerie shadows on the walls.

Julien jumped the last two rungs to land on a concrete floor. The room was empty, except for a lone figure seated in the centre.

The chair slowly swivelled around.

He locked eyes with its occupant.

Now he was looking at her, Julien wasn't sure who else he would possibly have expected Malik to lead them to.

But what he *wasn't* expecting were the words that tumbled effortlessly out of Eleanor's lips.

"Welcome to the Arcane Purifier's headquarters."

Twenty-Six

JULIEN

Behind him, Darcy gave a shriek of shock which she quickly muffled.

Elliot nervously chuckled, as if preparing to hear that this was all a strange joke.

Cinn mumbled curses under his breath.

All Julien could do was stare at Eleanor, waiting for the puzzle pieces to click into place.

They didn't.

"Explain," Julien said, his eyes unable to leave the woman's face. "Explain what is going on before I lose my mind."

Eleanor adjusted her thick-rimmed glasses. "Take a seat."

A stack of metal chairs sat in a corner. Malik leapt into action, placing them in a semicircle in front of Eleanor.

Julien couldn't bring himself to move. Nothing made sense. His world had been knocked off its axis, sent zooming off into the stratosphere. "Since when are *you* a part of AP?"

"Child, I *am* AP. Now, sit down."

Julien's heart was pounding in his chest, an off-rhythm thump that sent blood rushing through his ears. Cinn pulled on Julien's coat sleeve until he gave in, perching on the edge of a cool metal chair. Silence spread between the lot of them. Julien clenched and unclenched his jaw, waiting for Eleanor to begin talking. By Christ she had a fuck-tonne of explaining to do.

"Where do you want me to start?" Eleanor said at last.

Everyone turned their eyes on Julien—gazes weighted with a mixture of expectation and caution. He felt their stares like a pressure against his skin. Cinn stopped tugging on Julien's coat, his fingers still hooked on his sleeve as though ready to pull again if needed.

Why? How? How long? Why had Eleanor summoned them all here? Why now?

"Béatrice."

Julien's sister's beautiful broad smile unfurled itself from the shadows of his mind.

Why her? Why couldn't it have been me? Why did she have to leave me?

It was where all this started. They were the only answers that really mattered to him, in the end.

"I want you to know that I never sought her out for this, Julien. She found her way to AP of her own accord."

"You reassured me her death was a random accident!" Julien cried, not bothering to mask the tidal wave of emotion pouring out of him. "You told me to stop looking for answers!"

"Yes!" Eleanor bit back, running her hand over her tight grey ponytail. "Because Béatrice was dead, and it seemed rather insulting to Isabelle's memory to get both of her children killed!"

Julien considered Eleanor's expression, seeking small cracks of remorse in the face of his mother's close friend.

"Father Gérard rang shortly after you left his church." Eleanor composed herself, smoothing down invisible creases on her trousers. "Did you know, Julien, that your mother only told two people about your extraordinary abilities? Myself, and Father Gérard. Not your father, your own flesh and blood."

"My father doesn't care about flesh and blood," Julien spat. He couldn't wait any longer. He had to say it. Had to know for sure. "He killed Béatrice, didn't he?"

Out of the corner of his vision, Elliot and Darcy exchanged devastated looks. A hand found its way into his own, Cinn's fingers interlocking to squeeze tightly.

"Yes," Eleanor said softly. "I believe he did."

Now, Julien *could* bombard her with cries of outrage, demanding to know why his father was still walking around a free man. But he wasn't stupid. That wasn't how the world worked, not when you were as rich and powerful as Lucien Montaigne. Not with his connections, with half the consortium in his pocket.

"With her locket."

"Yes."

"Because she..." Julien trailed off.

Eleanor sighed. "Do you remember meeting L, that day you found us at the crevice, after the earthquake? Well, Béatrice was working closely with them."

A sudden recollection dropped into Julien's lap. "Hey! That L person told me that *you'd* murdered Béatrice!"

Eleanor's eyebrows knitted together lightning fast. "What? You're mistaken."

"*Non*, I..." Thinking back to it, that wasn't exactly what L said. "They said your name!"

"Yes, because L and I have had several heated arguments about involving Montaignes in AP business! They were likely trying to force my hand, dragging you into it against my will."

"So, it's L's fault that Béatrice got involved in AP?"

Eleanor sighed. "Julien, the sooner you stop trying to assign blame for everything, the sooner you can start to move forward. But yes. L recruited her, specifically because they couldn't resist the direct link to your father that Béatrice offered." Her lip curled up in disgust. "Béatrice hinted to L that she'd made significant progress in their line of enquiry. Then, she was summoned to the Philippines on her aid mission, and died before she could meet with L again."

"Line of enquiry..." Elliot repeated. "What was L getting her to do? Béatrice barely spoke to Lucien, especially in the last year before she died. She could hardly suddenly cosy up to him for information."

"Which was why she made herself so suspicious, and ended up paying the price."

Nausea rose inside Julien, mixing with the simmering rage that had embedded itself within him since the church. His father would get his just desserts for Béatrice if it was the last thing Julien did.

Cinn cleared his throat. "The priest told us about the machine. He called it 'the dark machine.'"

"Yes," Eleanor said, on a sigh. "That's the one. *Machina Tenebris*. Béatrice was supporting us by sourcing information about it."

"Father Gérard couldn't even promise me it was real," snapped Julien. "Béatrice might have died for nothing."

"I can assure you, it's definitely real. Surely the fact that Lucien had her removed suggests she discovered something. Regardless, we have substantive evidence the machine exists."

Eleanor wheeled her desk chair to the side, presenting them with a wall of computer monitors, all blue background and white text. She stood up, rolling her shoulders back in a long stretch. Malik stepped forward, but she waved him away.

A keyboard terminal with a dozen wires flying around it sat on a desk. Eleanor pressed a few buttons, and the largest display unit changed into a line graph.

"The obscure rumours about this mysterious machine started almost twelve years ago now, but we believe it was fully operational the day before your mother's death."

"What does it do, please?" asked Darcy, ever the epitome of polite.

More tapping of buttons on the keyboard, more displays show-ing wiggly graphs that Julien would need his glasses to read. Then Eleanor reached into her pocket and removed a small metal bar, identical to the one Malik used to unlock the door. "In the last ten years, motecells have wormed their way into everything." She held up the bar. It was seamless—there was no need to replace a motecell, usually. They were designed to recharge themselves by drawing am-bient motes from the air, ensuring a near-endless supply of power.

"The invention of motecells shortly predates the rise in climatic activity, both of which shortly follow the *Machina Tenebris* project being completed. AP believes the machine draws power from the shadowrealm to fuel the production of them."

Julien rubbed a hand over his bleary eyes. Being nearly two a.m. in this dingy secret laboratory was hardly ideal for making sense of Eleanor's squiggly graphs that all followed the same curve.

"Okay. This... machine. The motecells. The natural disasters. Keep talking."

"Lucien registered his patent for an early prototype of the mote-cell in winter, nineteen eighty-five." Eleanor moved to the next graph on another display. "Production begins the following year, coinciding with the Kamchatka Peninsula eruptions and the Horn of Africa experiencing their worst drought on record. We finish up eighty-five with back-to-back tsunamis across Southeast Asia, and then, in eighty-six..."

Eleanor sounded like she'd made this entire speech many, many times. She walked them through another couple of years, constantly referring to her motecell growth graph until Julien's eyes hurt.

"Okay, point proven," said Julien. "Your data makes a great argu-ment, I'm sure. So where is this machine? I'll take great joy in taking a sledgehammer to it myself."

"I've already explained to you that we don't know." Eleanor pursed her lips as if Julien was wasting her time, even though she was the one who had dragged them there.

Julien moved on to another thought. "Hold on. These motecells are used in motetech all over the world. Every single production company has access to them, somehow."

"HorizonTech produces and distributes every single one from its Paris site. But your father owns almost every company in the world, Julien, as you know." Eleanor sounded more irritable by the minute.

"How come you think this machine thing draws power from the shadowrealm?" Cinn stared at the array of glowing displays.

"Noir thinks—"

Cinn cut her off with a splutter. "Noir's in on this too?!"

"What do you mean *in on this*? This isn't a joke. We're a team, working from facts. And Noir presents a solid case that the umbraphage emergence is in direct response to this." Eleanor gestured wildly to the room at large, appearing for a moment like a crazed old lady.

Cocking his head at Julien, Cinn became lost in thought. "Huh. That kind of tracks, right?"

"So, what now?" Julien asked Eleanor, who'd finally sat down again.

"What?"

"You obviously brought us here for a reason. What do you want us to do?"

Eleanor stared at him like he was an alien. "Lie low and stay out of trouble!"

A groan sounded from beside him—Elliot shared Julien's feelings.

"And I only brought you here because Malik did such a poor job observing you, he made matters worse."

Malik shuffled on one foot, a sheepish grin crossing his lips.

"Are you aware my father tried to snatch Cinn from our hotel room in Paris? And then sent a car to run us off the road? All after he wanted Cinn's 'help' with something."

Eleanor leaned back in her chair. It took a fair few seconds before she replied, "No. That's interesting."

"It's not *interesting*!" Julien raised his voice to her. It was one of the few times he'd ever done that.

"No, no, sorry. You've misunderstood me. I meant that Noir would be very interested to hear that. I'll see what I can do about getting someone stationed near your house."

Cinn's metal chair shot forward with a loud scrape. "I'm not having a bodyguard."

"That's good, because I can't give you one."

A sudden, piercing beep interrupted Cinn's next words, erupting from one of the machines with an urgent, grating rhythm. The sound was sharp and relentless, echoing through the room with an intensity that commanded immediate attention.

Malik shot across the room like his life depended on it. His hands flew over a console, tapping and swiping with a speed and precision that was almost impossible to follow. Symbols and numbers flashed on the screen, an incomprehensible blur. Diagrams and charts followed, with Malik's face a picture of fierce focus.

"What's going on?" Elliot jumped up to stand behind him.

Eleanor rose to her feet with the energy of someone who'd just climbed a mountain, and was about to climb another one. For a moment, she and Malik consulted the screens, murmuring about fluctuating pressure systems and much more Julien couldn't quite catch.

"I think it's alerted them to rising levels of climatic activity," Darcy informed them, once it became clear Eleanor wasn't going to turn around.

"This is bad," Eleanor said, pressing her fingers against the screen.

"How long, ma'am?" murmured Malik.

"A couple of days? Three at most? Sound the alarm at dawn. We'll need to prepare teams. Maybe we'll finally get something this time, with events of this magnitude all happening at once."

Julien jerked his head towards the ladder. Whatever Eleanor and Malik were discussing, he doubted Eleanor wanted to explain it to them.

"We'll be off then."

"I'll be in contact," Eleanor threw over her shoulder.

Elliot looked like he was going to reach for Malik's arm until he caught Julien watching him, Julien's eyebrows raised in a daring sort of way. Elliot's expression darkened into a glower, his arm dropping before he marched to the ladder.

The climb back to ground level was a quiet one. Everyone was either stunned into silence or as tired as Julien. His eyes drooped by the time they reached the heavy metal door and spilled out onto the pavement. Julien glanced at the corner shop exterior. The revelation of finding Eleanor in some sort of secret AP basement had aged him about twenty years.

Still, at least many things made more sense now. Yet there was one question still left unanswered, looming large in Julien's picture of events: why hadn't Béatrice talked to him when she started getting wrapped up in it all?

Had L bullied her into silence? Did she think Julien wouldn't approve of her involvement?

"I think she was trying to protect you," said Cinn into his ear, making him jump.

"What?"

Cinn laughed. "I can see what you're thinking about. It's written all over your face." He nudged his hip against Julien's. "Plus, me and her have our bond. So I know her now. You were always protecting her. From your dad and stuff. So she wanted to protect you for once."

Julien swallowed around a thick lump that prevented any attempt to reply. He blinked rapidly, pushing back the sudden sting of emotion. He took a shaky breath, his chest heavy with a strange mix of intense gratitude towards Cinn and the aching regret that he'd never quite know the whole truth about Béatrice's decisions.

But as he caught Cinn shyly smiling at him, looking pleased with himself, Julien understood he could grow to be okay with that.

Cinn and his beanie hat disappeared into the Clio's rear seats.

There were much more important things to be worrying about.

Twenty-Seven

CINN

Exhausted wasn't a strong enough word for how tired Cinn felt after the roller-coaster of the last two days.

Cinn and Julien ended up back at Cinn's house after all, upon Darcy pointing out that staying at her cottage had the unfortunate side effect of endangering her as well.

Once they'd climbed into bed, Cinn refused point-blank to leave his bed before noon the next day, and then only left his room to cook or smoke.

Julien spent the day at the windowsill, twitching the curtain back every five seconds to survey the road, awaiting the imaginary next round of assailants.

By nightfall, Cinn lost his patience.

"Enough! If they come, they come. They're hardly going to walk down the road all obvious, are they?"

Julien heaved a sigh. He drew the paisley curtains closed, then put his hands in the pockets of the hoodie he'd 'borrowed' from Cinn back in London. There was no claiming it back now. Julien wore it religiously anytime they were in the house. Cinn had, so far, done an exceptional job of not teasing him about it. Probably because the sight of him in it, while deeply amusing, filled Cinn with a quiet warmth—his chest felt strangely light, like he was in on a joke only the two of them understood.

With a pout, Julien said, "I'm not sure this is how you show appreciation to the person you love who is trying to keep you safe."

Cinn adopted a pointedly confused expression. "Who said anything about *love*?"

A stray pillow found its way into Julien's hands, then Cinn's face.

On the bed, Cinn lazily swung his leg around to lie on his side. "Oh, right, yeah, you did mention something about that. A few times, actually."

One moment Julien was by the window, and the next, he'd pounced on Cinn, pushing him backwards, pinning him to the bed with his full body weight.

"I don't care how many times I've said it." Julien's eyes were dark, his expression deadly serious.

Cinn stilled, captivated by the curve of Julien's lips, the flash of his dimples.

"I am..." Julien's hand gently brushed Cinn's hair from his forehead. "Quite frankly..." He leaned down, his breath warm against Cinn's lips. "So fucking in love with you, it hurts."

Cinn's heart stuttered at the thick emotion clouding Julien's voice. "But I don't want it to hurt," Cinn whispered. And then, "I'm not going to hurt you."

"I know, *mon amour*," Julien replied, his voice thick with sincerity, and Cinn relaxed, pulling his apparently sappy-as-fuck boyfriend down to capture his lips.

As their mouths met, Cinn's chest became aglow with a starburst of affection that threatened to overwhelm him.

Julien's lips were soft, pliant, moulding perfectly to the contours of his own. The kiss said more than Cinn could ever put into pretty words for Julien. It spoke of promises, of tomorrows, of all the futures they might have together.

Cinn's eyes fluttered closed, lashes sweeping against his cheeks, as he poured every ounce of his devotion, his love, his very soul, into the press of their lips. Julien made a low hum, a needy sound, the vibrations thrumming against Cinn's mouth.

This feeling he'd forever savour—the velvety feel of Julien's lips on his, the vanilla taste of the chocolate chip cookies Cinn had baked for him earlier. Cinn could drown in this feeling. Was drowning in it. Cinn reached to find Julien's hips, fingertips digging into the firm muscle. He needed to anchor himself—he was submerged, blissfully so, in the feel of Julien, the taste, the scent.

They kissed, and kissed, and kissed, until the world fell away, until there was nothing but the slide of their lips, the rasp of their breaths, the thrum of their racing hearts. Cinn's lungs burned. His head spun, but he didn't care. Not when Julien was kissing him like he was the very air he needed to survive.

Cinn's lips were swollen, almost painfully so, when Julien finally drew back. He chased their absence, not ready to be done with the intoxication they offered, but Julien gentled him, pressing their foreheads together.

Julien trailed kisses to Cinn's ear before taking his lobe between his teeth. He slid his hand down to Cinn's tracksuit bottoms.

"Wait." Cinn caught Julien's hand with his. "I want to... Can I fuck you?" He cringed at the crassness. "I mean, can I... make love to you?" *Even worse.* Cinn's face burned in horror at his own awkwardness. Where had this even randomly come from? He'd been enjoying the sex he had with Julien, enormously so. But a sudden overwhelming urge to experience *everything* with him had him asking the question.

Julien shook with laughter above him.

"Hey!"

Abruptly, Julien pulled back, the dim light revealing a flush of surprise colouring his cheeks. He pressed his finger to Cinn's lips, mirth sparkling in his eyes. "Shh. I'm sorry. But your face, though."

Cinn's ever-so-amusing face scowled at Julien.

"*Oui*," Julien said, and it took Cinn a moment to realise he was answering him. "I would love that, *mon amour*."

Cinn swallowed, attempting to calm his stuttering heart.

"But, two conditions." Julien ran his hand down Cinn's bare chest, brushing his fingers around the shape of each tattoo that he surely knew from memory. "One. First I get to worship this beautiful body you've given me the privilege of loving." Cinn's skin prickled in anticipation, his body already responding to the promise in Julien's words.

"And the second?" he asked, breathless.

"I'm still on top."

The wink Julien gave him would ordinarily have infuriated him, but Cinn was well and truly under Julien's spell now.

Biting his bottom lip, Cinn nodded. Julien slipped out of his clothes, folding his stolen hoodie carefully before placing it on a chair. The room was warm—Cinn was continuing to take advantage of his free heating—yet an intense shiver shot through him at the sight of Julien's body uncovered, his cock already semi-erect.

Julien slowly peeled off Cinn's tracksuit bottoms, revealing his own hardening, aching length. Coiling his hand around it, Julien lightly stroked it before pressing his lips against it, mouthing up, then down. Cinn's cock gave a throb of appreciation, his hips coming up to meet Julien.

"Are you going to make it really good for me?" Julien's voice asked, a low growl that went straight to Cinn's groin.

"Yes," was all Cinn could rasp in reply. Besides still being on top, Julien clearly had no intention of stopping the dirty talk Cinn found immeasurably arousing, even if he didn't have it in him to reciprocate.

Julien engulfed his dick in response, surrounding it with rapturous wet heat. His tongue flattened, pushing up against the sensitive skin.

Cinn gasped, thrusting up to meet Julien's mouth. His boyfriend chuckled around his cock, then slid it out of his mouth, giving the tip a strong suck as he did so. Julien flashed Cinn his brilliant white teeth, before climbing up his body, his hand quickly replacing his mouth before Cinn had a chance to vocalise his complaint.

Languid, delicate strokes followed. Cinn opened his mouth, a deep moan escaping, only to be swallowed up by the beautiful man on top of him. Slipping one arm around Julien's back to press against the curve of his spine, Cinn cupped the back of Julien's head, tangling his fingers in Julien's riot of blond waves, already a mess from their kissing. He dug his nails into Julien's scalp and was rewarded with a throaty hum.

Julien dipped his head, his mouth skimming along the line of Cinn's collarbone, teeth grazing the sensitive skin. His hands mapped the planes of Cinn's body as reverent and worshipful as he promised, reducing Cinn to a trembling mess. His tattoos, his scars, passing tenderly over each of his healing wounds, the dips and curves of his muscle. Goosebumps rose in the wake of Julien's fingertips exploring every inch of his skin.

"*Si beau,*" Julien murmured, almost to himself. "I want you to be mine. All mine." A thimble of desperation leaked into his words.

It felt wrong, Julien's small sliver of insecurity. All Cinn wanted was for it to disappear, to never return. He wanted every point where Julien touched him to be a brand, searing his skin. "I *am* yours," Cinn said, voice rough. "All of me, every part. You can have all of me, Julien. I'm yours, yours, *yours...*" The words poured out of him, a litany, a promise.

How had Julien already reduced him to this? He wasn't even inside Julien yet, and already he felt drunk on sensations, on the feel of Julien's body against his, the slide of his thighs against his own.

Julien's eyes glowed, pupils blown with desire. He pushed himself into Cinn, sliding their dicks deliciously together, eliciting another gasp from Cinn. "I can't wait any longer," he said suddenly, reaching for the top drawer of the nightstand.

Julien reached for the lube, but Cinn was quicker, his hand closing around the bottle. "Let me." He pried it from Julien's grasp.

Though Julien's eyes widened, he swiftly obeyed, sliding off Cinn, dipping the mattress with his weight. A small, hesitant smile crossed his lips. Trusting. Vulnerable.

"I've got you."

Julien tipped his head back to face the ceiling. When the wet heat of Cinn's tongue pressed against his entrance instead of cold lube, Julien's back arched off the bed. Cinn flattened his tongue, sending it exploring the entire length of Julien's crack. Then he licked circles around and around the edge of Julien's hole.

"Fuck! What are you doing?" Julien rasped.

Cinn didn't respond, too focussed on his task. Cinn pushed Julien's knees up higher, his tongue swirling around Julien's rim, the tip breaching him slightly before retreating. His pointed tongue met resistance at first, then Julien's ring relaxed.

Julien hissed in pleasure, clutching madly at Cinn's hair, tangling in between his fingers before pulling hard. A surge of raw emotion—lust, need, desperation—pulsed between them like an electric current, setting Cinn's nerves alight in perfect sync with Julien's unravelling control.

Saliva poured from Cinn's mouth, soaking Julien. He reached for the lube, coating his fingers liberally, then gently pushed Julien's thighs apart. Julien's breaths hitched, his nails scraping oh-so sensually across Cinn's scalp as Cinn slowly, delicately, worked a finger inside him, all the way to the knuckle.

A whimper slipped from Julien's mouth. A demanding one. "Give me another." He tried to shuffle downwards.

Cinn shuffled up to kiss him on the tip of his nose. "Not yet."

A low, tortured moan was Julien's reply. Cinn's cock agreed with him—it was twitching jealously at the feeling of his tight, silken heat.

"All good things."

His impatient lover clenched around the intrusion. Cinn slid his lone finger in and out, in and out, rubbing and stretching every inch of him with gentle caresses that had Julien calling him every unpleasant name under the sun.

"*Espèce de... Je te déteste! Putain!*"

At least, Cinn assumed they were unpleasant.

"You'll think better of it next time you make me beg for it, huh?"

Julien hissed at him, so snakelike, Cinn almost laughed.

But Cinn wasn't cruel, and Julien was more than ready, his muscles completely relaxed, pliant. Cinn added a second, crooking and twisting, searching—

Julien's back arched, his head falling back as a wanton moan fell from his lips. "There, fuck, right—"

Cinn's lips curled into a smug grin as he rubbed mercilessly, sending Julien more wild than he'd ever seen him—eyes wide as saucers, hair a frazzled mess from writhing around.

"Please, Cinn, I—"

"Shh, I've got you—"

Cinn's words cut off as Julien abruptly sat up. He pushed Cinn off him, hard, before climbing on top of him. He thrust his hips against Cinn before capturing his wrists, pinning them by his head. His eyes reminded Cinn of a wild wolf. A hungry wild wolf.

Cinn swallowed.

"I need..."

Julien didn't complete his thought, his molten gaze speaking volumes.

Cinn's heart raced, his body thrumming, as Julien snatched up the lube. The cool slide of fingers as he slicked Cinn's dick had him trembling with need.

He'd only last a few seconds inside Julien at this rate. Cinn sucked his cheek between his teeth and bit down, hard. There was no way he wasn't going to make this as amazing for Julien as he always did for him.

Cinn only realised his eyes had closed when Julien brushed his knuckles over his eyebrow piercing, saying, *"S'il te plaît?"*

He opened them, forcing himself to hold Julien's gaze, though the intensity of it had him in a chokehold.

With a firm, steady hand, Julien lined Cinn's dick up, nudging his head against his entrance. The tip popped in. A simultaneous groan passed between them.

Then, ever so slowly, he lowered himself on Cinn's waiting cock, like he was savouring every inch.

"Cinn..." Julien said his name like it was a precious treasure. Then his head fell back, as he finally seated himself fully.

Circling his hips, Cinn's eyes nearly rolled back, his mouth falling open at the perfect tightness. "Fuck—" Cinn's fingers dug into the meat of Julien's thighs, the give of his flesh, still keeping that perfect eye contact Julien couldn't cope without.

But fuck, it had never felt like *this* before, being inside someone. But then, what he had with Julien felt so different, so uniquely theirs, that shouldn't have come as a surprise.

The tendons in Julien's neck strained as he arched his back. Then a tiny grunt of what might have been pain passed his lips, and Cinn looked at him in alarm, but Julien shook his head. "Fuck me," he said, on one unsteady breath. "*And* make love to me. I want everything."

Cinn thrust up, one fluid movement that caused Julien to cry out, pressing a palm against his chest. Cinn's heart pounded impossibly fast, his skin flushed, as Julien moved. He set a slow, sensual pace, rolling his hips, undulating. Cinn's own hips snapped up, meeting Julien's downward motions.

Another thrust, then another, each matched by Julien's cries, certainly of ecstasy now. He'd never been so noisy. That was usually Cinn's job.

Fuck. He'd gotten distracted and stopped moving. Julien leaned down to press his lips against Cinn's cheek, the wetness from the tip of Julien's cock sliding across his stomach.

"Allow me," Julien said, a smile audible in his breathless voice.

Steadying himself with a palm on Cinn's chest, Julien began pushing up before impaling himself on Cinn's cock again and again, a punishing rhythm that had Cinn seeing stars. So many stars. Sliding his hands over the contours of Julien's beautiful body, Cinn gripped his hips, guiding him up and down.

And there Cinn was, so close to coming, though Julien couldn't be far off, his face slack with pleasure. A part of Cinn wanted to tell Julien to slow down, to make it last as long as possible. Being connected to Julien in this way was more than he could ever have hoped for.

But there would be a next time, and another. More times than he could possibly count.

Cinn thrust up, ever so slightly at first, and then more, and more, relishing the sensation of filling Julien up. He captured Julien's cock, pumping it in time with his thrusts.

"Come with me," Julien whispered, sounding very much on the edge.

Without any more warning, his lover screamed, hot cum painting Cinn's stomach in thick, creamy ropes.

Cinn needn't have worried after all.

No reason to hold back, Cinn gave in to the pull, allowing that pleasure to build and build until his balls were tightening. His thighs drew tight around Julien, drawing them ever closer together as he spilled gloriously inside him, Julien murmuring streams of praise as he did so.

The oxytocin ride was high. Cinn sank deep into the mattress, drowning in its soft embrace as waves of pleasure wrecked his body. He was helpless against the blackness that came for him.

When Cinn came to, it was to shivers, and Julien's name on his lips, urgent, needy. Julien repeatedly kissed him, stroking his hair as he brushed a warm cloth over his stomach and legs.

Cinn grabbed the nape of Julien's neck, dragging him to rest in the crook of his own. Julien sighed as he obliged, rubbing small circles across Cinn's hips as their breathing slowly steadied.

Eventually, Julien rolled off to lie beside him. Cinn turned onto his side. Julien looked the very definition of a complete mess, and pride seeped through Cinn. He'd long since given up comparing himself to Julien's many, *many,* but it certainly gave his ego a tiny bit of fuel to see Julien in such utter disarray. His golden princeling hair was a tangled mess, his lips swollen. He lay beside him, eyes unfocussed, murmuring nonsensical things under his breath. Sweat slicked his skin, glistening in the lamplight.

"What?" Julien eventually asked.

Cinn offered him a smug smirk. "Nothing."

"Am I not allowed to be dishevelled after the best sex of my life?"

Who cared if Julien was only saying it to be kind? Cinn would take it, thank you very much.

Cinn shuffled his head to rest it on the same pillow as Julien, leaving millimetres between their heads. "So that was alright, then?"

"Alright?" Julien kissed the tip of his nose. "Are you joking?" He drew back slightly, expression turning serious, then pressed his palm to Cinn's heart. "Because I wasn't. I've always enjoyed sex. Enjoyed it a lot. But sharing it with you is like nothing I've ever experienced. Because sex with you is fucking amazing. Hell, cuddling you is fucking amazing. Just being in the same room with you is enough for me. Will always be enough. You're enough, Cinn. You're everything. And I never want you to think otherwise, not for one second."

A dizzying warmth washed over Cinn, beginning in his chest and swiftly enveloping his entire body, making him feel as if he were levitating above and observing himself and Julien from a distance. "Okay," Cinn whispered in reply, smile aching his face. "You're everything to me, too."

Julien's speech appeared to drain him of his last shred of energy, and his eyes closed, though his grip on Cinn didn't lessen.

Some time later, Cinn, mapping the outline of Julien's collarbone, paused mid-stroke. "I want to ask you something."

"Hmmm?" Julien said, eyelashes fluttering in his doze.

Cinn untangled himself from the contortion of limbs they'd created. He crossed the room to open the small chest that came with the place. Locating the desired object, he returned to Julien, sitting cross-legged on the bed.

"Are you ready to wear this yet?" Cinn dangled Béatrice's locket in the air, spinning the cool silver chain around his finger. The oval-shaped locket's stars twinkled at him. "I think it might help you. And I miss seeing you in it. But only if you're ready."

A complicated mix of emotions passed over Julien's face, and Cinn tensed. He'd overstepped.

Julien reached for the locket, closing his hand over Cinn's. "*Merci*," he said. "I do miss wearing it."

When Julien slipped the necklace over his head, it fell straight back into place upon his chest. Cinn's face broke into a smile. *There we are.*

With a kiss to Cinn's forehead, Julien slid off the bed. He straightened his back, then his eyes darted towards the window. Cinn's heart plummeted. Julien's anxious expression was back. Was this Cinn's fault for giving him the locket?

"Come back to bed," Cinn pleaded. "I need you here."

Julien sounded genuinely sad when he replied, "I can't, *mon amour.*" He twitched back the curtain, resuming his eagle-eyed watch. "I'm not letting them hurt you again. I'd rather never sleep again."

"Both of the attacks were in Paris," Cinn protested.

"*Oui*, but he has men everywhere. Who knows if his stretch reaches Salvatore Gallo and the gendarmerie even?"

Trying to muffle his sigh, Cinn closed his eyes. "Wake me up in a bit then, and I'll have a turn. Don't stay up all night, you'll go mad."

Cinn stretched his arm out to Julien's side of the bed, now cold without him in it.

The pull of sleep beckoned him, tugging on the edges of his consciousness.

He loathed to leave Julien alone, glaring moodily out of the window.

Particularly as a feeling was growing in the pit of his stomach.

A prickling sensation, like something was slightly amiss.

But he could only fight sleep for so long before he succumbed to the darkness.

He would have to deal with whatever was on the other side, on the other side.

Twenty-Eight

Julien

It was half-past five in the morning when Julien was ready to leave.

The sun wouldn't rise for hours yet. By the time the first light touched Cinn's road, Julien would be dozens of miles away.

Staring down at Cinn's sleeping body in the fragment of moonlight—stark naked, entangled with the duvet as if it were a passionate lover—Julien wavered in his decision. It would be so much easier to unpack his bag, undress, slip back into the bed beside him. Hold his warm body close. Kiss the spiderweb on his shoulder. Be there when he woke up, giving Julien that small smile he always blessed him with, before pretending to be grumpy at being awake.

Instead, he was sentencing Cinn to wake up alone.

His heart gave a painful squeeze, as his mind conjured the image of the moment Cinn realised what he'd done.

Putain, he'd probably kill Cinn if he did this to him.

Julien was going to be in so much trouble.

But this was the only way to keep Cinn safe. The man who he loved more than anything. The person who, quite curiously, loved him back.

He'd keep him safe if it was the last thing he did.

Julien couldn't spend the rest of time at the window, anxiety coiling in his stomach, waiting for the next strike. He couldn't wait for Eleanor's half-baked promises of protection. *Non*, he needed to do what he always did, and take matters into his own hands. Be in charge of his own destiny.

Finding the hoodie he'd folded up earlier, Julien pulled it over his head. It would be cold on the journey, but mostly he needed the comfort it would provide. Cinn had no idea, but Julien had been routinely swapping the hoodie out with random identical ones Cinn left strewn all over his house. That way, it always smelled faintly of him.

Julien placed the note on the dresser.

He pulled the covers up over Cinn to cover more of his body.

He kissed his mop of brown curls, the tiniest bit too firmly.

Tempting fate.

Cinn didn't stir.

So, into the stillness of the bedroom, Julien whispered, "I'll be back soon, *mon amour*."

Twenty-Nine

Cinn

*C**rash!*

The sound of cupboards opening and shutting downstairs jolted Cinn awake. He pulled the covers over his head.

Bang!

Julien must have been messing around in Cinn's kitchen again, despite being banned since he ruined the best frying pan by scratching the non-stick coating with a metal whisk while making scrambled eggs. Could he not have waited for Cinn to cook him breakfast like he normally did?

He channelled his annoyance into a heavy sigh, then Cinn was ready to drag himself out of bed. Pulling on some tracksuit bottoms, he padded across the room. He froze when he saw a note propped up against the mirror, Julien's elegantly looped cursive handwriting filling the paper.

No.

Anxiety gripped him with an iron fist. Though he couldn't make out the words from across the room, his instincts told him whatever was written on it, he wasn't going to like it.

Let's get this over with.

He forced himself to take one step towards the note, then another.

He snatched up the paper like it had personally offended him.

Mon amour,

Don't be mad. I've gone back to Paris for a quick chat with father dearest. It's the only solution to keep you safe. I wish I could have said goodbye, but it's easier this way. Elliot is downstairs. I'll be back before you know it.

All my love,

Your Julien

P.S. I took the last two cookies for the road. Sorry.

Cinn re-read the note. Read it again. No, he wasn't misinterpreting Julien's outlandish calligraphy.

Julien had left him.

Julien had *left* him.

His heart sank like a stone in deep water, the cold realisation wrapping around him like a tightening noose. The world blurred, his mind teetering on the edge of panic as the words echoed relentlessly in his head.

A quick chat with father dearest.

Now, Cinn was no expert on conflict resolution, but after Julien had threatened to kill his father several times during his breakdown at the church, he wasn't convinced a 'quick chat' was the likely result of Julien paying his father a visit.

Pressing two fingers to his temple, Cinn calculated possible outcomes. Best case—Julien killed his father. Worst case—that fucker killed Julien.

Great stuff.

Another noise downstairs. *Elliot.*

Cinn pounded down the stairs to find him rooting around in the fridge. In one hand, he held the bowl of leftover lasagna Cinn had cooked yesterday.

"What the hell, mate?" Cinn all but shouted at him, waving the note in the air.

Elliot's face twisted into a pained grimace, like he'd just bitten into a lemon, his eyes darting nervously between the lasagna and the note in Cinn's hand. "Am I still allowed to eat this?"

"This isn't funny! Why did you let him go?"

Elliot closed the fridge and helped himself to a fork. "Oh, come on, what was I meant to do, knock him out? You know what Julien's like!"

Cinn stared at him, speechless. What had Elliot been thinking? Cinn would happily have knocked Julien out to stop him marching off alone like some noble idiot. It didn't sound like Elliot had even attempted to stop him. Cinn clenched then unclenched his jaw, then folded his arms across his bare chest. "Why are you even here?"

"Uhh.. protection?" Elliot looked deeply offended. "In case you're attacked again. Look, dude, maybe this isn't the worst idea. Maybe this is a simple way to sort everything out. Julien isn't a delicate flower. His channelling abilities are *insane*. Like, seriously. You don't need to worry about him." Elliot was speaking very fast. Too fast. "And he reassured me he's got a foolproof plan. You know I wouldn't have let him go if I thought there was any chance of danger." Crinkles appeared in the corner of his eyes. "But he's not in any danger," Elliot repeated. But there was a tiny unspoken, *'Right?'* at the end of it.

"I'm not only worried he might get hurt," Cinn said through gritted teeth. "I'm worried about what it'll do to him if he hurts his father."

"That piece of shit? He deserves it, though."

Elliot really wasn't getting it, so Cinn clamped his mouth shut. His telephone caught his eye—the handle was off the hook.

Elliot said, "Oh yeah, Julien rang Darcy to tell her the plan. Then he hung up on her and left your phone like that so she couldn't ring back to yell at him."

Three knocks at the front door.

"That'll probably be her." Elliot put the bowl of lasagna down, one last bite remaining in it.

Cinn went to answer the door, even though Elliot was supposed to be there as his main line of defence. Indeed, it was Darcy on the doorstep: eyes blazing with fury, one hand clutching a coffee cup like it was a weapon. She pushed past him. Cinn followed her back to the kitchen, giving Elliot a smug smirk over her shoulder. It was two against one now.

The pair of them had it out for a good ten minutes, Cinn leaving them fighting to get dressed. By the time he returned downstairs, Darcy was bright red, and Elliot looked vaguely remorseful.

Darcy passed Cinn a mug of hot tea. "He's an utter fool."

"I know."

"But he'll be okay." The promise in her words was a fragile thread of hope that Cinn wanted nothing more than to cling on to.

Movement in the corner of the living room caught his eye. The shadow cast by the worn armchair was flickering. Expanding. Darkening.

Béatrice, in all her hideous, eyeless demon-cat glory, emerged from the puddle of darkness, then hissed a greeting, her form undulating wildly. Cinn expected her to pad up to him, wrapping herself around his legs as she often did. Instead, the cat arched her back, her shadowy fur bristling in frantic spikes as she let out a series of frenzied, distorted yowls, her erratic movements a desperate attempt to convey a message.

Cinn dropped to his knees and reached for her. Béatrice sprang towards him with a sudden burst of shadowy energy, her form writhing and twisting as she nudged her head against his knee, insistently. It didn't take a genius to pinpoint the source of her urgent distress. "She's telling us Julien's in danger!"

"Is she?" Elliot's voice was laced with panic, and it took everything Cinn had left in him not to shout at him for letting him go.

"What else would it be?" Cinn bit out instead.

Letting out another yelp, Béatrice circled the three of them, ignoring Darcy's soothing coos. Then, with a final disdainful glare, she jumped back into the armchair's shadow and disappeared.

Silence filled the room.

"We need to go, now." Cinn dared the other two to disagree.

Elliot tugged a single corkscrew curl away from his head, then let it spring back into place. At Darcy's expectant look, he said, "Okay. Fuck."

That just about summarises my thoughts.

"Let me... go back and talk to Eleanor and Malik, I guess. See what they say and go from there. It's too risky for us to go to the gendarmerie with this. Julien is right—though I'd like to think Salvatore Gallo can't be bought, we can't be sure."

Cinn seared his gaze into Elliot. "I'm going to Paris as soon as physically possible, with or without you." He stormed towards the stairs, unable to look at either of them any longer.

"We'll sort it, Cinn," Darcy called after him, but he was already taking his anger out on his poor staircase. He slammed the bedroom door for good measure. Julien should be the target of his fury, yet his image only conjured gnawing guilt. Julien charged off to face his father alone, all because he believed it would remove Cinn from danger. His idiot boyfriend had refused to even allow Cinn the chance to reason with him.

He let out a low scream of frustration, kicking the wooden bed frame, which groaned in protest. He sank to the floor. His threat to go to Paris alone was all well and good, but he couldn't drive, had no idea how to book a plane ticket, and wouldn't have the faintest clue how to go about charging up to Julien's father's mansion to save him. If that even was where he was.

There's no way Elliot and Darcy won't help you, he reasoned with himself. *They love him just as much.*

Across the room, his storage chest sat quietly, its battered, weathered surface a reflection of his inner turmoil.

Cinn scooted on his hands and knees all the way over to it. Then, reaching into the very bottom of it, his hand closed around a crinkled envelope. It, and the enclosed letter, had initially lived in his bag for weeks, but were now stored here so they didn't get further damaged.

He'd read Julien's letter so many times he could likely recite it by now.

But still, he wanted to see the words. *Needed* to see them. Particularly that line written at the very bottom, just above Julien's scrawled signature. The words that stayed with him always, etched into his heart.

Dearest Cinn,

I don't think you know this about yourself, but you have this amazing ability to make people love you the very moment they meet you. Maybe it's the quiet way you try and understand them. The way you see the best bits in people, even when they can't see it in themselves.

You have every right to be angry about what I did. I'm not going to pretend for a moment it came from a place of kindness or concern for Tyler's welfare. Instead, it came from a place of blind rage, of misguided selfishness, and of twisted possessiveness.

The truth is, I think I may have gone a little insane. When I look at you, every cell in my body shouts, mine, mine, mine. It's this all-consuming, primal feeling that I can't control. But I know that love is about more than just possession. It's about respect, trust, and partnership. I know we have a long way to go before I earn the privilege of calling you mine. But I'm begging you for the chance to let me try to get there. I can't promise you that I'll never hurt you again, but I do promise I'll live every day trying to be someone you're proud of.

Because I know you deserve someone who can give you everything. All of themselves, and more. I've often wondered how different I would be, if I'd grown up seeing love in the eyes of my parents when they looked at each other, rather than hate, or fear. To my mother, her marriage was a prison sentence. It's taken me a long time to understand that binding yourself to someone can be beautiful.

When she died, my heart hardened into a fortress that very few people managed to penetrate. Then you came along and slipped in like a thief in the night, bypassing all of my defences without me even realising it. You caused an avalanche of unexpected feelings to come crashing down on me, clouding my logical judgement.

After Béatrice was taken from us, I was plagued by shadows, lingering in the background of every happy moment, ready to engulf me. Then you came along. Though you'd been walking amongst shadows yourself, you so quickly dragged me out into the light again. With how you make me feel, it's hard to imagine that our meeting wasn't preordained by fate. I've spent my life doubting the existence of soulmates. I don't know if I believe in destiny, but you are the most compelling case for it I've ever seen.

All my love,

Julien

Elliot knocked on the door before slowly opening it to let himself in. Cinn carefully folded the letter as Elliot slumped down next to him.

"I'm really sorry, dude. Really fucking sorry. I've fucked up."

"It's alright," Cinn said, though it definitely wasn't.

"Nah, it's not. I've let you down, and also Julien as well." Elliot sat back with a long soft sigh, wrapping his arms around his knees. "I made him a promise once. The first day I met him. I promised I'd stick with him, and now I've let him run off by himself."

Elliot looked so mournful that Cinn's anger evaporated, replaced by a low, heavy melancholy. He squeezed Elliot's shoulder. "Well, it's as you said. I know what he's like. How persuasive he can be."

And defiant. And infuriating. And impossible.

But despite all that, Julien was *his* defiant, infuriating, impossible idiot.

Elliot nudged his leg into Cinn's.

No, Julien was theirs.

And they were going to find him, whether he liked it or not.

Thirty

JULIEN

From the fountain on the lawn, Julien stared up at his father's manor house, its darkened windows the hollow eyes in the face of a cold, unfeeling giant. The stone walls, once grand, now seemed to sag under the weight of decades of silence and gloom. There was no warmth in this place, no light or laughter had ever graced its halls. Julien's only comfort was that, in a couple of hours from now, this would all be over. This would be the last time he'd ever set foot in this house, the place haunted by countless ghastly memories from his childhood and beyond.

The sky had deepened into a bruised purple, the last traces of daylight fading. Upon arriving at the airport, Julien discovered that there were no seats available on any flights to Paris that day. Consequently, he flew to Brussels and then transferred. It really wasn't his day, as both seats ended up being economy. In hindsight, Julien should have driven the awful rental car all the way back, but he'd left it behind in case the others needed it. He really was a saint, truly.

Before he could unlock the heavy door, one of the cleaning staff opened it, cloth in hand. "I saw you from the window," they said cheerily. "Mr Montaigne is in the drawing room."

The woman disappeared, leaving Julien to navigate through the corridors alone. He found his father and Carrie on lounge chairs near the lit fire. Carrie's hand flew to her mouth as she stifled a gasp, jerking slightly in her chair. Her husband twisted his head, composing himself much more swiftly.

"Julien," Carrie said. "This is a... surprise." Then, with a glance at his father, she stood up, exiting towards the dining room.

After tentative, slow steps, Julien took her place opposite his father. The man appraised him in his standard way, eyes roving up and down before settling on Julien's scarf that he was loosening. "That scarf of yours is rather peculiar. Am I really to believe that *this* is in vogue, presently?"

Julien flashed him a wide smile. "Perhaps if you'd step out of your comfort zone, you'd discover there's a world of fashion out there, besides stiff suits."

The air grew heavy with an unspoken tension as they engaged in a silent battle of wills.

It was his opponent who relented first. "I presume you're not here to debate our sartorial preferences, are you now?"

"No," Julien said softly, his voice steady as he assumed a mask of impassive calm. *You've got this.* "I've been considering your offer—the one from before Christmas." He braced himself. Would his father really accept this direct conversational approach, bypassing any mention of hotel break-ins or car chases through quiet French villages?

"Go on," his father replied, his eyes betraying a deep calculation behind their lined facade.

"I've thought about it, and you were right. We *are* all each other has left, and that does count for something." The words sickened him to his core. "Plus, our interests and ambitions do align. I desire nothing more than to progress further at MEET, if the offer from Jonathan Steele is still on the table. Senior Executive, correct?"

Julien waited. His father nodded, idly swirling his whiskey glass.

"Jonathan knows the scope of my talents. He knows I can go all the way. Between the three of us, we can do great things. Keep improving the world, just like you said." Julien was rambling now. Laying it on too thick. He clamped his mouth shut.

His father inhaled the scent of his drink before taking a large sip, rolling the liquid around his tongue before swallowing. "You may recall, during our conversation at that... *quaint* café, I inquired about the possibility of Cinnamon Saunders assisting with a matter." His gaze pierced Julien like a knife.

"If I'm going to join you, I need to know exactly what I'm getting into first. I need all the information. Then I can decide if it's appropriate for Cinn to assist us or not."

His father's effort to hide the slight narrowing of his eyes was nearly undetectable. "Certainly," he replied smoothly. "As I mentioned, I'm confident this partnership will serve everyone's best interests."

"Alright then. I'm flying home tomorrow morning, so I want to see it all this evening. Learn everything there is to know about this project of yours."

His father's jaw twitched. Had Julien taken it too far with his demands?

"Well then, I'll see what I can arrange. Feel free to help yourself to a drink." Nodding at the cabinet, he left the room, presumably to make a phone call from his study. Julien did not take his father up on the offer of alcohol, as tempting as that was. This plan required the clearest head possible.

His father returned, marching straight back through the archway. He ran his hand over his salt and pepper beard. "Arrangements have been made. We can depart immediately."

Julien's heart rate rocketed. Was this all going to be that easy? *Surely not.* Calculating his next response carefully, lest he reveal any cards, he asked, "What? To where? Do you not have copies of the paperwork here?"

His father's eyes lit up in that way they did when he delighted in having the upper hand.

Ha. He'd bought it.

"For this, it'll be easier if I show you," he declared.

The *Machina Tenebris* was evidently something he enjoyed showing off: one of his father's many shiny toys.

His father collected his coat, then led the way to his garage. His driver had his feet up on the desk, newspaper open. Upon hearing their footsteps, he jumped up with a start, his face flushing with embarrassment. "Has there been a change of plan, sir? I thought we were done for the day. Where are we going?"

"Père Lachaise."

The driver wasn't surprised, but Julien was. Why on earth was his father taking him to the cemetery where his mother and sister were buried? But he kept quiet, slipping into the back of the car.

The drive was over half an hour of intense silence, against the backdrop of classical piano playing on the stereo. More than enough time for Julien to second-guess, third-guess, fourth-guess this ludicrous plan.

But it's working!

Is it, though? Is it really?

When it came down to it, Julien was banking on his father being egotistical enough to believe that, *of course,* his son had come to his senses and seen that partnering up with him was the logical thing to do.

They arrived at the cemetery, the car dropping them off before speeding away to park elsewhere.

Julien studied the enclosed perimeter of the cemetery, with its high walls and metal gate. When he'd dragged everyone here to dig up Béatrice's rib, they'd blasted the lock on the front gate. Now, he half expected his father to march up to it with a key. Instead, they walked on to where the tall stone wall descended into a line of bushes lining the pavement. With one glance around him, his father pulled a branch to one side. "After you."

Julien dove through the bush, battling the prickly branches that snagged in his hair. Through the darkness, a small hole in the brick wall revealed itself. He had to crouch down so low that it wasn't clear how his aged father was going to pass through it, but by the time he'd turned around, there he was.

The man brushed down his suit, glaring at a loose thread now present on his overcoat. "I seldom make this journey myself." His father sounded rather put out by the trouble.

"I can see why." Julien surveyed the rows of grave markers. "This... wasn't where I expected to find myself this evening."

"There are at least three access points to where we're going. This cemetery is but one of them. It is the most suitable for us on this occasion, however." His father chose a winding path. "It's not too far."

Although Julien didn't have the map of this place memorised, he had been here enough times to know they were heading towards his mother's and sister's resting places. They'd entered through a western edge, and so first passed Oscar Wilde's grave, with its modernist tomb and sizeable angel. When his mother died, Julien had been too young to grasp the vanity of his father securing plots in this exclusive cemetery. Now, he could laugh at the pretentiousness.

Cloaked in a twilight hush, they walked on through the pathways lined with weathered tombstones and creeping ivy. Shadows danced among the elaborate mausoleums and ornate graves. The whole place felt more solemn than last time, as if the graveyard knew the weight that rested on the visit that night.

They reached Division Twelve, and the spot where Béatrice's gravestone lay next to his mother's smaller one. Julien had never visited either grave with his father, and this was certainly an odd time to do so. For a while, the pair stood there, in cool, still air, accompanied only by the faint scent of damp earth mingling with that of the flowers that littered many of the graves.

"I know that we're not here to see *Mère* and Béatrice. I can only guess you built an 'access point' here, so that if you were seen, it would be viewed as though you were visiting her." Julien delivered the statements in a monotone.

"You're as perceptive as ever."

Gazing at the pair of headstones, he prepared for his father to have built some sort of contraption into his mother's grave—it could slide to one side to reveal a staircase or something. Then his father turned away, taking brisk strides to continue on the path.

The graves were a detour, not the destination.

After many more minutes of traversing the cemetery's extensive pathways, they reached the entrance to the cemetery's columbarium. Julien paused. Taller than the sea of graves, the building's imposing stone facade loomed like a sentinel above them. Shadows from the overhanging trees draped the structure in an eerie gloom, and its arched windows were dark, obscuring the cremated remains that were housed within.

"Seems like a fun place to hang out," murmured Julien.

From his pocket, his father pulled out an unlocking bar, not dissimilar to the one Malik had used yesterday to access the corner shop's basement. Thankfully, Julien was visiting a much more highbrow establishment this evening, swapping boxes of biscuits for rows of urns resting in the stone walls.

His father approached one of the columbarium's niches, seemingly indistinguishable from the others. With a swift motion, he pressed a hidden latch behind the urn, causing a section of the wall to shift. The stone slid aside with a muted rumble, revealing a narrow staircase spiralling down into darkness.

This is more like it.

"This way," his father said quietly, as the passage to the underground chamber opened before them.

Impressive. Julien restrained his excitement to ask, "What is this?"

His father glanced back at him with a glimmer of satisfaction. "This, my son, is a true Parisian secret," he replied as they began their descent.

What little light they had vanished. His father bent down for a moment, fumbling around in the dark until he found a disk-like object. He tapped it, activating the lumenmotes and providing a modest amount of light.

Julien almost offered to amplify the light, or even to produce the light balls he was fond of making—he had a lighter in his pocket—then caught himself. His father didn't know he was channelling again.

The stone steps were narrow and worn, spiralling down infinitely. His father's voice filled the cool, musty air. "The catacombs beneath this city are vast, a labyrinth connecting countless underground chambers. But after the World War Two bombings, it was assumed that the passages to this particular area were destroyed. That assumption has allowed us to operate something here, undisturbed, and away from any prying eyes at Auri."

Julien's breath caught in his throat. This unexpected turn of events was as twisty as the staircase they were walking down. As they descended deeper, the walls seemed to close in, and the echoes of their footsteps grew fainter. The pace they'd set had turned almost into a death march to hell. However, turning back was becoming a less and less likely possibility.

Deeper and deeper they went, the air growing chillier. Julien tightened his scarf around him, running his fingers through the threads for comfort. *This is all almost over,* he told himself for the umpteenth time. But as they navigated through the maze of ancient tunnels, he found that sentiment harder and harder to believe.

Flickering light from his father's lumenmote disk cast eerie shadows on the limestone walls. The silence was oppressive, broken only by the distant drip of water and their footsteps, muffled by the damp earth beneath. After what felt like an eternity, the narrow passage widened, revealing a medium-sized chamber, with many dark tunnels leading out from it. Julien avoided looking at the walls lined with carefully stacked bones, remnants of the countless souls who had been laid to rest here centuries ago.

In the centre of the chamber stood a large stone table, a colossus of cold granite. It appeared to be their destination.

"So, you said there were a few different access points to this place?"

A few different ways to escape, should I need to.

"Yes," his father replied with a nonchalant air.

Putain. The whole catacombs situation had slightly derailed his plan to destroy the machine and kill his father in one fell swoop. How on earth would he attempt to navigate his way back alone? He was too young and pretty to die, lost in a maze of bones beneath Paris.

A noise sounded from a nearby tunnel. A rat? An angry skeleton, reforming and coming to get them? His father leaned against the stone slab. He crossed his arms. Smiled.

"Do you know that you were named after my father, Julien?"

Warning bells burst into life. *Something isn't right here.*

"I did know that, yes." He'd never met his grandfather, but he'd heard the tale.

"You inherited your intelligence from me, and I from him."

Julien really didn't like where this was going. His chest tightened, a cold sweat creeping along the back of his neck. "Alright."

"However, on this occasion, you have demonstrated a truly shocking degree of naïve stupidity."

His father didn't move an inch.

Neither did Julien.

"It's laughable, really," his father added, a cold smile playing on his lips.

Julien's heart pounded louder than the distant echo of dripping water. The walls seemed to close in, the air suddenly too thin, too suffocating. His mind raced, grasping at any possible exit plan, but every thought was like a flickering light swallowed by encroaching darkness. He could kill his father in an instant, that much he was sure of. He could manipulate a bone from the wall, send it flying through his neck. In fact, he was fairly confident he could straight up explode his brain, if he worked his extraordinary motes in the right way.

But that still left the machine operational, its location undiscovered, and Julien lost in the catacombs.

His father laughed, a cold, mocking sound that echoed through the chamber, reverberating off the stone walls, an ominous chorus.

"What's so funny?" Julien threw out, buying time.

"Dear son. It's almost a joke." He stepped away from the slab, spreading his arms in mock grandeur. "The absurd notion that you could waltz into my house and win me over with a handful of insipid platitudes."

Julien's mouth dried. "I—"

"That you didn't think I had that priest thoroughly interrogated for every scrap of information he gave you."

Oh, God. Poor Father Gérard. Julien hadn't been the most polite to him, but he didn't want the old man harmed. "Is Father Gérard okay?"

A sharp-toothed smile was offered in response.

"You honestly thought I'd just walk you right up to the *Machina Tenebris,* and give you the grand tour?"

Why yes, yes he had. His father was completely correct—Julien's plan was downright stupid.

Without warning, both of his wrists were yanked behind him, a sharp click securing their bind. Cool metal touched his skin. A faint blue glow pooled on the floor.

If Julien could see his wrists, he'd find a pair of handcuffs identical to the ones he'd watched a gendarme attempt to bind his mother's wrists with in the church. Moments before Julien killed them all.

He tried to twist, to discover who'd snuck up on him, but the person grabbed his neck, then shoved him, sending him tumbling onto the hard floor.

"I'd really rather not rip these trousers." Julien's humour felt hollow, the fear in his voice obvious.

Bound by these cuffs, he wouldn't be able to channel. For a fleeting moment, he held onto the possibility that the motetech wouldn't block access to *his* motes. That dream promptly faded when he reached for them, to be rewarded with nothingness. He couldn't sense windmotes, even though there was a slight draft. He could see light emanating from his father's disk, but he couldn't detect a single lumenmote. For Julien's entire life, he'd sensed some form of mote constantly, wherever he was, at any time. Now, it was like he'd been blinded, stripped of a vital sense.

Jonathan Steele stepped out from behind him.

He was wearing one of the grey outfits often offered to people who'd used the Displacement Baths.

"Hello, Julien," he said in English. "I'd say it's nice to see you, but I'll spare you any games. I owe you that much, at least."

Julien gaped at his boss, the man he spent years working under. "*Non*," he whispered. He *pleaded*. "Don't do this."

A briefcase lay in the shadow of a wall. Clicking it open, Jonathan extracted a vial and a small cloth. He quickly soaked the cloth with the liquid.

"What is that?" Julien knew. He might have gotten himself down here, but he wasn't *that* stupid.

Closing the space between them, Jonathan knelt on the floor with Julien, pressing the cloth to his mouth. A pungent, unfamiliar scent filled Julien's nostrils, stinging and suffocating. He jerked his head backward, but Jonathan's firm press followed.

This wasn't how Julien imagined his death, far away from everyone he loved, his father leering above him, his final moments slipping away in a haze of chemical fumes and betrayal.

One thing was for sure—Cinn was going to track him down in the shadowrealm and murder him all over again.

Thirty-One

DARCY

If you wanted something done properly, you had to do it yourself.

It was the first lesson Darcy's father ever instilled in her; it was the motto she lived her life by. And it had never rung so true as it did that day.

So when Elliot started to spiral into a hopeless panic, and Cinn started threatening to leave that very second, Darcy demanded they go see Eleanor that exact instant.

As much as Darcy wanted to get to Paris as soon as possible, she'd never underestimated Lucien Montaigne. The man was ruthless, cunning, and always two steps ahead. If Julien really was in danger, they'd need more than the three of them—they'd want a small army to lead into battle. Darcy could almost hear her father's voice reminding her to stay sharp, to never underestimate an opponent. The stakes were high, and she wasn't about to let her guard down. Not now. Not when everything was teetering on the edge.

Eleanor might not be the army they needed, but she was a start.

So, she collected Cinn from his room, from his position slumped on the floor, leaning against the bed frame, staring vacantly at the floorboards.

Five minutes later, they were in the alley at the side of the corner shop, banging on the metal door with no handle and no lock. Harder and harder they pounded, determined that there must be some member of the AP down there who would eventually hear them.

"Hello?" shouted Elliot. "We need to talk to someone."

"What are you doing?" an accented voice shouted from behind him. A thick Swiss-German accent.

The three of them spun to find a balding, middle-aged man glaring at them.

"Hi," said Cinn. Then, of all things, he *waved*. "It's me. You know me."

"You?" spat the man, eyes wild. "Yes, you're in my shop buying my cheapest cigarettes, flour and eggs almost every day. Great for me. But this does not explain why you bang!" He shook a pointed finger at the door.

Did the shop owner know about the secret moteblessed organisation operating from the depths of its basement?

If Darcy had to guess, she'd say no.

The metal door flew open, hitting the brick wall with a crash. Specks of dust floated to the ground. From within the dark entrance, Malik stepped into the light of the alley. He smiled at everyone, as if not surprised to see a stand-off between an angry shopkeeper and the three suspicious people banging on his basement door.

At the sight of Malik, the man's expression changed from anger to mild annoyance. The pair of them proceeded to have a hushed, rapid conversation, which resulted in the shopkeeper huffing before wheeling around to head back down the alley.

"You three sure know how to make an entrance." Malik paused, frowning. "Where's your prat of a leader?"

"Julien's not our *leader*," mumbled Elliot.

"That's who we're here to discuss," stated Darcy calmly. Thank goodness she was here, or the whole thing would be descending into chaos. "We need your help. And we need it right now."

Madame Sinclair, sat on the very chair she'd swivelled around on last night, looking between them, obvious exasperation written on her face. Her usual impeccable demeanour had unravelled further since they last saw her—purple bags under her eyes, crinkles in her power suit. Had the woman slept at all?

Moments prior, Darcy had relayed, with impressive conciseness, the entire situation, and outlined exactly what she wanted from Madame Sinclair. Elliot and Cinn had stayed quiet the entire time. It was glorious. Even more glorious was how much she could get done without Julien dragging her down.

"I didn't realise you were capable of so many words," Madame Sinclair said eventually, appraising Darcy as if seeing her for the first time.

Darcy tipped her chin up. "Needs must."

"This is all extremely concerning. And very unfortunate timing."

Unfortunate. Darcy pressed her tongue to the roof of her mouth.

The older woman jerked her head towards her consoles and screens. "With the continuation of the calamities imminent."

"With respect, if we find Julien, we might be able to destroy the machine, and in turn, solve all of our problems at once."

"'Might' is the keyword there. Look, believe me, I care for Julien's safety more than you know."

Elliot did not contain his snort.

Madame Sinclair pierced him with a glare so fiery it could melt an iceberg. "I have no children of my own, you know. No siblings. Isabelle was the closest thing I had to a sister. I failed her, in so many ways, but when she died, I did my damnedest to look out for her children. Including sitting through dinner after dinner with their insufferable father, pretending for years we had a strong alliance. Including trying desperately to keep Julien away from all this for the last year."

"Now's the time Julien needs you the most," Cinn quickly interjected. "Surely it's enough that he's run off to see his father! How is that going to end well? Now he knows what he knows?"

Closing her eyes for a moment, Madame Sinclair leaned back in the chair. "I agree. Of course I'm concerned. If the entire gendarmerie hadn't been dispatched to tackle various umbraphage attacks, I'd be on the phone to Salvatore Gallo."

The screen behind her showed flashing dots over Hong Kong, New York, and a couple of other major cities. Darcy slid her eyes to Elliot, who twisted his lips. After Julien had summoned him to Cinn's house, he'd called in to work and made excuses. He probably felt terrible about it.

"Most of them correlate to locations predicted to be hit by climate disasters in under twenty-four hours. Manpower is at a premium right now."

Darcy made to talk again, silenced by Eleanor raising her hand.

"I didn't say I wasn't going to help. I'm explaining our situation."

Malik cleared his throat, shuffling slightly away from the console he was monitoring. "Ma'am? If I can support, I want to."

Madame Sinclair swung back and forth on her chair until Darcy itched to stick her leg out to stop her.

"I need four hours. Maybe five. I'll see who I can gather. It won't be many."

"No!" Cinn's voice was so choked with emotion that Darcy herself felt it. "That's not good enough! One hour, then we leave! We might be too late already!"

"Fine then, you leave in an hour. I'll take the Displacement Baths, and we'll see who gets there first."

The woman stared at Cinn calmly, awaiting his response.

"Fine," Cinn spat. "If you can get us into the Baths, I guess we'll do it that way."

"Go, quickly. You're delaying everything. We'll meet you outside the Baths."

Malik moved towards the ladder. "I'll show them out."

Madame Sinclair gave him a withering look, like that was obvious.

As Elliot and Cinn followed Malik up the ladder, Darcy called after them. "I'll be there in two minutes."

Cinn paused on a rung, giving Darcy a curious stare, then continued onwards when she revealed nothing. When she and Madame Sinclair had the room, the other woman waited.

It seemed strange that Darcy had once found Madame Sinclair intimidating. Now, the woman only looked time-worn, diminished, exhausted.

"I want a reassurance from you," Darcy started, choosing her words carefully. "If AP is successful in destroying the *Machina Tenebris,* then the world's supply of motecells will cease, correct?"

Madame Sinclair became statue-still. She regarded Darcy, unblinking. "You're worried about your father. The pacemaker your parents are fighting to get approved?"

The woman's face hadn't softened. Darcy hadn't expected it to. "Yes."

"I'm not sure why you think this is a negotiation."

"Because your negligence has resulted in Julien coming to harm, so now you owe me. You can fix it by helping another person I love. My father is the kindest soul I know. He doesn't have long left with us if they don't get the pacemaker fitted."

"I can't promise anything," said Madame Sinclair. "It'll be a brave new world if we succeed in destroying the machine. Decisions will have to be made on how we proceed."

"You're on the consortium. You'll be able to do *something* in his favour!"

"The point of the consortium, when it was established, was to ensure that no single moteblessed individual could wield unchecked power."

Darcy laughed. Madame Sinclair cracked a small smile.

"I know. We've come so far from that, haven't we? If we manage to take down Lucien, then we need to go back to making decisions for the greater good, not individual cases. I can't promise you anything specific. But I can promise that we'll consider the human cost in our choices."

Darcy's heart pounded in her chest. "The human cost is everything, Madame Sinclair. Don't forget that."

With that, she climbed up the ladder without looking back. Left to navigate the dark corridors alone, it took her a fair few minutes to reach the exit.

Her eyes adjusted to the brightness. Cinn lingered by a stack of compressed cardboard boxes, smoking. Elliot stood a fair few strides away from him, close to Malik. Very close.

"What's going on?" Darcy asked Cinn.

"I don't know. We were waiting for you. Though we've apparently got some hours to kill, anyway."

Cinn then had the audacity to offer Darcy the end of his cigarette. She glared his hand away, storming down the alley.

Malik appeared to be in the process of consoling Elliot—both of his hands were clutching the other's. "We'll find him," he promised, in a low voice. "I know we will."

"I hope so," Elliot replied, gazing at Malik in a nauseating way.

Hadn't Elliot met this random guy only the other day? He was milking this situation for all it was worth, clearly.

"We need to head back and come up with a strategy for when we arrive in Paris," Darcy barked at Elliot.

Malik raised his eyebrows, shooting Darcy a questioning gaze. "To your cottage?"

Darcy's stomach tensed at the familiarity in Malik's tone. How many times had he watched them all there, from the shadows? And now Elliot was putty in his hands, just like that? "I won't bother giving you the address. I'm sure you know it intimately."

"There's no need to be rude, Darce," muttered Elliot.

Cinn peeled himself from the wall to join them. "Yeah, Malik's on our side. He was stalking us on Eleanor's orders, but he's here to help, now. Right, mate?"

Shaking her head, Darcy strode off without a second glance back at them.

She'd need to save her energy, if this was what she was to deal with.

Thirty-Two

CINN

Cinn lay horizontally in the Displacement Bath, naked, breathing hard. Unlike the portable van-based tub he'd been displaced into last time, this time he arrived into Paris in a private pod, with a set of grey clothes hanging nearby.

He braced himself for vertigo as he slowly stood on shaky legs. The clothes—and trainers—fit him like a glove. Highly polished metal formed the four walls that surrounded him, reflecting Cinn's pale, glaring image. The sight of the deep wound on his forehead from the car crash still startled him. He pressed a palm against the wall's smooth surface, studying the deep frown lines etched into his forehead, the tight set to his jaw.

Cinn closed his tired eyes.

What if they didn't find Julien? Or if they found his body in a lifeless heap on the ground?

The image his brain conjured was horrific, and a low groan slipped out of him.

A series of sharp knocks on the cubicle door. "Cinn?"

Cinn blinked. That wasn't a voice he expected to hear, here in the Parisian Displacement Baths.

"Noir?" Cinn opened the narrow door to find the old man dressed in similar loose grey clothes. He looked so different out of his dark robes that Cinn snorted. "What are you doing here?"

"I'm the backup, lad." Noir flashed him a wide grin, revealing a silver tooth Cinn hadn't noticed before. "Don't look at me like that. I might be triple your age, but I can hold my own in a fistfight. Don't you worry."

Cinn rearranged the doubt on his face to something that could pass for gratitude. "Thank you for being here."

Noir squeezed his arm, gaze soft. "Of course. We wouldn't let you deal with this all by yourself." He added, "I'm in your corner, Cinn. Always."

An unexpected rush of affection hit Cinn square in the chest. He nodded at Noir. Cinn didn't trust Eleanor as far as he could throw her, but somehow this old codger always had a way of making Cinn feel safe. Feel heard.

A bath attendant complained at them in French, ushering them out of the tiled, chlorine-filled chamber. Elliot, Darcy, Malik, Madame Sinclair, and two strangers they'd been briefly introduced to back at Auri, were waiting by the exit. The circle made space to accommodate Cinn and Noir. A fresh wave of anxiety struck Cinn. What if he was expected to lead this motley band? He hadn't the faintest clue where to start, aside from storming Lucien's mansion.

As the circle quietened, all eyes turned to Eleanor, and Cinn's fear lessened, somewhat.

"Listen up." Eleanor commanded attention without raising her voice. Everyone shuffled closer. "I've received word that Julien Montaigne was seen entering his father's house at approximately six thirty p.m. today. Around thirty minutes later, Lucien and Julien left the estate in the back of a black Mercedes-Benz. Their current whereabouts are unknown."

One of the new people—Tanya?—made an obvious show of yawning. "Ma'am, it's late. If we have no active leads, may I suggest we tackle this at dawn?"

"No!" Cinn's cheeks burned under the heat of everyone's startled gaze. "I mean, you can go, if you want. But I'm not sleeping until I find him." Something in Cinn told him there wasn't time for that.

A pair of sympathetic green eyes found his. "To be fair to Tamara, we can hardly march up and down every street of Paris," Darcy said. "But I was wondering"—she glanced between Cinn and the others—"if our cat friend fancies being of use again."

"I can't summon her like a dog."

Noir hummed under his breath. He was going to be pissed off that Cinn hadn't divulged his shadowrealm companion to him. The rest of the circle appeared either bemused or confused at the mention of Béatrice. Why had Darcy brought this up in front of them? Cinn glared at her.

"Have you tried?"

What? Had Darcy gone mad? Cinn spluttered slightly. "Of course not!"

"Well, then!"

Cinn turned to Elliot for support, but he only shrugged.

Malik stood close to Elliot. "Worth a try, no?"

Attention remaining entirely on him, Cinn's face continued to flush. "Fine," he mumbled. "Can you dim the lights?"

Elliot tipped his head back, studying the strips of overhead lighting. A moment later, they flickered before dropping to a soft, ambient glow, casting long shadows across the room.

"I'll just... go try over there." Turning swiftly, Cinn beelined straight for a dark corner of the lobby, feeling the back of his neck prickle.

God, what he would do for his Walkman back right now. Or a quick cigarette. How was he supposed to focus on manifesting a demon cat when he was on the edge of an anxiety attack, images of Lucien cackling over Julien's dead body plaguing his brain?

To make matters worse, he had six pairs of eyes glued to him, like he was a circus show.

Stop fucking staring at me.

This was stupid. Béatrice wasn't going to magically appear for him. It didn't work like that. Randomly roaming the streets of Paris would be a better use of time!

The quiet, concerned chatter of the group reached his ears and Cinn clenched his jaw. How long until they got bored and pissed off? The warding band around his wrist warmed with his rising temper.

And there she was. Two eyeless sockets staring at him from the darkest recesses of the shadow.

The cat shifted slightly, her silhouette wavering like smoke.

Thank fuck.

"Hi." Relief cascaded through Cinn as he moved in front of her, shielding her from view.

The sound of footsteps behind him did not sound promising.

"Remarkable!" Noir gasped, reaching forward, hand outstretched.

When Béatrice hissed at Noir and jumped back, Cinn couldn't suppress his nervous, unsteady laughter. "She kind of only likes me." He shrugged. "I wouldn't touch her if I were you. She bites."

Behind Noir, the rest of the group shuffled about, trying to get a good look, while Darcy snapped at them to stay back.

Cinn dropped to the cool marble floor, lowered his voice to a whisper. "Okay, we're all here. Where to now? Where is he?" Then, because he couldn't shake the feeling that the sands of time were slipping away, grain by grain, he added, "Help me find him before it's too late."

Béatrice was still for a long moment. She let out a low growl that resonated deep within her and bolted towards the revolving glass door, paws skittering across the marble.

Cinn's heart jumped into his throat as he watched the creature's swift, determined dash. "Follow her!" he urged, already on his feet, moving towards the door.

Outside, the sign on the brick wall informed him he'd visited *L'Oasis*. Cinn sped past it, his borrowed trainers rubbing against his heel as he pounded them against the pavement—Béatrice was already at the end of the road.

"She's a speedy one." Running beside him, Malik sounded amused.

Cinn didn't waste energy replying. His breaths were coming out in quick, frosty puffs as they raced through the damp, cobblestone streets of Paris. Their writhing ball of shadows darted ahead like a dark phantom, weaving through the narrow alleyways and cutting through the beams of street lights that somehow only made her darker. Elliot was right behind Cinn, while Darcy and Malik kept pace, exchanging glances filled with urgency.

When Cinn glanced back, he found Eleanor, Tamara and that other bloke trailing far behind them. Noir, moving with uncanny grace for a man his age, was almost a shadow himself, blending into the night as if he belonged there.

Béatrice led them past shuttered cafés and sleeping boutiques, across bridges that arched over the Seine like silver ribbons under the moonlight. Though, as they dashed past a few remaining tourists still braving the frigid night, the cat slipping through the crowd like smoke, Paris's usual magic felt twisted, distorted. Like the city itself was bending around them, guiding them *somewhere*. The tug was palpable, a gravitational pull stronger than the fear of what lay ahead.

Just when it seemed the cat would vanish into the labyrinth of Paris forever, she stopped abruptly just outside a metro station.

"The catacombs?" Darcy said, on a gasp of air, clutching her chest. "Béatrice was never this fast before!"

Béatrice didn't seem bothered by Darcy's comment, quickly slipping through the bars of the ancient iron gate. The cat turned, her eyeless sockets locking onto Cinn, and with a flick of her tail, she disappeared into the darkness below, vanishing down the narrow stairway leading underground.

No! Cinn's heart stuttered as he lost sight of her. He gripped two of the gate's heavy bars, squinting at the entrance. Rough, aged limestone framed it, the words '*Arrête! C'est ici l'empire de la mort,*' carved deeply into the rock above, barely visible in the dim light.

"Move!" Elliot hip-checked Cinn out of the way, sending him stumbling into Darcy, who had her face pressed between two bars.

A deafening bang pierced the quiet air; Elliot smashed the lock. The chain fell limp, clattering against the metal.

Eleanor, who'd fallen behind, arrived and cleared her throat. Her grey hair, damp from the Baths, was now further dishevelled.

"You stay up here, ma'am." Tamara tightened the straps of a grey rucksack.

Eleanor exhaled a heavy sigh, like she could easily collapse on the ground. It was definitely a good idea that she stayed behind—she'd slow them down.

"No," Eleanor said, rubbing the base of her spine. "I think I need to come. If Lucien really is down there"—she pursed her lips—"I want to see him. Let's go."

Malik slipped through the gate first, heading straight for the narrow stone archway just beyond. Elliot caught his arm, pulling him behind him. Malik's face scrunched in mild annoyance, and Cinn would have found it all funny if they weren't on a life-and-death mission to save his idiot boyfriend.

Within seconds, a mixture of flashlights and lumenmote disks were thrown into hands, and then they were off.

When they first descended the spiral staircase into the greasy dark, Cinn feared there would be no Béatrice to guide them, that she'd leave them to fend for themselves in some cruel twist. However, she was waiting for them only a dozen steps down, tail flicking impatiently.

Down and down they went, the darkness closing in like a tightening veil, despite the soft light they carried. The cool air thickened with the scent of earth and history. And more than a few decayed bodies, Cinn supposed.

They reached the bottom, finding a narrow, dimly lit tunnel. The walls were lined with neatly stacked bones, skulls interspersed as morbid decorations. Of all the places in Paris they could have ended up, did it really have to be here? How and why was Julien in the fucking catacombs?!

They pressed on, each breath of damp air tasting faintly of limestone. The faint glow of their flashlights lit the slick, uneven floor, while the shadows of ancient remains stretched long and ghostly against the walls.

Cinn quickened his steps, the chill of the catacombs clinging to him like a breath from the grave. The tunnels stretched endlessly before him, and Julien seemed impossibly distant, hidden somewhere in their depths. A knot of dread twisted in Cinn's gut, tightening with every step. How long was this going to take?

"This isn't creepy or anything," he muttered to Elliot, who was practically jogging to keep up. Elliot laughed hollowly, but it did nothing to relieve the tension building inside him.

Treading carefully, they followed Béatrice through the next tunnel, but every step grated on Cinn's nerves. Their footsteps echoed against the low, arched ceilings, forcing him to duck every few paces, which only slowed them down further. The passage stretched on and on, narrowing with every turn, the neatly stacked bones giving way to rough, damp limestone that scraped against his arm when he moved too fast. The cold bit through his clothes, each breath turning to mist, and the distant hum of the city above was swallowed by an oppressive silence that pressed uncomfortably in his ears. Cinn's eyes locked on Béatrice's flickering form as she darted ahead with maddening ease, her graceful movements a sharp contrast to his growing frustration. She moved like she belonged here, while every twist and turn of the labyrinth only made him feel more lost—and more desperate to reach Julien.

They turned a corner, and a wider chamber opened around them, where the ceiling arched high above, disappearing into the shadows. The walls were carved with old, fading inscriptions and crude markings left by the hands of explorers from long ago.

Béatrice paused briefly, glancing back at them before slipping through a narrow crack in the wall—almost invisible in the gloom. A cool draft emanated from the passage on the other side.

"Here," Cinn shouted behind him, pointing towards the narrow opening.

"She's gone off map," said Darcy.

Cinn twisted in the narrow space to find her poring over a map of the catacombs. "Where did you find that?"

She didn't reply, only laid it flush against the wall, tracing the markings with her fingers. Noir joined her, humming to himself as he studied it.

"We're not going to fit through that crack," Malik murmured.

"Do *not* suggest we blow the tunnel up. I'm not getting buried alive today," Eleanor said.

Anger coursed through Cinn at the note of finality in her voice. "Well, we have to do something," he snapped at the woman. "We've come this far!"

"I'll thank you for minding your tone!" Eleanor retorted. Behind her, her two lackeys glared at Cinn.

Cinn glared right back. "I'm going to look around the corner. There might be another way to get there."

"There's not," Darcy said flatly, waving her stupid map in the air. "Come see for yourself."

"I'm just going to check!"

With that, Cinn marched off. He was done being slowed down. They didn't have spare minutes to fuck around with maps. He'd find another way, then quickly go back and get them.

Cinn's frustration carried him deeper into the winding tunnel, the damp air pressing against his skin. He turned one corner, then another, the dim light from the main group fading behind him, swallowed by the shadowed twists of the catacombs. The walls closed in, the passageway narrowing, the labyrinth turning more chaotic with every step.

He should probably go back.

Cinn spun, staring at a tunnel that split in two. Was it the left-hand side? Cinn strode quickly through it, retracing his path, but each turn felt identical, a dizzying maze of stone and bone. Panic began to creep in. Cinn now had no idea which way he'd come from, and the voices of the others were only a distant echo swallowed by the endless dark.

You stupid idiot. Now they'll have to waste precious time to come look for you.

The air stirred. A chill shot through him.

The shadows pulsed around him, gathering with a sudden, terrifying intensity. Without warning, a dark tendril shot out from the wall, wrapping around his arm like an icy vine.

In shock, he dropped his flashlight, which went rolling across the stone out of reach. He screamed; no sound came. The darkness tightened, tugging him off his feet and dragging him *through* the stone wall itself. The world around him dissolved into a swirling vortex of cold and black, a void that stretched in every direction. Each of his senses blurred—the feeling of the ground, of weight, of time, all slipping away like water through his fingers.

An eternity passed. Cinn tumbled through the darkness, unable to tell up from down, a sensation of falling and twisting through the unseen passages of the catacombs. Cold air rushed past him, stinging his skin, and faint whispers seemed to brush against his ears, though he couldn't make out any words. Suddenly, he was thrust forward and spat out violently, landing hard on cold, damp ground.

Cinn lay still for a moment, gasping for breath, his heart pounding in his chest as a horrible realisation sunk in—he was in complete darkness. No light, no sense of direction, just the thick, oppressive blackness pressing in all around him.

"Holy shit."

The blackness ate up his words.

Cinn sat up, resting his head against his legs. He allowed himself a low moan. That experience had been far worse than the Displacement Baths earlier. There, he'd felt weightless, fluid, whereas now he felt like he'd been a heavy stone that'd been repeatedly knocked against a wall.

He rubbed at his head, where a headache was forming. Then Cinn forced himself to his feet. The air here felt different—denser, older, filled with a deeper sense of dread. It was so dark, you could almost smell it.

Cinn pressed his hands against the rough, damp walls of the tunnel, the cold stone biting into his palms. The darkness was suffocating, swallowing everything in its path; he couldn't even see his own fingers in front of his face. He let out a slow, shaky breath, forcing himself to focus on the sensation of the walls, the uneven texture of ancient limestone beneath his fingertips. With each step, his heartbeat pounded louder in his ears, a frantic drum beat that matched the panic rising in his chest. No shadow cat to guide him now—only his gut, a primal instinct urging him to keep moving, keep searching, to find Julien.

His mind raced with images of the labyrinth stretching endlessly, trapping him down here forever, forgotten in the shadows, his body never found. The thought gnawed at him, a tightness coiling in his stomach.

But he couldn't stop, couldn't let the fear paralyse him. Julien needed him. Nothing would stop Cinn from getting to him.

"Get it together," he muttered, voice small in the consuming dark. Each step forward felt like a battle, the silence around him heavy.

A song burst to life in his head—"Dead," one of the tracks on his beloved Pixies cassette. The one that he'd worn out to the point of ruin. Then Julien's gifted replacement had burned alongside Maz, the precious treasure reduced to ash.

Cinn laughed to himself, the sound echoing wildly off the stone walls, a stark, jagged edge of hysteria in his voice. He pressed his fist to his mouth. Although he felt alone down here—truly, terrifyingly, utterly alone—he had no idea who was close by.

So, he mimed the song lyrics, imagining the frantic baseline thumping in his veins, the distorted guitar slicing through the air, drowning out the silence and the creeping fear. The song playing loudly within him felt gloriously comforting—his only possible defiance of the crippling terror threatening to consume him.

Armed with his music, he moved slowly onwards, feeling his way along the wall, praying his gut wouldn't betray him, knowing that if he stopped now, he would never find Julien.

Then he heard it—the soft, almost imperceptible patter of paws somewhere ahead, followed by a low, rumbling purr that seemed to vibrate through the walls themselves.

Cinn froze, his heart pounding in his throat, just as something sleek and cold brushed against his ankles. He flinched, feeling the unmistakable shape of the cat slide between his legs, her shadowy form curling around him like smoke. "Béatrice," he whispered, a shaky grin spreading across his face. She was there, waiting, guiding him again. Her presence was a lifeline, a tether to something other than his own fear. "I missed you, friend."

He paused to stroke her, scratching between her ears. She purred, a grateful sound which quickly deepened into something more urgent.

"Take me to him, please," Cinn urged. "As quick as you can! Go, go!"

Because, as he followed Béatrice through narrow tunnel after narrow tunnel, the feeling that they were running out of time only intensified.

Every distant echo of his footsteps became a relentless reminder of the urgency, each sound a reminder that they were racing against an invisible, unforgiving clock.

"Hold on, Julien," he said, to the skeletons of the catacombs. "I'm coming for you."

Thirty-Three

JULIEN

J ulien wasn't dead.

Yet.

At least, he presumed he wasn't dead. The afterlife *could* easily consist of being locked in a catacomb cell, but somehow, he doubted it.

A heavy fog clouded Julien's thoughts, making it difficult to piece together the events that had led him here. His head throbbed with a dull ache, each beat of his heart sending a wave of nausea through him as the lingering effects of Jonathan's special compound refused to fade.

The prison he lay in was a narrow, suffocating space carved out of the ancient stone, its rough, damp walls pressing in on all sides. The air was thick with the smell of mildew and earth, almost tangible in its heaviness. Nothing was visible to him, not even a single speck of dirt—the darkness was absolute, swallowing everything in its path. A constant reminder he was miles under the ground.

Composed of sharp, jagged objects, the disturbingly uneven floor moved under him as he shuffled. *Bones.* He was lying on a bed of bones.

The only sound was that infuriating drip of water. Distant, rhythmic. But at least it gave him something to focus on. It was easier to drum his bound hands against his back in time with the drip, rather than think about other things.

Like the fact he'd allowed his father to trick him so easily.

Like the fact he was going to be buried amongst the bones of strangers, forgotten and alone.

Like the fact he'd never get to say goodbye to Cinn. To Elliot, to Darcy.

What was worse was that they would likely come looking for him, eventually. After a week or two, he supposed.

Though… would it really be that long?

Julien had made it crystal clear to Elliot that he needed to stay put with Cinn. He'd promised Elliot he'd be twenty-four hours. What would happen when that time ran out?

Would they come straight to Paris? To his father's house? Would his father bump them off too? Finally, get his hands on Cinn, for whatever nefarious purpose he wanted him?

Although… was Julien being naïve? Would it even take twenty-four hours? If Julien had woken up to find Cinn gone, he wouldn't have followed the instructions of some silly note left on the dresser. He would curse him every name under the sun, then leave immediately to go find him by any means possible. Give him several slaps before kissing him silly.

You thought you were so clever, didn't you? Well, you're a fucking idiot.

Julien threw his head back against the hard rock, the sharp bite into his scalp not nearly an adequate enough punishment for what he'd sentenced those he loved to.

You're a useless piece of shit.

They'd all be better off without him, anyway.

It worsened Julien's nausea to think about, but with him gone, Cinn would meet someone who didn't make him want to tear his hair out on a daily basis. Elliot would finally make more friends, now that Julien was no longer holding him back. The faint frown lines on Darcy's forehead would smooth out. She'd have constant hot water in her shower.

Hot tears trickled down Julien's face, igniting fresh waves of anger. No matter what happened, his father would not see him cry. Julien blinked them back, rapidly. His mind reeled, searching for some glimmer of happiness to cling to.

An image fell into his brain—cool sunlight streaming into Maz, as Julien drove on a winding country road towards Paris. Julien accidentally singing that silly Wu-Tang Clan song. The look on Cinn's face when he realised—

A loud bang, followed by the sound of stone being dragged across stone. The memory of Cinn's delighted smile dissipated into smoke, leaving only the blackness behind.

Julien didn't have the energy to devise a cunning escape attempt, so he just lay there and waited for whatever was to come.

His body was rolled over, once, twice. Yanked roughly to the side. A flicker of dim light illuminated the space, revealing the shape of a tunnel, its walls lined with crumbling stone and dark, tangled roots snaking down from above.

Julien didn't bother to suppress his low moan of pain, his headache reaching sledgehammer levels. The person manhandling him wasn't his father, or Jonathan, but some unknown man with a thuggish face. He barely glanced at Julien as he dragged him to his feet. Another man joined them, another muscled brute.

"You can walk, or we can carry you, princess," he said. "Your choice."

Julien took one unsteady step forward, followed by another.

The man grunted in approval, pushing on Julien's shoulder.

Two twists and turns of the catacombs later, the three of them spilled into the chamber with the massive stone slab, where Jonathan had knocked him out. That fucker. After all the late nights Julien had pulled for him, all the designs and projects he'd seen to completion.

Julien paused, expecting his father to slip out of a shadow, smiling victoriously.

"Down there," a man grunted.

Squinting in the low light, Julien could make out a narrow set of steps descending from the far side of the stone slab, almost invisible against the rough-hewn surface. The slab wasn't just a table—it was a hidden doorway, its edges barely perceptible, leading to the dark mouth of another chamber below.

A few hard shoves had Julien flying towards the next staircase, then stumbling down the uneven stone steps.

When he reached the bottom, his eyes dashed around the space, dimly lit with several lumenmote disks propped against the catacomb walls. His gaze sought *son connard de père.*

The chamber was empty, however. Empty of people, at least.

Because there, dead in the middle, was something that could only be *it.* That goddamned machine. *Machina Tenebris.*

He would have loved to laugh at it, to say that it didn't look like much, after all this build-up. But that would have been a lie.

It dominated the chamber like some monstrous metal heart. Roughly the size of a compact car, its intricate structure contained an array of polished brass gears, darkened iron plates, and strange crystalline tubes snaking around its surface. At its centre was a core—a sphere encased in a lattice of black metal, pulsating with an unsettling blue light that seemed to draw the shadows inward. Tendrils of red flowed from the sphere, reminiscent of the shadowrealm's red vines. They coursed up through a series of glass conduits that stretched towards the ceiling, casting sharp, erratic patterns on the walls.

Julien couldn't look away. This was motetech, certainly, but motetech unlike he'd ever seen.

The air around the *Machina Tenebris* crackled with a faint hum. Its subtle vibration passed into the ground, thrumming beneath his feet.

"It almost seems... alive," Julien murmured to himself. Like it was a living, breathing entity.

"Doesn't it?"

The reply in French made him jump. His two security guards still clasped his shoulders, but Julien didn't need to turn. His father's voice was unmistakable, carrying that smooth, self-assured lilt that always seemed to mock him, even in rare moments of sincerity.

Instead, Julien's gaze remained fixed on the machine. A part of it caught his attention. An odd-shaped contraption protruded from the side of the machine—a cluster of metal appendages, each tipped with sharp, needle-like ports, bristling like the legs of some mechanical insect. This part of the machine looked different, as if crudely attached by a child.

A cool sickness spread throughout Julien as he stared at it. He didn't know what he was looking at, not exactly. But it wasn't good.

His father's voice broke Julien's horror-struck stare. "Bring him closer," he ordered in English, with a casualness that suggested he was asking for a cup of tea. He walked past Julien to stand near the machine.

Julien's heart hammered as he resisted, trying to plant his feet, throwing his weight back. "Fuck off," he hissed, straining against the men's grip.

But the men didn't relent, dragging him inexorably forward, the cold prongs of the stone floor scraping against his feet as the machine loomed ever closer.

"This has all worked out rather conveniently, wouldn't you agree?" his father said, his tone light, almost amused. "You see, acquiring Cinnamon Saunders was proving to be quite the tiresome endeavour."

At Cinn's name, a white-hot fury surged through Julien, threatening to boil over. *Don't give him the satisfaction.* His hands clenched involuntarily, nails biting into his palms as he struggled to tamp down the anger rising with the bile in his throat.

"When word reached me about the little... mishap with my men in that hotel room, I must admit, I found myself rather intrigued."

Putain. Julien should have tried harder to ensure that the third man on the balcony didn't live to tell the tale.

"It wasn't until that priest started spilling his secrets"—his father grimaced with disdain—"or should I say, *your* secrets, that things took a most intriguing turn."

Julien's heart sank faster than a treasure dropped in the Seine.

The secret he'd closely guarded since his childhood was no more.

"Father Gérard just... told you everything?" Julien blurted out. He couldn't imagine it.

"Not at first." He fiddled with a part of the machine Julien couldn't see. "I had to be rather persuasive. People can be quite cooperative when their loved ones are at stake, don't you think?"

Julien clenched his jaw so hard, his teeth ached with the effort. "Is that a threat?"

A loud laugh echoed off the catacomb walls. "In fact, your loved ones will be quite safe now, thanks to your efforts. As I explained to the priest, this resolves everything."

Part of Julien didn't want to encourage him to continue, but a larger part demanded answers. "What?" he spat. "Enough with the games, just tell me."

"We knew—Jonathan and I—that we couldn't continue like this forever." Tapping the metal surface of *Machina Tenebris,* his father sighed, looking at the machine mournfully. "We knew we had to find a solution."

"So... you knew that this... *thing*"—Julien jerked his head at the machine—"was behind the recent calamities... the umbraphages, even, and you didn't pull the plug on it?"

"Not immediately. It only became undeniable in the last eighteen months or so, when our increased output directly correlated to the increase in such events."

Julien's gaze drifted upwards to where the machine fed into the catacomb ceiling. Where did it go, exactly? To HorizonTech's motecell production site? It was on the other side of Paris, but the catacombs did stretch that far...

"Once we grasped what we were dealing with, we set about finding a solution."

There was that word again, making Julien's blood run cold.

"The very night Viktor Sturmhart caught wind of the possible existence of a shadowslipper, he contacted Jonathan. And so began the second phase of our project." He lifted up the cluster of metal appendages, marvelling at them. "To find a suitable, sustainable source of power. We originally thought only a shadowslipper would do."

"Would do..." Julien repeated, staring at the contraption.

His brain had been tirelessly working in the background to make connections that he now fought to suppress, unsuccessfully.

The bundle of thick wires his father held were arranged in a cruel arch. Julien traced their path, horror growing by the second. Three port-like attachments, with needles sharp enough to pierce skin. Skin and bone.

"No," Julien whispered, a full-body shudder passing through him.

"It will be quite painless, once we're past the initial installation. You'll become comatose."

As if on cue, Jonathan Steele materialised from the shadows of an adjoining tunnel, his face set in a grim line. Without looking at Julien, he walked behind the machine, to focus intently on something unseen.

"This outcome benefits all. With your body to power the *Machina Tenebris*"—Julien almost choked—"the planet's equilibrium will settle. The calamities will reduce to natural levels. The umbraphages will be no more." A sneer curled on his father's face before he pinched his lips in distaste. "This way, your precious *friend* Cinnamon remains unharmed."

If Julien had his hands free right now, he'd use them to strangle the crazy old man. He'd slam his father's skull into the stone again and again until it shattered. Press his fingers against his windpipe until it collapsed. Push his eyes against their sockets until they popped.

"Ready when you are," Jonathan quietly said. Then he moved around the machine to face Julien. "He's telling the truth, Julien. This really will fix everything."

Julien didn't stop his jaw from dropping. "*Fix everything?* Fix everything, with the caveat, I live out the rest of my days sealed in the catacombs, as a vegetable plugged into a machine?!"

"What's one life compared to all those currently suffering?" his father asked, quite seriously.

Breathe.

Julien forced himself to inhale the stale air, his breath unsteady.

"I'm your son!" he eventually got out. "Your last surviving family member."

"Since when have you cared about that?" His father sneered at him, as if he were a piece of dirt. "Your entire life you've barely treated me with respect, let alone anything close to love."

"Because you were a fucking abusive prick who mistreated every one of us!"

The words hung heavy in the cold air. For a long moment, the only sound was the soft hum of the machine. The oppressive silence of the catacombs swallowed Julien's voice, leaving nothing but the weight of his words echoing against the stone walls.

Anger glistened in his father's eyes, and he opened his mouth, where daggers undoubtedly waited to be thrown.

Julien was twelve years old all over again, hiding under the dining table, watching his father lift his mother off the floor by her neck.

"I know you killed them!" Julien screamed, before his father could offer any sort of pathetic defence. If this was the end, he wanted some shred of resolution. To hear his father say the words.

"Killed them? I fear you're mistaken. It was your actions that brought the church walls crumbling down on your mother."

The guilt that Julien had lived with for the last ten years surged like a tidal wave, shattering the dam Cinn had laboriously built, with his steadfast words of reassurance. It crashed over him anew with a force that left him breathless.

"As for my beloved daughter, well, she aligned herself with the wrong people and paid the price for her dangerous choices."

Beloved. He made a mockery of the word with his tone.

"You murdered her with this!" Julien nodded down to the locket around his neck. The side where the metal touched his skin warped from amplifying excessive motepower. "Her locket! Of all things! She burned to death! Her flesh melted!"

"Bring him here."

The two silent men pushed Julien forwards, and Jonathan raised the trio of needles, readying their position. Another shove, and Julien was mere inches from his father, the man he'd detested throughout his entire living memory. The man who'd killed his biological family, and tried to harm the one he'd built for himself.

Seizing his chance, Julien threw his head forward with all the force he could muster. His forehead collided with his father's face with a sickening crunch. The old man staggered back, his nose bursting with a violent stream of blood. He stumbled into the side of the machine, swearing under his breath as he clutched his face. The two men, momentarily thrown off balance, struggled to regain their composure while Julien's breath came in harsh, ragged gasps, his heart pounding with a fierce surge of rage.

"You're going to rot in Hell, you selfish monster!" Julien snarled.

His father wasn't religious. It still felt good to shout.

"*Mère* never loved you, and neither did we!"

The vile man paused, looking up at Julien for a moment, clutching his nose. Blood pooled down his wrist as his brow furrowed, like he was lost in some distant, fleeting memory. "No. No, I don't suppose she did."

"I don't know how you tricked *Mère* into marrying you!"

"Oh," he replied calmly, wiping his face with the black of his sleeve. "I had my ways."

At this, Julien screamed.

His screams tore through the catacombs, raw and primal, echoing off the damp walls. His body convulsed with frantic energy as he thrashed against his wrist restraints, flailing his limbs wildly. He kicked out, striking one man in the shin, sending him stumbling. Desperation fuelled his strength as he wriggled and twisted.

Julien wasn't deluded.

He understood the dark reality of his situation: there was no way he could possibly escape.

But he wouldn't die like a meek lamb, trotting merrily off to slaughter.

The men struggled to pin him down, their hands clamping onto Julien's arms and legs with grim determination. Julien's breaths came in ragged, gasping bursts as he struggled to suck in oxygen in between wailing further abuse at his father.

Distantly, a small part of him recognized that Jonathan stood closer to the machine now, and the ominous whirring of the *Machina Tenebris* had grown in volume.

Jonathan reached for the myriad of connectors, held them steady.

Julien's vocal cords felt as if they were being torn apart, clawing painfully at his throat. But with his limbs restrained, and the two muscle-heads carrying him towards the looming needles, his screams were all he had left.

So, he screamed. Raw, desperate.

He screamed for young Julien, who could only watch as his mother unravelled before him, a tragic victim of her cruel husband.

He screamed for the teenaged Julien, burdened with the crushing weight of guilt. Crippling guilt. Guilt that would taint the best part of a decade of his life.

He screamed for his darling sister, whom he had vowed to protect and failed. He hoped she'd forgive him.

Finally, he screamed for himself, and all the possible lives he wouldn't get to live now. All the love he wouldn't get to share.

The point of a cold, sharp needle was pressed into his skull.

Thirty-Four

Cinn

Voices.

Voices up ahead, in the endless dark void of the tunnels.

A faint murmur of voices, carrying through the darkness like an unsettling whisper.

Cinn abruptly froze, flinging his arms out to grip the wall, steadying himself.

And was that the tiniest shred of light, a faint glimmer seeping through a crack in the stone?

With slow, tentative footsteps, he travelled towards it.

The light grew brighter as he approached, casting distorted shadows on the walls and promising a glimpse of something beyond the all-encompassing dark. His heart raced with a mix of hope and trepidation as he moved closer, straining to catch the murmurs.

The voices grew louder, the frantic urgency escalating until one voice erupted into a rapid, angry torrent of French.

Julien!

Cinn's recognition of Julien's voice was instant, but the raw fury in it was something new, something dangerous.

Julien screamed, a raw, guttural scream that tore through the very fabric of the catacombs, and Cinn's heart. A scream so tangible it would be absorbed into the substance of the walls for eternity.

Panic surged through Cinn, propelling him into a frantic, fumbling run. Each scream that followed was more tortured than the last, slicing through his nerves and filling him with a visceral dread. He had never heard Julien scream before, and the sound was a piercing, agonising assault on his soul. Cinn let slip his own scream of frustration, hating himself for not being quick enough to prevent whatever was happening.

The light grew brighter as Cinn barreled forward, the darkness retreating. The tunnel opened into a large chamber, flickering light casting shadows over the stone walls. His breath caught as he took in the scene.

Lucien Montaigne stood tall, his shadow stretching across the walls like a sinister, twisted devil. Beside him loomed some sort of colossal machine. *The* machine. Julien had found it!

Julien.

Cinn's gaze locked on him immediately. Julien was on the ground, hands bound behind his back, struggling violently as two burly men dragged him across the rough stone floor. His clothes were torn, hair a tangled, filthy mess, and his face smeared with dark dust. Yet his expression was pure fury, twisted in defiance, every muscle straining as he fought with all he had to pull away from Jonathan Steele. Jonathan Steele, who was pressing an impossibly large needle into the base of Julien's scalp.

"Stop!"

The scene unfolding in front of him became a tableau as everyone froze. Pure, unadulterated shock rippled through the chamber, filling the air with a heavy, palpable tension.

Cinn's gaze collided with Julien's. He searched his expression, expecting to see relief there, or joy. Instead, he saw only devastation. Julien's face was a mask of utter despair: his eyes were wide, glazed over with a sheen of unshed tears, and the usually vibrant spark in them was replaced by a hollow, pained look. His mouth was set in a grim line, trembling slightly as if trying to form words that wouldn't come.

At the end of a very long moment, Julien shouted, "Run!"

Everything happened at once. Lucien barked orders in French, sending Cinn instinctively stumbling away from the two men who'd dropped Julien to step towards him.

A powerful burst of wind slammed into his left side, sending him hurtling through the air. His head smacked against the solid rock, a sickening thud echoing through the chamber as the impact sent a jarring shockwave of pain through his skull.

Every bone in his body felt shattered, every muscle pulled.

Julien screamed again. With all he had left, Cinn tried to sit up to show him he was alright, but it was no use. He didn't have the capacity. Stars swam in his blurry vision. Flat on his back, he faced the chamber's ceiling. He attempted to make sense of the outraged voices, shouting French at each other. The tense back-and-forth between them implied an argument. Were they debating what to do with him? Julien's voice cut through them. Oh, God—was he *begging*?

With immense effort, Cinn managed to roll onto his side, though pain pounded through his skull.

Julien was on his knees, hands still bound behind him—not just with any handcuffs, but those motepower-restricting ones now familiar to Cinn, since he'd seen that memory of Isabelle almost being forced into them.

Julien's eyes were wild, his words frantic. "*Je t'en prie, ne lui fais-pas de mal! Je ferais tout ce que tu veux, je te jure, mais laisse-le partir!*"

The sight of Julien's desperate plea to the father he despised for Cinn's life was a gut-wrenching display of sacrifice, the emotional cost too high for Cinn to fully comprehend.

"Julien," Cinn croaked out. He twitched his arm out towards him.

A familiar shadow flickered at the edge of his vision. Béatrice rematerialised, her shadowy form prowling closer. She slunk towards Cinn's shadow. For a moment, she simply perched there, then, her wavering fur extended, and she melted into a formless puddle.

Cinn felt her formidable power before he even understood what was happening—she'd melded with his shadow, just as she had on Westminster Bridge. An incredible surge of strength flowed through him, the throbbing in his head receding.

On shaky legs, Cinn climbed to his feet.

The five others stared at him. No, not at *him*, but at his shadow behind him. He didn't need to see it—he could *feel* it. An overwhelming, pulsating force, ready to be wielded. As he raised his palms, the darkness around him responded, shifting and coiling, a weapon at his command. He was no longer a defenceless victim; he was a force of shadow and strength, and he was *infuriated* with apoplectic rage.

Jonathan's hand still gripped the collection of needles attached to the machine. His face turned stricken as he realised he'd gained Cinn's attention. Releasing the appendages, they clattered to the ground at Jonathan's feet as he raised his hands in surrender.

Cinn didn't hesitate. He did not show mercy.

With a surge of will, he commanded his shadow to stretch out and wrap around Jonathan's arm, the one that he was going to use to hurt Julien, moments ago. The darkness twisted and tightened with brutal force, squeezing until the bone splintered beneath the pressure. A sickening crack echoed through the chamber as his arm was crushed. Blood poured out, a dark, viscous fluid that pooled on the ground, surrounding the needles. The man screamed, a piercing, agonised sound that was abruptly cut off as the shadow's grip tightened further, leaving him writhing in what looked like excruciating pain.

Lucien barked orders at his two men, who were staring at Cinn with twin expressions of wide-eyed horror. Without communicating, they simultaneously turned, and angled their escape towards the nearest tunnel.

Cinn sent his shadow surging forward, wrapping around the men with a forceful grip. In an instant, he'd slammed them violently against the tunnel wall, the impact resonating with an echoing thud. The shadow released their hold, and the men crumpled to the ground, unconscious, their bodies sprawled in a tangled heap of defeated limbs.

Nearby them, Jonathan had passed out from blood loss, or pain. Or he could be dead. Either worked.

Three down, one to go.

Cinn turned to Lucien, who looked between him and Julien. Calculation shot over his face, and he lunged for Julien.

How tempting it was to break Lucien's neck.

It took everything in him to resist.

Instead, he sent as much power through his shadow as he dared, slamming Lucien's head against the tunnel wall. He slumped to the ground, body folding in on itself.

I hope that hurt.

Breathing hard, Cinn basked in the sheer exhilaration of the shadow obeying his will, its pliant, dark form shifting with precision and force. Like this, he was untouchable. The power was intoxicating, and Cinn revelled in the rush. He hadn't touched any sort of drug in years, but the high they offered was the only thing he could compare it to. The sensation was thrilling, a heady mix of control and liberation that surged with each fresh command he issued. The raw, unrestrained power was an escape from the helplessness he'd felt for most of his life, being dragged into the shadowrealm against his will. Being told he was insane by psychologists. Bringing back malevolent entities that slaughtered people in front of him, while he was powerless to stop it.

So this? Yes, this was *exhilarating*.

And frightening.

Ever so terrifying.

But Cinn pushed it all to one side.

Julien needed him.

Julien stumbled slowly towards him, face a picture of desperation, like if he could just reach Cinn, everything would be okay.

God, how Cinn needed to touch him. Hold him. Never let him go.

Cinn threw himself across the cavern, wrapping him up in his arms. As Julien sighed into his ear, a missing piece of Cinn finally slotted back into place. He crushed Julien to him so tightly, as if holding them both close enough would prevent them from ever parting again.

"Smash these fucking cuffs off me so I can kiss you."

Cinn slowly let go, and Julien presented him with his back. With gentle fingers, Cinn parted Julien's matted hair, searching for a puncture wound. There was a tiny red dot, which he smoothed with his finger.

Time to get the cuffs off. A deep breath in, and Cinn was ready. He conjured a small tendril of shadow, careful to keep it controlled, and willed it to curl around the metal cuffs. He let the shadow pulse with pressure, testing the strength of the restraints. "Hold still," he muttered, concentrating hard. With a quick motion, he tightened the shadow's grip and heard the satisfying crack of the metal giving way. The cuffs fell to the ground with a dull clink, and Julien's arms dropped free.

"*Merci.*" Julien rotated and stretched his wrists, rubbing at where they'd been bound. Then he pierced Cinn with his gaze, intensity swimming in its grey depths. "You're a fool, by the way, coming here and endangering yourself like this."

"Are you joking? You're the asshole who ran off and forced me to come find you!"

Their gazes burned into one another, colliding like two stars caught in each other's orbit. Magnetic, unstoppable. Without a word, they closed the tiny distance between them, Cinn yanking on Julien's scarf to pull him closer even quicker. Arms wrapped around waists, hands found hair, lips pressed against lips. The brief kiss was filled with a desperate blend of relief and longing, Cinn pouring every inch of himself into it.

"I was so terrified I'd never see you again. It was all I could think about," Julien said softly into Cinn's ear. "I can't believe you came."

Cinn stepped back to stare at his mess of a boyfriend. After everything they'd done and said, how could that possibly be true?

"Okay, don't look at me like that. I can believe it. And for what it's worth, I'm sorry."

Cinn pressed their foreheads together, squeezing the nape of Julien's neck like he could slip away again at any moment. "You're a fucking idiot. But I love you. And fuck, I missed you."

"What did it take? Five minutes?" Julien's exhausted face attempted a smirk, and Cinn cupped his face to kiss both of his dimples.

"If you do this to me again, I will kill you," Cinn warned.

"I'd completely understand. But I promise, it'll never happen again."

Cinn would have liked to have Julien sign some sort of contract in blood, there and then, but in the background, the machine whirred. He pulled away from Julien with a sigh. "I better destroy this damned thing." Truth be told, he was looking forward to it.

Cinn's eyes locked onto the machine. A shiver of awe and dread rippled through him as he took in its monstrous form. *Machina Tenebris*. The name fit perfectly. It dominated the chamber, a grotesque fusion of metal and dark technology Cinn could only guess at. The machine thrummed with a faint, constant vibration, resonating through the ground and into Cinn's very bones. Somehow, he could sense its power, a deep, foreboding presence that made his own newfound strength feel insignificant in comparison.

The *Machina Tenebris* needed to be destroyed.

"Stay back," Cinn warned Julien.

Cinn's gaze bored into the pulsating core of the *Machina Tenebris* as he summoned his dark friend, directing the shadowy limb towards the machine's heart. His shadow slithered and surged, aiming for the core that surely powered the whole damned machine. However, as his shadow inched closer, a strange resistance became apparent. The blue light of the core flickered defiantly, and the crystalline tubes pulsed with energy, as if repelling his efforts.

Cinn tried again.

Again, the shadow failed to penetrate the machine's defences, its dark tendrils recoiling as they encountered an invisible barrier. Cinn could *feel* the resistance, akin to magnets repelling each other. The force that was almost sentient, pushing back against each attempt. Frustration and desperation surged within him.

"Stop!"

Cinn blinked, shaking his head. Julien had been trying to get his attention for some time.

"It's impervious to shadow."

You don't say. "I can see that."

"Let me try. I've been itching to since the second I saw it."

Is that safe? Cinn wanted to ask, but bit his tongue. Julien needed security and confidence, not seeds of doubt. "Are you sure? You don't look great." That was an understatement—his face was pale and drawn, his hands trembled slightly, and there was a lingering tension in his posture.

But Julien only stepped forward, eyes narrowing at the pulsating core of the *Machina Tenebris*. He extended his hand. In an instant, the chamber filled with pure, bright white light. Beautiful, bright light.

Sparks of light danced circles around him like tiny stars, and in that moment, Julien, with his mess of golden hair, seemed less like a man and more like a celestial being descended into the shadows—a vengeful angel.

His light grew brighter, intensifying with each passing second until it was nearly blinding. Julien's face was set in determination as he thrust his hand forward, and light shot through the air, a swarm of fiery sparks. They collided with the machine, embedding themselves in the metallic surface and seeping into the cracks and crevices of its structure. Flickering for a moment, they then flared with a sudden burst of energy, sending out a searing light that caused the machine to groan and shudder.

Cinn threw his arm in front of his face, blinking rapidly. Several parts of the machine burst into flame.

"Is this safe?" Cinn shouted, as the flames spread across the dark metal like wildfire. The crystalline tubes hissed and shattered, severing the red tendrils that snaked around the machine.

As Cinn took several steps back, wrenching Julien back with him, the core throbbed violently, the blue light flickering erratically as if fighting against the onslaught of Julien's motes. A sharp crack rang through the chamber, followed by a deep rumble as the core's protective lattice splintered.

Smoke filled the chamber, obscuring Cinn's view, but more importantly, choking his lungs. He coughed, spluttering all over Julien.

Julien doubled over, hacking violently as the smoke clawed at his throat, each cough racking his body.

"Ju—" Cinn tried to shout his name, but was rendered speechless by the smoke smothering him.

Another coughing fit hit Julien. He struggled against it, then managed to croak, "Hold on," pushing Cinn flat against a wall.

What was a minor draft passing through the chamber became a strong wind, then a violent, swirling vortex, whipping all the smoke away from them into the whirlwind encircling the machine.

The *Machina Tenebris* was no longer visible, lost in the churning mass of thick, grey smoke. The air crackled with energy, the swirling fog distorting the space around it like a frenzied mirage.

A deafening roar ripped from the centre. Cinn dropped to his knees and squeezed his eyes shut.

There was a series of snapping sounds, followed by what sounded like a pattering of glass raining down onto the ground. Then the raucous noise faded. Cinn peeled his eyes open to find the smoke dissipating—Julien was directing it down a tunnel. It left behind a pile of twisted, melted metal, jagged edges still glowing faintly with heat, like the scattered bones of a defeated beast. The machine was utterly destroyed, a lifeless, deformed heap.

A profound stillness settled over the chamber, wrapping around them like a heavy shroud. The change could be *felt*, deep within Cinn's bones, a palpable shift in the air. The oppressive weight that had filled the space moments before lifted, replaced by an eerie calm. Was he imaging this? He exchanged a glance with Julien, and was met with his answer.

Cinn found Julien's hand, squeezed it tight. "You did it."

Julien did not reply, and his hand slipped out of Cinn's to hang by his side.

"Julien?" Cinn dropped his voice down low, cautious.

Julien was still staring at the machine, his jaw clenched tight, eyes filled with a dark, simmering rage. His entire body was trembling, almost vibrating with fury, as if he were barely holding himself together. His chest heaved with rapid, shallow breaths, and his fists clenched so tightly that his knuckles were white. The strong frown etched into his forehead seemed to deepen even further, his expression hardening into something almost feral.

"*Non!*" Lucien's voice cut through the air like a blade, and Cinn almost jumped out of his skin. Lucien had gotten to his feet, his clothes covered in ash, a stream of blood trickling from his left ear down to his collarbone. "*Non!*" he shouted again, his voice raw with disbelief and fury. "*Qu'as-tu fait?!*"

Julien's head slowly turned, his glare locking onto his father, eyes blazing with a cold, terrifying intensity that chilled Cinn to the bone. His body shook harder, as though every muscle was straining to hold back an eruption. His lips curled back slightly, and his breath came in ragged bursts, barely controlled, a storm ready to break.

There was no denying it—Julien was no longer entirely in control of himself.

"*Adieu, Père.*"

A jolt of fear shot through Cinn's veins, sharp and electric. He stepped in front of Julien. "Wait!"

Julien made to push him out of the way; Cinn placed his hand on Julien's chest, imploring him with his eyes.

"He's a murderous, abusive cunt," Julien stated coolly, eyes looking straight through Cinn. "Move out of the way."

Vibration pulsed through Cinn. Julien, still shaking with fury? No, it was the very ground he was standing on. The ground trembled beneath them, a low, rumbling that echoed Julien's anger, growing stronger with each second, the catacombs themselves responding to the storm building within him.

"Julien!" Cinn's voice wavered with fear, but Julien didn't flinch, didn't even acknowledge it. His eyes remained locked on his father, the silence between them far more menacing than any words. A horrible chill ran through Cinn—Julien's indifference was terrifying, as if nothing and no one, not even him, could reach the man standing there, holding the weight of his rage like a loaded weapon. Lucien, thankfully, had the sense to stay silent.

The surrounding stones rattled. Dust fell from the ceiling.

Cinn's sense of dread grew as the shaking intensified, small rocks cascading from the ceiling.

"He deserves to die. He *needs* to die." Julien delivered the words in a monotone, the air around them thickening with the force of his fury.

"Listen to me, please." Cinn placed two hands on Julien's face, bracing to be shoved away. "Don't do this to yourself. Let's walk away. Darcy and Elliot are down here somewhere." Hopefully. "And Eleanor. Let her deal with him."

Julien's mouth twisted.

"Please," Cinn pleaded. "If you won't do it for yourself, do it for me."

The rumble beneath their feet grew stronger and the dust raining down upon them grew thicker, some of it being inhaled into Cinn's lungs, making him cough.

"You're scaring me!" Cinn cried, desperately clutching at straws, though it was the truth. He fisted the material of Julien's shirt. "You're going to bring the whole place down on us!"

Lucien staggered slightly, bringing a hand to his mouth as a harsh cough erupted from his chest. "Yes, listen to him. You love him, yes? You'll kill him. You'll kill us all!"

"How about you shut the fuck up," Cinn snarled at him, before turning back to Julien. He slapped his cheek lightly. "I know how angry you are right now. But don't be like him. You're so much better than that."

"I love you." It wasn't enough to make up for Julien's disaster of a father, but it would have to be a start. "I love you so much. Now stop shaking the fucking catacombs before you raise the dead."

Julien's face softened slightly, a crack of light piercing through the dark cloud that loomed above him. He made a loud, defeated sound, pressing his hands to his temple, then he slipped to his knees. Something heavy hit Cinn's head before tumbling off, and he glanced down to see something suspiciously bone-coloured on the floor. The ceiling still trembled, small fragments of stone still falling. A horrible cracking sound from somewhere deep in the catacombs boomed through a tunnel. What was happening? Why wasn't Julien stopping?

"I... can't!" Julien croaked out, still pressing his fingers to his temple. He unleashed another horrible scream. "I don't want this! I've never wanted it!"

Cinn joined Julien on the floor, grabbing both of his hands. "It's okay." If they were about to be buried alive, they would at least be found together. In one hundred years, archaeologists would find their skeletons entwined around each other, and declare them roommates.

A sudden loss, as if something had been ripped out of Cinn, made him lurch forward. His shadow suddenly possessed only its usual darkness, its usual shape.

"Béatrice?"

The cat didn't look Cinn's way; her beady eye-sockets locked on Julien's slumped form. Then Béatrice glided across the floor, her shadowy form moving with grace and purpose. She reached Julien, cocking her head. Slowly, her fur extended outwards and upwards, until she was no longer cat-shaped. Béatrice wrapped herself gently around him, as if offering an embrace. The dark wisps drew closer, and closer, enfolding Julien in a protective cocoon.

Julien's tremors eased, his noises of frustration calming as Béatrice's dark essence intertwined with him. She was, Cinn imagined, absorbing his anguish, her formless body melding with his own turmoil.

The shaking of the catacombs subsided slightly.

Yes! Keep going!

The shadows twisted around Julien, covering almost every inch of him. Eyes closed, his golden hair whipped around his face. Then the tremors lessened even more, becoming faint vibrations as Béatrice's shadowy presence enveloped Julien entirely.

The shadows unraveled from Julien, slowly loosening their grip. They swirled gently, like a soft breeze stirring dark tendrils, hovering close before retreating. Julien's eyes opened, locking onto Cinn's. In them, Cinn saw a quiet steadiness, the wildness that had gripped him moments ago now replaced by something grounded, resolute.

Cinn stepped towards him—

A pained cry shot through the room.

Lucien had seized his chance of escape, reaching the entrance to the nearest tunnel. But he'd tripped on something, landing in a twisted heap, clutching his leg.

Béatrice's shadow tore away from Julien, moving with a sudden, lethal grace. It surged forward, a mass of writhing darkness, intent and unstoppable. Lucien barely had time to register the movement before the shadows were upon him, wrapping around his body like serpents. They coiled tighter and tighter, a malevolent force dragging him down with a brutal snap. He hit the ground hard, his eyes bulging with terror.

The dark tendrils pulsed, growing more intense, more violent. Lucien's breath hitched into a choking gasp, his mouth opening wide in a silent, desperate scream. Then, with a sickening pop, his eyeballs sprang from their sockets, dangling grotesquely as blood streamed down his face like tears. His expression was frozen in horror, a twisted mask of agony as the shadow crushed him further.

Bones snapped with sickening cracks, limbs bending at impossible angles as Béatrice's shadow constricted him tighter and tighter, his body folding in on itself. The sound of flesh ripping echoed in the chamber, the shadows feeding on his form until all that was left was a grotesque heap of shattered bone and torn muscle, twisted beyond recognition.

Cinn's stomach turned violently, nausea roiling inside him as he took in the sight of the mangled corpse. His hand flew to his mouth as he doubled over, retching, unable to tear his eyes from the grim spectacle. The stench of blood and death filled the air, clinging to his senses as he heaved.

There was a whisper of words Cinn couldn't quite catch. Then, after one final shadowy flourish, Béatrice evaporated like mist.

The catacombs fell eerily silent, the shaking ceasing completely as the echoes of Lucien's final cries faded away.

"Fuck," Cinn managed to croak out. "Fucking hell."

Cinn's gaze snapped straight back to Julien, every muscle in his body tense, fearing he'd still be unreachable. But the storms swirling in his eyes were gone. Though clearly exhausted, he was back. Cinn tentatively squeezed his arm, eliciting a faint but heartfelt smile which filled the dark cavern with sunlight.

Julien's hand closed tightly around Béatrice's locket. "She's gone," he said. "We won't see her again. That's that."

Wrapping his arms around Julien's waist, Cinn pulled him tight against him. He rested his chin on Julien's shoulder. "She's at peace," Cinn said. Though he didn't truly know, it felt good to say. "But I'm going to look after you for her now."

"And he's gone." Julien stared at the unrecognisable lump that was previously his father.

"Yeah." Béatrice had killed him so Julien didn't have to, and for that, Cinn would be eternally grateful. "He had it coming." Cinn scrutinized Julien's reaction for any hint of regret, and found none.

Julien's fingers curled into the fabric of Cinn's shirt, clinging to him like a lifeline. "I wasn't sure I was going to come back from that. I almost..." He let out a massive exhale, the breath escaping him like he'd been holding it in for hours, the tension finally draining from his body.

"It's all over. You can rest now," Cinn assured him, cupping Julien's face, thumbs brushing away the dirt and sweat. "I've got you."

"I could sleep for a week." With a sigh, Julien sank into Cinn. His eyes fluttered shut. Ever so slowly, the tension in his muscles softened, the weight of the world lifting from his shoulders as he surrendered to the warmth and safety of Cinn's embrace.

Julien may as well nap—he'd need the energy if they were to find their way out of this place. Cinn wrapped his arms around him, squeezing him as hard as he dared. It wasn't until he felt the rhythmic rise and fall of Julien's chest that his own breathing finally steadied. Sat still on the ground, Julien's warmth seeped into him, keeping the chill at bay. Cinn's hand drifted across Julien's stolen hoodie, slightly torn in several places. That was okay. He'd give him another one the moment they got back home.

Time slipped away in that quiet moment. Cinn savoured the sensation of Julien nestled against him, each heartbeat creating a soothing rhythm, the chaos they had just faced already feeling like a distant memory. He lost himself in the softness of Julien's hair against his cheek, the way his body relaxed against him, and the gentle rise and fall of his breathing. Each second stretched into eternity, reinforcing the quiet sanctuary they'd created, and Cinn was reluctant to disturb it.

"What in the ever-loving—" a voice behind Cinn cried.

Cinn had thought Julien close to sleep, but he laughed, the rumble of his chest so great it shook Cinn. Untangling, they found six pairs of eyes staring at the scene in disbelief and horror. Mainly horror.

"Are they all dead?" Noir said, observing the bodies.

"He is, definitely." Cinn jerked his head at Lucien. "The jury is still out on the others."

Eleanor tore a hand through her hair, looking like she could easily rip it out. "You had to go and make a mess, didn't you?"

"Did you expect anything less?" Julien's lips twitched upward, and his smile almost met his eyes.

Darcy and Elliot climbed over bodies, melted machine parts, and piles of bones to reach them. Without a single word, they closed in around Cinn and Julien, their arms wrapping around them in a hurried collective embrace. Both of them were shaking—whether from adrenaline, fear, or exhaustion, Cinn couldn't tell. Their bodies pressed tightly together, squishing Cinn so much he could barely breathe. But he wouldn't have had it any other way.

"You look like shit," Darcy told Julien.

Julien grabbed her head to press violent kisses on both cheeks. "I love you too."

Elliot's face shone with sweat. "I would murder the pair of you if I had an ounce of energy left." He glared at Cinn, with a wide grin.

"How about we move past all the murder stuff now?" Cinn pulled at his baggy hoodie, soaked with blood.

Eleanor joined them, pinching the bridge of her nose. "Right now, we need to get out of here. I'll send people down for the bodies." Her voice was firm, but there was a softness behind it.

Darcy offered a weak smile, brushing a hand over Julien's hair as they pulled away from the embrace. "Come on, let's find a way out before this place collapses on us."

As the others began to move towards a tunnel, Cinn lingered a moment longer. He glanced at Julien, who was still resting against him, head nestled into his shoulder.

"You ready?" he asked softly, his fingers curling into Julien's.

Julien didn't answer right away. He looked over at the mangled remains of his father, the shadows of the past that had haunted him for so long now reduced to blood and bones. His grip on Cinn tightened, but there was no tremor in his hand. He took a slow breath, then nodded.

"*Oui.*" Julien whispered, his voice low but steady. "I've never been more ready."

They stood, Cinn offering a shoulder for support. For a moment, they just stood there together, Julien leaning into him, both of them covered in blood and dust, but still standing. Together.

Cinn squeezed his hand. "Let's get out of here."

They followed the others, leaving the cavern and its darkness behind. And as they walked, hand in hand, Cinn couldn't help but think that maybe, just maybe, they'd finally found their way back to the light.

Thirty-Five

EPILOGUE

Six weeks later

Cinn glanced up at the trees. The first hints of life were breaking through winter's grip. Buds, small and pale, clustered at the ends of slender branches, tiny promises of green yet to come. Shy things, barely open, with delicate, almost translucent leaves peeking out from their protective shells, hesitant but determined to face the world again.

The four of them were sitting in a courtyard near the library.

Darcy had magically produced a picnic blanket. Cinn brought cookies to share, his first attempt at a brand new recipe. Julien acquired four coffees from Café Curio for them. Elliot contributed absolutely nothing, but he'd turned up on time, so that was something.

It was the first day they'd braved the outside for lunch. Spring was coming early this year, if the sudden upturn in weather was anything to go by.

Cinn's headphones rested around his neck, quietly playing music only he could hear. Just the way the others liked it.

His new Walkman, a gift from Julien, was a major upgrade compared to his previous one. He'd gained auto-reverse, bass boost and even had a built-in radio. Definitely worth the agony of watching his old one burn to death in a blaze of glory.

Cinn's only complaint was that the Walkman mysteriously came with a John Coltrane cassette already inserted.

"Still no sign of the return of your motes, Julien?" asked Darcy.

"*Non*. Béatrice took them with her. A parting gift."

Cinn was slightly sad he'd never get to experience her awesome power again, but shadowslipping was more than enough adventure, he supposed. He hadn't slipped into the shadowrealm since the church, but Noir was fairly sure when he did, he wouldn't be seeing the umbraphages and the red city ever again—they hadn't been seen since the machine was destroyed.

Now, Noir was talking about Cinn working with the investigative department of the gendarmerie, travelling on-site with them to deliberately slip, to help gather evidence.

He'd finally be a real life superhero.

Julien had begun meeting with Noir weekly, under the guise of documenting the confounding motes. Noir had offered one theory, that his ability to access them had been triggered by excessive cortisol during the years prior. Now, it sounded like the sessions had turned more into therapy, based on what Julien had shared with Cinn.

Julien seemed a bit lighter every single morning he awoke in Cinn's arms, before he pulled back the curtains and demanded Cinn wake up.

"Incoming," Elliot announced, eyebrows raised.

"Afternoon." Eleanor stared down at them, eyeing the blanket, likely wondering what the hell they were doing, trying to have a picnic in February. "I'm glad I've bumped into you. Saves me a job. The consortium meeting just finished, and I can share a few updates of interest. Jonathan goes to trial in March, as expected. But Viktor Sturmhart's claim he knew nothing about the machine is going uncontested." Eleanor's lip curled into a sneer. "Looks like Jonathan is smart enough not to drag Viktor down with him. However, in other news, MEET will announce the new permanent director next week."

Julien, who'd come home moaning about the carnage at MEET for the last few weeks, brightened. "That *is* great news! I've got a list longer than my arm for them."

"Have you thought any more about our conversation on Monday, Julien?"

Lucien's death had caused Julien a problem, which he'd spent most evenings that week mulling over with Cinn.

Carrie had fled Paris, with the gendarmerie yet to locate her. This left Julien, who'd inherited a fifty percent share in HorizonTech, as the unexpected and reluctant heir to his father's empire. The board was already circling like vultures, eager to secure their influence or seize control of the company in the power vacuum that remained.

For Julien, the idea of running HorizonTech was almost laughable. The thought of stepping into Lucien's shoes, of managing the web of corruption and motetech secrets his father had spun, filled him with a dread that had almost reduced him to another breakdown, before Cinn had swept in to talk him down off the ledge.

Ultimately, Julien could either manage the company himself, or risk it falling into nefarious hands again.

"My decision still stands. I want to turn it into a cooperative. And allow the smaller companies to buy out of the HorizonTech umbrella, if they wish to."

Eleanor nodded once—she'd clearly expected this. "I'll help you sort the paperwork."

"Any further news?" Darcy asked, face set in a tense mask. Her dad's health remained on a downhill slope, and she spent most of her spare time on the phone to Scotland, demanding updates.

"I was just getting to that." Eleanor smoothed down her jacket, inhaling a deep breath in through her nostrils. "You'll be pleased to hear that until MEET determines a safe way to generate enough power to mass produce motecells on the scale Lucien did—if a safe way even exists—the consortium has agreed to prioritise distribution to the medical sector above all else."

"What about—"

"I spoke to someone this morning, and they're confident your parent's pacemaker will be approved for trial any day now."

"Thank you." Darcy dropped her gaze, fiddling with the hem of the blanket.

Eleanor shrugged. "I've barely done anything." As she turned to continue on her way, she paused to throw a line over her shoulder: "Oh, Cinn, Noir and I have agreed you're free to go back to London now, if you wish to. Just keep your warding band on and you're good to go."

Cinn's head shot straight to Julien, catching the tail end of a look of panic he quickly schooled. With a quick kick of Julien's leg, he said, "Don't be daft. You know I'm not going anywhere. Anyway, we're adopting that black cat from the shelter next week. It would be a pretty dick move to leave you with sole custody of her."

A scowl ruined Julien's beautiful face. "I did *not* agree to that cat and you know it. You told me we were going to look at coffee machines!"

"You'll come around." Cinn fluttered his eyelashes at Julien until his scowl deepened, and Cinn burst out laughing.

Elliot jumped to his feet, taking the last cookie with him. "I'm going to be late."

"Since when did you care about that?" asked Darcy. "Where are you going?"

"I'm meeting... someone."

Cinn almost spat his coffee out at the look on Elliot's face.

"Really? The same someone you met yesterday, and the day before that?" Darcy asked innocently.

"He could simply come sit with us, you know," Julien said. "I'll be nice, I promise."

Elliot raised his middle finger at Julien before setting off down a path, checking his wristwatch before increasing his pace.

"Never thought I'd see the day." Darcy scooped her bag off the grass. "I'm just returning some books to the library. I'll be back in a bit."

The second they were alone, Julien pounced on Cinn. "Well? Did you get it?"

Cinn leaned back on the blanket and propped his head on one arm. "Get what? You're going to need to be more specific."

Julien lunged for him.

"Hey! Watch out! Get your paws off me." Cinn raised an arm to shield Julien's impatient fingers, which were trying to pull up his hoodie. "Hold on." He carefully lifted his jumper up to show Julien the patch of skin currently under cling film.

On the left side of his chest, above his heart, lay Cinn's new ink—black line art, an exact replica of the moon and stars engraved in Julien's locket. Except, Cinn's version had the word 'destiny' in fancy calligraphy written above it, the letters weaving into the stars.

"The tattoo artist copied your drawing exactly."

"It's marvellous," Julien said, beaming at Cinn's chest, before tucking some of his hair under his beanie. "It's my new favourite tattoo of yours."

Cinn snorted. "It would be." He pulled out the locket from under Julien's shirt. *A perfect match.* He brushed his thumb over the cool metal oval. Julien had tried several times to take a photo of Cinn to go inside it, alongside the one of his family. Alas, apparently Cinn's smile was never quite wide enough, forcing Julien to try again, and again. Julien had amassed so many photos of him in his drawer, Cinn was starting to suspect something was afoot.

Hovering his fingers in the air, Julien traced the letters of Cinn's new ink. "Destiny, mm? What sort of lame person would get *that* permanently inscribed onto their body?"

Cinn shoved Julien as hard as he could, sending him tumbling back into the blanket. He shot daggers at Julien, face heating. After all, Cinn wasn't the one who'd written sentimental crap at the bottom of a letter, and started this whole 'destiny' thing.

"Someone who wants to keep their destiny close, right where they can feel it. Not that you'd get it."

With a laugh, Julien recovered quickly, swinging his leg over Cinn's, clamping his wrists to the ground with his hands. Julien's curtain of blond waves fell on either side of Cinn's face, sealing them off from the world. Pinning him to the ground with his weight, Julien studied his face, grey eyes intensely serious, and Cinn's breath caught in his throat.

If this is what destiny felt like, Cinn wanted nothing more than to surrender to it.

"Fear not, *mon amour*, I've got every intention of keeping my destiny very close." Julien pressed his lips to one cheek. "Tomorrow." Then the other. "Tomorrow." Julien sealed their fate with a kiss to Cinn's lips. "And tomorrow."

The End

Bonus Content

D id you catch the free bonus chapter which takes place between the two books, *An Interlude at Julien's?*

Scan the QR code to subscribe to my newsletter. Existing subscribers can find the link to my bonus material page in the footer of every newsletter.

Acknowledgements

Thank you so much to Lucie for your excellent efforts translating the French and acting as official French advisor™. Julien is tremendously grateful for your efforts.

Thank you to WH - Three whole books!!! I wouldn't have made it this far without you to keep me sane! Thank you for educating me on the really important stuff, like whiskey, and hot tub sex.

Thank you to Molly for being first to read this book! I'm glad you didn't want to stab Julien quite so much by the end.

Thank you KJ for your eagle-eye over my manuscript. Your feedback helped to make the book tremendously better! (Though Cinn and Julien are not very impressed with you, after you forced them to have more and more substantial injuries...)

Angela - your edits smoothed out the last few creases! Thank you so much. Your enthusiasm for my characters is deeply motivational!

And finally THANK YOU for making it to the end of the Shadow and Light duology! I hope you had a blast.

Also by TJ Rose

Bite Marks and Broken Hearts

An MM Paranormal Romance

What happens when a touch-starved vampire saves an Irish runaway with a broken heart from a demon? Find out in this fun-filled, humorous PNR with heat and heart. First in 'The Killigrew Street Case Files' – a series of interconnected standalones following the same found family as they solve paranormal crime.

Monsters within Men

An MM Post-Apocalyptic Romance

London, 2053. One of the last remaining civilisations in the world.

A decade on from the first wave of human-flesh-craving monsters that wiped out most of society, Noah finds himself stepping up to lead Squad E, part of London's East Regiment, fighting back against the creatures that threaten mankind. But between battling monsters, struggling with grief, and his rivalry with another lieutenant, Noah is sinking, fast. The last thing he needs is a young, weak conscript with an attitude problem to add to his issues. Especially when he can't seem to get him out of his head.

Zeke, Squad E's newest recruit, would rather do anything else than be conscripted into the dwindling military force battling to save humanity. But when his research assistant job abruptly ends after his boss is arrested under mysterious circumstances, he must learn to embrace his new life as a soldier. But perhaps his attractive commanding officer—whom he is forbidden from dating—might offer the silver lining he never knew he wanted?

As the crisis escalates, London's time begins to run out. Food shortages, riots, and secrets buried by leadership all push the city towards its boiling point. The ten members of Squad E, along with their faithful dog, Wolf, must band together if they're going to make it out of this alive.

ABOUT THE AUTHOR

TJ Rose is steadily turning her wild imagination into alternate universes, one happily-ever-after at a time.

By day, she weaves action-packed queer romances packed with vivid worlds and characters who dance between sugar, spice, and pure chaos. By night, she's either plotting doomsday scenarios or binging horror movies—sometimes simultaneously.

When not writing or daydreaming, you'll find her wandering through the British wilderness, coffee in hand, sunlight optional but strongly preferred.

Follow her on social media & sign up to her newsletter to stay up to date!